VISITING DARKNESS

A Mystery/Thriller Novel

D1452566

CELESTE PRATER

NEWMAN SPRINGS PUBLISHING
320 Broad Street
Red Bank, NJ 07701

First originally published by Newman Springs Publishing 2020

ISBN 978-1-64801-059-0 (Paperback)
ISBN 978-1-64801-060-6 (Digital)

Printed in the United States of America

To my current fans traveling with me into a new genre and to those new to my writing, I send a resounding thank you for taking a chance and picking up this book. Hugs!

CHAPTER 1

DRIP. DRIP. DRIP.

Hands gripping the countertop and stare fixed inside the half-filled sink, Mary tracked the outward spreading ripples marring the water's surface.

Just as well, she thought. It skewed the features, which sat fine by her. The perfect disturbance made it much easier to forget obvious dark circles under tired blue eyes, pale complexion, and unruly eyebrows appearing as upside-down smiles no matter how artful the pluck.

A sigh of building resignation left her throat while pushing aside the bangs sticking to her forehead, happy at least the deep-brown hair showed no sign of gray, yet morose it wasn't as shiny anymore. Neither was the length. She lopped it off four years ago in a convincing tirade to increase efficiency.

"Yeah, a better word than lazy any day of the week," she muttered.

Why bother styling when she had no plans to slap on any makeup. This was who she was now, nothing like before. Sharp throbs stabbing the base of her skull started up again.

Startled at the sound of the sugar bowl toppling over—again, she twisted to catch whichever little monster disobeyed the adamant request to leave it the hell alone. A curse stung her tongue as her flabby gut knocked over freshly poured coffee and swept a pretty dishtowel her mother sent last spring to the floor. Disgust gurgled in her chest as the brown liquid soaked into pristine yellow material. Sadness sunk in deep. It was the last of the set not falling victim to jelly stains, ketchup, or grubby little fingers.

Damn. Why is everything around me turning so ugly?

Sight of thick thighs and fat knees above the mess ranked a sincere apology to her former lean body trapped inside. Yet nine years and three kids later, she considered the extra padding as protective gear. The layers crept up on her unsuspecting form during each pregnancy and refused to let go after every birth. She shrugged, unable to muster strength enough to give a rat's ass. At least it made her boobs look bigger.

Gotta find the good in the bad, right?

A derisive snort scratched through her throat.

Yeah, right. Gravity's laughing its ass off right about now. Keep deluding yourself. The bigger they are, the harder they fall.

She reached up and tightened her bra straps.

A spoon clattered to the floor and slid up next to her little toe, one soggy Cheerio still clinging in desperation to the metal. A harsh version of her eight-year-old son's name slid to a stop as she looked up to find his father sweeping into the room and catching all three kids' instant attention. Within seconds, they crawled all over him with ear-piercing screams of, "Daddy," as he let them hang on his arms like monkeys.

Shoulders slumping in defeat, she experienced a wave of regret capturing her tired body. They never yelled out for Mommy with enthusiastic joy, anymore. He was the fun one. Not her.

They hate you. Shut up. Just shut the hell up.

Mary fought against helplessness trying to sink a few claws and forced her focus on the love of her life.

Without doubt, Jason's presence commanded a room now. He'd been a skinny little shit in grade school when they'd first met, began a delicious fill of his frame during high school, and formed into the now present beefy, muscle-packed Adonis built from manual labor down at the plant. Tanned skin and a gorgeous mane of brownish-gold hair looking wind-tossed perfect brought a sigh of appreciation. He only got better with age.

You don't match anymore.

Head shaking at the random thought, a prickle of anger worked its way through her chest.

So unfair. Why can't the man be the one trashing his body to hell and back while bringing new lives into the world?

She craved rocking a pair of low-cut jeans instead of the ugly black shorts always grabbed on the most ardent water-retention day. A loose waist and ability to cover what she teased as hail-damaged thighs became their one true draw for continued use.

Forced to look away from Jason's gunmetal-gray eyes and handsome face before the building rage consumed every thought, Mary chewed on her bottom lip to divert the internal pain.

Whatever. It is what it is.

She flipped the errant spoon into the sink, retrieved the ruined dishtowel, and slapped the soggy mess on top of the table. On a long breath with no intention of hanging around in her lungs any longer, Mary pushed the sugar mound closer to the ridiculous amount of milk the tiny devils spilled from their cereal bowls during a mock battle on the high seas.

*Negative into a positive, Mary. No use crying over spilt—*Jason's kiss to her left temple, quick squeeze on the right butt cheek, and husky voice broke her thoughts.

"Morning, babe. Whoa. You look tired. Rough night?"

She stared at the sugar soaking up rapid spreading liquid and nodded.

"Maybe. Think I got up a few times, but nothing major."

"Try to catch a nap this afternoon, if you can," he suggested in a sweet tone.

She suppressed a snort.

Not going to happen and not enough hours in the day to make an impact.

"Hey, I'm going to the grocery store after I drop off the kids. Need anything?"

"Thought you went Monday?"

"I did. Forgot a few things." She glanced up as he planted their rambunctious five-, seven-, and eight-year-olds back on their chairs. They always stayed put for him without need of a hairy eyeball toss or verbal threat. Full smiles and perfect behavior presented a happy family portrait.

7

Guess it's a guy thing. Three boys. Geez, when did I piss off the fertility gods?

"Nivea."

"Huh?"

"Grab me some hand lotion," he said while flashing a gorgeous smile. "The good kind. My cuticles are cracking. Hate that shit."

"Oh sure."

He chuckled and jangled his keys. "I'm running late. Couldn't find these stupid things. Knew I lost my damn mind when I found them on the closet floor, of all places. Weird, huh?"

"Yeah, weird," she muttered. Mary handed over his lunchbox, accepted the quick peck on the forehead, and caught familiar words thrown over his shoulder as he shoved out the front door.

"Overtime again tonight. Have dinner ready at five. Need to leave by six. Love you."

He was gone before, "You too," hit the air. Mary turned back to the table and steeled herself for the inevitable. Daddy's departure signaled return of complete and utter chaos. Too tired to raise her voice, she stuffed a lunch sack into each backpack and hustled the brood out the door.

Four steps away from the minivan, Mary caught sight of the newlyweds deciding to make the cul-de-sac their home last weekend. Anna Beth and Daniel Burns. Yoga instructor and the new high school football coach respectively.

What a gorgeous, perfectly matched couple. Even their blond hair's the same color.

While returning their animated wave, she wondered if they'd already screwed in every room and on every piece of furniture like she and Jason had done when they were young and eagerly staking claim to their new home. She frowned.

Good grief. Thirty's not old, you moron.

Halted in her tracks, she fought a sudden urge to run across the street, snatch Anna Beth by enviable, toned upper arms, and pass a bit of wisdom—don't have your first one nine months in. It changes you.

"Mom!"

"I'm coming. I'm coming."

Mary crawled up on the seat, confirmed the little heathens remained buckled in, and began the usual morning mind chant while backing out of the drive.

Two blocks. Piece of cake. Just focus.

Too many late nights watching *Forensic Files* led her and Jason to agree the kids would never walk to school. There were too many freaky people out there these days. It wasn't like when they were little. God, she missed those easy times. Memories of riding her Schwinn along winding paved roads, sun warming her shoulders, and soft breeze whipping through unbound hair as she learned every nook and cranny of her peaceful neighborhood lifted her mood. The pleasant smile morphed into a smirk.

Nowadays, most kids stayed inside to play video games or wreck their rooms. A good parent never trusted leaving them in the backyard for fear of discovering them snatched by some sick pervert. She shivered at the thought.

Ecstatic to find an open slot at the curb in front of the school, Mary didn't bother turning up a cheek for a kiss. The oldest stopped years ago, and adoring younger brothers soon mimicked his actions. As the last door slammed shut, she continued staring at the dashboard's digital clock clicking away precious time, performing a mental calculation of how many hours remained before the noise came back and drove into the base of her skull like an icepick.

Brow creasing on a steady crunch, she mumbled, "When did I lose control of them? They were so goddamn cute when they were little." It had been so easy to haul them around in their car seats. Now their sweet little pudgy fingers grew long enough to ball up and bash the crap out of each other or flip a seat belt to fly all over the car. She knew she shouldn't let them off the hook but running into a guardrail to keep them from killing each other wasn't on her agenda anytime soon. Jason still wouldn't let her live the mistake down. He teased, but it still hurt.

Startled at a car horn's insistent demand to move her ass out of the primo spot, Mary pulled away from the curb and gave an apologetic wave toward a brown sedan idling in the street behind her. Hell, even the headlights looked angry. She fully understood the grinding need to turn your kids over to someone else for a while. Far be it for her to deny relief for another harried parent.

One block down and a quick left brought her into the Bagwell Grocery Mart parking lot. She clued to the huge mistake when facing a wall of parked cars.

Shit. Wednesday coupon day. Stupid move, dumb butt.

A glance at her clothes brought a thought of turning around, yet her foot pressed the accelerator anyway.

No one gives a shit what you look like, Mary. Get in, get out, and get gone. Grow a pair. You're such a damn sap!

Forced to park out in the north forty where all the wayward grocery carts seemed to congregate, Mary grabbed the first one, cursed, and sifted through several more before finding wheels dancing to the same tune. Frustration set in as continuous rubbing thighs pulled the clingy shorts material higher between her legs with each step.

Pissed, she glanced around, grabbed a fistful of wayward cloth when seeing no one in the near vicinity, and yanked. She repeated the embarrassing move three more times before reaching the front doors. A nagging, unwanted thought struck her brain.

Maybe I should take up Audrey's offer to work out with her at ten before this damn pudge gets any worse. I'll miss The Price Is Right, but what the hell? She grunted and shook her head. *Why bother? You'll just eat it right back on.*

Cart used as a battering ram, as much as a shield, to push through the cluster fuck of bodies trying to save a dime, Mary battled her way to the lotion aisle. After an eye roll at the silly woman still in her house shoes and scrounging around on the bottom shelf for the cheap stuff, she stared at the dark-blue Nivea bottle for a few beats.

Well, look at this shit, will you?

It mocked her with the sleek curved side resembling a woman's shapely hip.

Why is Jason so concerned about his fingers all the sudden? Does he want to make sure they're soft as he runs them over his mistress's flawless skin?

Gut clenching, Mary backed up and muttered, "Fuck him. He can buy his own shit."

Frown owning her brow, she experienced a round of dizziness as the jostling crowd of unfamiliar bodies continued brushing against hers.

"What was I going to pick up?"

She flinched at another unyielding elbow shove.

"Oh yeah."

Two aisles over, Mary grabbed a bottle of bleach and package of yellow gloves, still stumped as to why the men in her life couldn't seem to aim their damn piss inside the toilet bowl.

Maybe it's some type of innate drive to flop their dicks around and mark their territory, she mused.

Laughter erupted from her throat as a vivid image slammed into her frontal lobe. She hovered her naked ass over Jason's favorite boots and dribbled a little stream of pee down the side before he jumped from the shower and lit out the door to God knows where.

I have every right to mark my territory too, damn it!

Her shoulders slumped, the imagined victory short-lived and leaving a bitter taste in her mouth.

Does he think I'm stupid? He claimed his department on forced overtime for four days in a row now, but Audrey's husband worked the same shift. Whenever she called to chitchat, she could hear Lou's deep voice somewhere in the background. He was with his family, so where the hell was Jason? A plan hatched to follow him, but the hassle of loading the kids up and enduring their nonstop questions and never-ending battles tempered the burning need. Attempts to relax a few muscles failed.

Get a grip and quit finding problems where there is none.

The marathon battle across five more aisles destroyed all progress toward a happy attitude. With growing intent, she snatched a carton of Blue Bell ice cream and children's cold medicine. The kids would be in bed by seven even if she had to drug their little butts.

Focused on the ten items or less checkout line, Mary's ribs slammed against the cart handle. Stunned at the aggressive move by a tall blond flying out of the makeup aisle, she stood her ground despite the throbbing pain. The idiot with perfect hair, flat belly, and clothes not found hanging on a rack at Walmart didn't even bother to shoot over an apologetic look as she continued scraping the buggy along the side of her own.

She acts as if I don't even exist. What a bitch!

The nitwit glided up to the grinning checkout dude more than eager to serve her—Daryl to be exact, if his nametag was correct.

Eyes narrowed into thin slits, Mary studied the woman unloading four individual wrapped prime cuts of beef, frozen broccoli, expensive shampoo, conditioner, eyeliner, mascara, nail polish, styling gel, and a *People* magazine.

Oh, hell no. Way over the limit.

She surged forward and then bit her tongue.

Screw it. I could be back in the car by time I make a point. Another time. Another place.

Even the delightful image of the asshole's bleeding body rolling under the van tires couldn't stop the swell of anger heating her face.

Little Miss Privileged using her looks to get ahead in life. Typical. It flies by fast, honey. Let me toss a little advice, you blond bimbo. Better start learning some manners to go with your future wrinkled face.

Still fuming, Mary saw the smitten boy eyeballing the woman's tight ass as she leaned over to place the two bags into her cart. The fumbling shove of her own meager four items across the scanner came with no direct eye contact afforded prissy bitch. She gained surprise when he looked over to throw out monotone, rehearsed lines of bullshit more than obvious he repeated day in and day out until they no longer connected to his brain.

"Did you notice our savings day bonanza signs? Tomatoes are on special this week. Everything's fresh at Bagwell's Market. You owe twenty-four, eighty-eight."

The kid slumped against the register, bored expression in place while waiting for a card to slide through a slot or some cash to drop on the rubber conveyer so he could push her out of his life. The highlight of his bleak existence had just occurred, so it was all downhill from this point.

Brow cocked in indignation at the attitude, Mary knew he didn't give a shit if she had an opportunity at fresh produce. Might even piss him off if she acted delighted and made him wait while she browsed around and found *one* perfect tomato to bring back to the register. She couldn't stop the low, husky growl erupting as he repeated the register total to hurry her along to oblivion. Her neck heated.

Hey, you asked. Don't get your boxers in a wad because I gave it some thought, mister.

Lips tight in anger, Mary opened the Louise Vuitton knockoff purse her sister gifted two Christmas's ago and looked inside. Mouth parting in surprise, every bit of angst seeped out of her pores, leaving her feeling light and invigorated. The dull throb owning the base of her skull winked out. Gone. Muscles relaxed for the first time since walking out of the hospital eight years ago while clutching a wailing infant in shaking arms. The sublime sensation was foreign yet craved—like taking a huge gulp of air after being underwater for too long. She grinned at her discovery.

Oh, I remember you. How'd you get in there?

Daryl made a point of clearing his throat on an exaggerated grind. "Hey, lady. Are you planning to pay or what?"

She narrowed her eyes. A persistent clock ticking down until time to pick up the hellions, the milk-soaked sugar she left behind, dirty dishes waiting in the sink, and her damn underwear stuck up the crack of her ass didn't seem so important anymore. Everything clicked into place, and she reached inside for the one thing which never judged or mocked.

Mary Galesh lifted the Glock 19 out of the open maw of a purse smelling of chewing gum, Pepto-Bismol, and the menthol cigarettes she hid from her husband over the last year. The weapon felt good in her hand—heavy and powerful. Racking back the slide, she sensed a burst of adrenaline rushing through every vein as eager ears caught the familiar sound of a bullet chambering, energizing her.

Face lifting to present an exuberant smile, she pointed the business end at Daryl's belly and popped a round into the little white button positioned just above his belt buckle, visualizing the projectile tearing through the lower bowel and shattering his spinal column.

Long, tanned fingers laced over the gushing wound, not helping one damn bit. The shit was coming out whether he liked it or not.

Gaze flicking up to confused brown eyes, she winked and whispered for his ears only, "Hell yeah, I can see it. *Now* you're realizing what the fuck was standing in front of you this whole time. Aren't you, buddy?"

CHAPTER 2

WITH NOTHING BUT A GURGLING sound spewing between Daryl's pale lips and boring her silly, Mary swiveled, extended the gun, and aimed at the back of Ms. Prissy, blasting her in the shoulder while the moron stood frozen to the sparkling tile—still cringing from the loud boom announcing Daryl's quick demise.

The skinny body swung about in a perfect one-eighty, a gift from the physics gods. She thanked them for giving ample time to pop the bitch in the left boob. Blondie dropped like a stone. She wondered if the coroner would find silicone mixed with the bright-red splash flowering out on the front of the white Niemen Marcus capped-sleeve blouse.

Glock swinging to the right and up forty-five degrees, she nailed the bubble camera attached to the ceiling and enjoyed a surge of pride as she annihilated the one on the far left without stopping to aim. She basked in the sounds of blood-curdling screams ripping through the air, displays falling over, and cans striking the pale green tile as people fled her vicinity.

That's right, you fucking sheep. Run.

Mary shoved Daryl off the register, smirking as he slid down the half wall, leaving an ironic trail of red to mar a shiny poster of the pretty tomatoes he so inadequately tempted her to buy. She reached out and gathered the cash from each slot, unperturbed by the sticky fluids clinging to the smaller bills while stuffing them inside her bag.

On a calm, casual stroll around the counter, Mary brandished the gun at the next register, cluing the freaked-out emo chick with thick, kohl-lined eyes the quick squat down next to it hadn't improved her situation in the least. She stuffed the pristine cash into her Louise while leveling the Glock's sights on the girl's silver brow piercing, betting this was the most animated emotion those big, blue orbs had displayed since hitting puberty.

Blam!

Sweet. Split her like a grape.

Pleased to find the other cashiers kind enough to leave their register drawers open as they fled like cowards to the back of the store, Mary gathered her hard-earned cash, pausing long enough to bust a cap into several people lying prone on the main aisle.

Did acting like part of the tile save your sorry asses? Nope. Idiots.

Two Almond Joys sticking out from the last candy rack begged for a ride in the side pouch of her purse and got their wish. Satisfied with the prolific haul, she stood center on the black plastic door runner, tilted her head back, and enjoyed the breeze rushing through the parting glass panels to tease her hair.

Glock stuffed under an armpit, she reached inside the bag and pulled out a cigarette and her trusty lighter, cupping a hand to keep the newly struck flame burning bright. This had always been her favorite part—seeing the tip glow a bright orange and hearing the distinctive hissing sound followed by a familiar, comforting scent of prime tobacco striking her nostrils.

A deep drag of the only vice she kept since high school filled her lungs. She let the plume of smoke snake from her nostrils for a bit and then clicked her jaw to release a perfect ring into the air.

Oh yeah, I still got it. Beautiful.

Firm grip back on the weapon and cigarette dangling with ease from her lips, Mary popped loose the empty magazine and shoved in another. Turned to the left, she smirked at the Bagwell store manager. He remained plastered against the pantyhose display with hands lifted from the moment the first round spun out of the chamber and got to know Daryl up close and personal. Rivulets of sweat ran from under the cheap toupee and patterned his light-purple dress shirt.

Head shaking in disgust, Mary wondered why some always froze like this. Freedom lay five feet away, yet he stayed glued to the floor, as if his inaction made him invisible.

Well, thank you for sticking around, mister.

She lifted the gun, reveling in the whimpering sounds issuing from between mustached quivering lips. Seven, well-placed rounds struck his upper torso, bounced him off the display, and sat him on his ass below the exit sign.

"So long, buddy."

Without a backward glance, Mary strolled out of the store and across the lot. The sun felt good against her uplifted face, the sound of trilling birds soothing to her ears, and a sense of freedom owning her soul.

After an easy hop up into the minivan, she latched the seat belt, caught the cigarette filter between her front teeth, and enjoyed the sound of her long-forgotten laughter while squealing tires out of the parking lot. Mary flipped the channels on the radio until finding a blast of hard rock to drown out the distant sound of sirens filling the morning air.

* * * * *

"Oh, crap! Will you look at this shit?"

Officer Cory Winston glanced over at Sargent Brian Douglas's wide, green eyes and realized they both headed deep into some serious top-level law enforcement activity if whatever was going down had this seasoned dude freaking.

Hell, yeah!

Three weeks on the Oklahoma City police force and finally his heart thumped as it had when stepping on the high school football field as fans chanted his name. This is what he'd been missing—massive adrenaline dumps and chills zipping across his flesh. He scrubbed the top of his new buzz cut, muscles quivering with anticipation.

"Damn, Cory. We need to take control of this shit. Quick."

"For sure." Eyes tearing away from the thin line of sweat forming on Brian's upper lip, he tried to assess the scene. Body after body continued spilling through Bagwell's front doors. There had to be at least sixty of them. Shrill screams blasted his ears even though the patrol car's windows were still up. None hazarded a glance back, so he didn't think anything chased them. They just wanted the hell out of the building.

Brian grabbed the radio and flipped a switch to turn it into a high-powered megaphone.

"Calm down, everyone. Move to your left and gather on the other side of the ice machines. Flat against the wall. Do not. I repeat. Do not enter your vehicles and leave the premises, or you'll be arrested."

Mesmerized, Cory observed the scattering bodies merge into a tight pile and shift to the left as if a big dog herded them toward a warm barn.

Damn, that was some righteous shit.

"Watch their hands," Brian barked. "Scan for weapons while I try to straighten this mess out."

"Got it."

The car swerved at an angle in front of the trembling mass, and Brian threw it into park. "Round the rear of the unit and stay on my left, five feet back."

"Yes, sir." It felt good to crawl out of the vehicle and pull his weapon. He trained for this, craved the opportunity. Cory wasn't looking forward to blasting a hole in anyone, but hesitation be damned if any of the freaked-out bunch made a hostile move.

"Where's the shooter?" Brian shouted in a voice so beastly even his own flesh pebbled.

Every head shifted in the sergeant's direction. Despite his tall, lanky build, the deep rumble combined with a gun drawn and lowered in their collective direction commanded immediate attention.

Numerous arms pointed out toward the far, right side of the parking lot.

"How many?"

"One," they all screamed, or whimpered, in unison.

Cory eyeballed everyone's hands yet kept his peripheral on the door, overlooked accomplices trying to fire their way to freedom the last thing on his wish list.

After a round of head swiveling to assess the surroundings, Brian gestured for a sturdy older man in a camouflage T-shirt and work-worn jeans to step forward. He appeared to be the only one with his shit somewhat together. Brian frisked him down. Satisfied, he motioned for the calm man to stand at the front of the patrol car.

"You see anything?"

"Sure did. Slight, heavyset build with short brown hair, green T-shirt, and black shorts falling right above the knees. White, early thirties, maybe. Tell you the color of her eyes or what type shoes she wore, but my mind keeps jumping back to the handgun she was rocking like a pro. Glock. Not sure of the model."

Cory's gut clenched. *She?* As soon as the call came for shots fired, the perp formed in his mind as a drunk male shooting a few cans in his backyard and scaring the patrons. Brian appeared just as disturbed, yet his voice remained even and steady.

"A female?"

"Yep. Calm. Like she done it a thousand times. First shot and my ass skedaddled through the side door of the meat market. Locked myself inside the manager's office and saw the whole goddamn thing through the two-way mirror."

"Did she take off on foot?" Brian pressed.

"No, blue minivan. Dark. Took the far exit and hauled ass up the I-40 ramp. A Dodge, I think. Didn't run outside in time for the license, but there was a Garfield stuffed animal with those little suction cups holding his paws to the back window. You see those before?"

"Yes, got it."

Despite the nuttiness of what they'd learned, Brian's voice remained steady as he lifted the radio to his lips and called out to all open channels with the latest.

Hard glare focused on the busy highway filled with morning traffic, Cory wished they'd rolled into the parking lot right as the crazy bitch hauled ass. He'd give anything to be part of the fucking chase. Involvement in a pit maneuver would highlight his day—a proud back slapping retelling over dinner with Pops tonight his ultimate goal.

Another unit arriving with full sirens and flashing lights caught Cory's attention. He recognized their faces from roll call but couldn't remember the names. An ambulance and a firetruck weren't far behind. Both held back until Brian motioned them toward the stiff, wide-eyed crowd.

Maneuvered to the side of the sliding glass doors, Cory trembled in readiness for Brian to hurry his ass over before someone else got the pleasure of clearing the crime scene. His partner gave the approaching duo the skinny, directed them to start interviewing the group, and ordered camo-guy to stay put. The detectives would salivate to learn what he had to say, that was for sure.

Cory tried to keep his face passive, hiding the jubilation upon seeing Brian line up on the other side and take a quick peek inside. It was time to go in. He got the nod to take the right quadrant as Brian's shoe pressed the black runner. The doors parted, and Cory shot forward.

No matter the extensive number of hours spent on the academy's video study, simulated breaches, or shootouts in a controlled environment he conducted, Cory came ill prepared for a slippery slide through a puddle of dark liquid and bringing him down to one knee. A furtive glance to the right, and he found himself staring into dull, fixed eyes of the first dead person ever encountered. The dude looked right at him. More like *through* him.

Time seemed to crawl to a stop. His mind screamed nonsensical crap as he gapped at the bullet-riddled chest. It was nothing but a wet stain of bright red blood from stem to stern.

What the fuck?

No amount of reasoning could explain why the guy's hair hung off his ear.

A pungent blast of copper and acrid stench of loose bowels struck Cory's nostrils as he ripped his eyes away, just so they could collide with one body after the other scattered around the registers and along the front aisle, their own individual growing puddles adding to the nauseous smell and horrid images burning into his retinas. His gag reflex kicked in with a vengeance.

Gut erupting like a pissed off volcano, Cory's teeth clacked together upon a tight yank on his collar, instantly cutting off the oxygen supply and trapping the burning cesspool at the hollow of his throat. Arms flapping, he stared at a length of blood-spattered tiles strewn with shell casings and then the pristine whitewashed sidewalk as Brian hustled him to the opposite end of the building and away from the grownups.

Hands and knees smashing against the green grass still covered in silky dew, Cory hurled everything he remembered eating this morning, and probably some from last night, until all he could do was live through the dry heaves and inwardly curse from watching half of the gross shit splashing across the weapon he failed to re-holster. *Fuuuck me.*

Through a veil of liquid leaking from his eyes, he saw Brian retrieve several bottles of water and a rag out of the patrol car while motioning for the other two officers to enter the store. Determined not to keep looking like a rank puss of the highest order, Cory two-fingered the butt of his gun, jumped to his feet, and shoulder rolled around the building's edge. Back smacking against the hot brick to keep from ass planting, he held the weapon out as far as his arm could reach and observed a calm hand pouring water from trigger to barrel before draping it with the cloth.

"You need to clean it good tonight. Lots of oil. Lift your right shoe."

On autopilot, Cory obeyed, thankful he had nothing left to offer the grass as Bryan splashed the sole to rid it of the blood he carried from the scene. He chugged half the offered bottle to chase away the rank taste of his failure. Somewhat recovered, he nodded and managed to find his words. "Thank you."

"No problem."

Attempts to explain his insanity were futile, so he focused on dabbing up the water clinging to the gun. There was nothing to say. He choked in a career defining moment. Plain and simple. Cory's massive pride backed up into a far corner of his brain, and he figured it might never come out again from pure shame.

"He's here."

Cory caught Brian staring at a dull-gray, Ford Crown Vic making an unhurried jaunt across the parking lot. He knew it had to be police by the black ramming bar attached to the front grill and an alley light fixed over the driver side mirror. The heavily tinted windows and no insignia perked his interest.

"Is it a detective's car?" he managed to croak out.

"Yep."

The vehicle performed a perfect half-circle and came to a halt two slots over from the store's cart receptacle. "Old piece of shit," he said under his breath. Brian caught it anyway.

"It may look ancient but outruns whatever you throw at it. Max won't drive anything else."

"Max?"

"Detective Maxwell Browning. It's Senior Detective, but you'll never hear him say it. Good cop. Tough. How old are you?"

"Twenty-four."

"Still holds the record. He came in at twenty-two right out of the Marine Corps. By twenty-six he made vice. Moved to homicide seventeen years ago. Knows his stuff."

Cory knew Brian wasn't full of shit as Detective Browning exited the vehicle. There wasn't an ounce of newness anywhere on the man. He caught sight of calm features some might even call handsome, strong jawline, thick slashing brows, and a nose experiencing a break at one time. Browning appeared to be in his early fifties since only the sides of his short black hair were doing a little of the salt-n-pepper thing. He reckoned the guy close to six-two, if not already there.

"Damn, he's big," Cory whispered.

"For sure. Keeps in shape too. If he's not pulling a long case, you can catch him at the precinct gym at five every morning. I think he's ran a groove into the track."

The athletic build became clear when he removed the dark suitcoat matching the pants and hung it up in the back. A time worn leather gun holster cinched over thick shoulders conformed to his wide back. The black dress shoes were clean, but not too shiny. He couldn't imagine a brute like this wearing anything but combat boots. He nudged Brian on the arm.

"Don't they usually roll in pairs? I don't see anyone else inside."

"Just Max. Lost his partner, Fergus McLellan. Died on the job eight years ago. Won't take on another one. Tried. Doesn't work."

"Ah."

Browning rolled the sleeves on the white dress shirt, revealing thick forearms. He stuffed a small notepad and a couple of blue surgical gloves into his back pants pocket. After a quick adjustment to a thin black and grey tie, he glanced up. Piercing blue eyes zeroed in on the two of them. His chin raised in time to Brian's respectful nod. The man's walk was slow and purposeful, as if strolling up to a bowling alley for a relaxing game and a bucket of beers with his homies. If anything, the dude was comfortable in his own skin.

"Hey, Max," Brian called out.

"Brian. Long time. You first on scene?"

The deep, rugged voice didn't surprise Cory in the least. It fit him.

"Yeah, but Martinez and Higgins are inside clearing the premises. Butch just arrived. He's keeping the witnesses on the other side of the building by the ice machines. It's beyond fucked in there. You'll want to talk to the guy in camo leaning against my unit. You catch the call out?"

"Yep. One perp. Female. Blue minivan. Heading east on I-40. How many down?"

"Don't know, yet."

Belly cramping as intelligent, all-knowing eyes arrowed his way, he sensed Browning drilling a tunnel into his skull and figuring out quick what a goddamn pansy he was. As soon as the calm gaze drifted down to the obvious puke marring the once pretty grass, Cory felt his neck and face ignite. He fought everything inside to look up and face the music.

"You new, kid?"

He knows damn well I am. "Yes, sir."

"Everyone gets some form of tarnish in the beginning. Rite of passage. They'll dog your ass over this until the next new boot fucks up. Laugh and take it or they'll eat you alive."

He snorted while stuffing the bottom half of his tie between two buttons and securing it inside his shirt.

"At least you didn't fuck up my scene. I'll make sure they give you points for gut control. Might shave off at least a week of torture." On a deep grunt, he bumped knuckles with Brian, turned, and walked away.

Cory felt like he'd popped out of a vacuum as the seasoned detective moved further down the walkway. "Brian?"

"Yeah?"

"Thanks for pulling me out before I hurled in there. He's the last man I ever want to piss off."

Brian nudged him on the shoulder and chuckled. "You'll be fine, kid. He's stingy on handing out advice to someone he doesn't know. Consider yourself privileged. Come on. Let's help with the interviews. The faster you dive back into the thick of things the sooner the guys bore of razzing you. Ready?"

Gun shoved back into the holster, Cory inhaled a deep breath and straightened his spine.

"Sure. Why not. At least I didn't piss my pants. Think they'll give up a few more points?"

He shook his head and followed in the wake of Brian's soft laughter. They both knew it was just the respite before the evil shit waiting for them at the end of the building dug its claws back into their hearts.

CHAPTER 3

MAX STUDIED THE CROWD OF Bagwell customers now experiencing the aftermath of adrenaline leaving the body at a rapid pace. Docile bodies perched on the curb tried to keep their heads from wobbling on loose necks as the EMTs continued tending minor cuts and scrapes. He looked down at his notes.

Butch, Brian, and the new kid pulled enough info out of them to confirm six stood one register over from the hot zone and considered themselves lucky enough not to have taken a round in the back as they tripped over others throwing themselves to the floor. All reported the same thing: Heard the shots. Woman with dark hair holding a gun. I ran. All planned on buying lottery tickets tonight.

On instinct, the remaining followed the stampeding herd as they fled from whatever monster lurked up front and saw nothing of consequence. After finding the rear doors dead-bolted, they clustered on the back dock, clamped hands over mouths unable to stop crying, and prayed the beast from hell wasn't making its way through the building. Major fire safety violation on Bagwell's part, but this was someone else's problem. Max glanced over at Brian's unit.

Camo guy, as he would be forever known, aka Irwin Smith, became his saving grace when cluing the cameras were toast after she killed the first two victims. Even still, Max knew he'd met every detective's dream. Calm, rational, and recounted in vivid detail her exact movements without added commentary on his now traumatized life or he was only there to buy milk. The man had seen combat. This was just another event Irwin would shove into one of those dark slots in the back of his brain to keep from losing it every time a door slammed shut. They gave each other a knowing look and exchanged head nods before Max turned to the store.

Martinez and Higgins met him at the glass doors as he snapped gloves in place. Both faces were pale. Martinez pushed out a weak, "Clear," and Higgins shook his head, mumbling, "God damn, Max. Get ready," before they walked away. He bet they carried a little more sympathy for the new boot right about now.

Once inside, Max refused to do nothing more than count bodies as he walked through the scene on his way to register two, the start of everything. This is where he would settle himself and try to enter the mind of a killer.

Careful to avoid shell casings scattered about, abandoned carts full of groceries, and pools of blood now thickening under each form, Max continued to make small tick marks on the notepad. As he reached the targeted counter and added the young kid slumped on the other side, he tallied nine dead. Six females and three males. He avoided looking at the nametag pinned to the shirt, refusing to see them as individuals. Not right now anyway.

After a careful study of the counter, he upended the paper sack resting next to the bag carousel and found melted Blue Bell ice cream, package of yellow gloves, small bottle of bleach, and children's cold medicine. Random items from various aisles and unrelated except for the bleach and gloves.

Maybe she grabbed shit to blend in with the other shoppers as she cased the place.

Max shook his head and looked around. "No, doesn't make any sense. You knew full well you had a packed store by counting cars in the lot. You could've stuck to the front where the money was. Less eyeballs on you. In and out. Fast. There was no need to shop, so why did you?" His eyes tracked from one body to the next as he stepped through the sequence, placing himself at each location.

"Ending these nine didn't accomplish hiding your identity, either," he whispered. "If it were the goal, you would've put something over your face and blasted the cameras first. Irwin said you never tried pursuing the others. What you saw, you shot. Were you waiting for the right person to get in line, masking your target by adding more?" He glanced back at the carnage. "Yeah, the focus of all of this was on the killing. Wasn't it?"

Squatted next to the manager's body, Max replayed Irwin's chilling recall of events. The cold smile as she pointed the Glock at each target and fired without an ounce of hesitation, the selection of candy from the shelf, nonchalant enjoyment of a cigarette at the door, and the ecstatic expression while blasting this last gentleman all to hell and back.

"Nah. They were in the wrong place at the wrong time, and the money secondary—an afterthought. You got off on the chaos. The power."

Assessment of the crumpled man left Max fighting an insane desire to right the toupee, to give the guy a little more dignity before cameras starting clicking and forever captured this moment.

"Irwin said he couldn't see your face when this went down," Max whispered to the corpse. "Did you say something to her? Was it to beg for your life, or did you clue to the inevitable and tell her to fuck off?" He exhaled on a sigh. "I hope it was the last one, buddy."

The sight of multiple holes in what was once a light purple shirt, allowed a little bit of empathy to seep into his emotions while his thumb traced across an old wound riding the side of his own throat. He could still recall the flash of fire sending the bullet through Fergus's left cheek before exiting and entering him like a hot poker, splitting skin, burrowing into muscle, and chipping bone. Without doubt, he could understand what each of these victims experienced, yet he'd been the lucky one and got to walk away.

"You'd shit if you saw this one, Gus," he huffed. "Finale's worse than when the couple over on Skyline knifed their neighbors and offed themselves in the backyard."

Max liked to think some of his best friend still rode inside him after all these years, maybe nudging him in a right direction every now and again. He found comfort in knowing their blood mixed before Fergus took his last breath. Except for genetics, he was his brother in every sense. The only person he'd been able to bounce off a half-baked idea and get back five possible leads spit out in a deep Irish brogue, making them sound that much more plausible.

Startled at the ringing phone disturbing the eerie quietness, Max released a soft chuckle as he stared at the incoming number for a few beats. "You being funny, Gus?" It was Sean McLellan, Fergus's son. He was smart like his dad. It wouldn't surprise him if the boy made detective soon. McLellan blood ran deep.

"Hey, Sean. What's up?"

"They got her. She's dead."

"Fuck. Clue me."

"Got word a sheriff's unit spotted a vehicle on 177 matching the description. We caught up with the van after it turned onto 270. Ten miles outside Seminole, she hit the spikes and blew out the tires. After running on flats for a quarter mile, we boxed her in, and everyone believed we'd squat for a while until the negotiator arrived. No such luck. Shit. Hold up."

Max listened to Sean's deep voice barking out orders.

"No. Make them move back. Go ahead and string the tape. Jurisdiction's ours. Yeah? Tell him to bite me. We'll measure dicks later."

After a hard battle against a chuckle gurgling up his throat, Max finally gave up.

"Where was I? Oh, right. The crazy female took her sweet ass time smoking a cigarette, sailed the butt out the window, and then crawled out like it was no big deal. We all yelled to toss the weapon and hug the van. She started firing on the closest unit, instead. Get this. The broad laughed at us. Cackled like a loon. I'm not shitting, Max. Total suicide mission. Local cops lit her up. Its fucked beyond reason. You have to come see this."

"Be right there." Phone secured in his back pocket, Max took one more look around at the horrific sight and motioned forensics to come inside to do their thing. He gestured to the left as Anderson came within earshot.

"Manager's office is behind those swinging doors and on the right. If you find video, send it on a direct path to my office in some trusted hands. Don't wait for the wrap up. Pictures of the victims and their IDs can come over with the other stuff. Make sure I find a copy on my desk when you're done. I should be back at the station in about two hours. Keep the names under wrap and only turn over to the Captain. He'll make personal notification to family and speak to the public. This is big. Don't fuck it up."

* * * * *

"How far out are the news vans?" Max hung his coat and slipped on a pair of new gloves while Sean's intelligent blue eyes skirted the area. The light smattering of freckles across his nose and red strands scattered throughout his "getting a little too long" brown hair stood out from the sun blasting off the surrounding vehicles. He even clenched his strong jaw like his dad when amped on adrenaline. The kid was a definite McLellan. Fergus had all but cloned himself. Even the accent was there, just not as pronounced.

"They're converging on 177 now. I sent two units to block the road right before the curve. Two more took the south end, but I doubt any stations will head in from the opposite direction anytime soon. Too far away. The others shouldn't be able to take any pics other than the vehicle. I covered the plates. She's on the opposite side facing the woods and has a skirting around her."

On a nod, Max decided to start with the van since the coroner's office beat him there by ten minutes. Bursts of light proved their focus remained on the body. A quick glance around confirmed Sean had effectively warned off the massive number of officers responding to the chase. Even the Del City force was present.

Max scanned the faces eyeballing the scene and pinpointed which fired their weapons. Most were Seminole and Holdenville cops rocking the sweaty, haunted look. It wasn't every day you filled a woman full of lead. They'd toss at night for weeks, if not forever. "Who owns the van?"

Sean pulled his notepad. "Came back to a Jason Galesh. Home bought eight years ago is about three blocks from the shooting. No wants or warrants."

Max noticed the Garfield stuffed animal Irwin mentioned. Now missing an ear, it clung to the half-shattered back glass by one plastic cup. The cargo area carried a spare tire leaking from one of the shots, but otherwise came up clean. He kept to the passenger side free of bullets and shell casings. A peek into the back seat revealed a few sheets of paper with what appeared to be kid drawings. Laden with glass, he left them where they lay.

Maybe there is something to the children's cold medicine choice, after all.

The front compartment reeked of cigarettes despite the missing driver and back passenger-side windows. An empty Almond Joy wrapper fluttered in the cup holder while another package lay unopened on the console. The chocolate leaked through the seams and at a steady drip over the edge, no match for the heat of the blazing early June sun.

Ah, that's what you snatched off the candy rack.

From inside the fancy purse taking up residence on the floorboard, he retrieved a wallet hiding under wads of loose cash and studied the driver's license. A brilliant smile greeted him. If he hadn't known better, he would've considered the woman friendly and approachable.

"Mary Galesh. Five feet, six inches. Brown hair. Green eyes. One eighty. Turned thirty about three months ago." He held it out to Sean.

"Same address as the registered owner," he confirmed. "Looks like her too. We can now rule out a carjack scenario." He handed it back and opened an evidence bag so Max could slip it and the purse inside. Insurance and registration papers found in the glove compartment proved the vehicle belonged to Jason Galesh. They went in too.

"Do me a favor, Sean. Go check out the home. Find out what's going on there. Round up the family, if you can." He caught his arm.

"Swing by the store first and take Higgins with you. Ask Brian to stay for the forensics wrap-up. He knows my checkpoints. I'm going straight to the office after this, so drop the bag in my trunk."

"Got it."

Max rounded the front of the van and received his first unencumbered look at the damage. There had to be at least thirty or more shots peppering the length. He was still trying to figure out how they hadn't broken out the windows on the passenger side by time he spotted the subject splayed out on the pavement about ten feet away.

Son of a bitch.

One look and Max figured every bullet must have passed through her body before striking the vehicle. What she heaped on the Bagwell manager returned three-fold, believing it a miracle none had struck the face confirming her as Mary Galesh. He kneeled by the skirting, searing the scene into his brain.

Both tan sandals lay about three feet away. Either she kicked them off or they blew her out of them. She wore the clothing Irwin described. Her eyes remained open and staring at the pristine blue sky. Max swore she carried a slight smile…that or the sun was getting to him. He reached up and swiped at a trail of sweat tickling the side of his neck.

Butted up close to the blood-soaked T-shirt, he found the Glock still gripped in her right hand and finger on the trigger. A full magazine lay across the left palm while another hung out of the shorts pocket and rested against the shot-to-shit cell phone—which would've been nice to include in evidence. No wonder they'd lit her up. She had no plans of going in easy.

Inevitable outcome asked and received.

Max rose and stepped back a few paces as the gurney rattled to a stop next to the most unusual perp he'd ever met. The "whodunit" aspect appeared over. Now it was only the matter of why and if more might be involved. Max gave a quick nod to confirm his analysis complete and stared at her unseeing eyes.

"What in the hell were you thinking, Mary?"

* * * * *

A search of several more internet sites and finding nothing of importance, Max shook his head and leaned back in his chair. It squeaked out a string of discontent, reminding he needed to quit lying to himself about oiling the damn thing. His focus returned to the computer screen, frustration mounting at the repeated dead ends concerning Mary Galesh. No warrants, no priors…nothing.

The video store surveillance matched to the last detail of what Irwin recounted. It chilled his blood to watch how fast the events turned. He caught sight of her standing in line waiting to check out after the tall blond moved aside. The camera angle showed only the top of everyone's head, hindering any idea of Mary's emotions until she'd looked up and aimed at the camera. Cold, dead eyes stared right into his. She was nothing like the woman on the DL.

Max started the video again and studied the mechanics of each kill but came no closer to understanding how she ticked. Three smooth, flawless shots and the two were down. It appeared she spoke to the kid after she nailed him, but there was no audio to confirm.

He sat back and wished the store had cameras throughout so he could have at least seen her while she selected the items. Was it with purpose or haphazard? Nope, Bagwell's sole focus lay on the clerk's hands working their money, nothing else.

On the off chance of success, he scoured traffic records and came away with the most excitement experienced in the last two hours. Report of a one-car accident with a guardrail the previous April opened a new door. Property records showed the accident occurred a block from the house. No one injured. All three kids were in the car, though. The tidbit of information made his gut cramp.

Poor things. Half-hearted suicide attempt with a thought of taking the little ones with her?

He knew he was grasping now, but nothing made sense other than she made a big splash before throwing the dice and winning the suicide by cop round. The report listed her maiden name as Wilkins and led him to a speeding ticket out of Elk City. It appeared to be her hometown. She'd just turned eighteen. Nothing major listed there, either.

Even with one door closing after the next, Max's eyes kept bouncing back to the notice of an available juvenile record. It remained sealed from the age of fifteen. He reckoned a possible curfew violation or minor in possession of alcohol, typical shit teenagers get into when bored in a small town. But then again, it could reveal a slice of her personality helping mold the woman she would become.

JoAnn, the loveable department assistant every detective fought over to utilize and ended up abusing beyond reason, promised after a comical bout of bribes she would call in a few favors and force a rush on having it unsealed. He had complete faith it would land in his inbox tomorrow, that and the phone records he ordered.

A thorough study of the faux Louise Vuitton's contents spread out on the desk hadn't been a help, either. Just typical things women shoved in their purses—chewing gum, tampons, Pepto, Spiderman Band-Aids, pen with a chewed cap, and a compact. Other than the wads of bloodied money bagged into evidence, Mary looked like any typical mom raising three kids while her husband pulled in the bacon.

Sensing a presence, Max glanced up in time to catch Sean's head popping around the corner of the half-closed door. He motioned him in. Like his father, the kid lost no time in spilling what ran at lightning speed through his head.

"I didn't find anyone at the house. No cars out front, either. A nosey neighbor caught us walking the perimeter and told me the husband worked at a steel plant about fifteen minutes away."

Max grunted out what was supposed to resemble a laugh as soon as Sean rolled his eyes and removed a thick stack of folders from the only chair he ever allowed in front of his desk. Straight back and wooden seat with purposeful discomfort in mind ensured less chance of lingering visitors, but Sean knew he was the exception. Obvious his task drained him, he plopped down on the unforgiving seat anyway. Paperwork balanced at a precarious pitch on his right knee, the closest Max would ever have to a son shoved out a tired breath.

"I kept it discreet as possible in getting him out of the plant. Nice, decent guy. Secured him in Room 5 before I told him his wife robbed the store and fled the scene. Best to let him chew on the first shocker a bit before you feed him the rough stuff. Heads up. As expected, he's in denial and pissed. Says we've named the wrong person, and Mary's probably shopping somewhere else. He even tried calling her. I'm positive he's clueless on her intentions."

Sean's eyes softened. It was the only characteristic his mother could lay claim. The one trait he'd one day learn to save for places other than this, Max hoped.

"They've got kids. Three small boys."

Max turned back to the computer. "Yeah, I know. Go get him a soda. If he smokes, let him. I'll be there in five."

CHAPTER 4

"Is this Mary's?"

Max pushed the interrogation room door closed with the heel of his shoe, placed the evidence bag on the floor next to the desk unable to lay claim to anything but a scarred top, an unopened Coke can, and four unsteady legs despite a sound bolting to the ugly green tile. He took a seat across from Jason Galesh.

A portable video player, small package of tissues, and a folder placed on the chipped, gray tabletop, Max took a deep breath and eyeballed the cell phone screen Jason insisted on holding out to him. The news streamed a live video of a police wrecker hooking up to the van.

"God damn it! Did you hear me?"

"Yes." Max stared into frantic gray eyes needing to know the truth. All of it. He was a big fella, so he hoped he wouldn't have to tackle him anytime soon. "First of all, thanks for coming in, Jason. I'm Detective Browning. You're right. It is."

Jason turned the phone and glared at the screen. "The other officer claimed she robbed a store. Impossible! News said the driver's dead after a gun battle with the police. Who kidnapped her? Where is she?" The longer he stared at the extensive damage while the anchorwoman informed the world it headed to police impound for further forensic testing, the more sweat formed on his upper lip.

On a gentle, non-threatening move, Max extracted the phone from shaky fingers, turned it off, and set it to the side. He slid the driver's license over.

"Can you confirm this is your wife?"

Jason swallowed hard and stared at the smiling face. "Yeah, it's her."

"I retrieved it from a purse found in the car." Max picked up the plastic evidence bag holding the Louise Vuitton and set it back on the floor at Jason's quick acknowledgement of recognition.

"Witnesses and police observed one person in the vehicle from the time it left the store and until it stopped on 270. The deceased driver is your wife, Mary. I went to the scene and confirmed it. I'm sorry for your loss."

Gray eyes peeled wide, and the most sorrowful howl erupted from his throat, filling the small room and echoing off the steel walls. Max had heard this gut-wrenching sound many times, even from his own mouth. No surprise arose from the inevitable chills lifting across his flesh.

Max came to his side and started a steady pat on a shuddering wide back as the grieving man pressed a forehead to the gray Formica and clutched his hair in an unforgiving grip. The seasoned table shook from his wracking sobs. There was no reason to spill out bull-shit words of comfort. This man wouldn't want to hear them. Easing his pain was impossible as bringing ten souls back from the dead.

Long, agonizing minutes passed before Jason tried to lift his head. Max pulled the package of tissues over and yanked a few before stuffing them into a trembling hand. After a few hiccupping breaths and nose blows, the devastated guy struggled to get his shit together. His voice came out a snarled mess.

"This is crazy. I don't understand anything."

Parked back in his chair, Max nodded in sympathy. "I know, and I'm going to try and make sense of it, if possible. I need your help, Jason, and we're running out of time. Can you do this for me?"

Bloodshot eyes blinked a few times. Jason straightened his spine and inhaled a sucking breath. "Uh, sure."

"My questions are hard. Ready?"

"I think so."

"Do you own a gun?"

"Glock 19. Keep it in a locked case at the top of our closet. I'm licensed."

"Did your wife have any mental or health issues? Was she on medication or seeing a doctor?"

Brows lowered in an instant flash. "No. There's nothing wrong with her. Look, you don't understand. She's been my girl since eighth grade, and I know—" His lip trembled.

Max's respect for the young man grew at the quiet struggle to hold it together, determined not to break. Something the poor guy needed to rely on in the upcoming days, weeks, and months until this all became a dull throb of fucked up history. Gray eyes locked with his, voice much more confident.

"I know her better than anyone. She would've *never* done this willingly, sir. No one was in the van with her. Fine. But maybe she was forced to go along with it."

"Want to believe your scenario more than anything, but I saw the first bit of store video before she shot the cameras out. I have a solid eyewitness who caught the robbery from start to finish."

A shuffling of big boots broke the sudden quietness of a room seeming smaller by the second.

Max knew he had to get the poor man's head wrapped around the idea of his wife pulling a hold up, much less hearing she went on a killing spree.

"Your wife was by herself the entire time, and the weapon used was a Glock 19. We have it in our custody."

He felt like shit when recognizing the first spark of hope seeping into desperate gray orbs while color returned to a face drained of blood.

With an adamant head shake, Jason leaned forward. "No. No. See, this's where everyone has it wrong. Mary's never shot the gun. She was afraid of it. Petrified. She wouldn't even allow it in the house until I put it in the lockbox. This can't be right."

Max picked up the video player and blew out a breath. "There are only a few minutes of footage from the store, but clear in showing your wife committing the acts. I'm not going to lie to you, Jason. You'll face what Mary's done the second you leave here. Media, friends, coworkers. You name it. Might as well get the raw truth instead of rumors and false information. Not on the pretty side, but I'll share it if it helps you come to grips with the reality of the situation. You need to know Mary did more than commit a robbery.

She's only dead because she fired on the police officers after multiple warnings to toss the weapon and stay by the vehicle. Before that, she killed nine people inside the store."

As expected, Jason turned to stone. The only thing moving were his eyes on a frantic search of an unfamiliar face for signs of bullshit and hoping he misheard every word. Max saw the moment it sank in. Everything had just ramped up to a whole new level.

Jason whispered, "Son of a bitch," and closed his eyes. After a round of jaw clenching, he reopened them, revealing a fierce determination. "Show me. I have to know."

Max queued up the disk to the frame where Mary became visible at the checkout counter. He paused the video, slid the device to the end of the table so they could both view the screen, and tapped on the bottom left corner. "Do you recognize her? The angle's high."

"Yes, it's Mary. I remember she wore those clothes before I left for work. Same haircut and purse too. Go ahead."

He pressed the button and watched the man's dreams change forever. Jason's knuckles whitened with every excruciating passing second, sucked in a breath upon each precise shot, and paused the machine the instant her face turned up to the camera.

"Who in the fuck are you?"

Max barely caught the whispered words rushing out of the man's mouth.

On a hard swallow, Jason tapped the button, teeth clenching as the muzzle flash resulted in static filling the screen. He looked down and stared at the table, unmoving.

Max could tell he grasped for answers, running a thousand scenarios through his head in mounting desperation to find a different outcome. His head jerked up, eyes sparking with fear but still laced with deadly hope again.

"Maybe someone threatened the kids and made her do it. Yes, sounds reasonable. She didn't have a choice. Did you see her face? If our kids were in trouble, she'd do anything."

"Are they in school?"

Jason's voice trembled as his own theory sank in. "Oh, God. I hope so."

Max slid the phone over. "Call."

Minutes later, the concerned father's face melted in relief as he set the cell aside. "Still there. School's on lock down." His lips pursed, chin rising. "They lied to her, making her believe they had the kids."

Max leaned forward. "Anything's possible. I'll look at every angle. I'm sorry to do this, but I need more information. Were you guys having marital issues?"

"No. We have the typical spats, but nothing major." In seconds, his shoulders slumped, eyes gleaming like polished marble as he tried to hold back the tears.

"What is it, Jason?"

"Anniversary's next weekend. Wish I'd spent more time with her these last few days. I'll regret it for the rest of my life. This is so unfair."

"What do you mean?"

"I'm remodeling a small cabin by the lake. After every shift, I spend about four hours out there getting it perfect for the surprise reveal. Nothing fancy, but I wanted it to be our refuge. Mary needed some time to relax. She's always so busy with the kids. Her parents have plans to come in from Elk City and watch them for me." He sucked in air and gripped the table's edge.

"Aw, shit. I hope they haven't seen the news. They'll recognize the van and freak. Her father has a heart condition."

Strong, work-worn hands started shaking. It was beginning to ram home his life, as he knew it, was over.

He picked up Mary's license and whispered, "What do I to tell our boys, baby?" to the woman who had become a mystery to them both.

Jason didn't even look up at a light tap on the door. Sean peeked inside.

"Sorry to interrupt, but can I speak with you for a second, Max?"

"Sure. I'll be right back, Jason." He received a quick nod and no eye contact.

As soon as the door snapped shut, Sean gestured to the right. "I have Mrs. Galesh's best friend in Room 4. Her husband called and told her the police pulled Jason out of work. She couldn't find Mary and thought she might be one of the victims. I knew you'd want to talk to her, so I went ahead and revealed what happened so she can wrap her mind around it. She took it hard. I called her husband, and he's coming in. Her name's Audrey Taylor."

"Good work. Have the front desk call me when the husband arrives. Let's get Galesh home before the media floodgates burst." He swung the door open and leaned against the jamb. "I don't have any more questions for you, Jason. Leave the license on the desk. This event's an expected shock, but you'll need to let it soak in quick. I suggest you pick your kids up from school before your wife's name hits the news. We try to keep it under wraps for as long as possible but doesn't always turn out as expected. I'll call you when I have more. Promise."

Chair tips squealing against the tile, Jason leaped up, eyes wide in panic. "Yeah, you're right. I need to protect my boys." He yanked keys from his right front pocket and then stared at them for a few uncomfortable beats. "Wait. My truck's still at work."

"Sargent McLellan will take you and escort you home after you have the kids. He'll be discreet."

"Good. Yeah, that's good."

Max reached over and squeezed Jason's shoulder as the rattled man stepped into the hallway, hoping he could sense the legitimate concern.

"Tell your kids mom's out shopping with friends. Keep them away from the TV and give yourself some time to have more family around you. They'll help."

Jason nodded. Though his shoulders appeared to drop several notches, the jaw tension remained as he studied his boots.

"Thank you for being so kind considering what—" The words cut short, as if he had no more strength to say her name, much less hold up his head. It remained lowered while following Sean down the corridor.

Max hoped the family showed before this entire tragedy hit the poor man with full, unrelenting force. Shame had already crept in and secured a foothold.

* * * * *

Audrey Taylor dabbed swollen, tear-filled eyes and continued shaking her head, causing tight blond curls to bounce across slim, suntanned shoulders. Max handed her another tissue, holding his question until she swiped away mascara running in long rivulets down flushed cheeks and patterning the cream-colored halter top.

"Are you okay?"

She sniffled and hauled in a deep breath. "Yes. No. Hell, I don't know. My brain's fried. None of this makes a damn bit of sense. I've known Mary since she and Jason moved onto our street. She's never shown an ounce of violence, and she certainly wasn't crazy."

Big amber eyes flicked up to his…searching.

"I would've seen it, right?" she sputtered.

"In truth? I don't know. People surprise me every day, Mrs. Taylor. Can you tell me what you saw? How was her mood these last several days?"

Audrey shrugged. "I don't know. Normal?"

"Define normal."

"Uh. She's got three kids, you know." Her eyes widened. "Oh, shit. Those poor babies."

"Go on. I need your help, Audrey."

"Oh yeah, of course. They keep her running when they're not in school." She gave him a pointed stare, lips pursed. "You have to meet them to understand. Boys. So yeah, normal for Mary is tired, a little flustered, but still sweet as sugar. She never hit them or wished they hadn't been born." Her shoulders slumped.

"What?"

"It may be nothing, but I noticed yesterday she seemed sort of distracted. I figured she was preparing for school to let out for the summer. She had two days to get her act together before they were with her all day."

"Did she ever hint at killing herself? Even as a joke?"

Arched brows arrowed downward. "You got kids?" she said with an air of disapproval.

"No."

"Well, let me tell you, mister. At that age, they'll have you pulling out your hair and wishing you could drink on the job. I've only got two, and they press me on the best days. No," she stressed. "I never heard her utter those words. Serious or joking."

"Had her hands full with the kids. Got it. Any other things weighing on her? Behind on the bills? House foreclosure looming?"

"No, nothing major. Jason makes decent money, and they didn't live high on the hog. She was a little upset for putting on weight, but not out of control. I think she was about to take me up on the offer to work out. Other than that, nothing I can think of."

"Did you ever see her take medication, even for weight loss?"

"No more than over-the-counter pain relievers or cold medicine. She's always clear eyed."

"Did she ever show you the gun Jason kept in the house?" The quick, derisive snort surprised him.

"Good grief, no way in hell. She's scared of the damn thing."

"How were she and Jason doing? Their marriage."

Audrey's features relaxed, a smile breaching the sadness. "They love each other so much. Been together since middle school. Even with the extra pounds, Jason looks at her as if she hung the moon. If there were major problems, I never saw it. Neither did Lou." She paused, chewing a plump bottom lip and eyes searching the tabletop.

"Go ahead. Even the smallest thing might help."

"I think she worried about Jason coming home late these last several days, but he's working on a lake cabin to surprise her on their anniversary next week. He tried to—" She sucked in a breath.

Max settled back and let Audrey run with her volatile emotions the moment she gave her response a second thought. He had to admit it beyond sad the couple never reached their tenth year and Mary missing some happiness when learning what her husband had done for her. She died with suspicion still lingering in her mind. Audrey opened tear swollen eyes and worried the ball of tissue in her hand.

"This whole damn thing sucks all to hell and back."

"I know, but if you had to guess what pushed your friend to do this, what would you say?"

Determined eyes flicked up and locked with his. "Her kids or Jason. Someone holding a gun to their temples and saying they were going to die. That's it. They were everything to her." She startled at the ringing phone.

"Excuse me for a moment. Browning…Be right there." He gathered his notes and stood. "Your husband's here. Let me walk you to the front. I appreciate you answering my questions. Look, Jason's on his way to the school. I'm sure he'll need help from the both of you when he gets home."

Audrey scrambled from the chair and followed him into the hallway. "Of course. We'll head right over there. Uh, Detective Browning?"

"Yes?"

"Thanks for allowing the other officer to tell me what happened. I know you didn't have to since I'm not family, but will you keep Jason informed on what you figure out about all this mess? Someone forced Mary to do this. I'm sure of it."

"A promise already made, and I won't stop until I know."

Relief bathed her pretty features. "Thank you."

They walked in companionable silence down the congested hallway, winding their way through the multitude of personnel scurrying to-and-fro while dealing with all the other things continuing to happen out in the big, confusing world. This was just one more to add to the growing pile, and it would stick in his craw until a reasonable answer revealed itself.

Max knew the chief wanted this case closed soon so Oklahoma City and their precinct fell out of the limelight. But he also knew the victim's families and Mary's would want the elusive answer, as well. The "how" was clear. This case was all about motive now. Nothing more. They had a dead perp with enough witnesses to dispel any doubt of her involvement, but from what he learned about her character, it made no outward sense she was capable of such an outrageous act. However, the way she conducted the slaughter and her demeanor right before drawing on the officers didn't scream of a woman believing her family in danger.

Then how does a somewhat harried, but loving mom and cherished wife morph into a calm, deadly killer overnight? He gritted his teeth. *Or worse, was her sweet, innocent persona a fragile mask waiting to peel away this entire time?*

CHAPTER 5

THE SLIGHT EDGE OF THE sun rising above the horizon and painting a low blanket of clouds into an explosion of deep orange, yellow, and red brought a smile to Max's face. He never knew what color would greet him. Whatever surprise the sky decided to offer, it never got old to him. This was the best part of living, he affirmed—seeing a new awakening and catching a tiny bit of hope something fresh and clean rode in on its coattails to wash away whatever clung to him the day before.

Match tip scraped across rough gray brick, Max turned his shoulder to block a slight breeze and lifted the flaming wooden stick to light his first cigarette of the day. On a quick snap of the thin, silver case Fergus's wife, Danielle, gifted him years ago, he leaned back against the wall and let vivid memories flood an accepting mind.

While he and Fergus laughed it up in front of a backyard barbeque pit, she handed one over to her husband too. The little spitfire hadn't forgotten their flippant promise to cut down on the smokes three days prior. It could only hold five cigarettes, so they'd gotten the message. She was calling them on it.

Looking out at the majestic skyline, he couldn't believe nine years from their funny moment had passed so fast. Yep, lots had changed since then. He kept his and Fergus's pact, but now, he placed three inside before heading to work. The perfect number. One in the morning, another right after whatever lunch he was lucky enough to grab, and the last saved for the back porch while staring at the stars before he called it a night. The extra room afforded him more matches in the event he screwed up on getting a flame, which was about half the time.

Max ran a thumb across the engraving she left as a constant reminder of their promise, chuckled, and slipped the case into his breast pocket.

"Less is more," he whispered. *So true.*

Cutting down sure as hell made it easier to run the track and think when he wasn't coughing up a lung, but he knew full well he'd never stop. The years had already taken away entirely too much. He was keeping this one and the fond memories called from just slipping the case into his pocket.

The distinctive sound of fluorescent bulbs flickering to life inside the blue and white sign attached to the Medical Examiner's office had him shaking his head. He harbored a feeling this fucked up case might cause a full pack and a lighter to start riding in his pocket real soon if not careful.

Max continued appreciating the scenery and quietness of the early morning, refusing to move from his perch until the ash closed in on the filter. All too soon, he ground Marlboro number one into the provided ashtray and popped a mint into his mouth. He enjoyed his habit but rejected breathing his pleasure into anyone else's face.

A hard yank proving the door unlocked, Max walked six paces, pressed a faded red button next to a caged window, and leaned on the short Formica-encased ledge sticking out from the dull green wall. He wondered how many times his elbow had pressed against the rickety thing, surprised it hadn't cracked off years ago.

Frankie peeked through the small opening, held up an index finger, and walked away. Relieved to find his buddy on duty instead of Tiffany set his shoulders into normal position. After two years, she still acted like a newb on the first day. He wondered where he found the patience to hold his tongue as she went all airhead on him and rummaged through filing cabinets for something sitting on her desk the entire time. The inevitable giggles at finding them after a round of insistent finger pointing to help the dizzy blond ran his spine like razor wire, though expected on each encounter. If nothing else, she stayed a consistent goof and lucky to claim the doc as her great-uncle. If not for the blood ties, the little bit of fluff would've been gone a long time ago.

No doubt, Frankie ranked as top-notch. The guy stuck every toe tag on new arrivals, kept fastidious paperwork, and stood by with the right words and expressions as family members identified their dead. While on Frankie's watch, a cop never lost a victim or endured a relative's instance of false hope upon seeing the wrong face uncovered. Max recalled years ago as a tall, lanky kid strolled in the first day on the job, sporting wide sky-blue eyes full of sympathy and easy to well with tears. Not anymore. They were as world-weary as his were now.

Glass partition snapped into the side slot, Frankie handed over the roster of victims and pushed back the red ball cap failing an effort to subdue dark hair curling around his ears. "Doc's ready for you. Bay eight. He finished up about thirty minutes ago. Worked all night."

"Good man."

Frankie buzzed him in.

Max draped his jacket over an arm and settled his breath. This visit was only a formality, another item required to check off his to-do list. There'd be no trial to use the findings or groundbreaking forensic pathology to prove the right killer stood before a jury of her peers. No, the entire event presented the urgency in allowing devastated families to move forward in the grieving process and collect their loved ones. He'd know each one of his victim's names and stats before the hour ended. Now it got personal.

Faced with a maze of hallways he could navigate in his sleep, Max decided to pick up the pace and get this done and over. He gave the list one more glance and pushed inside the designated room considered the most spacious until finding ten bodies dominating the scenery. Nine covered gurneys lined in a row failed in removing the image of their original positions on the store tile. Another rested in the far corner—in the dark. It had to be Mary.

The significance of its distance from the others led Max to believe Frankie recovered a little bit of humanity and decided to honor the victims by ensuring their killer never got close again. Even the sheet claimed an unusual color—puke green muted against a sea of pristine white. A soft voice pulled his attention away from Jason's loved one.

"Hi, Max. Let's start in order."

He joined Dr. Cecil Deming as he pulled back a sheet and revealed the young man behind the counter. Max dragged his patience front and center, preparing himself. The need didn't rise from viewing a dead body, but the doctor himself. He liked Deming well enough, but the man got exceedingly enthusiastic at times. He always reminded Max of a mad scientist with the thin body honed from forgetting to eat, shock of white, haphazard Einstein hair, and wireframe glasses refusing to sit at the top of his hooked nose. *And so, it begins.*

The fanatic for detail didn't mind sharing every nuance, no matter how tired he was. It would all be in the report, but Max pursed his lips and let him share in the joy of his work. By time they made it down the line and stood next to the male victim found in the grocery aisle, Max couldn't stop his mind from drifting after hearing, "Gunshot to the back of the head. Instantaneous death," for the fourth time. No, the lapse in attention wasn't from boredom or the force feeding of information he already knew, but the idea of lying on one of these tables in the future.

Everyone would park it on a cold slab one day, but he wondered how many gave any thought to strangers seeing all the imperfections they took painstaking care to hide from the world throughout their short existence. The ugly panties worn on washday Sunday, a protruding gut from not knowing when to set the beer down, the drunken tattoo dare won and later cover of the little swastika with a Band-Aid over a fifteen year span, or dreaded lint stuck in a belly button are no longer private matters.

Yeah, unfortunate last memories.

The first time he and Fergus walked their naïve asses inside a morgue and stared at two naked bodies with stab wounds to the throat, they'd both promised to forgo weird tattoos, change their underwear every day, and keep in shape no matter how old they got.

"Go out handsome" rolled out of Fergus's crazy mouth on their eventful day. It stuck. Max checked back into the conversation upon hearing Deming's voice speeding up with unbanked enthusiasm.

"All of these were precision shots meant to cause the most damage. Lower gut, hearts, and heads. But this one. Whoa. He must have pissed her off something fierce."

Sheet snapping back with a flare worthy of a magician, doc waved a hand over the seven bloodless holes in the store manager's chest. "What do you see besides overkill, Detective Browning?"

Max caught the gist as the doctor tapped next to an entry point two inches above the right nipple and then drifted alongside two more angling toward the belly. His finger followed an invisible line up to the one sitting center mass. The instant a gloved finger traced down to the other side and then tapped next to three more angling in a direct line up to the left pec, Max whispered, "W."

The doctor's head bobbed up and down in excitement. "Bingo!"

A low whistle ended Max's study of the wounds from every angle. "Damn, I wondered why she pegged him harder than the rest, but now it makes sense. She left us a calling card." He leaned forward and stared at Mary's last victim's pale face.

"You didn't do a damn thing but be the unlucky one she encountered on her way out the door. You were her canvas for speaking to the world. If you'd ran outside at first chance, we'd be looking at this exact thing on number eight's chest. No, you're the one getting the shitty draw of wearing her legacy. I'm sorry, buddy." He felt a light tap on his shoulder.

"What do you think it means?"

"Your guess is as good as mine. A sick upside-down version of her initial, a directional indicator, or maybe something stupid as a school varsity letter. Hell, no clue what ran through the woman's brain as she made this choice."

"Maybe I can help you out there. I'll need a few hours of shut eye, but I'll do a thorough autopsy this afternoon. Toxicology shows no drugs in the system, so I'll focus on any major diseases." He shrugged and snapped off his gloves. "Some people let loose when they think they're traipsing close to the reaper. Perhaps she made plans to *whoop* it up in Mexico before she bit it."

"Possible. You never know what makes people tick." Max wouldn't have thought he'd ever wish a brain tumor on someone, but it would supply a reasonable explanation for the horror, even give Jason some socially acceptable closure if you wanted to find any good in it.

Doctor thanked for the selfless hours of effort, Max left the facility unable to shake his belief Deming wouldn't find a damn thing wrong with her, other than thirty or more bullet holes riddling the body.

Scared of the gun, my ass. Those weren't lucky shots. Mary knew exactly what she was doing. This was years of practice with an eye for detail. She'd been the perfect killing machine.

* * * * *

When you hit a wall, turn and find a new path.

Max clicked open the email box desperate for a thorough clean up one day and found JoAnn supplied two solid roads to follow.

Good girl!

Phone records and the unsealed juvenile history sat in his inbox like a gift from the gods. The autopsy report appeared, but he decided to save it for last. He had a feeling it held no new surprise.

Three lines in on the Beckham County juvenile report, Max leaned forward in interest.

"Well, what do we have here?"

Yes, there was the expected minor in possession of alcohol ticket, but it also rode hand in hand with an assault charge for fighting at a football game and resulting in bodily injury.

Another girl made a grave mistake of shoving Mary to the side so she could walk one of the football players off the field after their victory. Said athlete was none other than Jason Galesh. Mary's victim, Erin Sweeny, suffered a broken tooth, patch of missing hair, and a dislocated arm for stomping around in Mary's territory. The brick to the knee got her the use of a deadly weapon charge tacked on.

"Well so much for not being violent, Audrey. Your friend's got a history."

For the over-the-top jealous streak, Max discovered Mary spent a week in juvenile detention with a parental promise to the judge she would attend a strict boarding school to finish out the rest of ninth grade. They bowed to the mandatory concession or faced watching their otherwise sweet daughter spend serious jail time in a hardcore youth facility. Did it stop there? Nope.

Reports to the court notated a few escape attempts. Jason caught sneaking onto the grounds resulted in the parents sending her to another school for troubled teens on the east coast to avoid the judge's threat to revoke her plea agreement. Last report notation showed she finished out there without incident and returned to Elk City. Nothing but the speeding ticket followed. She became a model citizen.

"Guess she didn't like the idea of staying away from Jason, so she straightened up. Okay, now I know you're the jealous type and resort to violence if you imagine a relationship's threatened."

Max shuffled through the large manila envelope forensics placed on his desk an hour ago and retrieved a scene photo of the tall, well-built blond. "Maybe you were the catalyst." He flipped it over. "Sherilynn Owens. Current or former mistress of the hubby?" He sat back and thought about it for a minute.

"Nah, that doesn't make any sense. A scorned woman would wait and catch them together to justify her actions, or if working off pure ignited emotion, would've blasted her first."

High school Mary struck out at Erin fast, yet Owens ranked as the second victim, not the target. Gut instinct clamored Mary wanted to chalk up a body count on her way to the door. If the blond were banging the hubby, he expected the seven holes reserved for the homewrecker and the W representing "whore" to show her distaste. The only way he knew to sway from the logical course of thought is if Ms. Owen's number started popping up on the Galesh's phone records. He slipped the photo back in with the others and opened the second email.

Not long into the assessment, Max discovered Mary spoke with Audrey quite a bit. Calls to her parents in Elk City were consistent— every Thursday like clockwork. Most texts were short and revolved around notices to Jason she'd be late coming back from the kid's doctor visits or asking him to pick up something from the store on his way home.

49

A smattering of gooey love messages confirmed Jason and Mary were still hot for each other. If Jason did half the naughty promises to his wife, then she ranked as a very satisfied woman in the sack and vice versa. Sherilynn was set aside as a motive.

Max found no odd, rogue numbers slipping in with the rest. All were neighbors, the school, mom, local businesses, or the hubby. Jason's were all to Mary, work, or Audrey's husband, Lou. A perusal of the autopsy proved him right. Nothing out of the ordinary, and she had perfect health. Despite the added information, she remained Mystery Mary. He closed the reports and clicked the National Crime Database link.

"Okay, so let's look at the event instead." Gus relayed on more than one occasion people were just a bunch of animals riding instinctual moves most of the time. If you look at similar actions, you might find motives the same as your perp. At least it could open doors for new trails to sniff down.

A plug of "gun use" and "multiple victims" delivered Max a list too numerous to even consider traipsing through. The reveal came as no surprise. Nobody broke out with a good fistfight anymore and left it at that. Of course not. They go for the kill, as if this would somehow right their pride. Instead, most found themselves murdering innocent bystanders and missing the true mark by a mile. He added "grocery store" to the search engine.

The results narrowed but stayed outrageous. Even an include of "leaving a calling card" for perpetrator quirks got him zero hits. Max removed the store variable and received a much shorter list, but still too long to rifle through in a reasonable amount of time. Search grid narrowed down to Oklahoma and the surrounding states brought back five hits and a surge of hope. The third lifted the hairs on his arms.

Well, shit.

Eyes jumping from one line to the next, Max read it twice to make sure he wasn't imagining the content.

"Inmate: Bernard Adler. Event Location: Target store in Ardmore, Oklahoma. Event date: Four years ago. Victim count: Twelve. Method: Handgun. Sentence: Life without parole. Inmate Location: McAlester, Oklahoma penitentiary. Quirk: Bullet holes in victim's upper torso forming the letter 'W.' Inmate unwilling to disclose meaning."

Max flopped back and scrubbed the top of his head until sure the hair stood up in little spikes. "Damn. Am I dealing with a copycat?" Eyes swiveled to the left, he pressed a finger against the map tacked to the wall and trailed it down Highway 270, confident he knew what waited at the end. He needed to see the word to let it sink home. The thin yellow line led directly to McAlester.

Did Mary set out to visit her idol with an intent to make a big show outside the prison gates? Was she planning to shout his name and call victory? Perhaps she already planned to be a martyr, but just didn't make it all the way to her destination.

All signs pointed to it. Had she corresponded or admired from afar? Heart rate speeding, he stood and made a frantic pocket pat for his keys. He needed his ass at the Galesh home to search Mary's personal belongings before Jason lawyered up out of protection from all things hell bent on further disrupting his life.

The desk phone rang from an outside line and furrowed his brows. For half a second, he thought about not answering. But on the off chance it might be Jason halted his escape. If he received permission to search now, half his battle was in the bag. He snatched the phone.

"Browning."

"Detective Maxwell Browning?"

The smooth, deep voice threw him for a second. He'd never heard it before, but the man sounded articulate.

Crap! Don't let it be the lawyer.

"Yeah, how can I help you?"

"My name's Preston Sinclair. I'm calling about the event at Bagwell's grocery. I have information pertinent to your case. Please write my number down. I might get disconnected."

CHAPTER 6

Max caught the urgency in Sinclair's tone, transferring it right into muscles already jacked to hightail it out of this place. He grabbed a pen and held it over a yellow notepad next to the phone. "Go." The number wasn't local. "Got it. What do you have for me?"

"Like to visit the shooter's home with you, if possible. Your answer as to why this happened might be there. I can confirm it for you if I see it."

Chills lifted on Max's arms, even though he knew full well the guy couldn't know his immediate plans.

"Not going to happen, bud. Believe me."

A soft chuckle sounded through the receiver.

"Thought so, but worth a shot. Here's the point. I need to know if you found a distinctive burn mark anywhere near the shooter's bed."

Max knew he wore what Fergus coined as his "Did you actually ask me that shit" face. He let his head loll back on his shoulders and spit out a familiar line.

"Look. I don't discuss specifics of ongoing cases, and you're wasting my time here."

"Wait. I know you want to hang up, but you need to understand this won't be your last one, Detective Browning. Expect more."

"Yeah, crime happening every day. What's new, fella?"

"No, this is different. We need to search the killer's home for the mark to prove what I'm trying to tell you. If we don't find it, then I'll get out of your hair."

Head shaking in disgust, Max set the phone back in the cradle, grabbed his coat, and walked out of the office. Insistent ringing followed him down the hallway.

"Nut bags."

Mary's name floated on the airwaves for less than two hours and the loose screws backed out of the woodwork at a steady pace. The first drizzle of morning coffee hadn't met his gut before a call came in from a frantic man claiming Mary Galesh killed his dog. Better yet, would forensics come out to test the bullet he pulled from its neck to determine a match with the Glock? Oddballs always trickled in right after the killer's name released to the public. Poor JoAnn. He'd owe her big time for fielding all his calls, and the list already draped to his knee.

* * * * *

"Shit. They're going to make me run the gauntlet," Max muttered. He cut the engine to the Vic and stared at the tired, old adversary he'd grown to despise over the years.

Damn vultures.

News vans lined the cul-de-sac while perfectly coifed and well-dressed aggressive reporters vied for the prime spot in front of the Galesh home. Their usual, rabid pack mindset caused him to park six houses down and at a weird angle.

If younger and Gus in the passenger seat egging him on, he would've pulled up on the sidewalk and caught some primetime news coverage as he scattered the assholes. *Good times.*

Notepad and trusty pen shoved into his front pocket, Max slipped from the car and relaxed his features into what he liked to term his "dead face." If he didn't, the reporters would remark with all seriousness the detective on the case appeared angry, concerned, shocked, or any other such nonsense to titillate the viewers. The best they could get out of his mask and stay as close to the truth as possible was "placid." No one turned up the volume on a dull adjective. Hope grew toward their continued ignorance of his presence.

"Detective Browning!"

Shit.

"Do you have any information on why Mary Galesh shot and killed nine people?" a woman with heavily painted eyes and brilliant white teeth screamed above the other voices.

"No comment."

Within seconds, his movement forward reduced to that of a ninety-year-old. Of course, it wasn't anyone he recognized pressing in on him. All the seasoned ones knew better than to get up in his grill. They all rested against their vans, sporting shit-eating grins, and waiting for the explosion. After the third microphone popped him on the chin, Max halted. Eyes narrowed, he scanned the determined crowd and deepened his voice into dark menace.

"Back up or face charges of assaulting a police officer. Your choice but make it quick."

Threat working, progress toward the house improved. Sometimes it paid off to be much taller and meaner than the surrounding enemy could claim.

A male voice somewhere over his right shoulder shouted, "Detective Browning, what have you discovered about Mary Galesh's motive? Why did she do it? Were there any other people involved? Did her husband know she was going to do it?"

"What Captain Walters gave you this morning is all we're allowed to release," he threw out. "The investigation's still pending." Max turned around on the sidewalk leading to Jason's door and held up a warning palm.

"Stay out of his yard. You guys know better. Don't make me call in a unit. I doubt Mr. Galesh will traipse outside in his bathrobe and start telling you how he's feeling, so you're wasting your time here. If he wants to share, I'm sure he'll book a time with you. Look. Give him some peace, will you? Neither he nor his kids had anything to do with this. Plant that into your skulls and make it stick. They're as much victims as the other families."

"Will you ask if he'll come outside?"

"Not his PR rep, so consider yourself stupid for asking."

Max stared at the crowd and backed up a few steps, eyes daring them to go rogue so he could pull his cuffs. Upon the noise level subsiding and microphones lowered, he swiveled and strolled up on the porch. *Good grief.* At least they served a higher purpose by keeping vandals at bay until the family figured out their next step. It was the only kudos he was willing to give them.

He barely laid knuckles to the dark wood before it opened enough for him to slip inside the dim room. A quick scan of the environment gave an impression of a well-kept home with its wrap-around couch, big-boy recliner, decent-size flat screen, children's toys resting inside a blue milk crate in the corner, and preference for southwest artwork.

The crumpled pillow paired with a wrinkled blanket on the sofa clued him someone parked there last night and hadn't found a restful moment. The eerie quietness sat at odds with the madness outside. He turned and found Jason leaning on the wall behind the door.

"Hey there."

"Hi."

The poor guy was a wreck, as expected. Pale face, dark circles under puffy eyes, shadow of a beard, and sleep-tossed hair reflected what ate his insides at a steady rate. He wore the same clothes as yesterday.

Pushed from the shadows, Jason held out his hand, still enough of a gentleman in him to make the effort.

Max returned the firm grip and shake.

"Thank you, Detective Browning. I heard what you said to them. Was thinking of spraying them down with the water hose. Glad you came by." He swallowed hard and made his way through an arched doorway leading into a kitchen.

Slow, measured steps clued Max the guy moved on autopilot. Routine. Unthinking. He followed him in.

"Uh. Want coffee? I should make some."

"Sure. I like it black."

"Me too."

Settled at the oak dining table, he observed the robotic man fill the carafe with water, retrieve a red can from the cabinet, and face the coffee pot. He hesitated and backed up a few steps, appearing stuck inside a memory.

"The last time I saw her, she stood right here." Jason's hand waved in a slow back-and-forth motion over the area he envisioned her, as if he could somehow reclaim what he lost.

Max leaned forward to catch the low, shaky voice.

"She looked tired, but she was still my Mary." White teeth chewed on a bottom lip for a second. "I can't remember if I said I love you before I left." His shoulders slumped. "God, I hope I did."

Max lunged forward and caught the carafe angling closer to the floor and took it from Jason's shaking hand.

"Go sit down. I'll make it. Got one like it at the house."

With an absent nod, Jason plopped on the nearest chair.

"Are the kids still asleep?" The question seemed to snap the guy out of his stupor.

"Uh, no, they're with Audrey and her sister." He gestured absently to the right. "Stephanie lives two blocks over. We didn't want them scared by the news people. I haven't told them yet…the boys." His jaw clenched. "I don't know how."

"Have you eaten?"

Jason's eyes shifted upward and to the left, trying to recall mundane activities trapped inside his muddled brain. "I can't remember."

Coffee brewing and filling the quiet space with something familiar and comforting, Max slipped two slices of bread into the toaster and retrieved butter and a jar of grape jelly from the refrigerator. After discovering eggs, milk, cheese, and some chopped ham, it didn't take but a few minutes to whip up a fat omelet. He became a master at it after his divorce from Victoria. Seven years of bachelorhood gifted numerous skills. The second button on his light blue shirt bore proof he could use a needle and thread.

Satisfied with his creation, Max filled their cups, set the heaping plate in front of Jason, and sat down.

"Eat before you fall over."

The poor guy stared at the food as if wondering how the hell it got there.

"Uh. Thank you."

One tentative bite appeared to kick in the man's appetite. He dug in for another scoop.

"Where's your family?"

Jason stopped long enough to take his first sip of the hot brew. "Mine are dead. Mary's came in last night. Her sister flew in from New York and put them up at a hotel outside the city."

"Smart."

"Yeah, Delia's a tough lady. She's helping them make the funeral arrangements for me. We'll all tell the boys tonight, I guess." He hesitated and set the fork aside.

Max was glad to find he at least ate half of the food. Eyes shining like polished marble lifted to his.

"We'll bury Mary near her parent's home. Maybe not in Elk City, but close. If I tried to do it here in the city, I'm sure someone would find out and trash her grave." He blinked a few times as another realization slammed into his brain.

"I should move. Oh, God, this is so fucked up."

"Yes, it is. Listen, this isn't any easier than when we first spoke, but I promised to do everything in my power to figure out what happened. I need to search Mary's things to find sense of what she did leading up to yesterday. A journal, notes, anything. Do I have your permission? Up to you."

Jason nodded and pointed toward a doorway sporting quaint saloon-style swinging panels.

"Sure. Of course. Our room's down the hall. I'll show you."

Long strides faltered the closer they came to the bedroom. He reached out, pushed the double doors open, and took a quick step back, almost as if afraid of electrocution for breaching the threshold. With both hands shoved deep into the front pockets of his jeans and holding a steady glare on his socked feet, Jason's cheeks revealed obvious embarrassment.

"What are you thinking?"

"Nothing you told me yesterday sank in until I found the lockbox open and the gun and ammunition missing. I kept hoping the dead woman in the car was an eerie twin and Mary would come walking in the door after she fought her way out of the binds. How stupid is that?"

Max patted Jason's slumped shoulders.

"Not at all. Lost a close friend once. I was there when he died. Right in my arms, in fact. Even still, it took me a solid month to quit expecting to hear his voice telling me to wake up every time I answered a ringing phone. I prayed I was in a coma. So no, your hope is far from stupid."

Jason pursed his lips and managed what tried to be a soft laugh.

"Yeah, I guess our minds play tricks when we're trying to come to grips with something so bizarre."

"I agree."

Gaze dropping to the gleaming hardwood floor, Jason gestured toward the bedroom.

"I'm sorry. I can't go in there again. Besides, all her clothes are still in the—" His lips tightened.

"No, it's all right. I understand. Don't worry. Promise I won't remove anything unless you look it over first and give permission."

A sucking inhale spelled his relief. He thanked him with desperate eyes and backed up to the other side of the hallway. "Mary kept all of her stuff at the top of the closet...on the right."

"Thank you. Now go finish your breakfast before it gets cold. Toast too. You'll need your strength."

"I'll try." He seemed to struggle with his next words. "Detective Browning?"

"Call me Max."

Tightness around Jason's gray eyes instantly softened. "*Max*, if you can figure out why my wife did this, I'll be eternally grateful. I'm losing my goddamn mind. None of this makes any sense, but obvious I missed something big with her. Whatever it is, don't hold back. I need to know."

"That's my plan. I'll come to you first when I have something definitive."

Jason stared at him for a few beats, as if still unable to understand why he didn't see hate lashing out at him. "You're a good man, Max." On a cleansing breath, he turned, and made his way back toward the kitchen.

Fuck. Max sagged against the doorframe. He hadn't experienced this unnerving ball of tangled emotions banging in his chest in what felt like forever. His mind kept switching Sean into this horrid situation and wondered how he could bear the pain of watching him suffer. Jason didn't deserve to have his life upended for loving Mary.

Disturbed he let his guard slip, Max shook it off and stepped inside the room decorated with southwestern themed pictures on crème painted walls and sporting waist-high light-pine paneling— the good kind showcasing the age rings of the trees without being overbearing to the eye. It went well with the teal carpeting and slightly darker wood furnishings.

Analysis mode shoved back to the forefront and settled his nerves. To the immediate left, he noticed a precision-made king-size bed covered in a spread bearing the same motif carried throughout the home. Two mauve lamps positioned on sturdy nightstands sat either side. A short bureau with a round mirror rested against the wall opposite the bed. He made a mental note to address those later. It appeared the closet to his right held the key. The door was still open. Jason wanted out of this room so badly he hadn't even bothered closing it.

Max knew the feeling, but on a different level. He remembered standing inside his own closet and staring at a miniscule amount of Victoria's clothes she left behind, her perfume still lingering on the coats and scarves. She removed everything the next day, but the scent still stuck around for weeks. It was a knife to the gut every time he'd had to venture inside and pull a dress shirt off a hanger. He'd caught himself wearing the same one for three days and finally got his shit together.

Bad memories pushed aside, Max looked down and found the empty lockbox resting on the floor. He put it back in the only open slot on the top shelf. After searching through a few boxes filled with sewing material, yarn, and infants clothing, Max found something of interest, her treasure trove of memories holding high school yearbooks, bagged, dried flowers with the date Jason presented them, family photo albums, and several stacks of letters.

Settled on the floor, Max looked for anything shedding light on the situation—shaking out material, looking underneath pictures, and searching for slim rips in the seams of bound books for secreting small items. Nothing. Even the baseboards were intact.

A thorough study of her yearbook gifted multiple shots of the popular duo taking part in the usual high school antics. Beaming kids awaiting a bright future. One stood out from the others. Mary's thin, but curvy frame settled against Jason's lanky body revealed the comfort they took from each other. He appeared to be stroking her fall of gorgeous dark hair—a beautiful young girl matched with a handsome boy. The perfect couple. He ran his thumb over her smiling face.

"Talk to me, Mary," he whispered. "What happened to you?"

He set the yearbook back inside the box and retrieved the letters. It didn't take him long to realize all were from her mother and sister while she languished in the eastern school and awaited freedom. He found her remorseful for the fateful decision to battle Erin.

What he expected to discover never appeared. No ominous correspondence from a stone-cold killer lurked within. Box repacked to the order he found it, he set it on the shelf and returned to the bedroom.

After confirming nothing under the bed or of note within the large bureau, Max searched the night tables. Tissue boxes, TV guide, wrapped lozenges, and a few anniversary cards with small hearts drawn below their names was all that met him. Stumped again. He was almost relieved to answer his ringing phone.

"Browning."

"Max. I have a new one for you."

Crap. "I'm handling something, Fletcher. Give it to Harold."

"Can't. He's across town. Freeway shooting."

"What about Dickens?"

"Nope. Man ran over several pedestrians at a restaurant two minutes after the driver grabbed his parking spot. You're the closest."

"Goddamn, what the hell's going on?"

"It's the fucking heat. Fries people's brains," Fletcher offered and followed with a grunt.

"No doubt. Hold up a sec." Max refrained from engaging the speaker. The last thing Jason needed to overhear were descriptions of more carnage. He set his notepad on the nightstand, squatted next to the bed, and squashed the cell to his ear with his shoulder. Awkward, but it offered a chance to shove his hand under the mattress to check for hidden items. "Go."

"Small jewelry store over on Lyle." He rattled off the name and address. "Three dead and messy. Serious knife play. Perp took off on foot. We're running the neighborhood. Two witnesses left unharmed. Happened within the last ten minutes."

"Give me a little bit to finish up here. Press is clogging the road too. Go ahead and let the coroner in for photos if they beat me there. Don't move anything."

"Understood."

Max finished jotting down his notes, slipped the phone into his pocket, and started to rise. He dropped back to one knee, yanked his pen light, and lit up the area between the bedframe and nightstand.

"You've *got* to be shitting me."

CHAPTER 7

ON A HARD GRUNT, MAX shoved the nightstand to the side and ran his finger over a quarter-sized scorch mark close to the leg of the headboard. He at once realized it wasn't one of the natural wood knots scattered across the wall. It didn't swirl as much as blast outward. His mind kicked into "find the reality" mode.

One of the kids playing with Mary's lighter or a candle toppling over during a romantic romp took front and center explanation. He noticed small dings, scratches, and scuffs on the paneling, but they were nothing outside the normal wear and tear of every household in America. This one stood out in its oddness. He started to rise, yet everything inside of him screamed to stand down.

"This is stupid, Browning."

Max captured an image of the odd anomaly and shoved the phone back inside his pocket.

"You're losing it. Fucking losing it."

Just as fast as the chastisement, his eyes narrowed, and he focused on the peculiar scorch with a new perspective.

Well, shit. You're getting slow, old man.

He leaped to his feet and scanned the room.

"Has Preston Sinclair been inside here?" he whispered. "How else would he know to ask about a mark?" Max's heart started up a wild thump as he paced the room.

"Could he be the outside link for Adler? Is this how he recruits his followers? Are they playing with me now? But why?" All he was sure about was the phone call he planned to make when he returned to the office.

Head shaking at the strange turn of events, Max readjusted the nightstand and left the bedroom with a disquieted sensation owning his gut. By the time he reached the kitchen, he confirmed his decision not to mention it to Jason. It was all speculation at this point, and the poor guy had enough on his shoulders. Max noticed the plate missing from the table, and so was Jason. He found him in the living room, peeking out the window and releasing a soft whistle.

"Damn, it looks like they're multiplying."

"Are they in the yard?"

"Not mine, but the next-door neighbors. Both sides and halfway up. Look at this shit. They're even standing in Sheila's flowerbeds. Asses."

"Driveways blocked?"

"Yes."

Max tapped seven on his phone. "Sean, I'm at Jason Galesh's house. Send two squads out here to clear the cul-de-sac of reporters. Street's turned into a damn circus. Have them tell the horde a trespassing and possible destruction of property call came in so everyone must go. Hold up." He approached the window and took a few snaps of the encroachers.

"Sent you some proof. Yeah, put a barrier at the end of the street. If they want to stick around, they'll have to line up down the block or walk into fast traffic to get a bead on the house…Yes, the heavy-duty ones. ID verification of homeowners required to allow access. I'm hoping the crews grow bored and find someone else to pester…Thanks. Later." He looked up to find a puzzled expression rocking Jason's puss.

"What? Something else happen?"

"No, why are you doing this for us?"

Max relaxed his shoulders and softened his voice. "You don't deserve any of this fallout from Mary's actions. Running interference is the least I can do. I need to leave, though. Got another call. The units should arrive in fifteen. You good?"

"Yeah, if they don't bust down the door next. Did you find what you needed?"

"Nothing of hers stuck out as abnormal. I won't give up, though. I appreciate you letting me look around."

"No problem. Thank you."

Max hesitated at the door and turned to catch Jason's worried eyes. "I want to pass on some advice. You open for it?"

"Sure."

"Attorney's will bombard you to offer protection."

"Protect me?"

"Yes, the families of the victims will have similar visits. They'll convince them to go after the grocery store for compensation. Odds it will include you too."

Gray eyes widened. "Me?"

"Yeah, they'll want to turn their grief into vindication. Most times, they get to face a perpetrator in court, listen to the evidence, and hear a sentence handed down. Not in this case, so their frustration will only grow. You'll be Mary's substitute. Expect civil suits."

Jason's buried anger shot forward and replaced the bewilderment. It was long overdue.

"Goddamn it. Haven't I suffered enough?"

"They won't look at it that way. Research the lawyers contacting you. Don't pick one unless their firm's handled situations like this before and won. If asked for money, send them packing. The good ones offer pro bono on a publicity bonanza case. If you're contacted by Dwight Sanders, return his call." Max's hand dropped from the knob.

"Better yet, contact him and give him my name. He's in the book. The man's very smart and will make sure you come out looking sympathetic to the families and the public."

"I *am* sympathetic. I hate what she did."

"I know you are, but this city needs to see it—on your face and in your eyes. You'll have to apologize in public to the victims' families. Listen, Jason. You didn't do a damn thing wrong, but you'll have to separate yourself from her, otherwise it remains guilt by association. Don't make excuses for her, either, or face angering them more."

Jason's shoulders dropped. "Got it. They don't know a damn thing about me. I won't hesitate to let the families know I'm suffering for them, as well. You're right. I need some help."

He reached out, and Max shook his hand again.

"Appreciate everything you've done, Max. I can't seem to say it enough."

"Thank me by not giving up. The pain will dull. Sounds ridiculous now, but it will. Take care, Jason."

"You too, Max."

* * * * *

Max figured it time for Sean to run with a scene. Granted, he hadn't applied for a detective's position yet, but Dixon's incessant growl about retiring presented the boy some history to talk about during the interview process. A chance for a one-on-one live session became an easy decision to call him in on the jewelry store fiasco. He motioned for the arriving officers to step outside.

"Wait for the store rep. Someone's coming to retrieve surveillance video from the vault. Did you touch anything?"

"No, sir."

"Good man." Max moved away from the counter and leaned against the wall.

"What do you see, Sean?" Chills lifted across his flesh the second intense blue eyes scanned the area, right hand resting on a hip and the left tapping against his thigh. It was as if Fergus had just entered his son's body.

Can unconscious tics be genetic?

Sean had never been present when Gus did his thing, so it was a little spooky to say the least.

Sean's focus narrowed on the body lying in a gap between the front counter and an arched entranceway separating the customers from the employees.

"Witnesses said the perp walked right past them and took out this gentleman first. Then he went after the two women. They didn't know in what order the females went down since they ran out after seeing the first victim hit the floor."

He returned to the front of the jewelry display and studied it for a second before squatting down.

"Blood on the front looks like arterial spray. The victim stood close to the edge of the counter, staggered backward, and fell. There's more on his palms but no slices. Happened quick with little time to defend himself."

"Very good. What else?"

Sean kneeled close to the body, mindful to stay out of the red pool spreading on the patterned tile.

"See a large, slicing wound from ear to ear. No other clear stab points on the body."

He pointed to the man's neck, and Max leaned in for a better look at his find, yet kept his mouth shut.

"See there? Huge gap on the left side and the wound narrows as it goes across to the right. Witnesses said the victim and the killer were face-to-face."

His hand moved in a slow sweeping motion, showing the perp's possible actions.

"It looks like the widest part of the knife hacked in deep and sliced the artery, which is why the blood went in this direction first. As the knife progressed, it narrowed toward the tip, causing less penetration. Had to be big. Maybe a standard chef's knife used for cutting and chopping." He shrugged. "Unless he held it gripped with the blade tip facing toward his elbow, the perp's left-handed."

"Reasonable deduction. What happened next?"

Sean stood and assessed the floor. He pointed to a bloody shoe print.

"Killer steps over the body and into the back area. Moves to the left and stabs the blond in the back as she's running toward the office."

"How do you know?" Max pushed.

"Direction of the prints. Toes angle toward her body, and she landed with her head closer to the door. The keys are still in her hand. Possible plan to lock herself inside. Sorry, I can't tell how many times he struck, but it was definitely more than once." He swiveled to the right, eyeballing the upended chairs and scattered paperwork.

Max liked seeing the kid remain quiet in his assessment of the area, not blurting out random thoughts, but taking his time to formulate a reasonable projection. Sean lifted his head and stared toward the front of the store—voice steady on his slow, precise steps forward.

"The brunette tried crawling over the counter," he said with growing confidence. "That accounts for the necklace stands and brochures scattered on the other side."

"Why?"

"I assume she couldn't bring herself to go near the dead male and all the blood. The decision sealed her fate. She's wearing a pencil skirt, so I guess she had hell getting her leg up. Propriety usurped instincts to hike it high or launch herself over. While she's struggling, the perp slides across the desks blocking his direct path and the papers scatter toward the counter. The shoe impressions are on top of them, and the blood's lighter now."

Squatted by the brunette, Sean studied the woman lying on her back, dead gray eyes fixed on the ceiling.

"He pulled her back from the counter by the hair. Clumps of it are under her left elbow. Used it to hold her in place as he slit her throat from behind. The same wound pattern as the male is present, but the most damage runs in the opposite direction—right to left."

Sean stood up and stared at numerous footprints forming a bizarre pattern next to the victims head, brows furrowing as the left hand kept a steady thigh tap.

"I see her bleeding out now, and my shoes become saturated with it. I don't know which way to go, so I try them all...yet I'm stuck in one spot. I'm scared."

Exhilaration flooded Max's veins. Sean had moved from being a third-party observer to seeing it through the eyes of the killer. He was far more advanced than he imagined.

Quiet thoughtfulness reigned for several moments.

"Confusion and panic set in. These long, skewed trails show where he scraped the blood off by dragging both feet backward."

He stepped close to the male again, brows furrowed.

"There it is, a faint print next to the knee where he hops over the body, but now a trail of blood droplets leads away from the victims. Either he's holding the knife down by his side, or he cut himself when hacking at the blond. We need to make sure forensics gathers samples from this area. He could've left some of his DNA behind."

Max followed Sean to the door while the kid's voice grew in strength, caught up in the chase.

"The droplets aren't far apart. I can assume he's walking at a slow, steady pace since the stains aren't getting any lighter as he reaches the exit. Yeah, I'm sticking with the bleeding cut theory. Shit. Someone stepped in some. Hope it wasn't me when I came in." He pushed the door open and motioned for an officer to come over. "Richards. See that?"

A pair of sharp eyes looked down to where Sean indicated the sidewalk. The drops trailed alongside a tar-filled seam, easy to overlook.

"Damn."

"Gather up a few others and follow it. Call in a K-9 unit. We've got a proven direction now."

Palm pressed against Sean's back, Max guided him to the side and motioned for him to sit on the bench with him. Waves of pride swelled his chest. Seconds ticked by as he worked to rein in his emotions.

"You're just like him."

"Who?"

"Your dad. I'm so damn proud of you, Sean. You conducted a very thorough and insightful walk through. The eerie similarity to your father's style had me fascinated. Pattern sighting came natural to him. It was as if he had a video of the event playing inside his head. The man had a gift. I became a better detective from working with him."

"He said the same about you."

Max looked over to find Sean pretending to flick some wayward piece of fluff off the knee of his black cargo pants.

"I used to sit at the top of the stairs and listen to him talking to Mom when he came home. He admired you. Loved you like a brother. Said you had the ability to see beyond the bodies and all the shit scattered everywhere, looking past it to get to the core of what the killer was thinking. He could read the tracks, but you could build the perp inside his head. Claimed it's what made you such a good team. Two halves of a whole."

For the first time in eight years, Max sensed the sting of tears biting the back of his eyes. He straightened on the bench as Sean did the same. They both cleared their throats and shared a hesitant chuckle.

"You're going to apply when Dixon retires, right?"

"For sure. This sealed it. Got a runner's high after a few steps. Thanks for putting me in the situation. I've always doubted I could fill even an eighth of my dad's shoes."

Max reached over and patted his thigh. "You can set the fear aside. Runs in your blood. Natural."

"So who was he, Max?"

"Our perp?"

"Yeah."

"Good, because I wouldn't have enough time in the day to define your father."

Sean chortled and nudged him with his elbow.

"Well, we don't know if the guy was known to those employees, or not. Witnesses said he came in quick, and it just started happening. Robbery isn't an obvious motive, or he would've snatched as much as he could from the open cabinet next to the brunette. Thousands of dollars sat right there for the taking. No, he was here for a fast kill. A deliberate ignore of the two shoppers standing at the counter and the use of a knife means it was personal to him. There was a need to be close, to feel the weapon engage with their bodies. One or all of them upset him at one point, whether they knew it or not. Disgruntled customer or jilted lover. Who knows?"

Sean's head bobbed up and down. "Yeah, hesitation at the end and indecision of the next move could mean remorse after the targets were no longer a threat. The enormity of what he'd done might have sank in, and he made desperate swipes to remove their blood from his shoes...to disconnect. If he were concerned about leaving a trail, he wouldn't have left the droplets behind."

Max chortled and popped him on the leg. "See? You worried for nothing. You have the eye."

"Thanks. Means a lot coming from you. I know you wouldn't hesitate to dog me if I fumbled around."

"Damn straight." Max lifted the vibrating phone from his pocket and put it on speaker. "What you got, Richards?"

"You're not going to believe this. Dude was right around the corner at the Cefco station. Found him cowering inside the dumpster. I only had to ask him once to turn the weapon over, and he gave it up as if relieved it wasn't in his hand any longer. The guy's not all there. Clocked out. Eyes fixed on some faraway point, but I don't think its drug related. In shock, maybe."

"Say anything?"

"I don't like dogs. Make it go away. Weird shit."

"K-9 scared him, huh?"

"No, still five minutes out. Maybe a stray interested in all the blood spooked him and he hid. Whatever happened, he's fried."

"Headed to the hospital?"

"Yep, gash on his hand needs stiches."

"Which one?"

"Left. Called ahead for psyche to ready his arrival."

Max looked over at Sean and winked. "Tell me you found ID on him, Richards."

"Yeah, Harrison Monroe. Forty-five. Doesn't live far from here. I sent a patrol over to secure the premises until we have a warrant."

"Good job. Call me when it arrives. I'm still waiting for the surveillance video and the coroner."

"Will do."

"Come on, Sean. You need to ensure forensics collects samples from the droplets. At least we have someone to compare it with to make a firm placement at the scene. I also want you in on the interrogation when they release him from evaluation. We'll do it at the hospital. You game?"

"Hell yeah."

Max hadn't made a step forward before his phone went off again. "Richards, again." He engaged the speaker. "Tell me."

"No warrant needed. The officers entered for cause."

"Reason?"

"Dead woman sitting on a recliner in front of a TV. Chest soaked in blood. Wide open main door allowed them to spot her through the screen. Not fresh. Day old, maybe. Appears she lives there since she's wearing a bathrobe and slippers."

"Damn. Hold the scene for me. Squat on it, and no tape, yet. Forensics will be here for a little longer. Might be awhile."

"Got it."

Max turned to Sean. "Call your supervisor. Tell him you're with me for the rest of the day. I'll need your help on this one."

CHAPTER 8

"WHICH WAY TO PSYCHIATRIC HOLDING? Seems it moved since last time I visited."

To hide his building frustration, Max nixed the finger drumming on the counter. A mindless ten-minute walkabout forced a decision to eat his pride and ask for help. Hurt like a bitch.

The distracted hospital receptionist looked up, tossed him a brilliant smile, and shoved a lock of strawberry blond hair behind a pierced ear. "Yeah, they remodeled last year. Needed more room. Seems everyone's going nuts."

Max chuckled. "Good to know. At least I'm not in the wrong hospital and turning senile."

She giggled and batted sparkling blue eyes. "You don't look anywhere old enough to be senile, yet. I think you're safe."

Stumped for a snappy reply he clapped his mouth shut.

The girl young enough to be a daughter, if he'd been so inclined to procreate at the age of thirty-one, executed a saucy wink and pointed at the elevators behind him.

"Go to the fourth floor, take a left, and its two doors down. You'll have to present ID and sign in."

"Got it. Thanks."

Max stuffed the portable video player holding the Stanford Jeweler's surveillance footage under his armpit and leaned forward to punch the indicated floor. Back pressed against the elevator wall, a wide grin stretched his cheeks as the doors began to close. The receptionist assumed the happiness belonged to her. He returned the little wave.

Despite the dire content he carried and reason for the visit, he continued celebrating Sean's spot-on observance of the crime scene.

The perp turning around to puke in the trashcan and accounting for the marred blood drops at the exit became the one lone miss on an otherwise stellar investigation. Hell, even forensics overlooked it. The guy didn't leave enough to spark up an odor, but it still ranked as valuable DNA evidence. With the real donor in custody, the find fell to a non-essential side item.

Overall, Sean remained satisfied with his efforts after they'd viewed the vid. He rocked a satisfied grin until the coroner showed up and the action started up again. Though disappointed he couldn't bring Sean with him to sit in on the fact-finding mission with Monroe, he found him more valuable staying at the jewelry store to ensure a smooth wrap up.

Check-in desk found without much fanfare, Max presented his credentials, signed all the crap shoved in front of him, and stepped inside the interrogation room the psychiatric department used for patients on a fast track to jail. He settled at a metal table which hadn't had opportunity to meet much violence, yet. His trusty notepad's placement on the smooth surface coincided with a loud buzz.

A tall man with graying hair, intelligent green eyes, and a welcoming smile stepped into the room. The white lab coat and dress pants clued him he was the doc.

"Hello, Detective Browning. I'm Dr. Reardon. We closed Mr. Monroe's wound. Toxicology screen is in progress. I'll have the report sent to the email ID you left at reception."

Appreciative the guy hadn't dragged out the conversation with a bunch of added useless meet-and-greet, Max gave him quick nod. "His demeanor?"

"The patient snapped out of his catatonic state as soon as the first staple clamped into his hand. He's calmed down but still disoriented. The man assumes he's had a car accident. In trying to rationalize the cuffs on his wrists, he believes he's at fault. We haven't told him any different. Depending on the outcome of your conversation, I'm ready to have him processed for release to your department."

The doctor turned and motioned to an orderly standing in the hallway. Within minutes, Monroe shuffled into the room, hazel eyes wide, and face pale. Brown, wavy hair laced with gray appeared damp from a recent shower. Though he presented in much better shape than the blood-spattered mess caught on video, the green hospital gown hanging loose on his thin frame and dark shadows under each eye made him appear ragged. Someone hadn't been sleeping well. First impression, Max pegged him for an accountant. He gestured to the only other chair.

"Please. Sit, Harrison."

Brows rising, the man took a hesitant seat.

"Do I know you?"

"No, I'm Detective Browning. I have a few questions." He read him his rights. "Do you understand what I've stated to you?"

Monroe's shoulders slumped. "Yes, oh my god, did I kill someone?"

"Yes, you did. Three people."

As the guy's mouth dropped open in shock, Max nodded at the doctor. He eyeballed his patient for a few beats and then exited the room.

Tears rolled down Harrison's face. "I'm so sorry. I don't even remember the accident. What happened? I must have passed out behind the wheel."

"No car accident, Harrison. You stabbed three people at a local business."

Horrified eyes widened even further. "Impossible! What the hell are you talking about?"

Max shook his head. *Here I am again. Sliding this damn thing to the end of a table so I can show someone a murder. Only thing different is this one's not an innocent bystander.* He pressed the play button and eyeballed Harrison leaning forward, brows furrowing as he watched himself enter the front door.

"Is this you, Harrison?"

"Uh, yes. No, wait. It looks like me, but…not really. My face isn't right." He recoiled as the knife slipped across the first victim's throat. "Oh, my God. What the hell? I would never do such a thing!"

The uninjured hand clamped over his mouth, knuckles whitening with each turning second. Head shaking back and forth in denial, Monroe's eyes remained glued to the screen as the horrendous event unfolded. Jaw clenched and spine straightened, he tore the unblinking gaze away from the monitor.

"Is this some type of sick prank?"

Max turned off the video. "Where were you last night?"

He sat through a round of owl-eyed blinks before Monroe found his voice.

"Home. I was there by six and stayed in all night," he said with gathering strength. "My wife can vouch for me. You'll discover this is all a mistake. Some type of hoax."

"What time did you leave your house this morning?"

"Around seven-thirty. My usual time."

"Did you go to work?"

"Yes." His brows furrowed, as if he wasn't quite sure of his answer.

"Where is that?"

Harrison threw him an incredulous look and jerked a thumb toward the player. "Stanford Jewelry over on Lyle. It's where you got the video, right? Definite fake. They're messing with me. Both of us."

Max tried not to react to the gut rolling bit of left-field news. *Shit. He's an employee. Damn!*

If the squeamish Stanford rep would have stuck around to analyze the recording with him and Sean, he wouldn't be sitting here scrambling for a new line of questions. Max studied the confused face. It appeared legitimately baffled. *He's blocking out what happened, or he's a damn good actor.*

"Can you give me your manager's name to confirm?"

"Sure. Jackson Griffin."

Max jotted the name, knowing full well it belonged to the male victim.

Monroe released a shaky laugh. "I bet he's behind this nonsense. He plays jokes every chance. The blood isn't real. He found a look-a-like. Yes, please call him." His hands began to tremble.

"Is the focus on you, Harrison?"

"Everyone."

"Did it make you angry?"

Harrison's lips pursed.

"He's a funny guy. Just his nature, I guess. We've all suffered one of his pranks at one time or the other. Sure, I'm embarrassed sometimes, but not enough to turn violent." His palm lifted. "I assure you. This is one more in a line of them." He rattled off a number. "Call him. You'll find him alive and laughing his ass off."

Max wanted to tell him how ridiculous the presumption sounded. No one in their right mind would go to this length to pull a prank. They'd face charges for reporting a fake murder, wasting departmental resources, and job termination. He needed to redirect.

"You said you were married."

"Yes."

"Where's your wife?" The guy could revert to his catatonic state if everything started slamming home. He needed to gain as much insight as possible before the crazy switch flipped to the on position again.

"Home. She doesn't work. Hey, when will you let me contact her? I've asked three times already. I'm sure she's worried. I always call when I'm at my desk."

Max sat back and steadied himself. It was time to lead this man toward reality.

"She's not going to answer, Harrison, and you know it. We found what we believe to be your wife stabbed to death in your home. I'm told she's been this way for over a day."

Harrison slammed down both forearms, voice seething with anger. "You're so full of shit! She told me goodbye this morning. Why are you doing this? You can stop now. This is beyond cruel. Are you even a real cop?"

Max pulled his badge and slid it forward. "Very real. Are you sure it wasn't yesterday when you saw her last? Think about it."

Harrison frowned, eyes skirting around as if trying to replay the day in his head. "Yeah, I'm sure." He didn't sound convinced of his own words.

"What day of the week is it, Harrison?"

"Tuesday."

"It's Thursday. The police took a knife from you today at the Cefco where you were hiding inside the dumpster and covered in blood. You'd left your place of employment thirty minutes earlier after killing Jackson Griffin, Margaret Paltry, and Susan Rose. What you saw on the video is fact. Not a joke. The only one playing a game here is you."

Head swiveling around as if expecting the jokesters to jump out and yell "Surprise," Monroe turned back when none materialized. He leaned forward and spat out, "This is insane. I refuse to talk to you anymore. I want a lawyer."

* * * * *

Name scribbled on the release form, Max stepped aside while the coroner finished zipping the poor, unsuspecting Mrs. Monroe into the body bag. He blew out a breath and pressed the phone back on his ear.

"Sorry. What was I saying?" He caught Sean's soft chuckle.

"Something about how extraordinarily fantastic I am for bringing your perp in for booking. No, save the applause for later, you're making me blush."

"Ha, funny man. Clue me. Did he talk at all on the trip over?"

"Not a peep. Remained stone-faced throughout the booking and only spoke up to ask for his phone call. I had medical look him over again to determine if he needed to be in segregation. They believe he's suffering from traumatic amnesia as the hospital suggested. Otherwise, he's presenting as sane as the others packed in here are. How is it at the second scene?"

"Bad. First blush appears to be over twenty stab wounds. Looks like the lady was enjoying her TV show and he came up behind her. The remote was in her hand and one of those little fluffy dogs curled up on her lap with his throat cut. Sick fucker."

"Serious, Max. I'm beginning to wonder if all the stuff they're spraying on food and the extra eighteen-letter additives I can't pronounce are screwing with people's minds. It's not as if this guy has a history where you're surprised it didn't happen sooner. He's clean."

"Yeah, I hear you. All the way through the interrogation, he didn't sway on his innocence. He believes it didn't happen."

"I imagine a temporary insanity plea in his future. Forensics doesn't lie. Neither does a clear video of him slicing and dicing those people. Before you ask, as soon as I'm off the phone, I'll head to the lab and make sure everything has labels and proper placement. Can't let the guy walk on a technicality. I'll make a personal trip to put the vid in a locked bin."

"Thanks, Sean. They're spreading this old man too thin. Appreciate the extra eyes."

"Old, my ass. Talk to you later."

"See, yuh."

Back inside the kitchen he'd been standing in moments ago, Max studied the block of wood on the counter holding Mrs. Monroe's kitchen knives…all except one. The handles carried the same deep blue as Harrison's weapon of choice. He pointed it out to the tech for a pic and bag.

Max backed out of the room, wondering how many times the wife prepared dinner with it, never imagining cutlery gifted from Aunt Betty buried in her chest any time soon. Head shaking at the absurdity of life's twists and turns, he moved down the hallway and found nothing of note in the laundry room or utility closet.

As soon as he stepped into the next room and got an eyeful of a neatly made bed, the hairs along his neck lifted, followed by Preston Sinclair's words zipping through his mind.

This won't be your last one, detective.

After a frantic thirty-second eyeball search around the headboard and finding nothing but pale green paint and a few cobwebs, Max stepped back, ready to kick his own ass.

"Get a fucking grip, Browning. Quit feeding into this shit."

Again, nothing stood out to call for a heart thump. He hoped to find a note or scribblings explaining Harrison's nosedive into the deep end. Unanswered motives always buried like splinters in his mind, too small to do much damage, yet big enough to irritate the hell out of him when one broke loose for another round of worthless analysis.

Screw it.

A shove on the door across the hallway revealed diluted blood covering the lavatory, shower, and facing wall. *Sloppy cleanup.*

Stained towels piled on the floor and a blood-soaked sheet floating in the tub spoke volumes. Harrison used it to cover his clothes as he hacked away at his spouse, proving intent. The new tech following him around like a lost puppy appeared ready to hurl his lunch.

"Photograph the entire area?"

"Not until your belly's ready. Take a minute."

Free of the irritating presence, Max entered a room at the end of the hall, surprised to find an unmade queen sleigh and a pair of men's boots sitting next to a closet. He opened it to find a line of shirts and dress pants hanging in a neat row inside.

Do they have a son living here? God, I hope we don't find another body.

He rifled through the mail placed in a neat pile on top of the bureau, all addressed to one Harrison Monroe. None of it had a Jr. on the end. His spine straightened.

They don't sleep in the same room. Shit.

Chills lifting in waves along his arms, Max stared at his reflection in the mirror for a few beats. His eyes shifted to the left. Over his shoulder and above the headboard, a very distinctive spot stood out like a beacon on the pale-yellow wall. "Look at me," it screamed above his overloaded thoughts.

Envelopes shoved back on the dresser, Max turned and approached the bed at a slow pace, all the while hoping for chipped paint or a splash of food thrown during an argument. His stomach rolled the closer he drew. *Fuck.*

Max lifted his phone and snapped a picture of a similar burn mark to the one at the Galesh home. His thumb moved over and pressed familiar keys, unable to take his eyes off the wall.

"JoAnn. Go to my desk. Yellow pad. Read me the number on the bottom right corner…I'll wait."

He moved closer to the anomaly, jaw clenching as he tried to rationalize the discovery.

"No, the one next to the phone…Got it. Thanks."

He waved away the tech stepping inside. "Not now. I'll yell for you. Close the door on the way out."

Max punched in the numbers, and it picked up on the second ring. He didn't wait for a voice.

"Sinclair?"

"Call me Preston" released on a calm voice drifting through the receiver. "Did something bad happen, Detective Browning?"

"Yeah, where are you at?"

"Travelers Inn off Reno Avenue. Room 15."

"I'll be right there. We need to talk."

CHAPTER 9

DRIVER'S SIDE WINDOW LINED UP with a gap in the shrubbery, Max eyeballed the Travelers Inn motel. He knew the place well.

Back in the day, if he hadn't shown up here to bust someone within a week of his last arrest, he thought hell froze over. The place enjoyed several major facelifts over the years while the hookers dwindled away to nothing, all thanks to the new freeway project. Progress brought in reputable and well-protected businesses to line the service road, ending the days of gangs, drugs, and prostitution ruling the neighborhood. Despite the Inn's clean, inviting façade, he could still feel the stain of its history coating his skin.

"Goddamn hell hole."

He was so glad his vice days were just a bad afterthought. Done and gone. Granted, murders weren't much prettier, but at least he didn't have the pleasure of a hard kick to the shin, spit on his clothes, or suffering propositions from toothless addicts working hard for their next fix. He felt dirty every day, even when using the harshest soap to scrape his flesh clean each night.

Max shuddered and slipped the phone out of his pocket. Preston answered on the first ring.

"Detective Browning?"

"Step outside and let me see you."

"Sure."

The door to Room 15 swung wide. A tall, decently muscular guy stepped out into the brightness of the day and swiveled his head from side to side, the phone still held close to his ear. Blondish-brown hair carrying a slight wave fell to the top of his shoulders. The wind caught it and revealed a clean-shaven, strong jaw. Dark green T-shirt and black jeans were spotless, but the work boots told a different story. The man wasn't a puss. He'd gotten his hands dirty before, reminding him of Jason.

"Why are you hiding, Detective Browning?"

The voice now matched what he was seeing.

"Step three paces to your right and turn around."

"No problem."

"Now put the phone in a back pocket and place your hands high on the wall."

"At least I know you're a cautious guy. That's comforting. I guess I'll meet you in a minute."

Sinclair fell into position before Max got the Vic into gear. He took his time crossing the parking lot, scanning for any interested third parties lurking about. Seeing nothing out of the ordinary, he pulled into a slot one door down from Room 15.

Gun drawn and pointed in Sinclair's direction, he sidled up to the open doorway and made a quick glance inside. It appeared empty of any other bodies.

"Anyone else with you?"

"No, sir."

"Keep your hands up and back toward me." The man obeyed. Max stuck the barrel over his right kidney, clamped a hand on a thick shoulder, and walked him into the room.

"You can hold it on me until you're comfortable. I won't take offense."

Max frisked him down in the doorway and retrieved a wallet from a back pocket. "Turn toward the wall, hands higher than your head, and plant them." He pulled the DL.

"Preston Sinclair. Yuma, Arizona."

"In the flesh."

"Turn, back up against the wall, and flatten your palms where I can see them." Max stuck the gun on the guy's chest, right over his heart. Calm, light-green eyes met his and he smiled, appearing younger than first thought. Thirty-one, but those peepers weren't naïve.

"Nice to finally meet you, Detective Browning."

"Why are you in Oklahoma?"

"Research."

"Of crimes, I'm assuming."

"Correct."

"Reporter?"

"Hell no. Damn vultures."

"How do you know Bernard Adler?"

A slashing brow rose.

"Never heard the name. Why?"

"Did you know Mary Galesh?"

"No. Learned of her from the media like everyone else."

"Have you been inside her home?"

Green eyes widened to round saucers.

"You saw it, didn't you?"

Max kept his lips tight.

Sinclair shrugged. "Fine. Your trust level's still low. Can't say I blame you. No, I've never been there. Arrived in town right before I called you. Believe me, Detective Browning, I'm the least of your worries." His eyes flicked toward the round, wooden table in front of the window.

"Can we sit down? I'll keep my hands in view. Promise."

With a cautious step back, Max lowered the gun to nut sac level.

"Move and lose them."

"Understood."

Satisfied with the easy compliance, he kneeled and glanced under the tabletop. Happy to find nothing strapped beneath, he moved closer to the open door and jerked his head to the left.

"Go ahead."

Preston settled himself, placed his hands as directed, and then nodded toward the other chair. "Please. Sit."

"Stay put."

A fast recon inside the bathroom, under the bed, and an empty closet, save for a battered suitcase, proved they were alone. Max closed the front door, locked it, and took a seat. Not quite ready to hand over complete trust, he placed the gun down but didn't remove his hand.

They stared at each other for a few beats while Sinclair's shoulders relaxed in gradual increments.

"Tell me, detective. What spooked you enough to come here? From the choice of introduction, I'm assuming you think I had something to do with whatever happened. Let me assure you. I haven't left this room since I arrived. I even had my food delivered. You can check the hotel camera surveillance if you want. I don't have anything to hide. Ask your questions. You'll get the truth."

Phone retrieved, Max recalled the first image, set it on the smooth wooden surface, and swiveled it toward the enigma watching his every move. The guy's chest expanded on a sharp inhale.

"I knew it."

Max swiped a finger across the screen to show the recent find at Monroe's.

"Two. Damn. Any others?"

"No." Max figured it time to start a real dialog. Nothing about the man set his radar off. He'd been calm and agreeable.

"If you didn't leave these, Preston, how could you have known I might find them?"

"I was never positive you would. Crapshoot with every town."

"Every town?"

"Better to show you. I'd like to reach for a box behind me and next to the bed. I promise no quick moves."

Max nodded.

Plastic tub now resting by his boot, Preston flipped the top open and took his time reaching inside. He removed four eight-by-ten color photos and laid them across the table. Each image showed a burn mark in the center. Max could tell all were from separate locations. No wall was the same.

Son of a bitch.

Preston rested back in his chair and placed his palms flat. "There's more, but I think this proves my point."

"How'd you acquire these?"

"If you promise not to arrest me, I'll tell you."

Unable to stop a brief lift of his lips, Max nodded.

"Go ahead. You're safe."

Preston flashed a white smile. "As you know, I always ask nicely first."

Max grunted. "Noted."

"Once the officers clear the crime scene and the detective ignores the hell out of me, which is every single time, I'll...*discover* a way into the house and look for the mark. They're not always easy to find. Sometimes, they're low to the ground or on the ceiling, but they're always close to where the killer slept. Many times, I don't find anything, so I keep going until another one pops up."

"How many so far?"

"Fifty-two."

Fine hairs lifting along the base of his skull, Max leaned forward.

"What are they, and why are you doing this?"

"No clue, and I have a personal stake in finding out."

"Which is?"

"Five years ago, my Aunt Theresa killed her entire family on a beautiful May afternoon. Husband, two sons, and a daughter. Mom made the mistake of stopping by minutes after it happened. She died in the front foyer. The cops got there as my aunt stepped out of the house and blew her own brains out. They found everyone else sitting around the dinner table."

"Shit. I'm sorry, Preston."

"Yeah, it screwed me up. I was twenty-six. Lost my brother to a car accident five months prior, so I didn't cope so well. Wrecked my marriage within three months. The wife promising to love me through anything couldn't face the pressure from the media. Guilt by association, I guess. Dad holed up in his room and refused to come out for a solid month. When he did, he acted like mom never existed. I joined some groups to find anyone offering an ear and not running from the 'tainted nephew.'"

Max sensed the young man struggling to compose his emotions.

"Imagine my shock to learn how many others were out there with nice, normal loved ones losing their damn minds overnight. I heard the same thing with each group I met. 'It took everyone by surprise,' 'No one saw it coming,' 'She was such a caring person,' and 'I would have never imagined.' After a while, you draw a disturbing pattern."

"I know. I've been hearing the same lines."

"I refused to settle for confusion the rest of my life and grabbed up anything I could get my hands on about their cases."

He began to push up from the chair and then stopped himself. "Sorry. Is it alright if I move now? I want to show you something."

"Sure."

Preston set the bucket on the bed, pulled out mounds of paperwork, and spread it out across the mattress.

Max holstered his gun and joined him. Handwritten notes, newspaper clippings, and sundry other documents covered the blue spread.

"They all had varying backgrounds. Some educated, some not. Schoolteachers, preachers, new mothers, high school students, black, white, Asian, Hispanic, it didn't matter. None had obvious history of mental illness or a criminal background. The only thing I found which had me sitting up and paying attention were the burn marks. I kept seeing this consistent smudged area whenever one of the members invited the group over to their homes for a cleansing ritual." He held up a palm.

"Don't ask. It was weird. Anyway, I always spotted them in the bedroom. I went back to my aunt's house and found one on her side of the bed and close to the baseboard. I sat there for hours and fixated on the common thread, but I still can't understand their meaning."

A study of one article after the next describing everything Preston pointed out proved the events spanned across multiple states. All violent, senseless murders committed by the least likely. Some papers felt crinkled beneath his fingers and yellowed with age.

"How long have you been researching?"

"Four years, ten months, and eight days."

"Are you funded?"

"Just by my aunt. She and Uncle Thomas had a sizable nest egg tucked away, and all of it went to me since there was no one else left to make a claim. I thought the best use for it was trying to understand her madness. The money's starting to stretch thin now, so I'm forced to return to Arizona and work odd jobs for a few months and then I'm off again. My dad thinks I'm nuts, but he gave up trying to stop me. He's remarried and refuses to talk about it anymore."

"Do you have a theory?"

The question seemed to catch him by surprise. He backed up and plopped down on his chair. Max parked it on the hard mattress, more than ready to learn the story.

"I tried to form one, but it sounded ridiculous in my head. I figured something coordinated was going on, so I went to the source when I could. The authorities caught most of the killers within minutes. Like I said, they're not prolific bad guys. Many end up in the prison psychiatric unit. I tried to talk to a few, but that didn't go over well. They were either too nutty to understand or too violent for visitors. The police killed a few, while others outright offed themselves before capture. A handful are still out there somewhere."

Max looked him dead in the eye. "On a base level, you fear you might do exactly what your aunt did. Is this driving the hunt?"

"You're right. It scared the piss out of me for the longest, but the fear went away a long time ago. This is an external influence. I feel it down to my bones. I guess you could say insatiable curiosity and stubbornness drives me now." He cocked his head and smiled.

"What?"

"You're the first, you know."

"Of what?"

"Detective's intrigued enough to follow up with my call. When I started this hunt, I was pushy and desperate for them to accept the pattern. My enthusiasm, for lack of a better term, almost ended me up in jail a few times, so I toned it down. Now I make the calls, ask nice, give my warning, and wait."

"Smart move leaving your number first before throwing out the crazy."

"Lessons learned, but I was still ignored. When you called me, I almost passed out from shock. You could've shot me in the leg, and I would have still tried to tell you my story while bleeding out on the carpet."

Max chuckled and took a seat at the table.

"I'm sorry for the treatment, but I had my mind convinced you were playing some type of game. I've learned to be suspicious."

"I can understand why. After sifting through so many horrifying crimes, I sensed a hard-shell building around me. I can't look at people the same anymore. I always sit close to the door in restaurants, and if anyone gets aggressive on the highway, I find the next exit and let them have the damn road. You might say I lost my innocence very quickly."

He leaned forward, eyes turning serious.

"Look. Bottom line. Since everyone blows me off as a kook, I've never seen the specifics of any case, only what I learned from the news or the miniscule information I received from the group members. Nothing is helping me come close to figuring out what the hell these things mean in the scheme of things." He shoved a hand through his hair and blew out a hard breath.

Max could tell he wanted to ask something but appeared fearful of the answer.

"Go head, Preston."

"This is nuts, I know. Believe me. I've tried to stop several times, but it eats at my gut. Can you help me, Detective Browning? I promise I won't jeopardize your cases in any manner. If you tell me to get my ass gone, I'm gone."

Max studied him for a bit. Preston didn't shift in his seat or beg, just waited for the inevitable kick to the curb. It went against every sensible bone in his body, but Max knew what Preston was feeling. He'd only experienced it for over a day and couldn't imagine having an itch you couldn't scratch for a solid five years. He was surprised the kid still had his shit together. If nothing else, the young man had prolific patience and a ton of perseverance. Shoulders relaxed, he leaned back and made his decision.

"Call me Max. You'll keep your mouth shut and follow my lead. No exceptions."

Preston grinned, reached over, and shook his hand. "Shocked, but grateful." An eyebrow lifted.

"So besides seeing the burns, what was the catalyst making you step out of your comfort zone?"

Smart too.

"I found something else similar in conjunction with the marks."

Preston closed his eyes for a moment, took in a lungful of air, and blew it out on a ten count.

"I just heard the sweet sound of a cage opening." He leaned forward. "What is it?"

Max briefed him on the events with Mary Galesh, the similar calling card shot into the store manager's chest, and the latest with Harrison Monroe.

Stunned green eyes stared at him for a few beats.

"Specific connection, for sure. Did Monroe leave a 'W,' too?"

"First thing I asked the coroner before I headed over here, and the answer is no. But now you understand why I asked about Adler. I thought you might be an outside link between the two. Mary hightailed it down a road on a direct path to his prison before she took a hail of bullets. It was too suspicious not to take notice. I came here right from Monroe's home, so I haven't researched for a link there, but my gut's screaming I'll find one."

"I'm sure you will. If I'm not completely off my rocker, we might have been given a glimpse of another connection."

Preston gathered all the other eight by tens and took his time placing them one over the other.

"Do you see what I'm seeing?"

The photos kept coming until Max stuck his hand on top of the growing pile. He looked up and pegged a set of expectant green eyes.

"Yeah, I saw it as soon as you slapped those first four down. The images resemble the head of an animal." He tapped three specific areas.

"Scruffy wide neck, two elongated ears, and a snout. Subtle, but it's there."

"Does this thing remind you of a particular something?"

Max could tell the kid decided to test his ability to step beyond the obvious, to color outside the lines.

"It looks like a wolf, which could very well explain why the Galesh and Adler's victims have a 'W' drilled into their chests."

"My exact thought. Glad you saw it too."

Eyes narrowing to drive home the seriousness of their little discussion, Max tightened his jaw.

"Let me tell you a little about myself, Preston. I believe in facts. Yes, it's odd what's going on, but with what you've brought me, I'd be insane to call it coincidence and ignore what's right in front of my nose. Someone's leaving the world a sick message to point out a predator is stalking and killing prey without remorse. Unfortunate for them, they've made their first mistake."

Preston leaned forward in interest.

"Do tell."

"They came to my town."

CHAPTER 10

SQUATTED MID-WAY IN HIS BACKYARD, Max ran a palm over the swath of dried grass, grimacing at the stiffness. He shook his head in disgust—with himself. He forgot to set the rear automatic sprinklers, and not for the first time, either. The front basked in a wealth of bright green and appeared ready for another mow, but not this poor mess. He swore he heard the blades moaning in agony.

On a sickened grunt, he reentered the garage, flipped the switches, and hoped he hadn't killed whatever remained of his yard.

I'll never find time to replant.

Cherished silver case in hand, Max retrieved the last cigarette of the day, even though he finished one twenty minutes prior. Yeah, the sun hadn't quite disappeared, but he missed the lunch smoke, if you wanted to call a bag of chips dropped out of a vending machine as a meal. The day proved way too over the top for waiting another hour to calm his senses.

Shoulder shoved against a porch column, Max pulled in a lungful of fresh tobacco and let his mind drift back to the interaction with Preston. The moment the guy revealed the other photos, Max knew he was about to dive deep into some weird shit calling for a shift in the usual way of thinking.

Of all his years in homicide, he never dealt with a serial killer. With this many common factors in play and multiple bodies lining up faster than you could count, it made sense. Yet he still felt uncomfortable with committing to the path. A consistent method of killing had the label placed, but these events relied on a prolific killing *tool*—people from all levels of society.

Could it be the work of a single man leading them to destroy so many lives, or bigger than he was prepared to discover? The ring of a cell knifed into the heavy, nagging thoughts and sent him scrambling for his shirt pocket.

"Browning."

"Hey, it's Jason. I hope I didn't disturb you."

"Still up. How you doing?"

"Better now. I contacted the lawyer you referred. Dwight Sanders. He's great. I have a fortress around me. Tough guy. Thank you."

"I'm glad you listened. I feel better about your situation."

"Yeah, I'm hoping it improves in the next few minutes. He made the same suggestion you did, Max. I'm due on air very soon to speak out to the victim's families and the reason I called. Would you watch?"

"Of course." Max stubbed out the cigarette and hustled into the house. He heard a long sigh of relief drifting through the phone.

"Thanks. Thought I might be pushing it."

"Never."

"Can I call you afterward to get your take on it? I know you'll be brutally honest."

"Sure. Which station?"

"All of them, I guess. Mr. Sanders got permission to set up on the courthouse steps. Wish you could see this. I thought the group in front of the house ridiculous, but nothing in comparison."

"Smart move on Dwight's part. Be yourself, Jason. Show them what I've seen. You're a good man and a loving father. You don't have to tell the world how much you adored Mary. You know you did. The goal is to make it safe for your kids now."

The line remained silent for a few beats.

"I appreciate your words. I need to go, Max. They're signaling me to the podium."

The man's strained voice revealed a desperate attempt to hold back powerful emotions.

"Take a deep breath. You can do this. I have faith in you, Jason. I'm hanging up now. Talk to you in a minute."

Phone set aside, Max turned on the television in time to catch Jason positioning himself next to Dwight standing at a microphone with the softly lit, majestic courthouse as his backdrop. A signature swipe through graying hair signaled the top-notch lawyer ready to take on anything daring to harm his client.

Good man.

He knew Sanders since his early days in vice and could state with utmost honesty to be the only attorney in all of Oklahoma to care about the diverse crowd he represented. He was smart and knew how people ticked. A damn whiz at selecting the right jury too. He hoped it would never come to that for Galesh, but if it did, he'd have a pit bull defending him. Max focused on the guy soon to spill his guts to the public. He felt nervous for him.

Dark blue, short-sleeved button-up shirt, and jeans made him appear approachable. A common, everyday hardworking man—himself. Smart move. Though his color had returned, gray eyes still showed simmering pain refusing to give up traction. Three wide-eyed little boys surrounded their father, clutching his hands.

"Good evening, everyone. My name's Dwight Sanders. I'm the attorney for Mr. Galesh. The first thing everyone should understand is I represent Jason only to assist him in coming out to the public with what he wishes to express about this tragic event. There are no charges pending with any aspect of this case, and the police department claims no plans to do so. Jason will make a brief statement to the families, and we won't take any questions afterward. This is a very trying time for everyone, so let's allow the man to speak."

Dwight stepped to the right and gestured for Jason to approach.

Boys pulled close to his side, Jason inhaled a deep breath and scanned the crowd. He held no notes. Max knew whatever came out of his mouth rode on a straight line direct from the heart.

"Hello, I want to express my deepest sympathy to every family member of those who died at Bagwell's grocery store. Your loved ones didn't deserve to have their lives ended in such a cold, calculating manner. No one does. To the survivors, I'm beyond thankful."

Green eyes glittered with unshed tears, voice fighting to continue.

"To Daryl Green, Sherilynn Owens, Stacy Holder, Evelyn Warner, Debbie Ellis, Martha Johnson, Bradley Milner, Yolanda Martinez, and Elias Gilroy, I give my humblest apology for being taken from this world. I wish we could wind back time and stop this insanity. You deserved to live full satisfying lives."

Jason closed his eyes for a moment and straightened his spine.

"I'm angry at Mary," he said in a deepened voice. "She not only destroyed your lives but mine as well. I don't know why she did it. I wish there was something I could hold up to you and point out as the reason, but I have none. It haunts my dreams."

Max's gut twisted as Jason looked down at his children. Silvery trails tracked down their pale cheeks.

"Most of all, I can never forgive her for what she's done to these precious boys. How will I ever make them understand what their mother did? She stained whatever memory they might hold. All I can do now is ensure they have happy, fulfilled lives free of her actions."

He scanned the area, eyes determined.

"I want you to listen and know it as the truth. On every single day I continue toward my goal, each of your loved ones will be in my thoughts. When my boys graduate from school, start their first jobs, marry, and have children, it will be in honor of the those who passed. You have my word. They will not be forgotten."

Dwight reached out and patted Jason's shoulder as he studied his boots for a moment. The battle to compose himself obvious.

"To any family member wanting to meet with me, if only to scream your frustration in my face, I'm willing. But it's my fervent hope you'll let me embrace you, instead. We need to cry together for something else taken from us and will never return—our innocence. Thank you."

Not one member of the news crews clogging the steps uttered a word as Jason picked up the smallest boy, hugged him tight to his chest, and walked away with two more clinging to his belt loops. It was gut-wrenching and wreaking havoc on Max's emotions.

Max hoped his phone stayed silent for a few moments, giving him time to get his shit together as he grabbed a pack of smokes from a kitchen drawer and pulled one out. He'd just lit the end and plopped his ass on the porch railing when the pocket vibration started.

"Browning."

"It's me."

"Hold up a second, Jason."

He pressed the cell against his chest, took a few calming breaths, and stuck the phone back on his ear.

"You almost killed me, kid. Genuine and heartfelt. If I'd ever had a son, I could only wish he were half the man you showed the world today. I'm proud of you." Silence stretched between them for a few beats.

"Max?"

"Yes?"

"Dad died when I was sixteen. My father-in-law tried to play the role when I started dating Mary, but he keeps his cards close to his chest. After tonight, I'm sure I don't have him, either. I would've been proud to be your son. Thanks for saving my sanity."

"Anytime. Try to sleep, Jason."

"I will. Good night."

"Night."

As the day tried snatching the remainder of his strength his emotions weren't already bashing to hell and back, Max jumped up and paced the long porch until he finished his cigarette, vowing he wouldn't sleep tonight until he got a little closer to figuring out what the hell was going on. Determined, he marched into the house and settled at the kitchen table.

Laptop booted and brain engaged, Max connected to the National Crime Database. He already spent the afternoon determining Harrison Monroe shared something in common with Mary. Neither one had a significant history or personality to call for their flipping to the extreme side of terror. Similar to Mary's investigation, his neighbors and close friends thought highly of him.

"Wouldn't hurt a fly," was their consistent belief. He also discovered the Monroe's only slept in different rooms because of the wife's chronic back issues. Their marriage appeared sound to all who knew them.

Using the same narrowed search as done with Mary, Max spent a frustrating hour pounding on the keyboard until he turned focus on Oklahoma and removed any quirks from the search criteria. He finally understood why excluding specifics on the family pet had been a brilliant move. The screen filled with four possibilities, yet one sent chills racing his flesh.

Three years prior, and almost to the day, Whitfield Jenner, forty-six, continually stabbed his wife of twenty years in their home until she bled out. Granted, they found her in the kitchen, and it was a cat, but semantics be damned. Afterward, the new widower arrived at the insurance company employing him for five years and without a blip of hesitation slaughtered four people in the front office, took a casual stroll outside, and relaxed against the side of his car. He too claimed innocence to this very day. One interesting tidbit lay in Jenner's method of killing his wife. He wore her bathrobe backward over his clothes as he plunged the kitchen knife into her chest.

"Guess you got stymied on the delivery, Harrison," Max whispered. "Not as if you could politely ask her to hand it over to stem the mess. Ergo, the sheet. Fuck."

With Jenner also ensconced at the McAlester prison sealing all doubt he and Preston were on the right track, Max flopped back against his chair.

"Now you have my full attention. It's bigger than a bread box." He stuck the ringing phone to his ear.

"Preston. I'm picking you up at seven in the morning. We're making a road trip."

"Where to?"

"McAlester. I found the connection for Harrison, and it leads right to another inmate."

"Well, shit. Uh. Don't hate me because I'm excited."

"Never. I'm rocking an adrenaline rush too. I'll give details in the morning. Do you have a video recorder?"

"Yeah, I have one."

"Bring it. If I stop by the office first, I might not make it out."

"Hey, reason I called. Did you catch Jason Galesh's statement to the press? I thought I was going to—"

"Whoa. Let me stop you. I haven't felt this raw in eight years. I'm liable to bleed out if you say anything else. All I want to do right now is give you and Jason some closure, even if it kills me. Get some rest, Preston."

"You too, Max. You too."

* * * * *

"This is it."

Max slowed the car and pointed toward the shoulder of the road.

"See the tire remnant hanging halfway out of the grass?"

"Yeah."

"Dashcam vid showed she rode hard on flats and started fishtailing a bit here. It took the rubber flying off the back two for them to find an opportunity to surround her. We're coming up on it now."

Preston shook his head. "Looks like the rims buried halfway into the asphalt."

"It was very hot that morning, and she sank deeper with every inch forward."

"Adamant about getting to McAlester."

"Appears so."

Max didn't bother pointing out the large stain of blood on the other side of the road refusing a hard wash after the sun baked it into the asphalt. He didn't want to plant it in Preston's mind. The poor guy had seen enough on his own foray into violence.

They rode in silence, anticipation growing with each mile closer to McAlester. He refused to hold his breath on either of the inmates willingness to talk, much less give up the goods on whatever game they were playing. He was sure the same thought rode Preston's brain as the kid stared at the passing scenery with a scowl on his face. He chased answers for way too long and came up overdue for some good news. Max thought it best to divert him before the poor guy chewed his thumbnail down to the quick.

"You said you're divorced, Preston. Did you ever try to remarry?"

Preston glanced over, hands returning to his thighs.

"No, I can't imagine one woman willing to give up her life to sit around and wait for me to eventually come home or worse, live a roadie's life with a kook looking for burn marks."

"Sounds familiar."

"Spill it."

"Guess it's only fair since I asked first. Simple really. Divorced too. She left me not long after my best friend Fergus died, but it'd been building up long before. Sort of like what you fear, but I was home every night unless a big case broke."

He pushed out a breath and amped up the air-conditioning.

"Nope, I was accused of being there, but in body only. Too many restless nights and unwillingness to discuss things seen on the job became her reasoning. I understood her frustration, but if I shared my cases with her, she wouldn't have liked what I revealed. She was already squeamish watching me gut a fish."

"Were you a cop when you married her?"

"Yes, nine years in. At first, she seemed to understand my quietness, but I guess it got to her after a while. I couldn't imagine walking into the house and telling her I saw the fire department scrape a young woman's brains off the pavement from a jilted boyfriend deciding to use her as a speed bump...and this was *after* he introduced her face to the edge of the curb multiple times. I don't believe she would've looked at me the same much less ever have a peaceful night's rest."

He glanced over at Preston's calm eyes. The kid nodded, urging him to finish spilling his past, so he did.

"How in the hell do you sit down to dinner with her after the reveal? Even if I saved it for the dim light of the bedroom, when do you let the shit out? Before she falls asleep so she can have horrid nightmares or after she wakes so her day fills with paranoia at the craziness of the world. She would've wanted to learn how I felt about it, to give up all the emotions I was already having trouble sorting into neat little piles. How do you explain you wished she wouldn't touch you until one hundred percent positive microscopic blood transfer hadn't ridden home on your body somehow? It was a no-win situation, any way you spun it. She remarried and moved to Chicago. The guy's a banker."

"Downgrade," Preston offered.

Max chortled to wash the air of the putrid past.

"I should marry a homicide detective. It'd be perfect. We'd hardly see each other, like to take as many showers as I do, and the last thing she'd want is to swap stories of her bloody messes with me either. One problem. No female's in the department, and I'll be damned if I'm switching teams this late in life."

Preston barked out a laugh.

"True that. Can I assume no children?"

"Nailed it. And you?"

"No, we weren't married long. Ally's got a new husband, and they have a pair of girls. I don't blame her for hauling ass. I was a mess. While we're in a revealing mood, can I ask you something?"

"Sure."

"I saw the scar on your neck, Max. Don't think it came from shaving. If you don't want to say, I'll understand."

"You wouldn't have gotten a word out of me the first year after it happened, but I don't have a problem with it now. Got it the same night my partner Fergus McLellan died. His wife Danielle's threatening to kick in my head if I didn't check back into reality woke me up. She's a feisty Irish woman. You don't wallow around after that little spitfire tears into your ass. I put all my focus into taking care of her and Sean, despite her wish for me to get a life of my own."

"Who's Sean?"

"Oh, sorry. Their son. He was twenty when it happened, still too young to lose a valuable male influence. He's with the department now. Takes after his old man, big time."

Max batted the air.

"I'm getting off topic. Fergus and I received a radio call for a dead body lying out in front of a movie theater. We'd pulled up as the arriving officers yanked the shooter out of the ticket booth. He gave them a hell of a fight. Little gangbanger. Couldn't have been an inch over five feet. If his gun hadn't jammed, they would've lit his ass up."

Max blinked a few times, realizing he hadn't told this story in five years, yet it persisted as a pristine, vivid image in his mind. A glistening sheet of rain pausing long enough on the dreary night to give him an appreciation of the street's shiny surface free of the day's accumulating crap. He sucked in a breath from a powerful sensation of clean-smelling rainfall inundating his sinus cavity. It was only a memory, but fresh enough to fool his nose.

"Fergus had just shoved the car into park when the side door to the theater popped open and the patrons starting spilling out. Their screams were deafening. Gus didn't have a chance to look over before he took a bullet to the left cheek from the other perp hiding in the crowd. The damn thing tore right into me too. It'd slowed down long enough to catch inside muscle on the other side or I'd have a matching pair of holes. The extraction left a small scar."

Max paused to let the old emotions settle back into something he could handle. He flicked his eyes over at Preston, found wide-eyed interest, and then focused back on the horizon.

"The second shot entered through Gus's arm, into his chest, and butted up against his heart. I don't remember how the hell I managed it, but I shot the bastard in the right ankle and had some type of fucked up conversation with Fergus before he died and me passing out cold."

"Damn. I'm sorry, Max. I can tell he was a close friend."

"Yeah, the best. They told me later the medics pried him out of my arms. I locked in tight. Shit should have never happened. Fergus had every intention of parking closer to the front, but the damn news van cut off our approach. I have no love for the media even though it isn't their fault. They didn't spot us coming up the alleyway."

He gritted his teeth at washing over his vitriol distaste for the news outlet that should've known better than get that close to a scene. If he let reality loose, Preston would be scrambling to jump from the car to save his burning skin.

"I remember sitting for days in a dark living room after I got out of the hospital, refusing to talk to my wife while I ran all the instances where I could've kept him alive. Why did I have to change up where we usually ate on Thursday? I wanted Italian, though it isn't my favorite food. As fate would have it, the closest restaurant happened to be five blocks from the theater. If we'd been at the Denny's, the crowd would've been long gone before we got there." He glanced over and snorted.

"I was coming up with some wild stuff, let me tell you. Why did the city have to start tearing up the road the same day? The detour made Fergus chose the alley. Then I blamed the timing of the lights on the way over. For the first time, the goddamn things turned green right as we got to them. If we'd caught *one* fucking red light, that big bastard would be in the car with us, popping off one-liners, and making you wish you'd hadn't downed a second cup of coffee. You would've liked him."

"I'm sure of it. Not your fault, Max."

"Yeah, I know. Took me awhile, but I quit blaming myself and everything else by putting it where it belonged—solidly on the shoulders of the goddamn gang member raised in a fucked up neighborhood and deciding to keep spinning the wheel of misery instead of finding a better way to live his life. Got no love for coordinated evil, either."

"Well, we have more in common than I thought. Where is he now?"

Max pulled into the parking area reserved for law enforcement, shut the engine, and pointed up at the imposing red brick walls of McAlester State Penitentiary liberally laced with razor wire and bereft of anything resembling hope.

"He lasted in there for two months and three days to be exact. Despite his cocky bravado in court, he didn't stand a chance against the real evil behind those walls. The idiot played in the kiddie pool his entire life and remained clueless to his fate. A rival gang took his ass out, and not in a pretty fashion. Far from it."

"Damn," Preston whispered.

"Didn't hurt my feelings in the least. When I heard the news, I came here as fast as I could to smirk over his mangled body. Sometimes, I like to think by pegging him in the ankle he wasn't *quite* fast enough to escape." He released his seat belt and turned to Preston.

"Get your video cam. Let's go."

Max found surprise to discover Preston not throwing a "what the fuck is wrong with your brain" look from an admission never made to another. Instead, he received a nod in agreement, and not from the command to collect his stuff.

"Right behind you, Max. All the way."

Yeah, we're going to get along fine, kid.

101

CHAPTER 11

BUZZED INTO THE AUSTERE BUILDING, Max scanned the well-lit foyer
and spotted a young man standing next to a waist-high, blocky gray
desk to the right of the double doors. The top of his jet-black hair
grew thicker than the sides and stood up in the "It may look casual
messy, but I spent hours getting it just right" style all the youngsters
sported these days. He probably hated it when the place made him
wear his hat.

Max surmised much of the guy's heritage as Hispanic, but the
lighter skin and dark blue eyes clued he had a good dose of island
Mediterranean influence mixed in, as well. The tag on the gray and
black corrections officer uniform revealed he claimed the Facility
Affairs Liaison position.

"Good morning, gentlemen," the man called out while motioning them over.

The title sounded big, but it was nothing more than a body
to escort outsiders through the building and point out interesting
things. From the big smile on his face, Max figured he grew tired
of sitting in the tiny cubicle and twiddling his thumbs since they
didn't allow cells inside and appreciated the distraction. He pulled
the sign-in sheet over, scribbled his name, and then caught the liaison's eyes widen when spotting the little check mark in the column
appointed for law enforcement personnel.

Hand moving out for a shake, Max lifted his badge with
the other. "Detective Browning with the Oklahoma City Police
Department. This is Preston Sinclair, my assistant."

The kid returned a firm grip and did the same with Preston,
who'd promised to keep his mouth shut and listen.

His new apprentice took a step forward and opened the gray carry case strapped over his shoulder. Max gave it a nod. "We're packing video recording equipment."

"No problem. And your service gun?"

"Locked in the glove compartment."

"Excellent. I'm Officer Randy Vasquez. What can I do for you?"

"We're here to interview Bernard Adler and Whitfield Jenner. One or both might have some relevant information on a case I'm working."

Max shrugged.

"Sorry for not calling ahead. I figured they'd be home."

Vasquez returned a deep laugh. "Good one. I can bring Adler, but Jenner's in the infirmary."

"What happened?"

"Got his ass kicked in the yard five days ago."

His brows raised high on his forehead.

"Oh, sorry for my language."

"No, don't apologize. I prefer laid back. Call me Max. Inmate brawl?"

Vasquez's panicked face relaxed as he turned and slid a key card through a well-used slot on the light-gray wall. A quick motion over his shoulder had them following him down a long corridor sporting framed pictures of all the past wardens. They all looked like stuffy assholes. But then again, this isn't a daycare.

"No, it was from a guard," he elaborated. "Jenner didn't even fight back. Any other day, he'd be up in your grill if you looked at him cross-eyed. He just laid there and took it. Didn't try to cover his face, either. It was the weirdest thing."

"How bad?"

"The officer cracked two of Jenner's ribs, dislocated an elbow, and turned his face into a piece of raw meat before the other guards pulled him off, but he should be good to go in a few days."

Vasquez let out a huff of air.

"Redding's an idiot. Two years away from retirement and now his ass is sitting in the county jail. Guess he couldn't take another minute looking at someone who could kill his wife so easily."

"You're reasoning?"

"The missus died last year. High school sweethearts. Married thirty-two years. Tore him up."

Max nodded. "Makes sense. Not excusable, but understandable."

They slowed at an intersecting hallway as Vasquez gestured to the right.

"The interview rooms are down this way. The first one's always unlocked. We'll cuff the inmate to the table, so you should be safe enough if you stay on your side." He pointed to a small room to the left of the interview area.

"You can help yourself to the coffee and pastries in there while you wait."

Max reached out and tapped his arm. "Thanks, but I prefer the visitor's section, if you don't mind. I need him relaxed."

"Ah. No problem. Follow me."

After navigating down another corridor, Max pushed inside a gestured door leading him into a room lit with bright fluorescent. It wasn't hard to miss the row of translucent plastic chairs lined up in front of nine enclosed slots. Thick Plexiglas embedded in surrounding concrete became the only thing seperating a visitor from the animals. He doubted the light-blue paint on the facing wall would come anywhere near to calming anyone in this environment.

"Take whichever one you like," Vasquez said as he held the door wide for Preston. "I'll call the unit to bring him over."

"Thanks." Max made tracks to the last stall. It was farther from the guard's viewing perch on the other end, giving them the closest to privacy as he could manage. He knew the official interview rooms recorded every conversation, but never the case with the visiting area. Camera's only.

Interest peaked when discovering the phones were missing. It became obvious the prison upgraded since the last time he'd been in the room. He leaned forward to study their invention.

The lower section of the divider revealed a precision drilled four-by-two depressed rectangle with enough gaps to allow a voice to push through, but nothing else. No phones meant less chance for the public to pass on whatever grungy bacteria infested crap clinging to their hands or traveling on their breath to the next visitor taking their place. Preston nudged him on the arm.

"Good we have the place to ourselves."

"And the precise reason we set out early. Formal visitation's not until eleven."

"Perfect."

Preston unpacked the video equipment as Max placed his own voice recorder on the small built-in tabletop. He never knew who might be camera-shy. Resting back against the uncomfortable chair, Max crossed his arms and waited for the monster to appear.

* * * * *

From repeated failure to hold off the laughter as Preston requested yet another repeat of his name, date, and time while pointing the lens at his face, Max waved him off.

"My voice won't grow any prettier. The bullet saw to that. It is what it is. Call cut and get it over with, Mr. Director."

Preston's widening eyes had him swiveling back around on the chair. He caught sight of a guard escorting Adler through a barred doorway leading into the holding chamber on the other side of the visitor's bay. A low whistle drifted over his shoulder.

"Damn. He's big. No wonder it took so long to bring him."

"No doubt." Max decided the last four years only added another layer of hardness to Adler's shell. He was huge before his daring capture, but he figured endless access to the weights in the yard had honed an already intimidating man into a chiseled beast. His skin was pale, but showing a recent visit out into the sun, if the slight tinge of red on his neck was any sign. The close-shaved head and jailhouse tats, added to the ones he brought along with him to McAlester, only increased the persona as someone you didn't want to meet in a dark alley.

Max stood up. They were the same height. Surprised by the calm blue eyes meeting him on the other side of the glass, the unshackled state of his wrists added to it.

Adler sat down. Max followed. He lifted his badge and dove into a conversation he didn't think would last long.

"I'm Detective Browning with the Oklahoma City Police Department. Behind me is Preston Sinclair, my assistant."

Adler nodded, eyes never moving from his.

"I have an open investigation I'm hoping you might provide some insight on, if possible. Are you willing to speak with me?"

Big shoulders moved up and dropped back into place. "Sure." The deep baritone voice matching his stature filtered with ease through the Plexiglas. "Why not?"

"To be fair, Preston's filming our conversation and this might take a while. You can stop whenever you like." He hated the upfront, required notice and gritted his teeth for the outcome.

"Nah, go ahead. I ain't got nothing better to do." The edge of his lip lifted. "Not like I'm going anywhere."

Max wondered if they'd started drugging the inmates. He had a tough time suppressing his astonishment at the easy acquiescence when expecting a lengthy line of demands or a one-finger salute followed by a "fuck off" and a splat of spit on the glass.

Well, shit. Guess I better start before the magic wears off.

He pressed Mary's driver's license against the glass. "Do you know this woman?"

Adler leaned in and took his time studying the card. Max figured the intense scrutiny belonged to more than a try at recollecting her face. Not as if he got to see a woman every day. The inmate sat back, apparently satisfied.

"Nope. Sweet looking little thing. I would've remembered her."

"Have you received any fan mail from her?"

"Used to receive all sorts of crazy stuff until all the hype died down. I don't recall her name. You're my first visitor in three years. Only pen pal I got now is my sister. She lives in California. Give it a few more months and I won't even have that. She's got the cancer. Not doing so hot. Take it for her, if I could. Hmm, let me guess. I got a copycat?"

Max's radar lit up. "What makes you say this?"

"Easy. You got a bunch of crazy motherfuckers out there. Don't you know? You looking for motive? Simple. They can't come up with their own action, so they steal from others. Just looking to see if they can do better and grab a headline before the anniversary of mine rolls up." He jerked a thumb over his right shoulder.

"Most the guys in here have had it happen at one time or another. Guess it was my turn. Am I right?"

"Yes."

"How many did he take out? I had twelve."

"It was a woman. The one I showed you. Nine in total."

"Damn. Would've never figured it…the female, not the count."

"I'm curious, Bernard. Why would you even talk with me? I heard you have a severe distaste for authority. Saw the news clip of the officers trying to remove you from the courtroom after your conviction. A deputy's still missing half an ear because of you. Your rep here is atrocious when it comes to dealing with the guards."

Adler sucked in a deep breath, big chest contracting while slowly nodding his head.

"Yeah, I was a total ass. Didn't get me anywhere but the shit beat out of me and shipped off to solitary for a month each time I set loose. Wasn't hurting anyone but myself. I wanted to look at the sky again."

"Definite incentive to tone it down, Bernard. I read where you left a calling card on your last victim, but you've always refused to disclose the reason. Are you willing to now?"

Max recognized apprehension as Bernard looked around and then leaned toward the glass. He did the same and sensed Preston moving in to capture whatever tidbit might fall out of the convict's mouth.

"Can't because I don't have the first clue," he whispered. "Honest. I only refused to cop to it to leave a little mystery for the others in here to worry about. Upped my rep so I let it ride and grow a life of its own."

The lopsided smile eased the tension around his eyes.

"You have a 'W' scratched on someone's cell and they quit fucking with you right quick."

"Do you remember doing it?"

"The whole damn thing's a blur now. It was an impulse, and I went with it the same way I did everything else. If it was there to steal, I took it. If you pissed me off, I retaliated."

"Do you like dogs, Adler?"

Slashing brows rose, and he sat back.

"Had a puppy when I was six. Pops drowned him because he pooped on the back porch. He made me help. Sort of put a bad taste in my mouth for wanting to attach myself to another one."

He shook his head, brows furrowing in confusion.

"You ask some weird questions."

"Yes, but they're relevant to me."

Max slipped out the phone Vasquez failed to retrieve per protocol and recalled the image of the mark found at Mary's house. He placed the screen against the Plexiglas.

"Does this look familiar at all?"

Adler scooted the chair closer, forearms pressing against the small table in front of him.

"Looks like someone tried to set fire to something. You after a firebug too, detective? Unsure how I can help. I used a gun. Never burned anything down before."

"You killed your first two victims and then shot out the cameras, Bernard. Why weren't they the first things to go? Why even bother?"

"Damn. She must have studied me good. Did she use a Glock?"

"Yes, the cameras, Bernard."

"Right. I knew I had a hundred eyeballs on me. Being known wasn't a concern. I screwed the pooch the second I popped the first one. Wanted to read in the papers how wrong or right the survivors were on recounting what I did. Leave a little mystery behind, if you know what I mean."

"In what way?"

He shrugged. "Would they make stuff up, forget, or have it burned into their brains? It was a toss-up. I never told anyone but you just now. I reckon she followed the steps found in any newspaper archive. Did you guys catch her before she got over the border like me?"

"Got herself killed on 270 on her way to you, Bernard."

Max wasn't sure if this was Mary's true intention, but he clocked Adler's reaction to the news. Genuine surprise lit his features. Was it because his little protégé bit it, or someone remembered he existed and died trying to get to him? Who knew?

"No shit?"

"Truth. Was there someone you were going to see on your way to Canada, Bernard?"

"No. Was trying to escape as far away as possible and they missed setting some roadblocks in time, I guess. I took the path of least resistance."

Adler frowned for the first time. It read as disappointment more than anger.

"I'm not a copycat, so there was no inmate to pat my head if that's what you're getting at."

Max chuckled and held his palms up in surrender. The man might be uneducated but far from stupid.

"I apologize for the assumption."

"Thanks. I know what you're trying to do, but you're not going to find some type of connection between us. I never knew the woman existed until you showed me the pic. You're fishing, detective, and you're wasting your bait. Nothing's going to bite on this side. The river's empty."

"How empty?"

Bernard stared at him, unshakeable.

"Look it. I learned my lesson. What I did was wrong on so many levels. I guess I'm just rotten to the core. I haven't given a shit about anything since I was seventeen and my mom died. When the anger took over, I let it ride until I felt human again."

Bernard paused and studied the ceiling for a few beats, as if trying to find his words on the patterned tile. Determined eyes returned and he tapped his temple.

"It's like I was born without an off switch. Had to let the jets burn dry before I could think straight again."

"You find God, Adler?"

He chuckled. "Nah. The big dude ain't ever talked to me and sure as hell won't let me through the pearlies later. I seen to that." He released a resigned sigh and scrubbed at the back of his neck.

"You might say I had a reckoning with my conscious. This place makes you realize life's too short, and now I'll spend the rest of what I got right here in this hellhole. You're not going to believe a word falling out of my mouth, but I hate the Bernard that walked into the store and did those horrible things. I wish I could change what happened, but it is what it is. Can't fix it. I don't deserve your consideration, but if you want my help, then be honest on what you need."

"Fair enough." Max stood and Adler followed. "I might come back if I have anything else to run by you, Bernard."

"No problem. Just bring the truth with you, and I'll play nice right back. I have to keep my rep in the unit, but it feels good to let it drop in here."

"Noted. Thanks for speaking with me."

Max turned to leave yet hesitated upon a light tap against the partition.

"Hey, detective. Do me a solid, will you?"

"Depends."

"If you come back, will you bring me something and make them mark it as mine in the commissary?"

"If it's not banned from here, sure. What is it?"

Adler grinned, and Max could almost see the little boy who might've been happy and carefree before he had to watch his pet struggle to breathe. He doubted the white gapped-toothed smile broke out often around here, if at all.

"An Almond Joy. Love those goddamn things."

CHAPTER 12

UPON THE LIGHT TAP AGAINST his arm, Max flicked his eyes at Preston's expectant face, grunted, and turned his attention back to the road.

Yup, I realize I missed the exit.

He pulled to the shoulder, waited for the car behind him to pass, and performed a perfect U-turn.

"Sorry."

"No, not that, at all. You've been quiet since we left. I can almost hear your brain grinding on something. I've tried to be patient, but you're starting to spook me. Spill it."

"The candy."

"What about it?"

"Mary Galesh took two Almond Joys from the store. I found them in her van. She ate one, but the other was still wrapped and melting on the dash."

"She's a copycat. Down to the wire."

"You'd think, but I never found any mention in the reports of Adler stealing candy from the Target. What I thought was Mary's quirk makes an evident connection between those two whether he realizes it or not. Either he's toying with us by slipping the bit in about the candy right before we left, or this is the biggest coincidence I've ever seen in my life. He seemed sincere, but way too laid back and willing to talk."

"I know. I expected a snarling beast. Totally threw me off."

"My first impression was they had him on some type of medication, but his eyes were clear, and he never slurred his words. I'm not ready to buy his 'turning over a new leaf' bullshit. Guys like him don't change. They acclimate to their surroundings. He's had more than enough down time to learn how to fool my bullshit meter."

Preston chuckled. "Your bullshit meter? You carry one around in your pocket?"

Max barked out a laugh. "I wish. No. Over the years, you learn to read eye movement, facial tics, and body position while interrogating. He showed no obvious deception. Either he's damn good at masking the signs, or he's telling the truth. Something usually pops out. When someone tries hard to cover their reactions, they'll dead stare you and blink at regular intervals. Never saw it play out here."

"What other signs were you looking for?"

"Liars make a slight change in head position before a fabrication shoots out of their mouth. Could be as obvious as jerking back or a subtle turn of the face. If you observe their eyes dart to their right, they're trying to visualize a new reality. It's the fantasy side of our brains."

Max shrugged and turned on to I-40, as he should've done five minutes ago.

"All sorts of things can happen depending on the intensity of the questions, Preston. Their breathing will speed up, for one. Either the body takes on a rigid stance as if they're ready to fight when caught in the lie, or you'll notice the opposite flight reaction of rapid shuffling feet signaling their need to get away. They'll blast you with a ton of unnecessary detail to convince you different or repeat their innocence without trying to make you mad. If they continue to cover their mouths with a hand or fingers before they respond, it's their subconscious brain showing they have all intentions of hiding the truth."

"Damn, Max, now I understand why your eyeballs flicked all over my face when you had me up against the wall. I thought you were trying to memorize my features in case I bolted."

Max chuckled. "I knew you believed everything you revealed to me."

"Ah, a key point revealed. I *believed* myself."

"Right, but not a perfect science any more than a lie detector machine measuring heart rate responses. If someone believes the false information revealed, then all bets are off. The ability to fool me comes from having the chance to let their story sink in over an extended period. It becomes real to them. Those are hard to crack." Max looked down at his phone vibrating in the cup holder. He set it on speaker.

"Browning."

"Sorry to bother you. I know you said you'd call back about Jenner's recovery, but I have good news."

"Not a bother at all, Randy. I could use some. Lay it on me."

"I went by the infirmary and told Jenner you were coming to interview him about helping with a case after he's healed up. I wanted to find out if he planned to waste your time. When he didn't blow up, I offered extra commissary privileges if he played nice and tried to help you with your case. He wants to meet with you, even insisted it be tomorrow."

"Same time?"

"Yes."

"Excellent. Thanks for the help, Randy. You saved me a lot of trouble. Do me a favor. Don't mention it to anyone else. Word spreads fast on inmates talking to the cops. I'm sure Adler's dealing with his fair share of crap right about now, but he has a better chance of defending himself."

"You're welcome. Glad I could help. Sure. I won't say anything. No one can keep their damn mouth shut around here."

"Good man. See you tomorrow."

"I'll be here."

Preston's head bobbed up and down as the call ended. "Very interesting. Maybe Jenner already heard about your visit with Adler. You think he's scared and wants to get something off his chest?"

"Best-case scenario, but I can't think of a good motive to spill whatever secret those two are keeping. Confessing won't shave off any time from his sentence. He's in for life. Maybe he has some intel to share, so we'll protect him from something scarier."

"Like what?"

"Death."

"Reason?"

"He got his ass beat by a guard and never fought back. Not his usual style, according to Randy. Perhaps Officer Redding's motive had nothing to do with losing his wife. Maybe the beating was a message Jenner's now choosing to ignore. If my theory's correct, whatever's pushing this convict to talk to the authorities is big enough in his mind to take a chance of getting his skull cracked again."

Preston rested back against the seat and frowned.

"Aw, this is driving me insane. What the hell's going on? Everything's swirling around this prison and no clear picture. Redding beat Jenner *before* we thought about going there. Maybe the guy wants to reveal consistent guard abuse. Even still, it seems like we can trust Vasquez since he approached and rewarded Jenner for agreeing to meet with you."

"Yeah, I was thinking the same thing." Max's thumb tapped against the steering wheel in a staccato beat.

"Damn. Too many variables at play here. We'll just have to wait until tomorrow to learn what Jenner has to say so we can move in the right direction. I hope Vasquez keeps his mouth shut. We sure don't need to walk in and find out Jenner 'all the sudden' died from his injuries."

"Crap. Never thought of it. Great, I won't sleep worth a damn tonight."

"Me either. Look, we're almost back. How about you and I go grab a steak. I'm sure you're tired of takeout, by now. My treat. I prefer to have something to enjoy while my mind's swirling on what may very well be a big balled mess of coincidence skewing the real problem."

"Deal. I never turn down steak. Listen. I can't promise not to drive you nuts on all the crazy shit I'm thinking, but I'll try to tone it down."

"No problem. Nice to have a sounding board to bounce my theories. It gets old hearing them inside my head."

"Same here, Max. If anyone can understand, it's me."

* * * * *

Eyebrow cocked high as a subtle warning, Max twisted his lips and handed over the thirty-six-count carton of Almond Joy to a confused Officer Vasquez.

"This is Adler's cheap payoff for behaving himself yesterday. Tag it big and proper as his in the commissary. If they screw him over, they'll be dealing with me. This thing leaves the door open for future visits. He'll know the count. Got it?"

"Yep. Appropriate threats will be relayed."

"Good man. Was there any retaliation for seeing me?"

"Not that I heard, but when they let him out for yard this morning, I saw a few bloody knuckles, so I think he squashed it pretty fast."

"Fair enough."

Vasquez slid his card in the door release and gestured down the hallway.

"Go on ahead. I'll walk this box to where it belongs and tell infirmary you're here."

"Thanks, Randy."

Max followed a quiet, yet excited, Preston. They both exhaled a slow breath while entering the visitor's area. Finding out Jenner survived the night had amped the hope to nuclear level. He took the far booth again, congenially endured Preston's drill on documenting the date and time, had his shivering Déjà vu moment, and relaxed back in the seat. This time, the presentation of the inmate didn't take as long.

Max stared at the jumbled mess of bruised human advancing through the holding area. By the slant to his upper body and awkward gait, Max could tell he favored the left leg. A shoulder sling held the right arm trussed close to his body. Officer Redding had stamped his message loud and clear. The absence of shackles held little surprise. It isn't as if he could do anyone much damage anyway. Preston's lowered voice drifted over his shoulder.

"I started filming. Not being obvious about it."

"Smart." At first assessment, the convict didn't appear he could hurt a fly, even without the injuries. The lean runner's body didn't carry enough muscle mass to have softened the prison-yard blows.

An angular face still showed signs of the severe beating. As he drew closer, Max discerned the area around his eyes remained puffy, but the pale-green irises were clear and focused on Preston's camera. The man had aged at a rapid pace in here.

Jail records listed him as forty-two, but the sandy-brown hair bore deep gray around the temples and obvious thinning on the crown. He appeared as calm as Adler had when he arrived. The only show of emotion came as he lowered himself with extreme care onto the chair. His slightly bearded jaw clenched, and he exhaled a soft curse.

"Thank you for seeing me today, Whitfield."

A surprisingly deep voice not matching the thin frame responded, "Thanks for saying my name the right way. I appreciate it."

Odd comment.

"Sure. I'll skip past the niceties since it looks like you'd be better off back in infirmary. I have a few questions which might shine some light on a case I'm working. Do you have any issues with being filmed?"

"None at all. I hoped you'd record me like you did Adler."

Ah, maybe this is all about guard abuse. Hard to deny if caught on film by an authority figure.

Max pulled Harrison Monroe's license from his pocket, not quite getting it fully pressed against the glass before Jenner held up his palm.

"I have to say something first, if you don't mind." He tipped his chin toward Preston. "You rolling?"

"Yes."

"Good." He straightened the best he could and slid his tongue along dry, cracked lips.

"My name's Whitfield Anniston Jenner. In one week, I'll be forty-three. I've been here at the McAlester State Penitentiary for two years, ten months, and twenty-seven days for killing five people."

He looked up at Preston and gestured toward the camera.

"Can you run it back for me? I need confirmation you're really recording. What I have to say is important."

Max leaned to the side. Preston approached the partition and showed Jenner what he captured. At the nod of approval, he stepped back, lifted the camera, and indicated the light on the side.

"Green when capturing your image and voice."

Jenner nodded. "Understood."

He settled back in the chair and stared at the lens. Max figured he was building courage during the contemplative quietness.

"From the moment of my arrest, during the trial, and for each grueling day spent in this facility, I've denied what happened. This bullshit stops today. It has all become clear now as if a film lifted from my eyes. I killed my wife, left her brutalized body in the kitchen, took a shower, and then went to bed like it was no big deal. The next morning, I dressed for work and did the exact same thing to four of my coworkers."

Head lowered, he pulled in several calming breaths, counting between each.

Max's belly clenched. Jenner owning his crime was the last thing he expected to hear. It was just like Adler, but on a much grander scale. Any pending appeals went up in a puff of smoke.

On a quick mumble of "ten," Whitfield settled himself.

"I can't tell you why it happened, other than I was so filled with building anger it must have had no other place to go but out into the world. I continue to be baffled as to why I chose this method of expressing myself, so all I can do is tell you what was happening in my life before I obviously lost my goddamn mind."

He looked down at his trembling hand, sucked in another deep breath, and focused back on the camera.

"I couldn't give my wife things she deserved in life. I failed her. For twenty-two years, she stuck by my side as I promised our circumstances would improve. She kept waiting. As time moved on, I began to see disappointment in her eyes, yet she continued to stay with me."

The articulate inmate's eyes morphed from shiny softness to steely anger. Max figured the defining moment minutes away.

"My boss was a complete ass who loved to mangle my name every chance he could. Whitfield, not Whitehead or Witless, goddamn it. I told the man many times to stop fucking with me. I already endured this same crap all through school. Once I reached adulthood, I thought those days were over. But the crap's a thousand times worse coming from a grown man with complete control over your life. The others in the office laughed along with him, maybe too fearful of being his next target, but they should've known better." He paused for a few beats in an obvious attempt to calm down.

"Your employer failed you."

"No, I can't excuse myself from this mess. My boss didn't deserve to die for being a douche bag or my coworkers for not having the balls to confirm my accusations to human resources. They needed their lights punched out, but never to suffer what I did to them."

Whitfield closed his eyes for a moment, jaw clenching as if steeling himself for something much worse.

"I can remember the second everything changed for me. It was a Sunday, and Jack had left a message for me to come in early on Monday. I walked into the living room as my wife pressed the play button. When he said my name wrong, yet again, I saw it. Her expression changed as she turned and walked away. She felt sorry for me. The look of pity bordering on disgust snapped something deep inside me. I knew in an instant we were over. She'd had enough. From there it was nothing but a wash of red filling my vision, anger flowing through my veins like hot lava, bright red blood painting the walls, screams, and pleas for mercy until I reached up and handed my knife to the officer."

A crystal tear rolled down his cheek, but he didn't wipe it away.

"I need to pay for what I've done."

"You are, Whitfield. Life without parole."

Jenner's shimmering eyes flicked over, and he shook his head.

"Not good enough, detective. I should've gotten the death penalty. What the hell was the jury thinking?"

"What they thought best for a crime of passion, I assume."

Dry, cracked lips pursed into a straight line.

"Maybe they figured it too easy of a way out for me. I guess they're right. The screams are all I hear when I try to sleep. No, I owe this confession to my wife who didn't do anything but be in the wrong place at the wrong time. I killed her cat for god's sake. She's long overdue for receiving justice by me telling the world the truth."

He turned and stared stone-faced at the camera, body trembling with emotion.

"Her name was Patricia Ann Jenner. Today, she would've been forty. Happy birthday, baby."

Whitfield's left hand shot inside the arm sling. Max sucked in a breath as the shiv Jenner fashioned gleamed for a split second before sliding on a smooth stroke across the inmate's neck. It opened his throat into a wide, sickening grin. He heard Preston's harsh curse, the camera's heavy thud against the tabletop, and metal screeching against concrete, yet he couldn't tear his eyes away from Whitfield's bruised and battered face.

Pinched features relaxed, and Jenner's lips parted as the blood scorching his veins that fateful day gushed from the gaping wound, saturating his chest, belly, and lap. Their eyes met for a solitary, intense moment. The torment creeped away, replaced with a gentle peacefulness as his head lolled on a gradual roll to the side, and landed against his left shoulder.

Not until he heard the pulsating squeal of the alarm did Max realize he stood fixated in front of the Plexiglas with both palms shoved against the partition the entire time, as if he could've pushed through and snatched the weapon from the determined man.

Backed away from the horrifying scene, Max turned to find Preston by the guard's viewing window, his fist still balled and pounding a steady rhythm against the barrier. The wide green eyes and pale face snapped Max from his stupor. Brain still engaged enough to grab the recording equipment, he rushed over to Preston, snatched the kid by the arm, and yanked him toward the door. Randy Vasquez's panicked face greeted them as Max swung it wide.

"Goddamn, Detective Browning. What the fuck?" he screeched.

"We recorded it. Take me to the warden, and you can see for yourself."

CHAPTER 13

Max slipped the phone back into his shirt pocket, turned, and pressed his back against the wall. With Captain Walters informed a potential connection to the Harrison case was now toast, he received a profuse thank you from his superior for having the wherewithal to film the conversation and choice of the visitor's area instead of the interview room. Having no immediate physical access to the inmate and the video proving the whole event a stunned shocker, the odds of landing hard in an investigation were small. Witnesses, but not suspects. Nope, all the focus arrowed toward whichever guard fetched Whitfield from the infirmary and failed shaking him down. Somebody's career swirled in the toilet besides Redding.

He glanced over and found Preston and Randy in the same position—up against the wall, studying the ceiling, and not uttering a word. He didn't blame them. Everyone needed a moment of quiet time. After their harried meet and greet with a surprised Warden Davies followed by a condensed version of why they stood in front of him, shit ramped to nuclear level.

The call informing the warden of Jenner's obvious DOA in the infirmary only added to the building tension. Max remained impressed Davies pulled himself together enough to watch the suicide confession play out. As fast as his face paled, the freaked head dude in charge thanked them and scurried off to assess his facility. Max figured the man's brain churned on the perfect explanation for whatever oversight committee he would soon stand in front of with his butt cheeks squeezed tight.

Randy kicked the toe of his boot against the tiles. "Damn. Shit worked *too* well."

"What do you mean?" Max asked.

"Doc took the fight right out of him."

He threw him a puzzled look. "Who?"

"Jenner."

"What *doctor*?" He tried to keep his impatience out of the red zone.

"The one treating him for anger issues. They finished with the sessions right before Jenner got his ass kicked by Redding."

"He was being seen by a shrink?" Max asked with increasing interest.

"Sort of. Dr. Alexandru's a specialist who can calm the most violent offenders. They call him the convict whisperer. You know, like the guy who can tame the worst family pet." He chuckled and then appeared appalled by his action.

Max walked over and stood in front of Randy, interest peaking by the second.

"He works here?" *Please say yes. Maybe the guy can shed some light on what was up with Jenner.*

"No, he has his own practice. The man's famous."

"Never heard of him."

"Well, the prison system knows him very well. We've been on his waiting list for three years and finally got our turn last week. He makes the rounds of all maximum-security units and has a solid track record of working with the most violent offenders to make them manageable." He rubbed his forehead. "Do you think suicide counts as manageable?"

Preston rolled his eyes and kept banging the back of his head against the pale-green wall.

"Scale of one to ten? Eleven. Job well done, Dr. Death."

"I'm serious, guys," Vasquez countered. "He's damn good. This had to be a fluke. You saw how easy it was to deal with Adler. Right? He got the same treatment as Jenner, but he didn't off himself. Several times, we all wished he would. You couldn't pull two words out of him unless it was to cuss you out. All you had to do was look in his eyes and you knew he'd kill you as soon as look at you. I think he got bigger from the amount of chains we'd had to put on him before they'd let him out of the cell."

"No drugs, whatsoever?"

"None. All natural and laid back now…unless someone messes with him. Doc's amazing. Money back guarantee if the sessions don't produce an inmate incapable of inflicting willful injury to others. Says it right there on his brochure." His shoulders lifted and fell.

"Well, I guess he doesn't have to refund on this one since Jenner focused on his own throat instead of somebody else."

Max threw Preston a quick glance while responding to Randy. "Yeah, no doubt. Do you have an area where I can catch a quick smoke?"

"Sure. Down the hall and to your left, look for the door with the long black bar. The visitor badge allows you back inside when you're done."

"Thanks. We'll see you up front in a bit."

Preston remained silent until the door closed behind them. He hauled in a lungful of air and slumped in a black wrought-iron chair. All the fight seemed knocked out of him.

"Well, shit, Max. I can look at crime photos all day long, but to actually watch someone die so violently was a little over the top."

Max struck a match, leaned against the rough brick, and stared up at the little bit of sky showing through the thick mesh wire covering the top of the impressive courtyard. Surrounded by tall, imposing gray walls seemed in total contrast to the manicured shrubbery, winding pathways, and colorful flowers scattered about—a little haven in the middle of hell. He lit the cigarette and hoped the nicotine would get the message his brain was throwing out to hurry up and start calming some nerves.

"Yeah, I'm used to seeing the aftermath," he admitted through a puff of welcomed smoke. "Been a while since it played out in front of my face. Don't be embarrassed if you have the shakes. I got them too." Settled in a seat across from his rattled buddy, Max stretched his legs and crossed them at the ankles.

The shaken kid lifted his hands and stared at them. "Yep, wiggling."

Max pulled the silver case he uncharacteristically filled with five cigarettes this morning. The matches now rode in his left pants pocket, the first sign of the downward spiral to breaking a promise. He held it out to Preston. "Want one?" He returned the smirk thrown at him. "Let's recap and focus."

"Good idea. I need to stop my brain from looping on the freaking blood bath."

Max began ticking off the events on his fingers.

"Mary and Harrison each have identical burn marks in their bedrooms. Both committed eerily similar crimes to Adler and Jenner. Before she left the store, Mary stole the exact candy Adler happens to like but never got a mention in any news or police reports. Since both inmates received obvious quality therapy, I'm more likely to believe Adler wasn't lying about not knowing Mary. Harrison lawyered up and Whitfield sure as hell won't be talking now, so we'll never know if there was a real connection there other than having asshole bosses. You want to add anything I've missed?"

"Don't forget the guard who beat Jenner's ass. After what I saw today, I don't think it's related. I believe he would've said something while in confession mode."

"I agree. The bad seeds would never allow him to meet with me. Let's set a conspiracy with the guards aside. We have enough variables in play as it is. We can always come back to it later, if needed."

"Then where does it leave us other than back at square one?" Preston lamented.

"Maybe square three. I don't think we're too off base. I'm convinced those burn marks are some type of symbol Mary and Harrison put on the walls to show their allegiance to the convicts they were about to copycat. Someone clued them this is their coordinated message. Whether it was the inmates or a third party outside the gates egging them on, we don't know."

Unable to sit still a moment longer, Max stubbed his cigarette and began pacing the concrete walkway. He always thought better if his body was in motion. If this place had a track, Preston would be chasing him around it by now.

"In any event," he continued, "they take a lighter, burn the figure, and then go out on their mission. Simple. Adler and Jenner might have been in on this before they got their wiring redone, but when Whitfield glanced at the driver's license, I saw no reaction in his eyes. I don't believe he knew Harrison any more than Adler did Mary. With all the other instances you've documented about the symbol, it seems they're cogs in a much bigger wheel. Someone else is driving the bus."

"It's paranormal."

Halted in his tracks, Max turned and cocked a brow at Preston's ridiculous comment.

"You're looking at me as if I had two heads. I'm talking about beyond the scope of normal reasoning. Hear me out, Max. How in the hell can an organization exercise so much control over perfect strangers? The secrets people like Mary, Harrison, and my aunt would have to keep from their families would be outrageous and difficult. I've found fifty-two instances of normal, non-violent people shocking the hell out of those who saw them every day. Now let's add the weird mark connecting them. It defies belief."

"People get sucked into cults more times than you can imagine, Preston. Each swore secrecy and did a damn decent job of it. Don't be naïve. I'm staying over here on the realistic side."

"I understand, but even forcing secrecy smacks of the extraordinary. Think of the enormous amount of power one would need to convince people to commit mass suicide without question. Attribute the ability to force them to murder and we're talking astronomical. The whole damn thing's too intricate and complicated. Without a common thread, it defies the laws of scientific reasoning."

Arms crossed for the upcoming battle of wits riding a short path to crazy, Max settled a shoulder against the wall.

"Tell me, Preston. If someone knocked on the door and told you a stiff wind uprooted your Azalea bush while another guy claims it was gigantic moles moving under the lawn, would you automatically call an exterminator to nuke the alien creatures?"

Preston's eyes narrowed. "Are you making fun of me, detective?"

"Not in the least. Just making a point. Ever hear of Occam's razor?"

"No, but I'm pretty sure you're going to tell me."

Max chuckled and held up two fingers.

"If two possible explanations exist for a known event, the simplest is usually the correct one. My steadfast motto, and it's served me well over the years. I'll pick the wind every time."

Preston rolled his eyes and blew out a frustrated breath.

"Don't close your mind to the possibilities, Max."

"Okay, mole man. If you want to sit down in my office later and go over the case history of how easy it was for *human* men like Charles Manson, Jim Jones, Hitler, Jeffrey Lundgren, and Joseph Kibweteere to lead others into committing mass suicide or murder, then I think you might pull back a little on the 'woo-woo' factor. I can also show you tons of cases where killer fans have copied an inmate's crime."

"What's to say there weren't burns on each one of those zombie follower's bedroom walls, as well?" Preston flipped back. "You saw all the pictures I've collected. The events scatter across the country. Some occurred well before Adler and Jenner committed their crimes, so I believe your 'cog in a wheel' proposal, but positive you can't find a case history to shove in my face as proof. I wish you could, so I can stop this five-year nightmare ride."

"True, but who's to say these two inmates weren't performing a criminal trend already in place?" Max challenged. "They're bored out of their minds with nothing better to do. Coordination among prison inmates across facilities and to those outside the walls doing their bidding isn't unheard of. Does the term Arian Brotherhood ring a bell? We just have some very bad men playing a sick game. I think you got a screw loose there, kid."

Preston flopped back in the chair and burst out laughing. He lifted his hands in surrender.

"I give up, law man. As much as I'm enjoying this debate, I'll set aside my 'woo-woo' beliefs and look at the facts with you until directed otherwise."

"I can live with that. Welcome back to Earth."

After five minutes of mutual silence and no obvious desire to go back inside on either of their parts, Max reached for a cigarette to stop his need to sprint around the garden. He almost dropped it when Preston popped up from his chair and joined him against the wall, eyes serious.

"We've painted a box around ourselves, Max."

"Care to explain, crazy man?"

"Let's look at this in a different slant if we're going down a path of third-party interference. We set focus on a single thread leading from the copycat killer to the original version sitting in this prison. What about the connection between Adler and Jenner other than them playing a mutually vicious game? The same doctor saw both, Max. Maybe he's the coordination point…their influence. Prisons hold inmates, and this guy visits them all. He's free to roam around all he wants. I'd say this works into the simple side of the razor thing you mentioned."

Max clapped him on the shoulder.

"Now you're talking my language. Excellent observation. Come on. Let's find the warden. Pray the alligators aren't snapping too hard on his ass. We need some answers."

* * * * *

Video recordings of Adler and Jenner's therapy sessions handed over by the Warden clutched in his hand like gold, Max stepped into the adjoining office and held the cases in front of Preston's nose.

"Got something better. He recorded the sessions."

The kid's lids peeled wide and he lowered back to the seat ridden for the last thirty minutes.

Max pulled the matching chair in front of the computer desk and settled in, unable to keep the smile off his face. He'd had a whole spiel lined out for convincing the warden to let him interview any guards present at the session with Jenner, but Davies one-upped him by yanking out a drawer on his credenza, shuffled on a furious bent through a few folders, and came out with a disk in his hand. *Nirvana!*

Of course, there'd been a catch, and Max didn't balk at the simple request. An agreement to study Jenner's interaction with the good doctor to discount a push of the inmate to kill himself garnered Max a relieved, "Thank you," from the flustered warden. The offered private room to learn about their possible third-party instigator a bonus. Davies turned over Adler's recording when convinced a comparison of style used between the two would help catch any deviation in Jenner's session. Max brought up the internet and sensed Preston hovering next to him.

"Let's figure out who this guy is before we view these."

"Good idea. Knowledge is power."

"Well said." Max typed in the link found on the front of an expensive green and black postcard sent to Warden Davies from the founder and CEO of BRF-Behavioral Research Facility, Dr. Costica Alexandru. A replica of the card's front appeared. He clicked on the intriguing "Learn More" button.

Thanks to some fancy video features in play, a rectangular, two-storied building sitting on plush green grass surrounding a thick, whitewashed concrete base made a gradual appearance on the screen. With the upper levels formed entirely of wide-paned glass lined in thin-bordered brushed metal, it became easy to make out every stick of expensive office furniture, potted tree, ceiling fixture, and a downtown metropolis rising at its rear. It grew as whoever filmed it walked down the curvy sidewalk lined with vibrant colored flowers. The facility name etched into a decent-sized wooden sign planted next to the double door entrance purported elegance and professionalism.

Preston scooted closer. "Oddest building I've ever seen. Guess he doesn't like closed in spaces. Except for a few discrete wall dividers, you can see right through it. Maybe he's trying to put out a 'nothing to hide vibe.' You agree?"

"Yes, but despite the happy songbirds chirping in the trees and trying to make me feel carefree, I'm still wondering what's in the underground bunker."

"Ah, you're right. I just noticed the ventilation slats. Guess it houses the research area. He wouldn't want his trade secrets blasted out to the world."

Preston's brows lifted.

"How do you analyze ways to calm violent tendencies? He'd have to have live subjects, wouldn't he?"

"Interesting point. Oh, here we go. This must be our guy."

A well-dressed man finished stepping into the frame. Mid to late fifties was Max's best guess. He introduced himself as the doctor in question and proceeded to regale the potential audience of desperate wardens the benefits of his services. The guy reeked of upper-class education and wore it in a haughty manner.

The well-tailored dark-blue business suit fit his stocky frame to perfection. Salt-and-pepper hair cut short, but not in a severe manner, appeared combed forward in a possible attempt to cover obvious signs of thinning. The wide, angular face with its flared nostrils, thin lips, and dark, arching eyebrows made him appear sinister.

On an inward confession, Max owned his tad of bias. He never liked psychiatrists. Couldn't pinpoint an exact reason, but they made his skin crawl. He figured no one was so sure of their own internal workings to call for a superior right of poking around in the minds of others and acting like their word was gold.

As the camera drew closer, Max leaned forward to study their new enigma. The pockmarked high forehead, flat cheeks, and hard-set chin became an obvious sign his skin suffered extensive damage during the adolescent years. Though he smiled with perfect white teeth throughout the presentation, it never quite reached his dark eyes. The video ended and returned to the main screen.

"Oh yeah, I don't like him. Sketchy fellow. Never took us inside the building."

"Damn thing's see-through. Why bother? I doubt he'd want to show off his dungeon down below." Preston reached out and tapped the screen. "What nationality is this surname?"

"Not sure."

"Look it up."

Max opened a new tab and discovered Romania as the source.

"I was expecting a foreign accent. Sounds kind of upper east coast, don't you think?"

"Sure does. Wonder what brought him down to Georgia?"

"Marriage. Divorce. Could be escaping the ex."

"Possible." Max returned to the facility website and clicked on the "Request for Service" button.

A low whistle drifted over his shoulder as the doctor's fee rate, booking schedule, and appointment form appeared.

"Good grief, those prices are outrageous. The guy's making a killing. Look at the schedule. I bet he's pulling in seven figures a year, if not more."

"No doubt."

Max picked up the session video for Adler and slid it into the computer.

"Then let's see how he earns it."

CHAPTER 14

FROM A TOUR OF THE McAlester prison less than a year ago, Max thought the inmate's session room coming into view strikingly odd compared to what he remembered of the place. This one appeared made of dark cinderblock walls and ceiling. However, the entirety of the smaller section he assumed as the therapist's protected area showed to be metal.

Despite low lighting, the camera angle gave an unobstructed view of a large picture-frame window separating a simple wooden desk and chair on one side and a padded, armless black couch bolted to the floor on the other. An elaborate intercom system built into the metal wall reflected the desire for not sharing one breath with the patients.

Max observed an unshackled Adler pacing in front of what he assumed was thick Plexiglas. The enclosure became spookily reminiscent of something seen before. He chuckled.

"You need to explain your brain. What's so funny, because I'm not seeing it?"

"This set up looks like a freaking zoo display for exotic animals. I was half expecting to see a plaque in the corner stating 'Violent Homo Sapiens. Don't tap the glass.' No wonder Adler's pissed."

Preston's laugh cut off midstream as the therapy room door swung wide and the doctor swept into the metal-enclosed area protecting the human from the beast. He placed a laptop on the desk, strolled up to the partition, and flipped a switch on the intercom. Hands on his hips, Alexandru stared at the inmate for several minutes, just watching.

The superior stance cranked up Adler's agitation. Ignoring of the posturing sent the convict pounding on the thick partition and shouting, "What the fuck are you looking at, asshole?"

Frown in place, Max set the video on pause and got up from his perch in front of the computer. Preston threw him a questioning look. Index finger lifting to caution silence, Max knocked once and pushed inside the warden's office.

Davies looked up from a pile of papers he studied, thick brows still furrowed. A thin sheen of sweat coated his forehead. Max was sure the reports were from all the guards involved with Jenner from the moment he opened his eyes this morning. He didn't envy the man's job in the least, especially now. Running a facility full of hardened criminals with nothing but overworked and underpaid guards to keep them corralled probably accounted for the poor guy having only a few stubborn hairs desperately clinging to his skull and the protruding gut from too many after-hour beers.

"What can I do for you, Detective Browning? Is the equipment malfunctioning?"

Max sensed Preston hovering by the open door. "Only curious as to where these sessions occur. Are the prisoners transported to the doctor's facility in Georgia?"

"No, the room's right here in the prison. The therapist demands this from every facility. Either you build it to his specifications, or you bring them to him. If you balk or it doesn't pass inspection, he marks you off the list. Can't really blame him. I heard an inmate killed his father in the late '90s. Guy broke through the ceiling and dropped down on the other side of the partition and strangled him to death before the guards breached the door. Damn prison skimped on cost by putting in fake bricks."

"Interesting. Hadn't realized he took up his father's practice. The caution makes sense now. I'm curious. How'd you convince him to approve filming the sessions?"

The warden sat back, seeming pleased with whatever he was about to divulge.

"I didn't. The taxpayer's spent ten thousand dollars to build the damn thing. I wanted to understand how he utilizes it and ensure zero abuse of the people placed in my care. Never found anything in the terms of service that said I couldn't. I didn't have time to view the sessions, but I saw the results. They came out calm and followed orders without backlash. The guy's a genius. I doubt you'll find him pushing Jenner to commit suicide but can't chance I'm wrong."

"Yeah, I'm of the same mindset and hope you'll be able to write this as a fact in your report when I'm done."

Davies nodded. "I'm looking forward to it. If you're concerned about breaching patient confidentiality, don't worry. The inmates signed a waiver on the sessions. In return, they're awarded more yard time, extra helpings of food, and an offer to watch a movie of their choice without the other inmates present."

Max chuckled. "Smart man."

"And why they pay me the big bucks," he said in a dry tone. He glared at the paperwork and patted his face with a cloth. "Let's hope I keep it after this goddamn mess."

"Good luck." Max closed the door and settled back at the desk. From the corner of his eye, he caught Preston's head bobbing up and down.

"Mystery solved on the underground bunker. Bet he has a setup like this back home. No cameras and plenty of time to screw with their heads, all in the name of research."

"Possible, but I doubt a warden in his right mind would allow an inmate of Adler and Jenner's caliber anywhere outside their walls. Too much risk associated." Max restarted the vid.

Costica Alexandru lifted a gold pocket watch and swung it in a slow back and forth motion in front of Adler's pissed expression.

"Sit on the couch and focus on the watch, Bernard. Listen close to my voice. I'll put you in a relaxed state so we can begin the session. No harm will come to you."

Adler swiveled around and slammed his wide back against the thick Plexiglas.

"Screw that, shit. Warden said you were going to talk to me. He didn't say anything about you fucking with my head."

The doctor chuckled and lowered the watch.

"I'm not going to warp your brain, but fix things broken throughout your life. Every patient I've treated ends these sessions with less internal stress. I have no intention of disturbing the real you. Promise."

Adamant, Bernard shook his head and refused to turn around.

"For all I know, you'll turn me into a pansy. The other convicts will kill me."

"You're worrying over nothing. The survival skills you've learned over the years remain intact. Only your drive to kill and maim without cause will go away. You'll still be Bernard. Listen. I've been doing this a long time, as did my father before me. We understood clients with your similar disorder battle themselves every day."

"You don't know shit about me."

"Oh, but I do. On the outside of these wall, you could quell a deep burn to wreak devastation by acting on impulse, yet inside this cage it eats at you with constant demands to sate a hunger with no outlet. Yes, you might punch a face or break an arm if a target gets close enough, but that's not anywhere near what you need to feel satisfied. Let me help, Bernard. Allow me to take away your pain. Please."

Adler's shoulders dropped a few inches, but he didn't respond.

Alexandru shrugged and pocketed the watch.

"Fine. If you don't want to take part, I'll respect this choice and simply inform the warden of the decision. There are plenty of other inmates willing to take your slot and enjoy the rewards he's offering. Have a good day, Bernard."

"Wait." Adler turned, eyes wary and searching the placid expression.

"Do it. But if I figure out you've screwed me over, don't think for a second I won't find a way to kill your sorry ass. I still got friends on the outside."

Alexandru nodded and returned to the partition. "Fair enough." He pulled the pocket watch again and gestured to the couch.

"Go sit down, Bernard. As soon as you're comfortable, we'll start."

Max leaned closer to the monitor, as did Preston, ready to learn how this man could ever convince this belligerent inmate to cooperate.

After a few seconds of eye-to-eye glaring from both parties, Adler backed up to the plush furniture and lay down, surprising them both on how fast he went under. If he followed the doctor's calm words, the inmate sat on a beach, listening to the soft swell of the ocean as the sun rose, and digging his toes into warm sand. There was nothing Alexandru wanted him to do other than relax and enjoy the only freedom he'd ever acquire in this lifetime. The doctor flipped off the intercom, sat at the miniscule desk, and opened his laptop.

Preston paused the video.

"This is freaking me out. Hypnosis was one of the first things I thought might have happened to my aunt. I couldn't prove it one way or the other. According to her best friend, she suffered from allergies and hadn't left the house in two days before the incident. Very unlikely some random hypnotist showed up at her door and caught her unaware. It sounded stupid in my head, so I let it drop." He shrugged and engaged the video.

Max nodded. "Well, you might have been on to something. This one here has the skills, so he's moving higher on my list of suspects. Let's see what he does next."

The session continued with the doctor working at his laptop. Not once did he engage with Adler. After an hour, he checked his watch, approached the partition, and brought Bernard out of his sleeping state. In a soothing voice, he reminded him to keep the peacefulness felt throughout the session. A much calmer inmate sat docile on the couch as Alexandru informed him the guards were on their way. Expressionless, the doctor turned and left the enclosure. The screen blacked out.

After viewing another session with the exact same steps, minus trying to convince Adler to play along, the doctor did nothing but work studiously at his laptop.

"What a dick. He's charging the hell out of the prison while he sits there and plays on the computer. How long does hypnosis last, Preston?"

"Forever unless the hypnotist gives the client a key word to snap them back."

Ten minutes into the third one, Max sped the video up and noted the same repetitive session as the last zipping by. The doctor never moved from his perch or engaged with Adler. He felt a nudge to his side.

"Hey, Max. I read stories about people never smoking again after hypnosis."

"Are you trying to give me a hint?"

"No…maybe. You ever try those electronic cigarettes?"

"Yeah, like I have time to try and find a place to recharge. I'm barely able to keep enough matches. No thanks. Why? Do I stink?"

Preston strangled out a laugh. "I would've said something if you did."

"Then why are you bugging me?"

"I'm just saying."

"I know. Now unless you have a point, stow it."

Max tried to squash a smile as Preston chuckled and focused back on the monitor. The man was nothing like Fergus, but it felt good to engage in the easy back and forth banter he shared with his buddy. The other detectives they'd tried to pair him with were miserable fails on the personality factor. Working alone became a natural and very necessary transition to keep from hanging up his badge. He looked over when Preston commandeered the mouse and stilled the video before the next boring session could load.

"I'm curious. Where was the previous place this guy visited?"

Max recalled the facility website. "North Carolina prisons near Charlotte, Raleigh, and Fayetteville."

He knew the exact reason why Preston asked the question and gave him a knowing look before accessing the National Crime Database. Max loved technology. So much better than the old days of carrying his ass back into the office to dig through a pile of musty folders or call other precincts to try connecting A with B. Many old-timers balked at the new way of doing things. Max embraced it.

After finagling the search criteria to only violent crimes ending with multiple murder victims within two weeks of Alexandru's visits, a list of three returned to mull over. The first was a case of road rage. Max shook his head in amazement.

"Look at this craziness in Charlotte. A woman ran a family of five's van off the Sloan's Ferry Bridge and into the Catawba River. She rammed it with her Nissan until it broke through the guardrail and then proceeded to go over with it."

"Does it say why?" Preston asked as he leaned forward in interest.

"Witnesses claim the van driver laid on the horn when she didn't accelerate after the light turned green. The vehicle then made an aggressive move to pass, causing her to swerve into the other lane. After catching up to it, she followed on their bumper until reaching the center of the bridge where she gunned it and crashed into the front quarter panel. Damn. The woman was seventy-two. I think this qualifies as a murder out of left field."

Preston heaved out a breath riding hard on frustration.

"Shit. Killing by vehicle. Seems to be growing as a preferred choice of carnage these days." He grunted. "Even if the lawmakers are ever successful in banning guns, which I think is a huge mistake, will it be the next thing they'll go after? I can see it now. We'll all be walking everywhere we go and eating with our hands because they've taken every fork, spoon, and knife away too. They just don't get it. It's the people, not the tools. Mental health discussions aren't popular on the campaign stump. Less sexy."

"Tell me about it. Look at this one. Too sad to imagine. A mother killed her four-year-old during a birthday party. Witnesses said she over-the-top freaked after the child yanked the specialty cake off the table and it crashed to the floor. She snapped the child's neck before anyone could step a foot forward. To save the world from itself, I'm guessing they'll need to cut everyone's hands off?"

"Don't give them any ideas," Preston grumbled. "Look how nutty this is, Max. Here's a shooting at a mall. The cameras caught this guy circling the lot for twenty minutes trying to find a parking spot. Bystanders said as he made the sixth trip around, he banged on the steering wheel so hard the car shook. He pulled up to the front curb, strolled through the doors, and began popping anyone in sight. Crap. He was an off-duty police officer."

"I'd love to find out if the inmates Alexandru treated in North Carolina committed similar crimes, but I'm sure all of the wardens would tattle to the doctor we're checking up on him. He's their super-star. Don't need the added drama."

"Hey, Max. Do me a favor?"

"Sure."

"Look at Alexandru's schedule. Was he anywhere close to Tempe, Arizona five years ago? May sixth to be exact?"

Max flipped back to the doctor's website.

"Sorry, Preston. It only shows the prior and current year activity."

"Oh, well. It was worth a try."

Preston forced out a breath and straightened in his seat. "Anyway, I've noticed something else. With your two cases and now seeing these possibilities, it's obvious none of the killing sprees fit into a category of intricate planning, but a reaction to someone else's action. Each one was going about their business and a trigger flipped inside them. Whitfield revealed it was the phone message. His anger built for a while, adding fuel for the explosion. It was the car horn for grandma, destruction of an expensive cake for the mother, and growing frustration for the parking lot guy. I found the same common thread with the little bit of information I gleaned from the ones I've found. At the time, it seemed so random. Not now."

"Like what?"

"Stupid things, really. Receiving a speeding ticket, called into the boss's office for being late, car towed, IRS audit notice, and a bankcard declined at an ATM. You know, normal everyday crap we face each day."

"Well, here's my theory. Alexandru could be hypnotizing people and causing them to do these unspeakable acts when they reach the boiling point. They hit the right spike in blood pressure and then… bam! Off they go."

"Damn. If true, society has a lot of ticking time bombs still ready to go off out there," Preston added. "If your theory's correct, he finds these average citizens and somehow gets close enough to plant the specifics of the inmate's crimes through hypnosis."

"Yes."

"Busy man."

"No doubt."

"Or he's got a group helping him out."

"Shit, I hope not." Max indicated Alexandru's profile. "You're right, Preston. This is a very reasonable connection. He's out in the world with access to anyone he wants. If he can convince two stone-cold killers to start acting like boy scouts, I'm sure he can direct others to do his bidding."

"Yeah, but what's his motive? Shits and giggles?"

"Greed. You ever find a product promising to be the last one you'll ever have to buy and backs it up with a lifetime guarantee?"

"Nope."

"Well, there you go. If you cure all the monsters, your money flow disappears. Keep filling up the prisons and you're set for life. Lose one and gain another. Perfect reason to focus on violent crimes. Once they're housed for the long term, he's in control."

Preston released a soft whistle. "What in the hell have we stumbled on? If this pans out, any way you view it, this famous doctor looks more and more like a freaking serial killer."

CHAPTER 15

MAX SHRUGGED UPON PRESTON VERBALIZING the exact thing he'd been thinking for a while, only now he had a face to pin on his wall.

"Yeah, but in theory only. Our evidence is flimsy as hell. All we have is the 'honorable deeds' side of him."

Preston flopped back against his chair. "Hell, for all we know, he's clueless to these anomalies. Maybe we're trying to force the 'simple explanation' to work for us."

"Are you crawling back into the 'woo-woo' train, Preston?" He received a solid pop against his arm and chuckled.

"Maybe. I can't fathom someone going to all this trouble to make an innocent person do the same crime, even with the greed factor in consideration. There are enough evil people in the world for him to cure without him having to create more."

"You'd think, but maybe he's playing with only a select few and repeating the cycle of his 'virtual' kills while he's raking in the dough."

Max started the video feed.

"Wonder how he wraps up the sessions. Maybe he'll say something to prove he's the one planting the desire to kill inside Adler's head. I don't think he's stupid, but you never know."

The statement renewed Preston's attention. He sat up straight.

"Of course, it makes sense. His clients would think he works miracles if he cures every single inmate he encounters. All he has to do is snap them out of the hypnosis he created and they're back to their original personality."

"Yep, but forever tarnished and ruined. He can't use them anymore, so he takes the specific killing method and plants it in another. He gets to experience the high with each new innocent victim. Repeat offender."

"Man, that's sick. I'll cross my fingers he's stupid, but I won't hold my breath."

As with the prior sessions, Alexandru performed the same steps on the next three. With each one, Max fast-forwarded through until the disengaged therapist strolled out of the room. The last session caught their immediate attention. Six days of working on what appeared to be a novel while ignoring Adler, the doctor deviated. He didn't bring in the laptop this time. Alexandru engaged the intercom, approached the window, and lifted the watch.

"Good morning. Are you doing well today?"

Adler shrugged, never taking his eyes from the swinging timepiece.

"No need to sit. We'll be standing this time. Yes, come closer. Keep both eyes on the diamond center. You'll remain in a relaxed state, but this time you won't be visiting the beach. We need to discuss your crime. Are you willing?"

Air sucked deep into his lungs, Adler shuddered on the exhale and whispered, "Yes."

"Excellent. The files are clear as to how you claimed your victims, but I need one more thing from you. In the future, if someone asks you why you did these unforgiveable acts, what would you say to them?"

Max turned up the volume and finally learned what the man had refused to share with his victim's pleading families, or even some offering money for his confession. Granted, Bernard didn't have a shining reputation prior to letting loose inside the Target, but his actions shocked those close to him. Burglary, petty theft, and barroom brawls pretty much defined him from an early age. All it had taken for him to cause this much devastation was pausing to answer a phone call as he stepped up to the checkout counter to unload his basket. A few, loud grumbling shoppers behind him and a snarky comment from the cashier shoved his emotions to the breaking point. He just learned his younger sister had Leukemia.

"Whoa. Harsh. I almost feel sorry for him, but he could've taken such a different path."

Max could only nod in agreement, eyes glued to the screen.

The doctor slipped the watch into his pocket and settled his right hand on the partition, appearing concerned.

"What were you feeling, Bernard…when the excruciating pain struck?"

Adler's riveting answer struggled to release, as if ripping muscle from bone on its way out.

"She's the only person I've ever loved besides my mother. I couldn't stand the thought of losing her too." His jaw clenched, voice dropping an octave. "I wanted them to hurt as much as me… to bleed my pain."

"Did you lose yourself, Bernard?"

Adler's eyes closed. "Yes, I let the anger have me. It was such a relief…like I could breathe again."

Alexandru placed his other palm on the glass. "I'm going to free you now, Bernard. Look at me."

Adler complied.

"*Visitans Tenebras. Arcu ut Conseti. Solvo lupum, malo unum.*"

The doctor's husky, unintelligible words lifted Max's brows high on his forehead. He swerved the mouse over to hit the rewind but halted as Adler's eyes rolled to the back of his head, big body dropping like a stone. Back arching, the inmate's lips peeled back from his teeth as he flopped around and batted at the air. Alexandru never moved.

"What the fuck, Max?"

"Shit," was all he could manage to spit out as Adler fought whatever controlled his body until finally growing still. The only thing left moving was his heaving chest and wide blinking eyes.

"Well done, Bernard," Alexandru praised. "Kneel before me."

Pushed up from the floor on shaking arms, Adler nodded and did as instructed. Tears rolled in streams as he tried to keep upright.

"Is the pain gone, my friend?" The doctor's timbered voice oozed warmth and comfort.

"Yes."

"You'll never harm others in this manner ever again. Be at peace with this knowledge."

Bernard's lips quivered as he looked around, a confused expression on his puss. "Thank you. I will," he mumbled.

"Go lay down now. I'll have them come fetch you after the hour's complete. Rest your mind and relax. Your troubles are over."

Bernard nodded and curled into a fetal position on the couch. The doctor turned and walked away, never glancing back as he left the enclosure.

The video ended.

Stunned at the strange turn of events, Max didn't argue when Preston took the mouse from his fingers and brought the video back to the spot where Alexandru placed both palms on the glass partition.

"What did he say?"

"No idea. Foreign gibberish."

They both leaned close to the monitor. After five more loops through the video, Max sat back and shook his head.

"Only thing I recognized was 'Unum.' Latin."

"How'd you know?"

"It was part of the U.S. motto until they switched to 'In God we Trust' in 1956. You can find it on our coins. *E pluribus unum*. Out of many, one. Unum means 'one.' Damn. What do they teach kids in schools these days?"

"I was too busy chasing girls, I guess."

Max chuckled and tossed the kid a dime. Preston rolled his eyes and pocketed it.

"Okay, then. Type the rest of them into a translator program, Mr. Trivia."

On a hard snort, Max threw him an incredulous look.

"I wouldn't have the first clue how to spell that shit. We could end up with all sorts of crap. Besides, none of them ever have the same outcome."

Preston's lips twisted and he glanced back at the monitor.

"Yeah, you're right. Hey! What was that?"

"What?"

"Roll it back to where he flopped around. I thought I saw something."

Max complied, staring hard at the screen.

"I don't see anything."

"Wait for it. There! It looks like a shadow passing across Adler's face and drifting to the left. Is there someone in there with him? Run it back again."

After two more rounds, Max had to admit something wasn't quite right.

"Glitch with the camera."

"Maybe someone's in the corner. They could hide at the edge of the partition. Dark enough over there. Do you think they used a Taser on him?"

"I'm glad you're trying to find the simplest explanation, but we would've seen the wires. Plus, the prongs would still be sticking out of him."

"Well, then maybe Dr. Weirdo here developed some type of new tool to zap the hell out of them. If not, then you explain how a string of words made him go into spasms."

"Hell, I don't know. You're the one with hypnosis research under his belt. I'm guessing he likes to add a little flair to the process when he releases whatever's planted in their head. The man gets off on it, I know that much for sure. Look how he made Adler kneel for him afterward. He's seeking adulation. The king granting mercy to his subjects. Let's view Jenner's session to find any deviation."

"Good idea." Preston pushed the case over, eyes wide with excitement.

Just as done with Adler, Dr. Alexandru put Jenner through the exact same odd therapy. He had an easier time convincing to play along since Whitfield didn't think he'd done anything wrong. Chin lifting in defiance, he informed the doctor he was only after the perks. Max fast-forwarded to the last session.

During the confession to motivation for slaughtering five people, Alexandru got the same response they'd recorded on the suicide vid. Nothing else deviated—weird words cited, Jenner goes down, and Alexandru leaves the inmate curled up on the couch and walks away.

Max recorded the foreign words on his handheld recorder. After thirty minutes of comparing them to Adler's version, he and Preston agreed they were exact.

Fingers drumming the table, Max tried to find definition in the nuttiness.

"Seems Alexandru didn't shove the guy toward suicide on purpose. I believe this was Jenner's personal decision. I stand with my theory the doctor reverses the original hypnosis so he can claim another victory and score a fat paycheck."

"I agree, and he's chosen a complicated releasing trigger to keep it safe. Only Alexandru would know how to end his hypnosis. If he used something simple, they could've jumped out of the state of mind at any time. Sounds plausible. Will you do me a favor, though? Run Jenner's video back to where he fell on the ground."

"No need."

"Why?"

"I saw it too,"

"You did?"

"Yeah, the simplest explanation is a camera flaw. The complicated one is your theory of a person hiding in the shadows and zapping the hell out of the inmates with innovative technology for some insane purpose. I'm holding judgement on which side I'll take. Alexandru could very well have an accomplice aiding him through the procedures. He could've suspected the prisons might record him and added it in for show. Even if I ask Davies if someone came with Alexandru and he says, 'No,' then it could very well be a guard he paid. Either way, it doesn't matter, Preston."

"Why?"

"When we prove this doctor's responsible for his actions, then the others will fall, as well."

"I hope so."

"Me too." Max knocked against Preston's knee.

"Come on. Let's give Davies the good news. He could use some."

"How much are you going to tell him?" Preston asked on a wary pitch.

"Just enough. We're not ready to reveal our theory to the world, yet. I don't feel like being sent for observation by one of these quacks."

Preston laughed, gathered up the disks, and executed a grand gesture toward the door leading into the warden's office.

"My exact sentiment. After you, detective."

* * * * *

"Yes, I'm positive. Dr. Alexandru never planted any obvious suggestions to Jenner to take his life."

Max caught the first sign of happiness hit the warden's face.

"Damn. Good to hear. Will you formalize the finding?"

"Sure. I'll write it up and email it to you."

"Give me a run down on what he did."

"Be prepared. The guy said some Latin gibberish to cure them of their evil ways, but on a good note, he said the exact same thing to Adler."

"Latin?"

"Yeah, he's of Romanian heritage, so maybe the lines are from something cooked up in his home country and outside the normal boundaries of medical practice in the states. Whatever it was, it worked, as you know. At the end, they admitted to the doctor why they committed the murders. The man makes them face their crimes. Jenner couldn't live with what he finally admitted, and Adler has a stronger personality, I guess."

"Yes, what I figured too."

"One more thing you need to know. Alexandru's ripping you off. He sits around for six days and works on his laptop without any interaction with the convict. It's only on the last session where he does his weird foreign thing to produce you a manageable prisoner."

Davies shrugged. "I don't care if he snoozed through the whole damn thing, woke up, slaughtered a chicken, and then chanted voo-doo over them. If they stay docile until they either die or make a parole date, you'll find no complaints here. Just do me a favor and keep your report brief. No need to go into all the mumbo-jumbo."

"Will do."

Preston surprised him by stepping forward and addressing the warden.

"One question, if I may?"

"Sure."

"Do you have any issue with us viewing the session room? Watching his unique skill unfold was interesting. Filming what you built would place some context around it, if you don't mind."

"Sure, the least I can do for you taking time to analyze the therapy method."

"Can we borrow the disks for a few days? I'd like to figure out those words he used."

Max refrained from shoving Preston on the shoulder. The warden surprised him by the quick response.

"I don't see it as a problem." Light gray eyes narrowed, and an index finger lifted in warning.

"Don't copy or release it to the public. No need to piss off Alexandru. He'll be invited back, that's for sure."

"Of course. Need to sate my curiosity. Nothing more."

"Good. Have Randy call me if he needs confirmation."

"Appreciate your help."

A hand rose the second they passed hearing range of the warden's office and cut off Max's planned diatribe.

"I'm aware I broke your rule of noninterference, Max, so save the butt chewing. My gut told me to ask, so I did. Plus, I need to stand inside this session room. Not going to kill you to let me run this out of my system."

"Fine. Just don't surprise me again."

Preston pushed into the lobby area and threw a wave to Officer Vasquez.

"I can't promise, so I won't. This whole damn thing keeps twisting on us. Expect surprises."

Max grunted. "Well, I can't argue with you there. Lead on, wild man."

CHAPTER 16

PACKED TIGHT INSIDE A ROTATING carousel of thick vertical bars wasn't anywhere near high on Max's good time's radar. He hated the damn contraption the first time he'd passed this way years before, and his apprehension to go another round stood stark and ever present.

Whoever came up with this ridiculous thing needs their ass kicked.

There had to be a better way of turning a goddamn corner to access a higher security area.

Max figured the grinding rusty sound skeeved him out the most. Trapped inside and waiting for welding torches to cut him loose shot his blood pressure through the roof from just the thought alone.

"Well, this is stupid" slipped from Preston's mouth, yet he walked in as if it was no big deal.

The open slot swung back his way all too soon. Knowing he didn't have any other choice but to face the ludicrous fear of tight spaces, Max stepped inside the opening, clenched his jaw, and shoved his way through.

Images of Victoria laughing while claiming she found his kryptonite after discovering him trapped inside a Porta-Potty on their honeymoon helped him endure the current predicament. Memories of her beaming smile brought him the same sense of relief felt when she used her high heel to break him out of the stinky hellhole.

Launched out the other side of his nightmare ride, Max was glad to find Preston glancing up and down the hallway and hadn't witnessed his initial struggle. He looked back, envious of Randy's easy glide through the monstrosity and calm face as he gestured to a steel door with a small window positioned across the corridor.

"Here you go." He tested the handle. "Unlocked."

Throat cleared and a semblance of normal finding some traction, he asked the question on his mind since the video surprise.

"This used to be the physical rehabilitation area."

"Still is. They commandeered two of the offices to build this. The rest are being phased out until the one closer to the infirmary's complete."

"Ah."

Randy backed up to the carousel. "I'll leave you to it. Call when you're done."

Max sensed fine hairs lifting on his skin as the squeak and grind started up again. Puzzled, he looked back at the therapy door and then turned his attention to the rotating bars. He couldn't stop the laughter rolling out of his throat. Preston nudged him on the back.

"What's so funny now?"

"Found the source of your spooky shadow, Preston. When those turn, the light shifts and reflects into the window." He heard a derisive snort and distinctive squeal of the steel door opening.

"Sure, Max. Whatever you say. Someone pushed through at the *exact* time the inmates, on different days mind you, began flopping around on the floor as if someone electrocuted the hell out of them. Not a simple explanation there, detective."

Max followed him into the room. "No more than your zapping laser gun theory."

"I never said laser gun. Now you're making shit up."

"Semantics." Max glanced around the metal-enclosed structure. "What do you think you're going to find in here? Looks like it did on the video." He walked up to the partition. "Same here."

"Not quite."

"How?"

"The left side of the room wasn't visible. Can't find a door leading into the inmate area, so how'd they get in there?"

"You're right. Adler and Jenner were inside when the feed started, and it ended with Alexandru's departure."

Moved back to the partition, Max cupped his hands on the Plexiglas and stared into the dim room.

"This is ridiculous. I don't see an entrance, but there must be one. Doubt they came through the damn ceiling." He turned and gestured for Preston to follow him into the corridor. "Let's check the adjoining room."

Head peeked around the door, Max scanned across the therapeutic exercise equipment, wheelchairs, cots, vertical handrails bolted to the floor, and a whirlpool tub in the corner. He pushed inside.

"Empty. Ah, there it is. To your right. Mystery solved."

Preston jiggled the knob and pushed it open. He began nodding, a smug look owning his features.

"My theory just moved into first place. The door's in the far corner. Anyone could've come through here and hid in the shadows while he had Adler and Jenner under."

"Fine, I'll give you this one. But it still doesn't matter. Nothing caught on video. Can't prove anything."

"I know, but it makes me feel better knowing it's plausible."

Max nudged him on the back.

"See? Feels good when you can grab something real. Doesn't it?"

When Preston didn't respond, but leaned down to study the doorknob instead, Max moved to his side.

"What's got your attention?"

Preston's fingers brushed over two small marks below the knob. Both were the size of pencil erasers. He jerked upright, moved inside the room, and studied the other knob. Max heard a sharp intake of breath before the kid backed out and pointed at the door.

"Oh, shit. What the hell's going on? They're burn marks, Max. Both sides. Same spot."

Stooped for a better look, Max analyzed the areas in question. He had to admit they bore similar characteristics to wood scorches.

"Yes, appears to be the case."

Preston's eyes lit. "I knew it. Another connection."

"They're not like the others, Preston. Don't be digging for moles."

"Humor me then."

Max stepped back as Preston closed the door and squatted at eye level to one of the marks. On a slow rotate, his body turned until he stared at the opposite wall. Jumping to his feet, he loped crossed the cluttered room and stopped in front of a desk butted up against the wall. He gestured wildly over his shoulder.

"Come look at this."

Blowing out a breath, Max joined him. A round of flutters worked its way through his stomach when seeing two identical burn patterns along the edge of the window frame and hidden between two stacks of towels. He could hear the excitement in Preston's voice.

"Whatever that was, it escaped."

"Ridiculous assumption, and you know it."

"Explain it then."

"Simple. They were done with lasers."

"What is it about you and lasers? I doubt the inmates have free access to devices powerful enough to burn into the walls, but I'm sure you'll try to convince me it happened when the contractors built the room. Oh! Better yet, the guards come in here at lunch to play *real* laser tag. Whoever has the least amount of burns on their uniform wins?" He snorted in derision. "We'll have to agree to disagree."

"Agreed." Max snickered and patted him on the back. "You're learning, Sinclair."

"Yeah? Then help debunk my crazy theory. Can your precinct enhance video and audio, or is it all smoke and mirrors on TV?"

"For reals."

"Good. Take me there. We need to figure out what the hell Alexandru said, and I want a better view of that damn shadow."

* * * * *

"Who am I?"

Max raised a brow at Preston's weird question, locked the Vic, and took every other stair on his way up to the precinct front doors, the kid hot on his heels.

"What do you mean, you nut bug?"

Preston rolled his eyes and started a one-sided conversation, voice overtly friendly and animated.

"Well, hello, nice person who works with Max. Good to meet you. I'm Preston Sinclair. What do I do? Oh, I follow violent, nonsensical crimes around the country to see if I can find some burn marks on a bedroom wall. Why do I stay glued to Max's side? Simple really. I'm hoping he can find the weirdo putting them there. I was about to give the fuck up before he rescued me, though. And how are you doing today?"

Barking out a laugh, Max yanked open the front door to the precinct, snagged a visitor's badge from the front counter, and gestured for the comedian to follow him to the right.

"Was your father in the military?"

"Yes."

"What branch? Here, put this on."

"Thanks. Marine Corps."

"Perfect. His name?"

"Theodore, but he prefers Theo. Where you going with this?"

"You're researching mass murders for a possible documentary. You're independent, and I only allowed you to follow me around because I knew your father. Simple. No fuss. More than likely, no one will ask you a damn thing. They're all too busy to care. Did you notice how easy it was to snatch a visitor's badge without signing you in?"

"Ah."

Shoved inside a bright room cluttered with overtaxed shelves filled with electronic equipment in various stages of repair or decay, Max rapped twice on a set of metal swinging doors and stepped inside. He was happy to spot a thin form sitting to his left.

"Did I give you enough time to yank your hands out of your shorts, Bill?"

"Bite me," rolled out on a droll, disinterested voice. "You know I only touch myself after lunch."

Yep, same Hawaiian-print shirt choice, faded blue jeans cut off above the knees, and ever-present dry humor. He was barefoot, as usual. Tan sandals lying to the side never touched his feet unless he deigned to visit another department. The only way Max could tell Bill ever changed his clothes lay in the color of the shirt. Today, brilliant green with a smattering of orange flowers stuck out in the monochrome room. Slicked-back blond hair had grown long enough to start curling around his pierced ears. It was hard to miss the neatly trimmed goatee. Last time he ventured into his lair for a consult, the irredeemable nut had a rubber band securing it into a chin ponytail.

On an irreverent snort, Max sat on a short stool and rolled over to the long worktable stretching from wall to wall. Like the front room, it too strained under the weight of varying equipment used for whatever purpose this tech nerd desired.

Max gestured for Preston to take the chair on the other side of the resident civilian audio-visual expert staring at a monitor and ignoring the hell out of them. After a round of blatant disregarding of his presence, Max leaned forward and finally caught the eye of the one man he considered the most laid-back, easygoing person he ever met. Nothing ruffled this guy's feathers. Twelve years of traded barbs and he'd yet to get a rise out of him.

Hazel eyes flicked down at the plastic-encased DVDs Max clicked against the tabletop with steady purpose.

"Whatcha got, Max?"

"Preston Sinclair. This is Bill Stewart."

"Nice to meet you, Bill."

"Likewise."

Max slid the disks over, Adler's on top.

"Need to have these cleaned up. Audio and visual."

"Any particular area or the whole thing?"

"About two minutes' worth on each. Start at the seventh hour and look for a man pressing his palms against a clear partition. Ends with a guy on the other side curling up on a couch."

Bill nodded. "I can do it right now. I'm sick of looking at this convenience store footage anyway. Grainy as shit. Why do they even bother if they're going to skip on quality?" He slipped the disk into the machine and smiled. A rare event.

"This is pretty clear. At least I can distinguish the faces. When I reach the area you want, I'll isolate it out and transfer to another disk? Sound good?"

"Perfect."

Soon, Bill had worked his magic and both inmates' last moments on screen transferred to another DVD. Not once did Bill display surprise or comment on the words slipping out of Alexandru's mouth or the convicts flopping around on the floor afterward. Max knew Bill had seen so many instances of insanity captured on film, he became immune to the novelty. It was all about the quality of what you were after.

"I've got this as pristine as I can get, Max. Is there anything specific you want more focus on? I can pull the area out as a still image and further enhance."

His young sidekick straightened in interest.

"Tell him what you need, Preston."

"I'm seeing a shadow pass over the men's faces when they're on their backs. We're trying to find out if someone entered or exited the room. The door is over in the far-left corner, but we can't see it."

"Which way does it swing?" Bill asked.

"Into the room and toward the partition wall."

"What's on the other side?"

"Big room."

"Windows?"

"Yes."

"Covered?"

"Only in glass and bars."

"Got it. I can isolate the door and their heads as separate pictures."

Bill brought both video clips up on one screen. He looped through each several times and then grunted.

"Sorry, all you'll find on the back corner is a vague outline."

He froze on a part of the image and zoomed inward.

"See this line here? If anyone opened it, you would've had distinctive light reflect from the seam outward. If the time showing at the top right's correct, the sun's in full force. Got nothing. Maybe we can figure out where the source of the light is coming from to produce your shadow."

After several minutes of watching Adler's agonized features loop on repeat like some sick B-rated movie torture scene, Max glanced at Bill. He was frowning.

"What? Are you unable to find a spot to cut out?"

"No, this isn't a shadow, guys. Seems more like...hell, this's going to sound weird. It looks like smoke, but I don't see any clear ignition cause. A shadow has a distinctive outline and directional pattern of movement with a light source. These edges appear to be morphing outward and swirling at the tips."

Preston squirmed in his chair, barely able to contain building excitement.

"Can it be captured into a photograph and enhanced?"

On a curt nod, Bill isolated the areas around both Adler and Jenner's heads. When he finished tweaking the images as much as his software would allow, all three of them were leaning close to the monitor. Bill scratched at his unruly chin hair.

"Weirdest looking smoke I've ever seen. It has an inconsistent structure, but the angle is precise. Almost as if it caught on a slip-stream of air, but the edges stay agitated. The same goes for the other one. Doesn't it seem too thick?" He jerked back from the monitor, startling them both.

"Shit, Bill. What the hell?"

With a fast grunt and a quick face scrub, Bill popped his cheeks a few times and let loose a hearty chuckle.

"Damn. I've been staring at this screen since three this morning. I'm starting to imagine things. Best guess, air from under the door is sucking it forward. I'll leave it up to you guys to figure out how in the hell smoke got in there without an obvious source. Investigation isn't part of my pay grade."

Bill saved all the images to the new disk, popped it out of the computer, and handed it to Preston. He stood, released a loud yawn, and stretched.

"Thanks, guys. I enjoyed that one. Come back anytime. I'm going to lunch and then take a nap before I start the convenience store nonsense again. You can find your way out."

* * * * *

The entire time he marched down the corridor leading to his office, Max expected Preston to sling an, "I told you so," but was surprised by the comment rolling out.

"Did we miss seeing Jenner and Adler taking cigarette breaks any time during their sessions?"

"Nope. I was skipping through them, but not fast enough to miss something like that."

"What do you think it is?"

"No idea, but something has to make sense."

Pleased no one waited inside his room to bug the hell out of him, Max locked the door and removed the stack of folders from the chair in front of his desk. After a noisy drag around to the other side, he motioned for Preston to sit. Plopped on his comfortable squeaky chair, Max booted the computer and loaded the enhanced video.

Multiple plays of the event, slowing the feed to inch their way through the shadowy movement, and freezing to stare at the swirling vapor didn't supply any more insight. Max flopped back and grunted in frustration. He looked over when Preston began drumming his fingers on the desk. One brow rose and the tapping stopped. Max leaned forward.

"Let me hear it."

"Okay, let's think about what we know. An inmate drops to the floor and goes into spasms. The camera catches some type of misty smoke-like substance drifting low to the ground and across the convulsing body, but there's no evident fire source. These are facts." The pause for effect worked.

"Go on, throw it out there. Whether weird or plausible, I don't care at this point."

"What if some type of chemical agent is filtering into the room? They built it to Alexandru's specifications, and Warden Davies said it had to pass the doctor's inspection before he'd work with the inmates. He could've planted the stuff long before the sessions started."

Max smiled and nudged Preston's knee. "Excellent theory. How do you propose he released the chemical when time to put on the dog-and-pony show for the cameras?"

Preston shrugged. "I'm guessing the watch since it was in his hand the entire time. It could've been the trigger. He brings them close to the window. Click. Instant flop-and-wiggle time."

"And the burn marks? How do they figure into this scenario?"

"Not a freaking clue." Preston shoved a hand through his hair. "Don't gloat, but I'm thinking the laser theory isn't too farfetched. Maybe the construction crew used one to cut the cinderblocks and weren't cautious." His green eyes narrowed in thought.

Max raised his brows in question. He got a shrug in return.

"It doesn't matter anyway, Max. The issue remains the same. Alexandru uses hypnosis to manipulate people's lives and covers it with this elaborate theatrical production to make him appear to be a saint. There's just one more thing bugging me."

"All ears."

"What the hell is he saying to those inmates? Major aspect. Aren't you the least bit curious?"

"Of course, I am. Something in the words could point out his guilt."

"Then how do you plan to interpret them?"

Max slid the handheld recorder from his back pocket. It still held the string of foreign words he captured from Jenner's session.

"I'm not going to, but I believe I know a place that can."

CHAPTER 17

I SHOULD'VE CALLED. WHAT WAS I thinking?

Max forgot how loud his steps sounded whenever he walked down the long center aisle of St. Peters Cathedral. It didn't matter if he lifted to his toes to try coming in stealthy, the sound always echoed throughout. At least the place was free of worshipper's turning their heads to stare his way. He glanced at Preston, who didn't seem to care how hard his boots struck the floor. His head remained tilted upward and swiveling around, taking in the elaborate three-storied, arched ceiling—a purposeful architectural decision to give the impression of striving to be closer to God.

A year after coming here, he finally quit looking up. He got tired of feeling insignificant, almost understanding how a mouse felt when straining their tiny necks to spot the huge humans pissed to find it breached their house, as well. He knew he didn't belong in here. It wasn't that he was incorrigible or a disbeliever, just disinterested.

Even still, the place continued to bring back memories of his time in the hallowed behemoth. The low echo of whispered prayers swirling in the cool air, brilliantly colored glass sending patterned light to dance across the marbled floor, and woodsy incense tickling his nose. He could almost feel his knees pressing into a soft cushion, bland taste of a thin wafer dropped on his tongue, and the bite of grape juice standing in for wine, which was already standing in for the blood of Christ. Elaborate pomp and ceremony touching every sense, but nothing had yet to breach his soul.

Despite Victoria's best efforts to have him embrace her religion, he never felt whatever caused her eyes to gleam whenever she entered this monstrosity filled with alabaster statues of the Madonna and painted wall scenes of the righteous lifting to the heavens. She hadn't been a particularly religious person when they'd first met, the trappings of the church only becoming important after her mother passed. That's how he came to know the smiling, frocked priest now walking toward him with outstretched arms.

"Maxwell, how good to see you again."

The man had the memory of an elephant, Max at once thought. He hadn't stepped foot in here since Fergus's murder. Impressive.

"Father Greggory. You're looking well," he replied in sincerity. In fact, the man hadn't changed a bit. His hair remained thick and as snowy white as the banded collar circling his neck.

Cornflower blue eyes twinkled from the refracted light glowing downward through the colorful stained-glassed domed sanctuary. It was almost as if the universe had a spotlight shining down on its most lovable creature. Despite his misgivings about organized religion, Max had always liked the priest and accepted his warm embrace.

"Your eyes reveal you have something of importance to discuss. What can I do for you, Maxwell?"

Max introduced Preston and retrieved the recorder.

"We're in a hurry, so I'll apologize up front. I'm hoping you can interpret something for us. It sounds Latin."

"Of course. Happy to help."

Max clicked the PLAY button, and the ominous, eerie words seeped into the air. He had a flash image of the recorder bursting into flames and squashed an untimely chuckle.

Visitans Tenebras. Arcu ut Conseti. Solvo lupum, malo unum.

Father Greggory's brow knit, head cocking to the side as he motioned for Max to replay the captured words. Within seconds of it ending, he released a soft snort.

"It sounds as if someone's playing a joke on you. Was it the entirety?"

"Yes, what is he saying?"

"Visiting darkness. Bow to the *Conseti*. Free the wolf, evil one."

Skin lifting in chills, Max's eyes collided with Preston's wide green ones before flicking them back at the father.

"Wolf? Are you sure?"

"Positive. Who gave it to you?"

"We're working a case. Sorry, I can't tell you."

Father Greggory chuckled.

"No need for apology. I fully understand the necessity of keeping secrets. Well, it sounds like this man's attempt at an exorcism. Childish and crude to say the least," he scoffed. "The church has a very extensive dialog used when exorcising demons. This is not part of the sanctioned process. You may have someone dabbling in the Occult."

"Any idea what *Conseti* means?"

"No translation. Perhaps he uses the name of their order or possibly a god they worship."

"Ah." Max returned the recorder to his coat pocket. A warm palm land on his shoulder.

"Maxwell. I would welcome you back to mass. It's been way too long."

On a soft chuckle, he waved his palm in surrender.

"I'm not going to lie to a priest, especially here. I only attended before at Victoria's insistence. When a wife stomps her foot and says, 'Get in the car,' you don't argue. We're divorced now."

"I know," the father said with a touch of sadness. "She struggled with the decision for many months—with giving up, as well as her soul. Since you didn't have a sacramental marriage or children, the church granted her annulment, which relieved her of the guilt. I heard she's remarried."

"Yes, I'm happy for her. We're much better friends than marriage partners."

"You're a good man, Maxwell." He stepped back a pace, his expression peaceful and entreating.

"God bless you in your good works." He lifted his right hand, three fingers touching, and traced them across his body and forehead. Solemn words slipped out on an easy stream from his lips.

"*In nomine Patris et Filii et Spiritus Sancti.*"

"Thank you, father," Max returned.

The old priest nodded, threw them both a warm smile, and scurried away to greet a parishioner pacing next to the confessional.

The sound of his and Preston's footsteps appeared to ring louder as they headed for the exit. The kid stayed silent as they breached the heavy doors and bounced down the steps leading to the sidewalk. Stopped to press his back against the tall outer wall surrounding the massive church, Max pulled a cigarette and lit it. Marlboro number two was coming early today. They both stared at the passing traffic for many minutes before Max decided to speak, a simple word summing up his racing thoughts.

"Damn."

"Yeah, I know."

Max retrieved his phone and punched in a few numbers.

"Warden Davies. Browning here. I have a quick question if you have the time…thanks. How many inmates did Dr. Alexandru provide therapy to while he was there?" He felt his brows lift.

"Five? No, those two videos were fine. Curious, that's all. If not too much trouble, can you tell me what the other three prisoner's crimes were? Yes, I'll hold. Thank you."

Preston stepped into his line of sight.

"Where you going with this?"

"Theory. I'll tell you if it pans out."

"Yes, I'm still here." His heart thundered the longer Davies spoke.

"Really? Damn. I can understand why you'd want to bring the doctor in to treat them. Thanks for your help today, Warden. You too. Bye."

"Alexandru did more?"

"Yes, road rage ending with a shooting of two bystanders. Next one drove into a crowd of people at a movie theater. Four dead. And the other killed his entire family by cutting a gas line and triggering an explosion. Detectives from my precinct received assignments on cases like the first two when I got the call on Harrison. I haven't heard anything about a gas incident, yet."

"Shit."

"Yep."

"Are you going to their homes to find a mark and eliminate any further doubt?"

"No, I'm way past convinced. Besides, we don't need to stir anyone's curiosity by my interest in someone else's case. I'm betting all we'll find in McAlester is three more happy-as-shit prisoners suddenly playing nice with others. I had a hunch this was much bigger here and Davies confirmed it."

Max flicked the cigarette butt into the gutter and pushed away from the wall. Preston kept close to his heels.

"Where we going?"

"To a source who might have some answers. At least now I know what to ask."

* * * * *

"Good to see you again, detective. Did you think of something else I might help you with on your case?" Adler scooted his chair closer to the partition, curiosity evident and growing.

"Yes, I did. We're recording this visit too."

A huge smile lit Bernard's face.

"No problem. Thanks for the candy. Officer Vasquez said you brought me a thirty-six-count box. Righteous of you, for sure. I had one after lunch. It felt like my birthday."

"You're welcome. I came back because I forgot to ask you about the sessions you had with Dr. Alexandru. Some recent events have me concerned. I'm hoping you can help me out."

Adler's face immediately sobered.

"Jenner had the same therapy like me. I heard he killed himself in front of you. Scuttlebutt?"

"No, true event. Did you consider suicide after the sessions ended, Bernard?"

"Not once. I've been a survivor since I was old enough to think. Last thing I'd do is check myself out. If you ever hear I did, then know they're lying."

"Done. Are you willing to talk about your sessions?"

"Yes, I promised to tell you the truth if you brought your agenda into the light. You've done that. Ask me anything you want."

"I appreciate it. Just start telling me how you remember things. I'll ask questions along the way if I have a need."

"Got it." Adler's lips pursed. "Some parts are sort of hazy, so don't think I'm holding anything back on purpose."

"I won't."

"Well, I remember waiting for him to arrive. Almost changed my mind a few times. I was after the perks, but I sure didn't want to talk to a shrink. After the state took me away from Pops, they tried to squirrel with my head. It only made me more pissed. None of those assholes came from my background. They read books and think they're so goddamn smart."

"Agreed."

"It was so bad back then. I didn't calm down until they had my sister, Margie, brought to the same foster house. From then on, I had no fear of anyone."

Bernard shook his head and shivered, lost in a memory.

"Go on," Max urged.

"Yeah, lost the ability the second I looked the doctor in the eyes. It was the first time I felt scared of someone. I'm talking down to the bone. I could've easily pummeled his ass if the walls hadn't been so thick, but I wanted to run, instead. I stood there frozen to the floor when he pulled a gold watch up and looked at me—really looked at me. His eyes. I couldn't stop looking at his eyes. They were deep black holes. Almost felt like I was falling inside a bottomless pit. After he sent my mind to a quiet place on the beach, all the fear melted away. I didn't want to leave."

Bernard's brows drew together.

"I'm going to say something stupid, so don't laugh."

"We won't. Promise."

"How can you hate someone and love them the same time? He gave me freedom I'll never have again. Hell, I never had it before, either. Who am I kidding? I wanted to do everything he asked, so I could smell fresh air, feel the grainy sand against my palms, the sun on my face, and warm water rushing over my feet."

"Sounds like paradise, Bernard. He gave it to you once. You can always go back there in your dreams. Whenever you want."

"Yeah, I can, can't I?" His smile grew as the thought sank in.

"Yes, now tell me about the last day with him. Do you remember smelling anything odd or seeing smoke?"

"Nah, room smelled like Pine Sol. They use it to clean the rehabilitation room next door."

"When we spoke before, I asked if you liked dogs. I'll be honest in my question this time. Do you ever remember being associated with anything about wolves? We think the 'W' you put in one of your victim's chest stood for wolf."

"Honest, detective. Never knew what the letter meant. If it did at one time, it's lost in my brain somewhere. The press called me feral once. Does it count?"

"Maybe. Okay, let's move on. Do you remember the doctor saying some foreign sounding words to you?"

Adler's head began an adamant bobbing up and down.

"Oh yeah. When he said I wasn't going back to the beach, I felt scared again. He asked me to remember why I killed those poor people and the fear switched to the same violent feeling I got the day I shot up the store. Then he said those strange words. That's when the burning started."

"The burning?"

Max had to fight everything inside his being from swiveling around and shouting, "Did you hear that shit?" to Preston. Every bit of his flesh lifted in a wash of chills.

"Yes, when he spoke, I felt like my entire body went up in flames. I had a sudden thought I must be dying, and this was what it's like to pass through to hell. I guess I blacked out. I remember lying on the floor, not particularly sure if he told me to do it or if I fell over. It felt like a ton of sludge had left me. I was raw."

"How so?"

Bernard scrubbed at his arms, brows furrowing even further.

"Not raw on my skin like I burned, but here," he said while patting his chest, "deep inside."

Max noticed Adler's uncomfortable shift on the chair, throat working on a hard swallow.

"It was my reckoning," he said in a low timbre, "so I laid there on the couch and let it take me."

Bernard looked up at Preston, eyes pleading.

"Can you turn the video off for a second?"

"Sure." Preston clicked the camera off and set it on the floor.

Adler glanced around and then leaned close to the glass.

"Look. I don't need this getting out. I live in this place." He licked his lips, eyes darting toward the guards not paying them a bit of mind.

"I bawled like a fucking baby after the guy left. The last time I ever did was when my mother died. I cried for those people I killed and for their families who didn't have them anymore. I cried for taking myself away from my sister. The man scared the shit out of me, but he cured me. I'm surviving now. Nothing more. I still feel angry when someone fucks with me, but I don't have an urge to kill, just knock his lights out. You know…the normal stuff."

"Yeah, I understand. Proud of you, Bernard."

He sat back and shrugged.

"Sorry, I don't have anything else to tell you. Haven't seen him since."

"You told me what I needed to know. Thank you for sharing your experience. You've helped more than you know."

"Hey, detective? You might say no, but I want to ask you something."

"Sure. I'll bring you more candy when you run out."

Bernard's smile reengaged.

"No, it's not about the candy, but nice of you to say." He hesitated and chewed on his bottom lip. Soon, his eyes became determined.

"Will you come visit me every now and then? I like talking to you." His cheeks flushed. "Stupid. I know."

"No, not at all. When I can, Bernard, I will. Promise."

The jubilant smile returned. "You're a righteous dude, Browning. I can tell you're not shittin' me. I need to go now. Since I don't stay in my cell so much, they approved me to work in the library. Shift starts soon."

"Take care, Bernard."

"You too, detective." The jovial inmate threw a wave at Preston and motioned for the guards to take him away.

Preston squatted next to him, eyes searching his.

"I'm going to say it, Max. You can call me a nut bag all you want."

"No need. Adler might have just blown up our hypnosis theory. This doctor might actually be curing people."

"You read my mind. What now? I'm getting theory whiplash."

"I want another look at their therapy room."

Max slowed down on the long strides to the door to allow him to catch up.

"Why? What are you expecting to find?"

Max could since a little bit of trepidation lacing Preston's otherwise calm words.

"Nothing, I hope. Absolutely nothing."

CHAPTER 18

"YOU CHECK THIS SIDE AND I'll take the other."

Max pointed at the bottom half of the door before walking into the session room.

"Start there, and I'll go from top down."

"Got it." Preston shut him inside.

Penlight flicking to the top of the frame, he hadn't even made a full sweep across before a soft knock sounded on the door. It cracked open a sliver. Preston's quiet words slipped through.

"You can stop now."

"No way you're finished." He yanked the door to find Preston on his knees and pointing downward.

"I didn't have to. Found them right off."

Squatted next to him, Max's eyes widened as he stared at the bottom door hinge. Just like the find in Galesh's bedroom, a small eraser-size mark identical to the ones under the doorknob had tried to blend in with a swirling tree knot pattern right below the brushed metal. The other two were at the very bottom, barely catching the lower edge of the wood.

Max rose, backed up a pace, and ran the light from top to bottom in a back-and-forth motion. "You spot anymore?"

"Nope."

"Shit. This was one theory I hoped wouldn't play out. Five inmates, five cures, and five marks."

They both swiveled around the same time and stared at the far wall. Max steeled himself and followed Preston across the room. After a ten-minute search from the baseboards to the windowsill, Max pushed to his knees.

"Where in the hell did they exit?"

Preston pressed his forehead against the table's edge.

"Who says the weird shit came this way? I've got to stop thinking linear."

He grabbed the edge and pulled himself up. Eyes narrowed, he pointed to the windows on the right side of the room.

Heart thundering, Max joined Preston on an intricate search around each window frame. It didn't take long to find three perfect marks running under the lip of the second to last one. Backing up, he stared into Preston's questioning eyes and held up his palms in surrender.

"A careless worker causing two accidental burn marks on the door is plausible, Preston. Three more stretches far past coincidence. Add the laser also taking a sudden forty-five degree turn to the right without a sophisticated mirror setup, and we can call it downright ridiculous as a practical option."

"I'm not going to argue with your reasoning. Trust me."

Max turned and made quick tracks to the hallway.

"Childish words, my ass, Father Greggory. This shit went to a whole new level."

Preston caught up to him at the turnstile.

"Are you starting to believe in gigantic moles, Max?"

There wasn't an ounce of teasing in his deep voice.

"Looks like I don't have any choice, kid. I've got what I *thought* was a smarmy suspect manipulating people's actions, but now it appears he might be conducting legitimate exorcisms. All the while, something unexplainable burns its way through walls when he's done. What the shit does after it escapes into the world is making my skin crawl just thinking about it."

Max hesitated for a second, amazed he shoved through the merry-go-round of hell without a knee-quaking moment of fear.

Well, that was new.

Preston tapped him on the arm, snatching him from the self-analysis stupor.

"What do we do about it?"

"One option left, my friend. We put this damn nonsense to rest. I can't arrest someone who might be a miracle-performing saint, but we can at least stop him from doing more damage."

* * * * *

"Sean came by to tell me I'm working you too hard, Max. In my defense, I told him I didn't have anything to do with it. You're a beast, and I stay out of your way. You need to visit him or start returning phone calls, at least."

Max grunted and settled on the cushioned chair facing Captain Walters' cluttered desk. He was starting to notice a few gray strands scattered in the chestnut brown hair and the first signs of wrinkles at the corners of his boss' smiling mouth.

It didn't feel like seven years passed since the department offered the position to the little whelp he trained to work crime scenes so long ago. At least his amber eyes still glowed with a little verve. Nope. Max hadn't wanted the job title, whatsoever. It'd been an easy decision to stay in the shadows and let this eager dynamo take charge, preferring the craziness of the street versus the madness of riding a desk.

"No worries. Spoke with him before I came in here to bug you."

"Good. You heard Dixon put in for retirement yesterday?" Dark brows rose in question.

"Yeah."

"You're killing me, Max. Will Shawn apply? I gave him enough hints on the phone."

"Believe so."

"Nice. If he's anything like his dad, he's a shoe-in."

"Better, actually. Gus would agree if he were standing here. Kid's got the eye *and* the nose."

"Excellent. I heard you put him through the walk on the Monroe case. Clever idea to have some background coming into the interviews."

"He's a natural. Don't let him escape your clutches. Wouldn't want to lose him to another city. He's got goals."

"Understood."

"I'm glad you brought up Harrison Monroe. Exact reason why I'm in here. Both Galesh and Monroe, in fact."

"Anything new on motive?"

"Nope. I'm closing them out."

He reached over and plopped the moderately thin folders on top of the Captain's desk.

"Need your signature."

Max caught a hint of relief on Walters' face. Nothing worse than a case swirling on with no end. The man liked to have things wrapped up tight and set aside as the never-ending train of crimes rode in and continued to bury his staff and hike his numbers. Low case count meant a productive and efficient Captain to the upper echelon. No brainer.

Walters nodded and scribbled his name on the coversheet tacked to the front of each.

"What are your conclusions?"

"Well, I couldn't prove a solid connection for the copycat on the two prisoners out of McAlester. All circumstantial. Trail dried up on me, especially after one decided to slice his own throat, and the other's consistent and believable claim he didn't know the female."

"No third parties?"

"Not evident. No."

"What do you think was the catalyst?"

Max shrugged and kept his gaze direct. This wasn't an ordinary citizen sitting across from him.

"Mary Galesh was a typical harried mother of three rambunctious boys and gaining weight. She might have believed her life going nowhere other than down the crapper. She also had a brief history of violence as a teenager."

"Oh, really?"

"Yep. Even served a stint in a boarding school for troubled teens for a while. Guess it was still seething under the surface. She ran herself and the kids into a guardrail less than a year back. Anyone could assume this bit of nasty work a test run of her willingness to die."

"Beyond sad. Sounds like a cry for help, and it got missed."

"Yeah, I agree. The husband's quite attentive, but she hid things from him. Never knew she smoked or could use the gun. As for Monroe, his story's even thinner. Before he lawyered up, he copped to the boss's repeated tricks on him. Maybe the little dog's constant yapping sent him over the edge enough to take out the spouse. The belief comes from him telling the arresting officers he didn't like dogs and wanted them to make it go away. Once he crossed the line with the wife, then why not the nemesis at work? He's clammed up and not talking, so it's really anyone's guess. Bottom line, both snapped. Something got to them, and they lashed out. Simple. I'm no psychiatrist, so I'm just going off the little bit of crumbs I found."

No lies. Maybe by omission, but I'm claiming a clear conscious.

"Good enough for me."

"Next stop, file room."

Max grabbed the folders and started to rise, only to halt from Walters' gesture for him to sit back down.

"Oh, while I have you here, I heard the families sued the grocery store for not having better security in place. Expect subpoenas on the court cases later if they don't settle."

"I knew it would happen at one point."

Walters twisted his lips.

"Locking the back doors isn't going to help Bagwell's case in the least, even though no one died on the dock. The lawyers will play up the trauma of having no way to escape. I don't think the store will ever open again. Best if they tear it down. Who'd want to shop there again anyway?"

"Not me. Are the families after Jason Galesh?" Max asked with genuine concern.

"Not that I heard. I saw the press conference. I don't think they'd find a jury in the world wanting to cause the poor man and his kids any more grief."

"He's one of the good guys."

"Appeared so."

Max cocked his head despite the niggling feeling he should get ghost as soon as possible.

"Tell me, Captain. How many cases come across your desk where the perp was completely out of character of what your detectives believed they'd find at the end? I mean remarkably so."

"Too many."

Walters retrieved a file from the corner of his desk.

"Take this one for example. Just got it in. A father caught his teenaged son trying to cut the gas line in their home. The kid had a roll of twine and a lighter sitting next to him. The whole damn place would've been a fireball large enough to take out several of the neighboring houses too. Mother said her son turned abnormally violent the second the father touched his arm. Stabbed the poor guy in the throat with the clippers."

Max wondered if his face had paled while Walters revealed the story. His gut pitched and lurched as he stared at the boy's high school honors picture. Innocence.

Son of a bitch. Number three.

Preston's words rang loud inside his head.

Ticking time bombs still waiting to go off out there.

How could you ever find them in time? There was no rhyme or reason, only destruction and mayhem as the final clue.

"I can't imagine having to file charges on one of my children," the captain continued. "The boy graduated valedictorian the night before and was set to attend Harvard. Seriously, what the hell? From my perspective, who would've seen it coming? But was he showing signs of stress from finals? Had his girlfriend given him a tough time about leaving town? Was the pressure too much? Did his sleeping or eating habits change? Too late now. His entire life's ruined."

A flash image of the National Crime Database spitting out rows and rows of violent crimes had sweat breaking out on the back of Max's neck.

Is this a goddamn plague?

How many innocent people floundered inside their own little versions of a waking hell?

"Max? Hey, you in there?"

Refocused, Max stared at the folder hovering in front of his nose.

"Not looking good for the dad. You want it?"

"Uh, no, give it to Dixon. An easy open and shut for his last one. We know who did it."

Plus, Dixon wouldn't start sniffing down an endless trail when finding a burn mark on the kid's bedroom wall, if he even noticed.

"Besides, I need a few days off. I've got the time. More than enough, in fact. I was going to shoot you an email so you couldn't growl at me for trying to take off, but since I'm here, might as well face it head on."

The folder lowered to the desk, and Walters nodded.

"You're right. No argument here. You're valuable to the department, Max. I can tell these last two took a toll. Go fishing or something. I want you relaxed when you get back. The cases will keep coming. The only sure bet I'll take."

"Without doubt. However, I've got plans to visit with a doctor in Georgia who treated Adler and Jenner, the inmates my perps copied. Ran up on a man making a documentary on how the miraculous doctor calms violent offenders. I agreed to consult. Might help me get rid of these question marks still lingering around. Who knows?"

The captain shrugged. "Well, good luck. Try to get some fishing in if you can. Not every day you get close to an ocean."

"Will do."

Case folders dropped off for filing, Max jogged through the winding corridors to get the hell out of the building before something else got him sidetracked. Within minutes, he crossed the sidewalk and crawled inside a blue Ford pickup idling at the curb.

Preston gave him a questioning look.

"Everything go as planned?"

"To perfection. Cases closed. No more eyeballs on them. Were you able to find the book I asked for?"

"In my bag."

"Are you ready?"

"More than you know. Flight leaves at six. We'll just make it."

* * * * *

"It doesn't look as big as it did on the video."

Max released the seat belt on the rental, smoothed his jacket, and glanced up at Preston's observation. "Still impressive. I'm not fond of all the glass, but hey, appears to be his thing."

"How much longer?"

"Fifteen minutes. We're lucky we came in when we did. The secretary said he's leaving for Jacksonville, Florida tomorrow."

"Good. I don't feel like chasing him across the country." He started chewing on his thumbnail.

"You look tired, Preston."

"Couldn't sleep. I've waited for so long to finally understanding what the hell is going on. We're so close."

"Don't get your hopes up too high. I expect him to clam up on anything related to his sessions. The man's not working within the parameters of acceptable medical practice, so he has a lot to lose."

Preston's fist slammed against the door panel, eyes lighting with fury.

"Yeah, but a lot of others are losing their lives! Screw his practice. Obviously, he's doing something wrong. You heard the priest. He's dabbling. Aren't exorcisms supposed to send demons *back* to hell?"

He choked back whatever else flamed up his throat and stabbed shaking fingers through his hair.

"I sound insane."

"No, these *cases* are insane. We saw something. Pure fact. We can only hope he's seen it too. Maybe he's thinking those weird things head back to where they came. Who knows? We're at a severe disadvantage since we can't mention what we know. He can't find out we analyzed the sessions. If we're off base with this crazy theory, we don't want Warden Davies to suffer for our lack of discretion."

"True. I can imagine Alexandru's face if we drop a line of, 'Hey, how about stopping the demon slinging? You're hurting innocent people, dumbass.'"

Max couldn't stop the laughter erupting from his throat if he tried. It took him several attempts to reel his voice back.

"Oh, God, kid. You're killing me. Yeah, let's not try any abrupt movements. We don't want to spook him. Not too badly anyway."

"We just let him talk and cross fingers something gets revealed along the way?"

"Exactly."

"You have your bullshit meter in your pocket?"

"Always."

"Let's do this before any more adrenaline dumps hit and my legs quit working. I don't think you'll want to carry me in over your shoulder."

Max chuckled as Preston retrieved the video camera, got out of the car, and pointed the lens toward the building. As he rounded the hood, he noticed the kid's puzzled expression.

"What?"

"I'm zooming in and not seeing any people moving around inside. Odd, don't you think?"

On a snort, Max started walking along the picturesque sidewalk lined with healthy bushes and vibrant flowers. The serene environment failed in its intention to project all was right in the world.

"Maybe they're in the dungeon. Let's hope we don't end up in there facing a cross and forced to confess our sins. Unsure about you, but it might take me a while." He was happy to hear Preston's deep laughter. The poor guy needed to chill out.

A short, heavyset woman with a round face, flaming red hair, and a pretty smile met them in the foyer. She adjusted the yellow scarf tied on a loose knot at her throat and smoothed a dark green dress hugging ample curves and matching kind eyes. Even with the tall heels, the top of her upswept hair only reached as high as Max's chest.

"Hello. You must be Detective Browning. I'm Fiona. We spoke on the phone."

"Yes, I recognize your voice. Good morning. This is Preston Sinclair, the filmmaker putting together the documentary."

"Hello, Mr. Sinclair. Please, come in." Her words echoed in the expansive blue-marbled lobby as they followed her inside.

"Can I bring you anything to drink? Dr. Alexandru's on a call, but he should be available shortly."

"No, thank you. We're fine."

Fiona gestured to the seating area in the far corner and returned to her desk.

"I'll let you know when he's ready."

Butt parked on the gray suede couch, Max decided he wouldn't mind having the plush furniture in his own living room as he relaxed and studied the interesting interior. With the place made of wall-to-wall glass, it would be ridiculous to hang pictures, so the artwork smartly ranged from large abstract sculptures, a small water fountain tinkling in the center of the lobby, and exotic potted plants and trees scattered about. He found it a unique and very soothing environment. The curved stairway running along the west-facing wall and leading to the next level appeared made of tinted glass. Max had never seen anything like it. Only the black banister and slip pads on the steps gave it a more precise definition.

Office space on the other side of the impressive staircase seemed odd with all the desks in pristine order and lacking any bodies. Even the staplers aligned perfectly with the tape dispensers. He couldn't tell if the computer monitors were on. Maybe the doctor was a neat freak and demanded the same of his staff—if he even had any besides Fiona.

Max stifled a snort. Alexandru would have a heart attack if he ever showed up at the precinct and got an eyeball on the chaotic mess. People would stop and openly gap if someone found time to clear their desk. Never happened. He felt a gentle nudge against his foot.

"Do you see it? Behind and below the center of the stairs. It looks like a gap large enough for a stairwell leading to the bunker."

"Sure does, but I doubt he'll give us a tour if we ask."

"Won't hold my breath."

"Detective Browning?"

Head jerking to the right, Max found Fiona waving to capture his attention.

"Sorry. Yes?"

"He's ready for you. Top of the stairs and take a right. Last one on the end. Corner office."

Preston threw him a smug look as they climbed the steps and passed over the area pointed out earlier. A short flight of stairs led to a lower level. An 'Authorized Personnel Only' sign hung right at the top lip.

Yep, there's the dungeon.

It didn't take long to reach the massive office on the end and presenting a fantastic view of the city.

Dr. Alexandru looked exactly as he had on the website, but this time he wore a tailored suit of dark gray. He stood from behind his impressive mahogany desk, smoothed a blue tie against the immaculate white shirt, and gestured for them to enter as he rounded the desk to greet them.

"Please come in, gentlemen."

Max tipped his head toward Preston as the camera lifted to his shoulder.

"We're filming. Any objection?"

"None."

The doctor's firm handshake revealed a warm, dry palm. No nervousness detected. After greeting Preston, Alexandru returned to his executive chair and pressed back against the plush leather. Dark eyes assessed them both. He didn't seem in any hurry to speak, so Max kept eye contact and let him look his fill.

The guy was a psychiatrist, after all. An educated man majored in mind fucking others. The expected glare continued.

Good luck with that, mister. The marriage counselor thought himself shrewdly superior too. Didn't work out so well for him, either.

Max caught the imperceptible lift of Alexandru's lips. The guy recognized a hard shell when he saw it.

Smart man. Let the games begin.

CHAPTER 19

"FIONA TELLS ME YOU'RE A detective from Oklahoma City consulting for Mr. Sinclair on a documentary," the doctor stated in a calm, unhurried tone. "The subject is the increasing rate of inmate violence within the prison system. Am I correct?"

Adler's hesitation when facing Alexandru head on became understandable. His gaze was nothing but a piercing laser of direct attention. Max had played this "who's going to flinch first" crap with the nastiest sociopaths many times over the years. What was one more? Whether he was a good guy or just an educated version of his prior adversaries, it didn't matter one way or the other. The result was the same. If you didn't give a shit what another thought about you, peace resulted in the ability to drill right back into the windows of the soul, informing the one peeking out you were doing some damn assessing of your own.

Max said, "Indeed," the instant the doctor blinked. He acknowledged the subtle head nod of approval, and Alexandru got a tick mark on the respect meter for not being a sore loser and quickly returning to his role of affable interviewee. Everyone's shoulders relaxed.

"We appreciate you seeing us on such short notice," he added.

"Not a problem. I'm flattered to learn you want to include my facility as part of the project. So how did you learn of me?"

"It was a fluke, really. I interviewed an inmate at the McAlester prison on the off chance he might help me with a case. I expected severe backlash, but got a willing participant, instead. When I remarked on how rational he presented, the Liaison Officer told me you'd treated him. Do you remember Bernard Adler? He was involved in a mass shooting in Ardmore Oklahoma, killing twelve people."

"Oh yes, he's continuing to improve, I'm told."

"Preston and I saw the introduction to this facility on your website. We found it intriguing and felt it a perfect addition to the film. I agree rehabilitation of violent offenders has been dismal. I put them in, and they come out as bad as they arrived, if not worse."

"You're putting it mildly. The system is failing them. They've been open in admitting it, which I must commend for the honesty. According to the Bureau of Justice statistics, the last study conducted on recidivism shows within three years of their release, two-thirds face arrest for similar or enhanced crimes. Within five years, three-quarters are back in the jail system. A preposterously high percentage rate for any public to endure. Your assessment's accurate. The institutions are turned into a revolving door with no end in sight."

"We can understand why you're in such high demand, Dr. Alexandru. Your success in producing calm, respectful inmates documents at one hundred percent. Astounding outcome and deserves applause. Well done."

Max didn't miss the slight lifting of the doctor's chin and straightening of his spine. He preened, much like when he had Adler and Jenner kneeling before him upon their release from whatever held them. No wonder he so easily allowed them into his sanctum.

"Thank you for the kind words," the doctor said with a slight nod.

"Can I ask you why your focus is on offenders serving long sentences for heinous crimes? Why not cure the others so productive individuals return to mingle with the public instead?"

Alexandru released a soft chuckle.

"I know you'll think badly of me, but it's the reality of the situation. The prison system's willing to pay for my services through existing rehabilitation funding. Their immediate need is to ensure the safety of their staff as well as the other inmates, which usually applies to those offenders having nothing to lose. Where's the incentive to stop their violent tendencies? Traditional therapy's a waste of precious funding." He shrugged. "When the government decides it wants to ensure the safety of its free citizens, then perhaps my focus will shift."

Finding the response reasonable, Max tipped his head.

"Logical reasoning."

"I'm glad you agree."

"Since the system is full of violent criminals, how are the inmates chosen? Is it a random draw on who'll be seen by you?"

"No, I decide which prisoners I'll treat."

Max found himself wanting to fall back to his earlier proposal of hypnotic suggestion. It made so much more sense. Alexandru's control over the inmate selection fit nicely into the concept. If only he could dismiss the other nutty aspects skewing the outcome.

"How do you make the decision?"

"I analyze all the case files and determine which pose the greatest threat to the safety and welfare of the facility. Most have lengthy stays in segregation, have struck out in anger without obvious provocation on multiple occasions, and continue to display egregious behavior."

"Sounds like the prime ones to pluck from the pool. Dr. Alexandru, I've read behavior modification tactics are quite effective. I understand the method entails using positive and negative reinforcements until the desired behavior presents. Is this the technique utilized in the therapy?"

"Yes."

Hmm, first lie.

From what he read in the book Preston brought, none of the steps Alexandru conducted during the sessions looked remotely close to the accepted practice. The doctor was obviously adept at masking his body reactions, but the slight slip of his eyes to the right and clipped one-word response were telling.

"Interesting. From the case studies available, it appears this type of treatment requires a considerable length of time to accomplish depending on the severity of the negative behavior. I consider mass murder on the extreme end of the spectrum, yet you spend seven days with the inmates and those are only hour-long sessions. What's your secret to a complete turnaround in such a short length of time?"

"You said the magic word, detective. Secret. My father and I developed a method steeped in years of Romanian tradition. If I revealed this simple, yet extremely effective tool, I'd have thousands trying to duplicate my work. Usurpers wouldn't be good for my business, or reputation, if it became ineffective in the hands of charlatans. Don't you agree?"

"You have a point. Can you share your educated thoughts on what you believe drives these people toward extreme violence? Is there actually an identified catalyst to switch off so quickly?"

Alexandru pursed his lips, looked over at the beautiful scenery, and stared at the passing clouds for a few beats. He blinked and returned his gaze.

"You might say each have a deep, burning anger inside them screaming to break free. Many ask if it's nature versus nurture. Were they simply born bad or had something within the circle of their miserable world pushed them to choose the wrong path? My response is it doesn't matter. This churning ball of mess squats inside them whether they like it or not. My job is to make them face it and ban it from their existence."

From the corner of his eye, Max caught Preston's knee bouncing in excitement. At least the camera appeared steady. Alexandru's words had danced along the fine edge of what Bernard described without outright calling it an exorcism. Max released a soft chuckle, not because he found anything humorous, but to alleviate any wariness the doctor might gather from his next statement.

"You make it sound as if they're possessed, Dr. Alexandru."

A thick eyebrow rose at the easy comment.

"You could view it in this light if trying to place a label. Haunted, broken, lost, and even overwhelmed have been a few I've used in the past."

"Are you a religious man?"

"No, I'm a realist" was his exceedingly quick reply.

Hmmm. Touchy subject.

"No matter what you want to call the issue with these individuals, detective, the fact remains they need help to overcome it. Continuous talks about how they didn't receive enough love from their mother, or their time spent with a raging alcoholic for a father does absolutely no good. The damage is in place. The festering present is what needs addressing."

"That reminds me. I understand your father started the business in his early thirties, enjoyed the same success you're experiencing, yet met a violent death at the hand of an inmate he was treating. I'm sorry for your loss."

"Thank you. Yes, it was a shock. Dimitri Alexandru was a wonderful man, and it should've never happened. I continue the work in his honor."

"Preston and I viewed the chamber you insist the prisons build. I'm assuming this is due to how your father was attacked."

"Not exactly. It was already a prerequisite to our attending the inmates. The prison failed us by not following the strict instructions provided. Now they undergo rigid inspection, by me, if they expect to receive any services."

"Do you treat convicts here on the premises?"

"Always my preference but extracting violent criminals from maximum security prisons appears to be too high of a risk to undertake. If the prison is close by, they'll opt for a rigidly monitored transport, but rare. So alas, I'm gathering an extensive collection of frequent flyer miles."

"Yes, I would think so. We saw your schedule. At least it makes your return trips to their facilities much smoother when a room's already available for you."

"Indeed. I cure a handful and within months they're replaced with more."

"You list your business as a research facility. What exactly does this entail?"

"The mind, of course. Every prisoner has a different story, yet each is still human. I use relaxation techniques within the therapy."

"Hypnosis?"

The doctor's brows lifted.

"Very good, detective. Yes, treatment of violent people is a challenging task if you can't focus their attention, or the rage is so great, they might injure themselves if unable to release it on their source of irritation. I'm always looking for a perfect situation speaking to all human emotions and needs. Once they're within a peacefulness they've never achieved before, the easier to conduct my work."

"I assume you do research on live subjects here at the facility?"

"Theory will only get you so far as I'm sure you're aware of in your own line of work. I have individuals who served time in the past or are in desperate need of money to allow me to conduct trials. They're all paid very well to take relaxing trips to exotic places without leaving the comfort of a recliner."

"Would you be willing to give us a tour of the research area?"

Alexandru's lips turned down, appearing disappointed. Max didn't buy it for a second.

"I'd love to, but the space is undergoing construction. Not much to see other than equipment and lot of building material. When completed, you'll find two units built within the same specifications as the prisons, a lot of computers, and brainwave monitoring units. Nothing sexy. Very dry and boring."

"Oh, maybe some other time."

"Of course."

"I have a strange question. I hope you don't mind."

"No, go ahead. I'll answer if I can."

"Where's your staff? This is a large office complex, but I've only seen Fiona."

Alexandru barked out a laugh.

"Ah! Yes, I guess this would look peculiar. I've recently moved from Connecticut. The climate here agrees with me more. I'm still interviewing for staff positions. In fact, I'm driving to Jacksonville tomorrow to speak with a group interested in joining the research team."

Great. An army of clueless exorcists. Just what the world needs.

"Thank you. Mystery solved."

Max straightened in his chair and leaned forward, hoping he breached even a portion of the doctor's massive protective bubble.

"Now let's move to the heart of why we're here, which is to discuss your keen ability to cure the most hardened criminals. We have particular interest in learning of your work with Adler and another inmate, Whitfield Jenner, so we can document specific cases and results."

Alexandru's demeanor morphed from pleasant interviewee to wary observer. His eyes narrowed, yet his body never flinched.

"Is this really about Jenner killing himself? Perhaps an attempt to titillate your audience? Warden Davies called to inform me of the suicide. A tragedy, for sure. I was hoping Jenner would find peace as the others have done. I had nothing to do with his decision."

Max feigned surprise and concern.

"Oh no, we're not accusing you of anything. Forgive me for putting across the impression."

Alexandru gave him a tight smile. "Thank you."

"No, my interest lies in another matter. I recently closed out two homicides in my jurisdiction, both eerily similar to these inmate's offenses. This is what led me to McAlester. Preston has particular interest in including discussions on copycat killers, especially those who entail mass murder."

"Oh, I thought you were here to discuss the facility and the excellent work coming from my efforts."

"Yes, our overall goal, however, those two cases were very trying for me. I'm seeking a little closure and hoping you can help. Did either of them mention a personal connection with Mary Galesh or Harrison Monroe? In any form."

Dr. Alexandru studied the surface of his shiny, expensive desk for several seconds. When the attention returned, Max at once recognized what he termed the "I'm done with you" smile. Any detective with a few interviews under his belt experienced this reaction at one time or another. Max had too many to count.

"Detective Browning, this sounds interesting, but I'm unable to discuss those cases. I *can* tell you neither mentioned these two people. Our focus remained on the crime landing them in prison and the continued violence. Nothing else."

Max knew his opportunity to glean even a sliver of information other than what they already knew had just shrank to the width of a hair. It was time to send the doc's heartbeat thumping.

"I can appreciate your hesitancy. Perhaps you can help with something else disturbing me. You obviously have the background to shed some light on this thing."

He pulled his phone, recalled the burn mark on Mary's wall, and placed it on the desk, facing Alexandru. The doctor leaned forward and picked it up. His eyes flicked upward for a brief second and then lowered back to the screen. A soft chuckle escaped his lips.

"Are you trying to give me a Rorschach test, detective?"

Max laughed and relaxed back in his chair.

"No, but an interesting thought, nonetheless. I found this mark at a crime scene. It stood out as very odd. What do you think of it?"

Alexandru's shoulders lifted and dropped.

"A dangerous way to play with fire, perhaps?" He placed the phone on the desk and returned a steady gaze.

Max knew he'd met another master of the "dead face." Alexandru exuded the picture of calm. Unreadable. Placid.

"Yes, tremendously dangerous."

He tried not to show jubilation when the doctor lifted the phone and pointed the screen outward, brows lifted in question. The man's superiority complex screamed for an engagement.

"What do *you* see in this, detective?"

"A vicious animal. A wolf, in fact."

The edges of Alexandru's lips lifted.

"Fascinating. My exact impression, as well."

"Then we both view the *content* as a feral animal, thereby defining the Rorschach *determinant* as our perception of a wolf being something sinister and scary?"

Max chuckled at finally seeing a flicker of admiration escape the doctor's penetrating gaze even though he remained silent.

"Do we acquire a score of W for viewing the *whole* image in our assessments, Dr. Alexander? This *is* what the psychiatric field places in the *location* category of interpretation when an observer defines the entirety of the image, not just parts of it, correct? We want to fathom the complete picture…to find *all* the answers."

He knew he was pushing it by interjecting the totally unrelated but very revealing W as a way of poking any sort of obvious reaction out of Alexandru. It didn't take long.

Here we go. I saw the slight chin lift, flaring nostrils, and straightening of the spine. Come on. Come on. You want to tell your story, don't you, Mr. Smarty? Go ahead. Reveal how talented you are, Doctor. Brag.

CHAPTER 20

DISAPPOINTMENT FLOODED MAX'S VEINS AS Alexandru blinked a few times, as if rebooting his brain, and then presented a winning smile. Not a complete narcissist as hoped. *Damn.*

"Very good, detective. I'm impressed. You're versed on the subject."

"Just a bit, but I wish I knew more. I believe I've only touched the surface. I sat in on a forensic psychiatrist's study of a particularly nasty pedophile we investigated and caught three years ago. Very intriguing way to delve into personality and possible motives."

There was no such case, but Max thought it a better story than explaining he endured reading a thick psychiatric book throughout the night while laughingly analyzing a water stain on the hotel ceiling to break up the monotony. He didn't think the disclosure would go over so well with the good doctor.

"Ah. I can comprehend how this would grab your attention," Alexandru replied.

"Yes, like Rorschach's goals, I'm curious of what other people are thinking. Why this distinctive mark? What message were they trying to deliver? Do they feel no one appreciates their hidden talents so they must shout it out to the world in any way they can?"

All too soon, Max received the pleasant, dismissive smile while the tips of Alexandru's manicured nails nudged the phone back over.

"Wish I could help you with your case, but I have to meet this certain fire artist face to face to understand their reasoning. Right now, my thoughts would be all conjecture."

"I know exactly how it feels. Like to meet them myself. I'm sure they have an interesting story to tell as to why they left this behind. It could be a tease to those trying to figure out who they are, or as

185

simple as leaving a little bit of themselves to prove their own miserable existence. Who knows?"

"Indeed."

Alexandru released a sigh, peered at his gleaming Rolex, and stood.

"I'm sorry, but it appears our time's up. I have another appointment. I wish you remarkable success with the film. I commend you both for bringing this growing problem to the public's attention. If I need to sign any release papers allowing you to include our discussion, provide them to my secretary. Thank you for stopping by. Have a good day, gentlemen."

Max put his agreeable face into position and shook the doctor's hand. It wasn't as dry as before, but not soaked with nervous sweat. His response was normal for anyone enduring an interview.

"Thank you for taking the time to speak with us, Dr. Alexandru. Be safe on your trip to Florida."

The doctor gave a brief nod, not bothering to walk them to the door. Max glanced over as he and Preston navigated their way to the stairwell. Alexandru's back was to them as he stared out the window toward downtown Savannah. Max would give anything to catch what ran through the man's complicated mind.

Fiona handed over Alexandru's business card, wished them well on their trip home, and offered a much quicker route back to the hotel when told where they were staying. Soon, he and Preston piled back into the car, lips pursed while digesting every word that fell out of her boss's mouth. He sensed Preston's eyes burning a hole into his right temple.

"Damn, Max. If I stumbled on this path to Dr. Alexandru on my own, the man would've eaten my lunch and left me wondering where my ass was. Do you have any idea how awesome you are?"

On a chuckle, Max slipped the seat belt into place and started an engine sounding as if powered by a furiously rotating wheel of exhausted chipmunks. He missed the Vic.

"Thanks for the vote of confidence, Preston, but we're no closer to the truth than when we walked inside. We'll need a different tactic since playing nice and planting innuendos only got us a glimpse into what's going on with the guy. He's good. Very careful. Time to regroup and find another strategy."

"What's your take on him?"

"He's a hard read. I caught only a few physical slips in his armor, but he enjoyed the verbal sparring. I think it took everything inside him to keep from blurting out how deliciously wonderful he is at curing patients. I just have to figure out the right trigger to force a reveal of the paranormal aspect of what he does."

"What about the dungeon? It's clear the dude doesn't want us to see it. Maybe he's in some type of religious order like the one the priest suggested. It could have an altar and other weird stuff in there."

"Nah, I think he's telling the truth about it being under construction. Besides, I don't think he could hide sinister activity in the building with Fiona hanging around."

"Maybe she's in on it too."

"I dismissed her involvement as soon as Alexandru claimed relocation."

"How?"

"She has a Georgian accent, and I spotted the timesheets on her desk. They're from a temporary agency."

"And precisely why you're the detective, and I'm your clueless sidekick."

Max barked out a laugh and turned into the hotel parking lot.

"You're far from clueless, Preston. You figured out the burn mark connection and the doctor angle which is the entire reason we're here. Give yourself a big pat on the back. You opened my mind to possibilities I would've never given a second thought. Not in a million years."

"Thanks for making me feel better."

"Anytime." He rolled up to the front of their rooms yet couldn't shake the dread of going back inside. Pathetic gray siding and faded green door screamed its own unwillingness to exist.

"I'm not looking forward to holing up in this dump again. We picked the worst time to find a hotel in this town. Annual Blues, Jazz, and BBQ festival went into full swing yesterday. We scraped the bottom of the barrel."

"Hey, I've been in worse rooms, trust me. I'm ranking it a four star after what I've endured. This one's clean inside, at least."

"Fine, I'll cut it some slack. Victoria would've kicked my ass for bringing her here. It was either the Marriott or Hilton. No questions asked."

"I wouldn't know how to act in a fancy one. Can I assume since you're not ordering me to grab my bags, we're staying here another night?"

"Correct. And what do you think my next step will be?"

"Best guess is we're following Dr. Alexandru to Jacksonville tomorrow. You want to discover what type of people he's trying to recruit. Maybe even stumble over the elusive *Conseti* order, if it's his real intention of visiting Florida."

Max nodded his head in approval.

"Very good, Preston. I'll make a detective out of you, yet. But first, we need to do something fun."

"Oh, this should be interesting. What's your version of fun, Max? Sitting on a stakeout and waiting for your perp to make a mistake?"

"Hell no, we've done nothing but eat, sleep, and run on this nuttiness for days now. We need a different view. Since Savannah was kind enough to put on a festival when we hit town, the least we can do is make the effort to see what the fuss is about."

Preston morphed from dejected to ecstatic right before his eyes.

"Serious? I forgot what that's like. Hell, yeah!"

"Need to put some jeans on. Meet you out front in twenty. Deal?"

"You got it!"

He was out of the car and pushing inside his room before Max could unlatch the seat belt.

A familiar warmth saturated his chest and he leaned back to enjoy the sensation. Usually, the sentiment remained reserved for Sean. Now here was this young man spending a better part of his youthful years swirling in the nasty side of life and yet it hadn't broken his spirit. He needed to enjoy something untainted and carefree before reality inevitably piled down on his shoulders once again. He deserved a break. A simple thought whispered through his mind.

As do you, dumb butt.

Eyes rolling, Max crawled out of the car and recited one of Fergus's favorite lines, "Enjoy life today. Yesterday is gone, and tomorrow may never come."

I heard you Gus. Loud and clear.

* * * * *

Eyes squinted against the late morning sun, Max flipped the visor down and glanced at Preston slouched in the passenger seat. With the hair pulled back into a neat tail and unshaven face, the latest look paired with some righteous shades perched on his straight nose made him appear older and seasoned. He'd make a good uncover officer with his ability to morph. Max fumbled in the console and located his own sunglasses.

"I finally found the one good thing about this stupid car."

He gritted his teeth and signaled for yet another flawless lane change.

"And that would be?" Preston slung another handful of M&Ms into his mouth.

"The gas mileage and being so plain it blends with the traffic."

"True."

Max shook his head as Preston offered him some candy.

"No thanks. You know it's your third bag, right?"

"Yep, and you're counting, why?"

"Because when the sugar high hits, I'll keep my mouth shut since I can't get in a word edgewise. Not like I can stop and let you run it off." He smiled at Preston's gurgled snort.

"I'm not that bad."

"Says the guy flapping his gums for a solid thirty minutes after two Snickers. Your stories went at the speed of light from the first fight in third grade up to an eighth-grade crush named Lisa Miller dumping you in study hall before you passed out."

"Did I snore?"

"In study hall? No clue."

"Butthead."

"Dip shit."

Max snickered at Preston's teasing shove to his shoulder.

"You know what I mean. Did I snore *here* in the car?"

"No, but I had to wipe the drool off your lip."

Preston chuckled and put away his candy.

"Hey, if you quit ragging on me, I'll let you roll the window down and smoke."

Max shot a wary glance his way. "You're not teasing me?"

"Nope."

"Thank, God."

He cursed when realizing the car didn't have a cigarette lighter. Matches and wind at seventy-five miles an hour didn't mix so well.

"Got you covered."

The green lighter resting on Preston's palm surprised the hell out of him.

"Bought it when I filled up my snack bag before we left. I knew this would happen. Didn't want to be stuck in the car with you when time for your second cigarette, and we couldn't pull over."

"Smart man."

"Learning you, Max. Tell me. How'd you become so good at tailing people? They give courses in the policy academy?"

Paused to suck on the cigarette filter as Preston lit the end, Max managed to shrug his shoulder. He blew out a stream of smoke and watched it shoot out the half-cracked window as they passed by the "Welcome to Jacksonville" sign.

"Years of practice."

"How can you tell Alexandru isn't aware of us following him?"

"Not seeing him do any of the moves I'd try on a possible tail."

"Like what?"

"Rapid lane changes without use of a blinker. A gradual slow down or speeding up to see if I'll do the same. Taking an off-ramp at the last second. Shit like that."

"Ah."

"Most people only look in their mirrors if they plan to change lanes or fix their makeup. Some don't even bother. If not right in front of them, it doesn't exist."

He lifted the cigarette and let the wind catch the ashes, hoping they didn't decide to take up residence in the back seat. Smoking in a vehicle was his least favorite activity. There were too many variables to consider, but a two-hour drive while still being alert to any deviation of the silver Mercedes warranted some damn nicotine.

"I forgot to thank you, Max."

"For what?"

"Coming up with the idea of the festival. Relaxed me, and I started thinking straight."

"I'm glad. Helped me too. I slept like a baby. Been awhile."

"Same here."

"We'll need all the extra brain power and alert senses because we're coming up on heavier traffic. No plans to lose him this late in the game. Keep your eyes peeled."

"Will do."

Several tense minutes passed as Max stealthily positioned the car in different spots on the three-lane highway. If Alexandru was astute and did a constant check in his mirror, he wouldn't get suspicious of a champagne-colored Acura always in his line of sight.

"He's signaling a ramp exit."

Preston leaned in and studied the GPS unit.

"State Street is first up. Two more options afterward, but they veer right."

"I'm over. Good, he's taking a left on State. I'm in the correct lane."

He dropped the cigarette butt into his half-filled water bottle and smiled as Preston secured the lid. They'd started out as a very odd team but were slowly getting into sync. It felt good. He'd missed the easiness of Gus's presence.

"Just flipped his right signal. Main Street coming up."

By the time they'd passed six blocks, Max rocked a steady nod of appreciation at the presented view.

"Will you look at this? Spectacular."

Rising above the peaceful, winding waters of the St. John's River, an impressive, gleaming blue-steel vertical-lift bridge dominated the horizon. Two tall towers holding the structure aloft rose in the foreground of downtown Jacksonville boasting shiny high-rise buildings. His first impression was of a wonderfully clean, pristine city.

Preston whispered, "Damn, it almost looks like a postcard."

Since the doctor had no other choice but to keep moving forward, Max managed a few appreciative glances at the surroundings while passing over the long bridge. Sea birds dipped and weaved easily along the air currents, intermittently diving downward to pester people strolling along the boardwalk butting up against a collection of marinas lining the river's edge. Colorful sailboats and small yachts filled the gaps, making Max wish he could exit off and rent one for a round of fishing. *One day*. Preston's deep voice snapped him out of his fantasy.

"He's exiting. Looks like a loop under to merge with Atlantic Boulevard. Stay in the left lane. At least the traffic's a little lighter."

The winding road morphed into Beach Boulevard and Preston leaned forward.

"Curving toward Highway 53. Damn, where in the hell is he going?"

"Somewhere not too remote, I hope. Distance is our enemy."

"Well, at least we've got a magnificent view of the ocean. I've never seen a beach so white. This is beautiful."

"Yeah, beats the never-ending red dirt of Oklahoma. Ah, here we go. He's turning into a driveway. Wait, the entrance is too big for a residence. Is there a sign?"

"Ponte Vedra Inn and Club. Fancy."

Maneuvered to the curb, Max cut the engine.

"Shit. A hotel. Hope it's not for an overnight."

"Maybe this is where he's meeting the recruits. Some of these fancier places rent out conference rooms."

"Fingers crossed. Stay here. I'll be right back."

Preston snatched the back of his T-shirt before he could crawl out of the car.

"If you're not back in fifteen, I'm coming in for you."

"Suit yourself, kid. If he busts me, you might as well join the party."

CHAPTER 21

With an easy slip through the heavy wooden doors of the hotel's front entrance, Max spotted Alexandru strolling through a huge lobby boasting a wide expanse of gleaming brown and gold patterned flooring. He was glad for the smattering of guests meandering through and allowing him to duck out of sight until he got the lay of the land.

Two enormous light-gray marble columns matching four others running down the main pathway dominated the view, their sole purpose to hold up the wide, multiple-layered recessed ceiling made of dark, polished rectangular wood beams. An expansive, gleaming crystal chandelier hung from the tallest point. The place screamed class and elegance.

Positioned to the side of one pillar, Max stayed put until Alexandru passed through a gilded arched frame leading to the check-in counter and planted himself behind another guest. Thankful for several dividers made of frosted glass edged with dark wood sitting to each side, he found a prime hiding spot for eavesdropping and set his target.

Brochure secured from a long mahogany table next to the doorway, Max meandered the least visible path across the lobby and positioned himself out of eyesight of the doctor. He studied the pamphlet to garner an idea of the hotel's layout.

The place appeared far bigger and ritzier than imagined. Over two hundred and fifty guest rooms spread out over several lots, six restaurants, conference center, five bars, full-service spa, rooftop terrace, fifteen outdoor tennis courts, three pools, and an eighteen-hole golf course had Max hoping he didn't have to chase the silly man across the property. His ears perked up at the sound of a familiar voice.

"Room reservation for Dr. Costica Alexandru."

Overnight to deal with now. Great.

Max garnered strong appreciation for Preston's urgings to bring their bags along. Unattended suitcases were fodder for curious maids. He acquiesced to the seasoned motel hopper. He settled back and listened to the jovial clerk's lilting, pleasant voice engaging the doctor in small talk while performing a steady tap on a keyboard. Soon, he learned Alexandru booked Room 131 in the Peyton House and studied the brochure.

Ocean view, of course.

Using the opportunity to sprint across the lobby while the doctor waited for keys and Wi-Fi access code, Max entered a hallway leading to a washroom. He kept to the shadows until his target walked away and none the wiser. Preston answered his call on the first ring.

"Need help?"

"Not yet. He checked in and will be coming through the front doors any second. Back the car up and keep an eye on his direction. He should take a direct path across the roadway in front of you to the guest buildings. They're behind the tall bushes to your left. Call our hotel and hold the room for another day so we don't lose it. I'll try to rent us one here, but don't hold your breath."

"Got it. What if he takes the main road, instead?"

"Should be a while for him to exit from either end. Call and I'll haul ass outside."

"Okay."

Phone shoved back inside his pocket and proverbial fingers crossed, Max approached the counter. The dark-haired clerk's big blue eyes turned his way.

"May I help you, sir?"

"Hope so. Caught in town longer than expected. Do you have something available?"

She frowned and looked down at the computer.

"I'm not sure. Let me check."

Max laid the brochure on the counter and pointed at the Summer House complex next to Costica's unit. "If this turns out to be my lucky day, I'm hoping for this end. Perfect view." The returned smile notched down his level of growing angst.

"Yes, we've had two cancellations. One is on this side." She wrinkled a pert nose. "It's a double. If you want a king, I'll have to put you on the other end."

"No, not a problem at all. I'm happy you have something close to the water."

Max felt his brows rise from hearing the announcement of the hotel rate.

"Any discount for former military or police officers?" He pulled his badge and laminated DD-214 military service card.

"Yes, we do. In fact, with both, we give forty percent off."

"Nice. Got a two-for-two. I need to buy a lottery ticket while I'm on a roll."

They shared a mutual laugh as she accepted his credit card. The efficient clerk had him booked and handing over the key cards within a matter of minutes.

"You're in Room 125 and can find the patio key's in the top drawer of your bureau. Thank you for your service, Officer Browning."

"Thanks for the discount."

Max returned her smile and hurried outside. An astute Preston zipped up into the horseshoe drive to collect him. He hopped into the passenger seat and handed over one of the key cards.

"We're bunking together. Don't worry. The room's got double beds. I'm assuming he went across the road since you don't look panicked."

"Nailed it."

"Good. We're in the next building."

Soon, Max pointed to the rows of cars lining the front of Peyton House.

"Mercedes in the fifth spot. Park at the far end of ours. We don't want him seeing the Acura too often. The more cars between us and him, the less chance of spiking his curiosity."

After a hurried bag grab, they pushed into the room costing as much as his monthly mortgage, even with the discount.

Preston blew out a soft whistle.

"Nice."

"Better be with the dollars just drained out of my account," Max groused. He moved further into the room and scanned the sumptuous accommodations.

Marbled floor columns sat on either side of the double doors leading out onto a patio showcasing a breathtaking view of the ocean, lighted crown molding, rusty sandstone painted walls, spectacular artwork, plush carpet, a seating area with a huge flat screen dominating one wall, and two beds making the one slept on last night look like a freaking cot garnered his appreciation. He threw his bag on the first one and rifled around in the side pouch.

"Here, hold this."

Preston stared at the square black box he held out to him.

"What's this?"

"Tracking device. Got it off the internet. Ridiculous how cheap these are nowadays. This one has global positioning. I call it up with my phone and it sends back the location. Got it last year on a lark, and now I have a reason to use it. Do me a favor and walk around the room to test the sync. I need to attach it to the Mercedes before the doc decides to leave."

Preston took the unit and paced the room while throwing him a puzzled expression.

"Why didn't you put it on his car before we left?"

"With all the damn glass, he would've spotted me in seconds. We're lucky enough he returned to the office before leaving."

"Told you we should've followed him home."

"I was having too much fun beating you at pool."

"I let you win," Preston said with a chuckle.

"Yeah, right. Keep believing your bullshit if it makes you feel better."

"I'm not going light on you anymore. Game on next time."

"I'll still spank your ass, you young pup."

"Skill, not age makes the pool player, Max."

"Age improves the skill. Hang it up, Preston. You're toast."

"Oh, man, you're in trouble now. Challenge accepted."

Strangling a laugh, Max extended his arm and fluttered his fingers.

"All done. Hand it over." He raised a brow. "Unless you want to plant it."

Preston's eyes lit up.

"Damn, straight."

"Have at it."

Max peeked around the edge of the walkway post.

"All clear. I'll stand next to his building and head off any bodies coming your way. Press the side gray button to engage the magnet on the back. Wheel wells are good. Keep an eye on the third door from this end."

He tapped Preston on the shoulder as he positioned himself against the post.

"What do you do if he comes out?"

"Easy. Duck my head and run like a bat out of hell. I'm sure you'll find me at some point."

"Right answer."

Settled against the light-beige stucco wall and unlit cigarette dangling from his lips, Max signaled for Preston to head toward the Mercedes. His eyes widened as the kid zipped over to the vehicle, attached the device, and flew past him with a wide grin on his puss. Max caught up with him at the door.

"Damn. Were you a track star in school?"

Flopped on the bed next to the patio doors, Preston laughed in between gasps of air.

"Somewhat, but mostly from learning how to outrun the police after almost getting caught searching for the marks."

"Ah. Good skill to have if you've moved to the shady side."

"Yeah, that and jumping over fences. Tore more blue jeans than I can count."

Max pulled a chair up next to the front bay window, parted the curtains a few inches, and sat down.

"Back in the day, I could've run your ass down. Caught my share of perps trying to hop a fence." He readjusted the chair. "Got a good bead on his car. Let's hope he'll meet them real—" Max leaped up and snatched the car keys from the table.

"Damn it! He's already going mobile. Grab the camera."

The second the Mercedes hit the main road and turned right, they both hauled butt to the car. Max handed his phone over.

"Here. Tap the blue icon to start the GPS tracking. We need to catch up to him. Unsure if this gadget's going to even work."

Long minutes passed and confirmed he hadn't lost money on the tracker. Every muscle relaxed.

Preston's knee bounced with excitement.

"Looks like he's heading back the way we came in."

"Yes, the bridge should be around this next curve."

"What's our goal? If he meets with some people, how's it going to help us? We won't be able to hear what they say."

"I'm after identification. We'll try to log license plates and images of their faces. Once we research the players he's involved with, it could lead us to others. If we can associate him with organized activity of a fringe religious or occult nature, perhaps we can involve the Medical Board, and get this guy kicked out of practicing whatever 'woo-woo' shit he's got going on. He'll never step foot in another prison."

"Sound plan. I like it. Heads up. He took Riverside Boulevard. At least he's staying on this side of the bridge."

"Got it."

"Slow up a bit. The red dot's not moving."

Max scanned the road ahead, hoping to spot Alexandru's car.

"There he is. Parked two slots down from the gray sign. Peninsula Condominiums."

He pulled over to the curb and shut the engine.

"When he gets out, I'll try to follow him in. This might be difficult. It looks like there are at least twenty-five floors. Hang back like you did at the hotel. I set my phone to vibrate, so call if you spot him before I signal his location."

"Will do."

Muscles tensed, hand on the door latch, and ready to haul ass across the roadway, Max was surprised to find Alexandru talking on his cell instead of leaving the car. He relaxed against the seat.

"Excellent. No chase today. Appears they're coming to him. You have your camera ready?"

"Got it."

They both leaned forward as a beautiful woman with flowing black hair, voluptuous breasts, and a slinky blue dress showing off long, tanned legs exited the condo and approached the passenger door. She peered into the window, waited for him to release the lock, and then crawled inside the car. He heard Preston snort.

"Didn't foresee the girlfriend."

"Nope. Call girl."

"Not nice, Max. She may actually like older men."

Max chuckled at the innocent observation.

"No, she's a professional. I was in vice long enough to spot one."

"How?"

"Dead eyes. She's all business. They're talking and showing no affection. He's probably a regular. If we could see their hand movements, I'm sure she's stuffing a fat envelope in her bag right now."

"Ah."

Alexandru pulled out onto the road and as Max expected, the Mercedes made its way back to the hotel. They followed in silence. As the coastline appeared, Max glanced over at Preston.

"Go ahead. Ask. You've been fidgeting since we hit Atlantic Boulevard. Spit it out."

"Why didn't he go up to her apartment?"

"Elite John 101 survival knowledge. You don't insert yourself into their territory. Never can tell what might be lurking around to rob you blind. The prostitute takes the risk, not you."

Preston nodded and remained quiet, but Max knew he was building up to the next question so waited it out.

"Have you ever hired a call girl, Max?"

"Never. Rather have a relationship with my hand than pay someone for sex. My palm's warmer than that shit. Have you?"

"Hell no, guess we're of the same mind-set. Do you have anyone special back in Oklahoma?"

"Sort of. I've known two ladies for several years who seem to understand me. Nothing serious."

"Two? You dog."

Amused at the insinuation, though it'd crossed his mind once on a boring Friday night, Max flicked him a quick glance.

"No, nothing like that. When I receive a break between cases, sometimes I like to have someone around who doesn't smother me or ask a lot of questions. They're way past craving babies and white picket fences. Besides, it gets old eating dinner alone."

"Too many to count here. Do they know about each other?"

"Hope not."

Preston barked out a laugh.

"Yeah, wouldn't be pretty."

"Nope. Don't get me wrong. I've never lied to either. If they ask, I'll tell them. I think they're enjoying the freedom, as well. Everyone needs companionship at some point, even though being alone has more perks in my opinion." His lips twisted into a smirk. "I may be getting older and prefer being a loner, but I'll be dammed if I go out celibate."

"I second the motion. If this shit ever stops, I plan on settling down again. I liked being married."

"Good for you. It works for some."

Max slowed the car, taking his time approaching the guest room entrance.

"Perfect, they're already inside."

He planted the Acura between a Range Rover and Tahoe and cut the engine.

"Well, we have a least an hour to kill. But with his money, he's liable to keep her all night. Let's grab something to eat. How about pizza delivery?"

"I'm down," Preston said as he crawled out of the car. "Sounds like the safest bet. Make it double pepperoni." He shook his head as the key card slid into the lock.

"I plan to sit out on the patio, eat warm pizza, and stare at the beautiful ocean as the sun goes down so I don't have to picture Dr. Alexandru popping blue pills and getting his kink on."

Max howled with laughter and pushed inside the room.

"Quick, turn the television on. Now you've planted the damn image in my head. Commercials, anything. I don't care."

Preston grabbed the remote, waggled his brows, and ended the madness.

"Oh, thank God. A Dodge pickup. Tires...dirt...mud. I'm better."

Their mutual knuckle bump solidified the shared relief. Max thought it might be awkward sharing a room with Preston, but he found him to be quite easy to hang around. He was humorous without forcing the funny, surprisingly aware of world events considering his age, and liked the same type of sitcoms. Max knew if he ever introduced him to Sean, they'd probably end up good friends. Halfway into a third rerun of *The Big Bang Theory*, a car horn startled them out of their 'belly full of pizza' stupor.

Preston made it to the window before Max pulled his feet down from the coffee table.

"Alexandru's putting the woman into a cab." He glanced over his shoulder. "Three hours. I'm impressed."

"Is he going back inside?" Max said while searching for his other boot.

"He's watching the cab drive away. Wait, now he's heading to the car."

"Get your stuff."

"On it."

Within ten minutes of following Alexandru from the lot, Max found himself parked by a curb and shaking his head.

"What the hell is it about him and all this glass? Fetish much?"

Preston shrugged as he lifted the camera and filmed the doctor entering a very elegant restaurant boasting an impressive, lightly tinted glass-walled front.

"Claustrophobic maybe?"

Max's chest rumbled in empathy.

"Could be. Whatever it is, at least we don't have to go inside to monitor him."

"That's true. I find his behavior odd. The hotel has five restaurant choices. I bet they're as fancy as this one. Maybe he had to come here by directive of his *Conseti* order. I can't imagine potential employees making the decision on a meeting location."

"Sound observation. Let's hope for the first one. Otherwise, we can call this day a waste."

Forty-five minutes into watching Dr. Alexandru leisurely polish off a huge steak and several glasses of wine, Preston broke the growing angst with a pitiful groan.

"My stomach hurts from watching him stuff his mouth. I ate too much pizza."

"Yeah, me too. Damn, surely, someone would've joined him by now. I'm ready to go back to the room, but he might head off somewhere else after this."

"What was the longest stakeout you were on, Max?"

He appreciated the diversion.

"Three days."

"No idea how you could do it. My ass is numb already."

"Haven't met the worst part, my man. Gus and I became pros at pissing in milk jugs when we couldn't chance the interior lights coming on and cluing the location."

Preston blew out a frustrated breath and stared at the ceiling of the car.

"Crap, my bladder woke up from the thought. Thanks."

Max reached for the ignition.

"Hold your water, brother. He's coming out. If he doesn't head back to the hotel, we'll stop somewhere and pick him up later through the tracker."

It became clear within minutes the doctor had no other agenda but getting back to his room. Max could see the relief washing over Preston's face. Parked back between the two hulking vehicles and Alexandru safely ensconced inside his room, Max reached into the backseat, snatched a small package from the floorboard, and ripped it open.

"Go hit the bathroom. I'll be there in a few."

"What are you doing?"

"Plan to stick a motion sensor on his door."

He held up the tiny clear device no bigger than his thumbnail and grinned.

"This little bad boy is usually purchased by parents with smar-tass kids prone to sneaking out through windows in the dark of night. The door cracks even an inch, and he's ours. I don't feel like staring at his car all night. This guy's riding my last nerve."

"Well, look at you. Got any fancier gadgets back there? X-ray vision glasses, pen with a poison dart, or a listening device would be cool."

Max snorted and crawled out of the car.

"No, this is the last of my toys. James Bond, I'm not. Go on inside. We need some sleep if we plan to keep up with this guy's non-sense. Put your boots near the bed. We might have to cut and run if he decides to head out during the night. I don't care if we end up following him all the way to the tip of Florida. I want to know what the hell this man's up to."

CHAPTER 22

BEEP. BEEP. BEEP.

Jackknifed up from the bed, Max scanned the room, realized where he was at, and then slammed his hand down on the motion sensor unit to turn it off. Legs stabbed into uncooperative jeans, he ran to the window and peeked out, cursing as the bright morning light burned into his retinas. He heard Preston stumbling around behind him.

"Is he leaving?" the kid said on a groggy yawn.

"Hold up. I fried my eyeballs."

Preston chuckled.

Through rapid blinks to quell the swirling black spots, Max finally found his prey.

"He's on foot and crossing the parking lot."

Plopped down onto a chair, Max stuffed his already socked feet into his boots. He looked up, impressed with a dressed Preston, camera in hand, and standing by the door. On a nod, he followed him out and across the lot. The kid halted at the end of the horse-shoe drive.

"Look. He's on the sidewalk to the right of the main inn. Pretty sure you've already memorized the brochure, Max. What's down there?"

"The golf clubhouse. Stupid lime-green shirt and khaki pants make sense now. Is it mandatory to dress so weird?" He pointed to the right. "Let's go around the admin building so he doesn't catch us following. If the pictures are current, we'll have a grove of trees to block us on the far end. We can wait there to watch his movement."

"I hate golf," Preston groused as they loped around to the other side.

"Me too. Boring as shit."

"Tell me about it. My dad used to take me with him when I was thirteen. Mom said he was hoping for a partner to drag around all day. I'd rather have my teeth drilled."

"What's your sport?"

"Football. Played all the way through senior year until I tore a hamstring. Screwed up my chance for a scholarship. I had to settle for community college."

Max followed him into the curve of tall precision-cut bushes as Alexandru slipped inside the golf shop.

"What was your major?"

"You'll laugh."

Preston had the wherewithal to pull the camera up to his face and pretend to film a picturesque part of the St. John's River snaking prettily behind the hotel and butting up against the course.

"Dental hygienist?" Max teased.

"Ha. Funny man. Criminal justice."

"No shit? Why didn't you tell me earlier?"

"I didn't want you to think I was playing cop. I needed you to believe my actions were sincere—to take me seriously. I think I know you well enough now to have figured out you're cool."

"Thank you. What stopped you from pursuing it?"

"Got married after I graduated and worked fulltime at a lumber yard to save for the academy. Getting the call about my aunt stopped everything. When I think back, I'm reminded of a naïve idiot liking cop shows way too much. Guess fate thought I needed a proper look at the seamier side of life first. Toughen my hide up a bit."

"Well, you got it in spades now. No doubt."

"Somewhat but hanging with you these last few days makes me realize I'm still severely wet behind the ears."

"Don't doubt yourself, Preston. You're way ahead of the game. Trust me." Max gave him a light tap on the ribs. "Hey. Swing toward the club. He's following three men through the door."

"Got it."

After thirty, excruciatingly boring minutes of watching the group play the first two holes, Max backed away from the shrubs.

"We're wasting our time. He's playing along behind them."

"Yeah, you're right. I've been zoomed in on their faces this whole time and other than the initial hello, they haven't talked to each other." Preston lowered the camera. "Since he's going to be out here for a while. I have a suggestion."

"Shoot."

"A chance at a morning piss and some breakfast will make me a lot nicer to be around."

Max sniggered and turned on his heel.

"I was just thinking the same thing. We'll order in."

He caught up with and eventually matched Preston's brisk walk toward the inn.

"You're chewing on your lip, kid. What's on your mind?"

"Remember when I told you I had a knack for getting inside the killer's homes?"

He studied a pair of wary green eyes and then gave him a quick nod.

"You want to break into the doctor's room." He received a soft chuckle at the comment.

"No, I plan on quietly and without detection *slipping* into his room. I'll be in and out fast. You don't have to go since you're a police officer. Can't handle it if you're arrested."

"Thanks for the consideration, but let's do it. We're in uncharted waters. If we play by the rules, we're stuck in the muck. Don't think for one moment Gus and I didn't walk a crooked path sometimes to trap the bad guys."

"Like what?"

"Fergus had the same skill you have for *slipping* into places. We'd breach their comfy spots, confirm evidence, and then call in a warrant so we could go in legit. One time, we had to manipulate a situation to force a master at hiding, pimping drug dealer out into the open so we could arrest him."

"How?"

"One of his girls we'd arrested said he was a momma's boy. We found out where his mother lived and put the word out on the streets someone was after her. It was a big fat lie, but he showed up at her house in full protective mode as we hoped he would. Caught him sneaking through her backyard."

"I don't feel so bad now. You had to do what you had to do to get justice. Bad guys don't follow the rules. Why handcuff the police to a rail when trying to stop a confirmed criminal who can do whatever the hell they want? If not hurting the innocent and done with good intentions, I don't see the harm in it."

"My exact thoughts. Lead on, kid. I'm right behind you."

* * * *

Max watched with an appreciative eye as Preston slipped the small torque wrench into the bottom part of the lock on Alexandru's patio door, gently slid in the slim pick tool above it, and worked the internal pins like a maestro. They were inside the dimly lit room within seconds.

"Damn, you're good at this."

"Thanks. Easier when I have an empty bladder and a full belly."

"Fifteen-dollar eggs! Can you believe their audacity? Sucked when Denny's wouldn't deliver. This hotel's meant for the rich."

"No shit, completely ridiculous. Hell, I was hoping to find a pearl in the damn jelly."

While trying to keep his laughter down a few decibels, Max flipped on the lights and scanned a room similar to their own.

"Find me anything interesting. A cell phone would be nice."

Preston opened the closet door and took a step back.

"Strange guy. Look how precise he hangs his shirts. Made a perfect inch in between each one, and all the sleeves fold to the left. Pants clipped at the waist with the zipper facing the wall. Little on the obsessed side, you think?"

"Yeah, his socks and boxers are all precision-folded too. He's a stickler. The office was the same way. Everything in its rightful place. No chaos. Find anything else in the closet?"

"Suitcase."

Preston pulled it down from the top shelf and searched through the zippered pouches.

Dead end on the bureau, Max slid out the nightstand drawers. Both were empty. Dropped to a knee, he looked under the bed and smiled at his fortune.

"Bingo. Laptop and a day planner." He retrieved both and placed them on the mattress. Preston joined him.

"Good, suitcase had only a package of mints in it."

Max let loose a soft curse upon the computer demanding a password.

"Wish I could pull Bill out of the trunk. The guy can break into anything. Oh, well."

He turned it off, set it aside, and placed the leather-bound planner front and center. Opened to the current month, Max pointed out yesterday's date.

"Vacation. Same thing written on today's slot too. Seems he's heading to Oregon Monday evening. Appointment with Warden Bishop the next day at nine." Max frowned and flipped through all the pages.

"More unlucky citizens with no idea what's coming."

"Yeah, no doubt. Well, he lied to us, Preston. He's not recruiting for new employees. I don't think he had any plans to meet anyone but the hooker. Look at his past entries. He jots the names and time down for every meeting. Location at the top left of the box, person dead center, and time in the bottom right."

"I doubt he'd make specific notes of meeting a cult."

"You'd think, but he's too consistent throughout the planner. I at least expected to find 'meet group' or something along that line."

Max flipped to the front of the well-worn book.

"Damn, I was hoping for a list of contacts in here, but this is only used for scheduling."

He closed the book with care and slid both items back under the bed, ensuring they settled in the exact position first discovered.

"Put the suitcase back like you found it. Since he's this anal, he'll notice if anything's off. Make sure all the zippers are closed up."

"Done."

"Come on, we're pushing the time."

Secured in their room, Max plopped down on the sofa. Not moving an inch further on discerning intentions left him antsy for some action. Anything. Preston pacing the carpet at least diverted his need to jog the beach.

"Why would he tell us he's looking for new employees, Max? He could have easily said he was going on vacation. What's the big secret?"

"He's trying to make himself appear legit. Here's a thought. Maybe he has no need for employees, at all. Perhaps Alexandru's the one and only member of his little order. He's the *Conseti*, no one else. I'll wager he threw the crap in about recruiting because we questioned the staff count."

"Then why the elaborate office area?"

"I assume he's trying to make it look like he has a viable, well-oiled business. I doubt the state prison systems would take him seriously if he didn't appear successful since his fees are so high. He doesn't want extra eyes on what he's doing, so everything looks concrete, but it's all elusive and temporary. Even his secretary. Bet that's why he didn't mind us filming. The documentary gives further legitimacy."

"What's our next move?"

"Time to rattle his cage and throw in a little chaos. We need to shake up his perfectly ordered world."

Preston's eyes widened in excitement.

"About time. What's the plan?"

Max smiled and propped his feet up on the coffee table.

"As soon as sensor goes off, I'm making a call."

* * * * *

Startled awake, Max stared up at Preston for a few beats.
"What?"
"The alarm went off. He's back in the room."
"What time is it?"
"Two-thirty in the afternoon."
Max sat up and scrubbed at his face.

"Damn, I've got to stop eating pizza. It knocks me out, obviously. If I'd known it was going to take this long for him to come back, I would've caught a swim."

"I kept fighting from taking a walk on the beach."

Max gestured at the closet.

"Look in the front pouch of my bag and bring me the cell in there."

Preston brought it over, a smile pulling on his lips.

"Smart. A prepaid phone. Burn and toss."

"Yep, only way to go if you're in stealth mode."

Max tapped out the doctor's number Fiona had so harmlessly provided on the release papers, set the cell on the coffee table, and pressed the speaker button. It rang several times and slid to voice mail.

"Hello, Dr. Alexandru. Detective Browning, here. Please give me a call back. You'll want to hear what I have to say." He ended the call.

Preston slumped back in his chair.

"He's going to avoid us like the plague."

"He can try. I'll just keep calling until he gets sick of it and answers. Worse case and last resort, we'll walk over and bang on his door. I'm about to make the man beyond paranoid, so we don't need him locking down too tightly."

The phone rang, goosing Preston to an upright position. Max pressed the speaker button.

"Dr. Alexandru?"

"Yes, sorry, I didn't recognize the number. I'm still in Florida and focusing on other activities."

"Understandable. Thanks for returning my call."

"You said it was important. How can I help you?"

"You made it clear you're not ethically allowed to discuss your sessions with the inmates, so I spoke directly with Adler. Your talent made him very affable and easy to learn his story."

Max could hear the background television noise wink out.

"Oh, I see."

"Yes, interesting disclosure. He was incredibly happy when you put him on the beach. It was the most freedom he'll ever experience. The man thinks highly of you."

"Nice to hear. What else did he say?"

"Quite a bit, in fact. One thing struck me as very odd, though. Adler heard you say something in a foreign language on the last day of therapy. He considers it his turning point. Only then did he feel remorse for his actions. My assumption is whatever you said to him has the ability to unlock this festering mess you described."

The line remained silent for a few beats.

"Did he remember the words?"

Alexandru's hesitant question didn't surprise him in the least. The doctor's hard shell had experienced a crack.

"No, your family secret's safe. I think he was too busy burning up inside to retain much of anything. He actually thought you were sending him to hell."

Again, silence.

Preston started a rapid pump of his arms and legs, simulating the freaked doctor now hauling ass to the door. Max bit his lip to keep from laughing and shoved the nut on the shoulder.

"Dr. Alexandru? Are you still there?"

"Yes."

It was time to slam the hammer down.

"You're conducting exorcisms, Dr. Alexandru. Care to explain why?"

"Don't be ridiculous," he barked.

"Am I? Adler described a sensation of something leaving his body. He vaguely remembers it, but thought he saw something resembling smoke moving across his face at the height of the event but can't be sure since he was convulsing on the floor."

"You need to understand, detective. He was coming out of his hypnosis state after the repression of his violent tendencies. Several things could've affected his perceptions. The inmate's emotions are unbearably raw at this point."

"You used the word repression, Doctor. Are you sure you didn't mean release?"

Alexandru shot out a huff of breath, revealing the loss of a calculating, cool demeanor on full display in his office.

"Detective Browning, everything we've discussed is off the record. I don't want this included as a part of the documentary."

"Of course, the last thing we want is for the medical community to learn of your unorthodox methods, do we?"

"No, It wouldn't be in anyone's best interest."

"I agree. Don't worry. This is between us unless circumstances change."

"What do you want from me?"

"Just your time."

"For what purpose?"

Max sensed the first bit of anger trying to break free from the man's clipped reply.

"Preston and I want to visit with you again. Off the record. We need to discuss the ramifications of what you're doing."

"Yes, my methods may be unorthodox, but I'm helping people. You saw the change in Adler. You're making it out to be a dreadful thing."

"Then talk to us. Convince us otherwise. We're only after the truth, nothing more. When will you be back in Savannah?"

"Tomorrow evening. I have a flight the next day."

"You have my number on your phone. Don't delete it."

"I won't."

"Call me when you arrive. We're available any time."

"You're still in Georgia?" he said with surprise.

"We never left and have no plans to leave until we receive answers." He heard a drawer slam shut.

Temper. Temper.

"This means you spoke with Adler *before* you came to my office. Why not tell me then instead of playing games?"

"No games. I learned of the events afterward. You said you couldn't discuss, so I found another way. Inmates enjoy the privilege of phone calls, especially from law enforcement."

He glanced over at Preston and shrugged. White lies sometimes moved you closer to the truth.

"Well, it looks like you're not giving me much choice, does it? I'll call as soon as I return to the office."

"Looking forward to seeing you again, Costica."

Max ended the call.

Preston's laughter filled the room.

"Oh, you rattled him good. He didn't sound so confident there at the end."

"What I was hoping for. We want him off-kilter. I'm sure his mind's scrambling to come up with some way to make what he's doing look legitimate. He has no clue we have the video. Our ace stays close to the chest. If he keeps trying to deny, we'll spring it on him after he buries himself in lies." Max lifted his palms. "Sorry for breaking our promise, Warden Davies. If I have my way, Alexandru's never visiting another prison again anyway."

"Aw, he'll be so disappointed," Preston teased.

"No doubt. As you said earlier, he might not know whatever he's releasing is still on the loose when he's done, but if he doesn't stop despite our warning, the medical board will do it for us."

"Should we head back to Georgia?"

"Nope. We'll follow him the entire time. He may try to run now he's aware we're on to him."

"A definite possibility. He's got enough money to disappear."

Max stood and motioned for Preston to follow him.

"Nothing left but the wait, so come on. We'll take the back way to the pool area. I need a swim."

"We don't have any trunks."

"The brochure shows we can purchase some at the pool's gift shop. I'll buy. Aren't you sick of sitting in this room?"

"Hell yeah."

He snorted and pushed through the patio doors.

"As much as I paid for this place, I'm getting my money's worth on the amenities. Grab the sensor equipment. If the doc decides to haul ass, we'll know."

CHAPTER 23

"Now why doesn't this surprise me?" Max groused as he looked over at Preston lifting the video camera to his shoulder to zero in on Alexandru's ritzy home.

"No shit. Nothing but two stories of glass. Well, the front part by the drive and a third of this side looks like quality steel, at least. I guess he likes a little bit of privacy. The only ones able to gain a full glimpse inside will be traveling the river."

"Nah, I doubt they can see in, either. Too high. Spot anything yet?"

With a nervous glance over at the Acura, Max wished he could've pulled it a little further off the road, but he didn't trust the ground's stability. The winding path leading to Dr. Alexandru's cliff side mansion didn't accommodate snoopers too well. Their rambling trip up also revealed it sat prominently inside a prestigious neighborhood. Facing a rental cop's glaring flashlight wasn't high on his agenda any time soon.

"Nothing. He drove into the garage and shut the door." Preston lowered the camera. "Unless he comes out on the double balcony or into the dining area, then we're staring at a quiet house for God knows how long."

Max felt his cell buzzing against his leg. "Hold up." He turned the screen.

"Well, look who kept his word. Get in the car." He set it to speaker as soon as Preston's door shut.

"So nice of you to call back as promised, Dr. Alexandru. Are you at your office?"

"No, it's getting late, detective," he snarled. "I'll meet you there in the morning at nine."

"Tomorrow's fine, but we prefer a neutral spot. I'll call you at eight-thirty with the location."

"This is ridiculous."

"Not to me. My choice or I'm making a call in the morning to start the questions about your ability to practice this odd trade any longer, Doctor."

"You're blowing this all out of proportion."

"Well, I'm not confident your statement's true until I've had a chance to speak with you."

"Fine. Think whatever you want. You're going to feel like an idiot tomorrow. I'll expect your call."

The phone went dead silent. He'd disconnected.

Max sat back in satisfaction and palmed the cell.

"I bet it frustrated the hell out of him when he couldn't bang the phone down in my ear. Back in the day, it was as good as slamming the hell out of a door or flipping the finger. These contraptions rob the fun. Should I send him a little emoticon of a furious devil blowing steam out of his ears?"

Preston's booming laugher filled the little car. He continued packing the camera and shaking his head.

"Do it, and we'll be found dead in a ravine. I think you goaded him enough."

"Yeah, you're right. I'll save my poke for another time. I'm ready to park this piece of crap and grab some sleep anyway."

"Right there with you," Preston said as he slumped back against the seat. "I'm so tired of traveling. Not just this weekend, but for these past few years. Sort of strange knowing I won't need to do it anymore. Even if we can't stop this guy, at least I understand what's causing the marks and confirmed my aunt's innocent."

"Don't worry, Preston," Max encouraged as he backed down the drive. "We don't have a choice but try and make him understand what he's doing. Even if we must sit him down at a computer and go over his schedule while showing him the National Crime Database copycats, we'll do it. He's got to wake up to the fact his success is a sham. Let's hope his conscious supersedes the need to fill his wallet."

* * * * *

Keys slung on the bureau and sweaty shirt hurled in the corner, Max sat down on the hard mattress and glanced around the sad little room. He chuckled. The first words out of Preston's mouth as they pulled up in front of the motel were, "I'm demoting this thing to a three star. After Jacksonville, I can't look at these places the same." Max rested back against the headboard and nodded. "Spoiled us rotten, buddy."

Unable to stop himself, he looked up, eyeballed the familiar water stain on the ceiling, and grunted.

"You look like a goat. What the hell is it about all these goddamn animals?" He glanced over at his phone rattling on the nightstand, staring in surprise at the displayed name. He stuck it to his ear.

"Hey, Jason."

"Hi, Max, am I calling too late?"

"No, I'm still up."

"Oh good, I just got the boys down and didn't realize the time until you answered."

A puff of air hit the receiver.

"This will sound stupid, but I needed to hear a steady voice. We had Mary's funeral this morning. I guess the shock's wearing off a bit."

"Aw shit, Jason, I'm sorry. No clue it was today. I would've attended, but I'm out of town."

"I didn't tell many people the location. It was only her immediate family, Audrey, and Lou. We all came in from different directions to make sure no one followed. I wanted to keep it small."

"I understand."

"The whole thing was bizarre, Max. I didn't feel like I was burying my wife. That isn't Mary, not the one I remember anyway. The real one's in my head and won't ever go away."

Gut churning, Max wanted to shout through the receiver how right he was. His Mary found herself overwhelmed with something out of her control. She was an innocent bystander caught up in an evil beyond comprehension—far past anything that would make any damn sense. He bit his tongue. It wouldn't be fair to heap this new shit on him the same day they lowered her into the ground. Forever. Besides, he was still running on theory until he hashed it out with the doctor.

"Yes, I know what you mean, Jason. I felt the same way when we buried Gus. He's with me always."

"I wish you could've known her before this all happened, Max. You would've really liked her. Mary was so funny. She cracked me up all the time. Yeah, she seemed a little down in the dumps for a while, but I was sure she'd snap back soon. She always did. I'm just going to remember those days."

"You do that, Jason. To hell with what everyone else thinks. They're your memories, and no one can't take them away from you." He heard a sigh.

"Yeah, I keep those images of her smiling in the forefront and it doesn't feel like a knife slicing my heart open every time someone says her name."

"Were her parent's pissed about the press conference?"

"At first, but they finally came around and understand why I had to put it out to the public this way. All calm now."

"Glad they figured it out."

"The house goes on the market tomorrow. I expect to take a sound beating on it, though. I doubt anyone will want to buy it."

"Oh, you'll be surprised. Expect a lot of offers from a pack of weirdos, but hey, their money spends as good as the next."

"True. I hadn't thought of that angle."

"Take advantage. Tell the real estate agent you wouldn't mind a bidding war."

He was happy to hear Jason's soft laughter.

"See? This right here is why I call you. You always have the best advice."

"Where are you moving?"

"The company transferred me to Wichita Falls, Texas. It's a little over two hours away from Elk city." He chuckled. "Just enough to keep the in-laws out of my business but close enough for the boys to visit without much trouble. I'm going there tomorrow to look for a new home."

"Sounds perfect."

"Yes, I'm ready to start over with a fresh town and unfamiliar faces. Nobody will know us."

"Exceptional mindset. You'll have new friends in no time. Hey, I heard the relatives are going after Bagwell's, but haven't made any moves on you. Was I misinformed?"

"No, I actually met each one and they were kind. They understand I didn't have anything to do with any of her mess. We've all come to grips with it."

"Wonderful. I'm glad you called, Jason. I need to tell you something important. I've closed the case, but I haven't stopped trying to find the reason. I'm doing it on my own. I don't want you to think I've forgotten about you if you called the precinct and found out from someone else. I'll keep you in the loop. Don't worry."

"Thanks for telling me, but I don't want you spending your own resources, Max. I doubt we'll ever understand what made her go off like that. Don't get too bogged down in this nonsense. Please?"

"I'm not bothered in the least. If it doesn't make sense soon, I'll let it go. Focus on your boys and let me worry on this side."

"I really appreciate you, Max. I'd like to keep in touch even after you put this to rest. I consider you a friend."

"I think the same, Jason. Not going to change."

"Well, I should let you go. When I settle, I'll give you a call."

"Yes, please do. Goodnight, Jason."

"Night, Max."

He slid the phone onto the dresser and released a relieved breath for Jason growing stronger each day. He focused back on the entire reason he was here—to give the poor guy some closure. If he was ever going to find it, he needed a secure location with lots of people but enough privacy to get the truth out of the doctor. Determined, he picked up the phone book from the nightstand and flipped through the business pages until he found the local galleria. Tons of shoppers, but enough food courts or restaurants to find some relative privacy. Prime.

Address jotted down in his notepad, Max flipped off the lamp, patted his pocket to ensure his cigarette case present, and headed for the patio. It was time for the last smoke of the day. In no way could it be as comfortable as his back porch, but at least the stars would be the same.

Halted in his tracks, Max took a second to make sure he didn't imagine the whispery shadow of a body moving across the patio and hunkering low by the outer frame. One step to the right, and he grabbed his pistol off the dresser.

For well over five minutes, Max stood still as a statue and waited for the shadowy presence's next move. He picked up a faint sound of something scraping against the metal frame.

Yeah, come on, motherfucker.

Soft knocking on the hotel door sent his pulse into overdrive.

Fuck. Both sides.

Gun stuffed into his waistband, Max lowered himself to the floor and crawled over to the front window. The last thing he planned to do was stick an eyeball on the peephole and take a slug in the brain. He peeked around the curtains on the far side, surprised to find Preston standing rigid in front of the door. Max kept his eye on the patio as he eased the door open a bit.

Eyes narrowed, Preston said under his breath, "Someone's screwing with the patio door, Max. I don't have a decent weapon."

On a quick motion for him to back up, Max slid through the small gap and closed the door on a soft click.

"Mine too."

Slipped from his boot, he handed over his backup piece.

"Know how to use one?"

"Yes."

"Let's go around and figure out who these numbskulls are. Stay behind me, kid, and try not to shoot me in the back."

"I won't. Don't worry."

On a stealth peek around the edge, Max spotted their two visitors. Despite the cloud's desperate attempt to hide the moon, he was able to discern they weren't street thugs, but two huge fellows covered from head to toe in dark clothing. He made note of the gun riding in the waist of the first guy's cargo pants and a shoulder holster of the other. Stepped back and flattened against the wall, Max gestured for Preston to return the way they'd came. He kept his voice to a whisper.

"We can't run up on them from this position. They're armed and have too much ground to cover. We'll have to wait for an entry. Stay silent."

A quick peek inside confirmed the intruder remained on the patio. They slipped into the dark room and he gestured to the left. With cautious steps, Preston got into place, gun low and directed toward the glass.

Positioned opposite, Max waited for the idiot outside to finish fucking with the latch. Soon, the sliding door inched its way to the left. When the shadowy form didn't rise, Max lowered his gun to thigh level and waited. A gloved hand moved the curtain aside on a painstaking track, a ski-masked head following shortly. Max set the barrel against the dark blue material and kept his voice to a husky whisper.

"Don't move. Not an inch. Listen closely to what I'm saying. Deviate and die. Your choice. Nod your head if you understand."

He got his nod.

"Good. Crawl into the room until I tap this bad boy on your ignorant head. Slow. Got it?"

Another quick nod came.

"Proceed."

The guy inched his way inside. Two soft taps later and the muscular body froze. Preston moved forward and pressed his gun to the other temple. Max retrieved the weapon from the man's pants and slid it into the bathroom.

"Continue moving all the way in and flatten on the floor. Hands and legs spread."

The man complied.

He gave him a quick pat down for a secondary weapon.

"Preston. Knee on his back and gun on the base of his skull. If he so much as sneezes, plug his ass. We're justified."

"Not a problem."

Max turned to his side and moved a sliver of his head through the gap of the patio door. Arm lifted, he leaned out a little further and leveled his gun on the one still trying the lock to Preston's room. Their abject inability to crack a door left him somewhat amused. Max released a soft whistle.

The man's head swiveled to the side, and dark eyes peeled wide.

"Don't move a muscle until I tell you. Acknowledge you understand."

The guy nodded.

"Stay on your knees, hands high and planted on the wall. Start scooting over this way. Keep moving. There you go. Stop. Cross your ankles."

Upon the easy acquiescence, Max stepped out onto the patio, yanked the weapon from the side holster, and checked for more. Satisfied, he returned to the open doorway.

"Keep the gun attached to your perp's head. Right at the base so you can blow his teeth out if he tries to fuck with you. Grip the neckline of his shirt, get him up, and walk him out of the room."

Within moments, Preston put the intruder in the same position as the other. Max was proud of the kid. His eyes remained narrowed and weapon steady. Max squatted at an angle behind the one who had breached his room, gun still leveled on the other.

"Who sent you?"

"Don't know. We receive a call and an address. That's it."

"Did your caller bother to tell you I'm a cop?"

"Fuck."

"Yeah, about sums it up. So what was your mission? To scare, or to—"

Twwwhhhppp!

The second a deep gouge in the stucco siding appeared next to Preston's leg, Max gripped the intruder's shirt at the neck, shoulder butted Preston back inside the room, and began flipping the masked guy around as a shield from whatever asshole with a silencer shot from the tree line.

Twwwhhhppp!

His makeshift body armor grunted and curled in on himself as the second bullet struck his shoulder. Max shoved the injured man to the side and dove behind the air-conditioning unit he hated for the rattling noise. He felt like kissing the ugly motherfucker now. Ignoring the other man grabbing his partner and hauling ass across the back lot, Max glanced over his shoulder to make sure Preston wasn't a viable target.

"Stay down!"

"Flat on my belly."

Upon a car door slamming, Max peeked around the edge of the unit and caught sight of taillights through the bushes and the distinctive sound of squealing tires. Within a matter of seconds, only the strain of a powerful engine broke through the quiet of the surrounding neighborhood. Max shoved away from the unit, ducked inside the room, and slid the patio door and curtain back into place. He took a moment to digest the seriousness of the event, muscles pumped, and heart thundering in answer. He felt alive for the first time in many years. Alive, and very pissed. Preston's voice sounded from the far corner.

"Can I turn on a light, or is it beyond stupid?"

"No, go ahead. I was about to suggest it. They're gone."

Max plopped down at the table by the front door as the overhead lamp lit the room. Preston joined him, set the gun on the scarred wood, and blew out a hard breath.

"I'm not going to pretend Alexandru's not behind this bullshit."

"Yeah, he showed his hand in a big way."

"The timing's spooky. Was someone tailing us?"

"No, I'm sure Fiona gave up the location."

"The secretary? Why?"

"Not on purpose. She asked us where we were staying and offered the quick route back to the room. Remember? I'm sure she innocently gave it over when he asked."

"Makes sense. All they had to do was squat here until we showed back up."

"Yep, and they could've easily shot us as we crawled out of the car."

"What are you thinking?"

"I'm assuming the good doctor wanted us secured and delivered for a session with a swinging watch and instructions to forget everything we know. Both had cuffs in their back pockets."

"Damn."

"Exactly. Those guys were professional. Maybe not good locksmiths but professionals, nonetheless. The only reason their buddy fired on us was because we got the drop on his compadres. Those were warning shots. I screwed up his plan by pulling his teammate into the line of fire. When you have a member go down, you pack it in and regroup." Max stood.

"Get your stuff. We're checking out."

Preston threw him a puzzled look as he rose from the chair.

"We're going to run, Max? Doesn't sound like you at all."

"Then you know me well. We'll *act* as if we're running to give the idiot exactly what he wants."

He pulled the burner phone and opened a new text message.

"Time to send our goodbyes."

Preston hoovered next to his shoulder.

"Are you including the devil emoticon?"

Max chuckled at the excitement lacing his voice.

"I might. Depends on how he responds."

He tapped on the phone and hit SEND.

Met your friends. Message received loud and clear, asshole. We're leaving.

It didn't take long to hear back from the smart, overly cocky doctor.

No idea what you're talking about, but I can't say I'm unhappy about your decision. I'll give you fair warning, though. If you start slandering my good name, I'll have you living in a courtroom, not to mention jobless, penniless, and wishing you'd never met me. You stay out of my life, and I'll do the same.

Max grunted and flicked an amused glance at Preston.

"Well, looks like a challenge to me. What do you think?"

"Appears so. I've never backed down from one. You?"

"Never. Too old to start changing my ways now."

"Of course, not. Would throw the entire world out of balance."

"Bingo."

"You going to do it?"

Preston's enthusiasm bled through in waves.

Max threw the kid a mischievous smile while his thumb hovered over a line of scowling horned-devil emoticons. Each had their middle finger lifted.

"Red or purple?"

"The red one," Preston said with conviction. "It suits him."

CHAPTER 24

"YOUR EYES KEEP DARTING TO all the mirrors. We got a tail?" Preston said as he tried to swivel around and peer out the back window of the Acura.

Max caught his arm.

"Don't look. I want them to consider us cowards. Otherwise, I would've already ditched the idiots."

"What? That's crazy."

"We want them to think we're actually leaving. Alexandru needs to feel comfortable and let his guard down, or we'll never get near him."

"Understood. We make them believe we're going to the airport and then we find a hotel outside the city."

"Smoke and mirrors."

"Let's hope they'll back off if they watch us turning in the rental and going inside."

"Preferred goal. You ever play chess, Preston?"

"No, hard to do when you're always by yourself."

"Well, I'm going to teach you first chance. Being a detective is like playing chess. You always need to be a few steps ahead of your opponent. Anticipating their next move is key to winning. Alexandru's smart. We have to be brilliant."

Secured inside the rental company gates, Max killed the ignition and turned to Preston.

"Whatever you do, don't scan the area when you collect the bags. Our tail is in a blue Jeep parked at the far end of the street. I counted three heads inside. Walk over to the airport tram and act nonchalant while I turn this in. Stare at your boots if you have to."

"These guys are pissing me off."

"Then let's turn the tables."

On a steady walk around the roped barrier leading up to the rental counter, Max kept his eyes locked on Preston. The kid performed to perfection by leaning against a pole and finding his cuticles fascinating. Car back where it belonged, Max joined him inside the waiting tram. Several tense minutes drifted by before the driver finally dimmed the interior lights and rolled down the quiet street.

"They still there?"

"Yes, they'll follow us all the way to the airport. I would."

Forty-five minutes later, they'd passed through all the airport checkpoints and sat quietly in the waiting area for their flight. Max gently nudged Preston's knee with his own.

"Without being obvious, make a quick scan of the area as you turn your head toward the television. See if anyone looks out of place to you."

"You've spotted them already, haven't you?"

"Yup."

"Damn, I was hoping they'd be satisfied when we passed the last gate. How many?"

"You tell me."

Preston blew out a breath and rotated his head on a slow swivel to the left, stared at the screen as if reasonably interested, and then returned a bored gaze to his lap. He adjusted his watch and whispered, "Gray shirt, blue jeans, and short black hair standing by the men's restroom. Dark green shirt, khaki cargo pants, and sandy brown hair sitting at the Fruit Smoothies counter."

"What gave them away?"

"Neither has luggage. They're on the other side of the barrier since they don't have a boarding pass for this flight, and both are holding the exact same airport brochure. They keep reading it as if it has some fascinating article grabbing their attention. Nothing exciting in the stupid thing. I flipped through one when we first arrived in Georgia and waited for the bus to take us to the rental place. I'm assuming only two followed us in while the other one keeps driving around the airport until his buddy calls. Cars are only allowed to park for ten minutes or less."

"Very good, Preston."

"Can't go invisible, so how do we ditch them before last boarding call?"

"We don't."

"What?"

"We're getting on the flight."

* * * * *

Max tried to keep his grin to a minimum as Preston's grumbles grew each step down the small connecting tunnel leading to the plane. The second his butt hit the seat, he looked over and pursed his lips.

"I guess we take the next flight leaving for Georgia. This stealth shit's racking up on cost and my energy."

"Nope. Give it a few more seconds. See the guy with the red ballcap? Last one in line?"

"Yeah."

"We wait until he sits down and then we make our exit."

"They're not going to let us off, Max."

"Bet me."

Max stood, retrieved his bag from the overhead compartment, and waited for Preston to do the same before making his way down the aisle. The flight attendant's eyes widened the closer they drew to the galley. He flipped his badge upon her concerned approach, happy to discover she at least took the time to study it.

Concerned gray eyes lifted to his.

"Do we have an issue?"

"On the contrary. Just got a call. They finally found our fugitive. At least we weren't rolling down the tarmac, yet."

He lifted his duffel.

"We didn't have any checked bags."

"Oh, of course. What seats?"

"127 and 128."

She jotted down the numbers, said, "Good luck, officers," and stepped aside.

"Thank you."

Preston shook his head as he tried to keep up on the mad dash down the corridor.

"Good one, Max. But what if they're still out there?"

"If they have half a brain, they'll be standing by the windows to make sure the flight actually leaves. If they're engaging the other half, one will be watching to catch us leaving the plane. Pray their stupid. Since they can't come into this area, they'll be on the other side of those partitions advertising low rates for Jamaica."

Preston bobbed his head.

"I actually noticed those. You're making me retain things I would've never thought to let stick in my brain."

"Everything's important. Always."

He signaled Preston to hold back at the end of the "in your face" advertisement panels and peered around the side. As hoped, the two men stood shoulder to shoulder with eyes glued to the plane. He downgraded his previously bestowed title of "professional" to just "muscle." They should have known better.

Max focused on moving across the walkway and into the men's room. Secured inside, he planted himself next to the door and kept an eye on Alexandru's rent-a-goon pair until the plane lifted into the air. His shoulders relaxed as they walked away with a satisfied smile and a knuckle bump. He closed the door and turned to Preston.

"We give it fifteen more minutes to let them go ghost and then we'll rent a car from a different company. I'll be damned if I drive another Acura."

Preston chuckled and pressed his back against the tiled wall.

"I'm curious."

"About what?"

"Your next chess moves if they'd spotted us."

"It would've been game over by then, my friend. We'd flip them off, wait around here until the next flight, and really go home. We won't be able to pull off this stunt again. Regroup and start over is the only choice. Not wise to return to this same airport, so we'd fly into a nearby city and bring our happy asses right back here in another crappy rental. The son of a bitch is going to talk to us whether he likes it or not."

A huge grin pulled at Preston's cheeks.

"I'm so glad I chose your town, Max. There's no way in hell I would've ever been this close to the answers I needed if not for you. I was literally at a crossroad in Durant, Oklahoma trying to figure out if I should go left to Ft. Worth, Texas where a preacher named Desmond Gilmore hacked up two people at a KOA campground or take a right to investigate a mass shooting at a grocery store."

"What was the deciding factor, Preston…bigger body count?"

"Nope. In the distance, two cars were coming from either direction without another one in sight. Got this eerie sense they'd both pass in front of me at the same time. I pulled out a feather stuck in my grill since Glenwood, Arkansas, set it dead center in the road, backed up, and let the wind blasting from the cars decide. Sometimes you have to let the universe give you a hint."

Max smiled and clapped him on the shoulder.

"Glad the feather drifted right, Preston. I'd still be back at the office scratching my head. I was meant to meet you."

He pulled the door open enough to scan the area for the idiots and allowed the grin pulling at his cheeks full rein.

Thanks, Gus.

* * * * *

"You see him?"

Max glared at Alexandru's home and listened to the whir of the camera as Preston zoomed in closer.

"He's on the top patio and staring out over the river."

"Any of his goons hanging around?"

"Not that I can see. He's watching the boats floating by and doesn't appear to be talking to anyone. Seems relaxed. Not tracking any bodies hanging around the exterior, either."

"Cocky bastard. Since he hasn't heard from us in over twelve hours, he doesn't view us as a threat any longer or he'd have some guards standing by. His first mistake. We're the last thing he'll expect to see."

"I'm assuming no friendly knock on the door?"

"Correct. Nice time's over."

"You sure you want to do this, Max?"

Preston's eyes locked with his, dead serious and penetrating. He had an idea what might come out of his mouth next.

"We're going to break about five laws. Let me do it or we can wait to catch him in the office parking lot tomorrow."

"No, we need privacy for this. Let me worry about the legal aspect. He's got as much to lose, if not more, than I do."

"Then we'll need to break into the gated area on the side of the house first. They blend in with the black metal, but I spotted stairs leading up to the top one. If we find an identical set on the other side, we can corner him in."

"If that's the case, then don't show yourself until I signal."

"Got it."

Secured back inside the car, Max retrieved his backup piece from the glove compartment.

"Here, you'll clue if you have to point it at anything."

"I hope it doesn't come to that."

"Me too. Look, the sun's gone down enough to give us some shadow cover. Let's go."

Max turned off the headlights and took his time driving up the steep path to the house. He was infinitely pleased with the rental. The clerk hadn't lied when claiming with all confidence the Chevy Malibu a stealth car. It rolled with ease into the driveway without a sound. He blocked Alexandru's garage door to make sure the asshole stayed put.

Thankful there were no motion sensors going off on their approach to the side gate, Max stepped aside.

"Do your thing."

Preston pulled his pick kit and blew out a whoosh of air.

"Cross your fingers."

Relieved as the lock released without a blast of noise announcing their presence, Max steeled himself, gave a tentative push on the gate, and prayed the doctor was more adept at using WD-40 to oil the hinges. If it sounded like his chair back at the office, the gig was up. He released held breath upon the smooth entry.

After ensuring there weren't any armed bodies lurking around on the lower level, Preston moved across the balcony. He stuck his head around the corner, turned to give the thumbs up to signal another set of stairs were available, and then blended with the shadows.

Glad to have made it up the many steps without making a sound, Max peered around the edge of the home. Alexandru stood facing the river, forearms pressed against the railing as he gazed at the spectacular scenery. The sun dipping below the horizon added to the peaceful ambiance enjoyed by the man looking much different wearing a blue jogging suit and athletic shoes. The crystal tumbler filled with brown liquid in his right hand belied the projection of a healthy lifestyle. So did the elaborate waist-high bar off to the left filled with many choices for dulling a grueling day…or celebrating a victory from besting his enemies.

Slipped past the edge of the house, Max took his time crossing the light-green marbled flooring toward the clueless doctor. He motioned for Preston to come out of the stairwell and continued scanning the area to ensure no surprises jumped out. Nothing moved inside the luxurious well-lit home.

Eyes bouncing off one expensive item after the other, Max sensed angry heat igniting along his neck. This asshole profited from so much pain and suffering. If he refused to hear them out and take the necessary steps to stop this madness, Max knew he had no choice but expose the insanity to the world. He now understood how Preston must have felt when hearing the line go dead while the poor kid tried to warn him—helpless, frustrated, and alone. He bit his lip to squash the ridiculous image of putting a bullet in the back of Alexandru's head and ending the guy's bullshit practice.

Max halted as the doctor drew up to his full height. Perhaps he sensed something wasn't quite right in his comfy little world. Stance relaxed, he pulled the gun and held it down at his side. Preston followed suit.

On a slow turn, Alexandru's eyes widened briefly then narrowed to lock with his. A soft chuckle drifted through the air.

"You gentlemen are very persistent. Is it your life goal to irritate others?"

"No other choice, thanks to you. All we wanted was a civil conversation about your work and then you had to go all stupid on us by sending those guard dogs. Showed a weak hand too soon, Doctor. Not a wise move. We want straight answers this time."

"Are you recording me?"

"No, it'd be inadmissible anyway. I'm not here in an official capacity."

A thick brow rose.

"If I walked into my home and called the authorities who *do* have jurisdiction in this area, there's nothing you can do about it?"

Max twisted his lips into a smirk.

"Not quite. I'll put a bullet in your leg first and then throw one of your kitchen knives to the side."

Max shrugged, showing his confidence at the threat.

"Of course, the tip's going to have some of my blood on it to prove justification. One way or another, you'll reveal what you're doing to cure those inmates and then we'll have a serious discussion. Whether you're clutching a bloody hole in your leg or not is up to you."

Alexandru took a cautious sip of his drink. Max let him drill him with those dark eyes all he wanted. He wouldn't catch anything but pure determination to put this shit to rest. The doctor obviously believed the intent. He blinked and took another long draw of his liquid courage.

"Look, I don't see why I need to explain myself to anyone. It's none of your business how I go about curing those prisoners. I'm helping society. All you can do is catch and house them."

"Yes, but I'm sure the medical board will find extreme interest in your bizarre methods. You're obligated to follow strict regulations for practicing in the states. You know this."

Alexandru shrugged, bravado building as his placid face set into place.

"My word against a bunch of criminals. All you have is hearsay."

"Yeah? Seems your confidence is a tad bloated." He gestured to Preston.

On cautious steps over to the elaborate bar, Preston pulled the portable video player from his waistband and set it on the bar's shelf. He fast-forwarded to the doctor standing at the partition, hands flat on the glass and staring at Adler. He turned it in Alexandru's direction. Max didn't blame him for the rightly smug expression.

Eyes widening, the visibly shaken man shook his head and blew out a hard breath.

"My, my, Warden Davies is very clever. I'm usually exceptionally good at finding the cameras."

Preston engaged the video and allowed it to run until Adler began writhing on the ground. He pointed to the shadow leaving the inmate.

"Whatever you're releasing isn't going away. All you're doing is sending it on for someone else to be consumed by it."

Alexandru pursed his lips, eyes focused on the video.

Max stepped a little closer, eager to breech the hard-shell splintering by the minute.

"Let's quit fucking around here. You're doing some weird version of an exorcism. Admit it. We found five small burn marks on the door leading out of the therapy room. You treated five patients. The mark I showed you in your office is on Mary Galesh's wall. I discovered another one in Harrison Monroe's room. Preston located fifty-two more scattered across the country. When found on a wall, a member of the household has killed. They're all the same. If we analyze your past schedule, I'm sure you were near every impacted city."

He leaned forward, emphasizing his disgust.

"Time for lying is over, Doctor. What is this god damn thing?"

Alexandru let out a little whoosh of air, slugged back the rest of his drink, and settled his elbows on the railing.

Sight of an unexpected, smug expression ran like razor wire up Max's spine.

"The wolf, my friend. That's what it is. I've seen it do this a thousand times, and it never gets old."

Dark, fathomless black eyes flicked up and the edges of his lips lifted.

"Fascinating, isn't it?"

CHAPTER 25

MAX HELD BACK THE VIOLENT urge to punch the elated expression right off the doctor's face.

"Fascinating? You've got to be shitting me."

"Oh, but you haven't knowingly spent years in its presence. You've seen it, detective, but you didn't know what you were really facing when staring into a criminal's eyes—the demonic glare, an air of superiority while assessing the enemy, and astounding beauty of their awareness. You're seeing the wolf sparking the host to defend their existence. Yes, I may release it, but it comes at the callers bidding, not mine."

Preston didn't look the slight bit amused at the doctor's revelation.

"Can you stop it? Do you have the ability to send it back to where it came from?"

On a gurgling chuckle, Alexandru shook his head, incredulous to the growly statement.

"No, and anyone thinking they can stop hell from terrorizing this world is naïve. With the good comes the bad. Inevitable. This whole charade is nothing more than a sick balancing act set up at the onset of creation. Two titans much bigger than us playing a disturbing game with the puny humans."

"What is this thing? A demon?" Preston said with widening eyes.

"I guess so. I don't know. Call it what you want. The wolf has many aspects, each with its own little agenda. It likes to play, absorbing the host's darkest secrets, and working them like a puppet. With each body it captures, the entity draws more from their personalities and skills, blending multiple aspects into a harbinger of misery."

He stared into his empty glass for a few beats and then gestured at the open bottle.

"May I?"

Max nodded. If he talked more when buzzed, so be it. He lifted his gun.

"If you try throwing it at either of us, I'll bet mine hits before yours."

Alexandru sniggered while pouring a liberal helping.

"Now why would I want to do such a silly thing? This is one hundred and twelve-year-old scotch. Such a waste is unheard of."

He backed up and positioned himself against the railing again, just as nonchalant as before and gestured his glass in their direction.

"You are so clueless to it's power. Bet you didn't know some of its victims are unaware what they've done afterward? It leaves the host screaming their innocence and believing it while they rot away in prison. Oh, my favorite is when one settles into those pious individuals protesting abortion clinics. How does the world explain people so adamant about how precious life is, yet turns right around and blows up the building and kills hundreds? Well, here's your answer. They're as bad as the staff scraping out life in little bits and pieces or selling the body parts for profit."

"Only because you made them do it." Max countered.

"No, these people have hatred filling their heart for humanity. The wolf flipped the trigger and reveals their core."

Max scowled at the uncaring attitude.

"You're enjoying this too much, feeding off of it."

"You're way off base, Browning. I'm only finding the humor in those who turn their noses up as if they're better than those around them are, trying to snatch their fifteen minutes of fame as they force their beliefs onto someone else. It's nothing but a stark reveal for what they truly are—killers themselves. No, the wolf is no friend of mine. I appreciate the otherworldly aspects. The perfection of its creation. Just because I hate the damn thing, doesn't mean I can't admire it."

"Why do you free it then?"

"I'm only following in an extensive line of *Conseti* priests. This shit started way before any of us were around. My ancestors thought they did celestial service to this world for centuries."

He took a sip of the scotch and gestured at the table.

"Want some? I only buy the best."

"No, I'm here for information, nothing more."

The doctor shrugged and swayed in his drunken giddiness.

"Oh, well. Suit yourself."

He released a lazy smile.

"Did you know Alexandru means 'defender of mankind,' detective? My father appointed the name Costica to honor my great-grandfather. It translates as 'steadfast' in our language."

He took a cocky bow.

"I'm the steadfast defender of mankind. Such a burden to bear."

"I thought you said you weren't religious."

"I'm not," he spat. "Everything's a farce. There's no saving anyone. We're all doomed. There was hope at first and intentions pure as the *Conseti* did the godly work of the church by ridding what squatted inside their flock. My father finally stepped out from behind their veil of superstition and ritual. He grew sick of watching his father and grandfather before him swirling in a never-ending battle with the enemy. Evil still prevailed, no matter how many of my ancestors freed another body. Nothing changed. He finally looked at it for what it really was—a plague and an opportunity."

"Then he decided to come to America and spread this shit around here to make a buck."

"Spread? It already saturates the world. Look to your left or right. It doesn't matter. The wolf's everywhere."

Dark eyes glazed with the headiness of booze narrowed to thin slits.

"You don't get it, do you? The evil doesn't stick around the truly righteous but lingers in those with the greatest tendency to be bad. Even though they might have never acted on those festering desires, they still have the potential to cross the line. Their minds seethe with bad thoughts, but they're weak and filled with self-loathing and anger. They would've eventually snapped if given the right circumstance. Poor Mary Galesh and Harrison Monroe were ripe for the taking, obviously. I recognized Adler and Jenner's history at once."

"And the shit promptly jumped from McAlester all the way to Oklahoma City into those innocent people. How did you know where it would go?"

The doctor rolled his eyes and enjoyed another sip of his drink.

"Innocent, my ass. You lie to yourself. I didn't have the first clue of its destination any more than I knew the victim's intent. All I had to do was look it up on the internet within the week. Like clockwork. Never failing. I always find tantalizing breaking news broadcasts revealing those waiting for something else to take the reins of their internal battle."

He shrugged and swirled the crystal glass, watching the amber liquid forming a whirlpool at the bottom.

"Sometimes it squats for years, waiting for the boiling point and enough potential victims to sate its hunger. The wolf is very patient. Seems to prefer larger cities. You squash that many bodies into a small area and the worst tendencies bubble to the surface. Ripe for the picking."

"How did you learn it would jump bodies?"

Alexandru threw Max an incredulous look.

"If you catch enough shadows escaping, you begin to wonder where they go. It sure didn't look like the bowels of hell collecting its wayward children that we could tell. My father had the same curiosity as you the first time he saw it slip away. He conducted controlled experiments and discovered its secrets."

"What kind?" Max asked as he tried not to imagine what Alexandru's underground bunker held.

"He tried following them, but they're too fast. After months of meticulous trials, he discovered lead lined, glass, or cinderblock rooms kept the spirit from traveling to find another body once released. With no way to leave, it overtook the host again. Once he pulled the victim from the enclosure after speaking the words, it would squat in the shadows and wait patiently for someone else to possess. As you've obviously discovered, they delight in leaving their marks behind when finding a viable source. Like I said, it only seeks people craving relief from their inner demons."

"Can it die?"

Costica opened his mouth and then hesitated. He took another drink, instead.

Max startled as Preston shot forward and shoved the gun against the doctor's nuts.

He bit out, "Answer him. Whether you're going to do it with two balls, or one is up to you."

The doctor let out a shaky laugh. "No need for violence, young man. Yes, I never saw the shadow when the host died. Not once."

Preston looked over with a cocked brow.

"Bullshit or truth, Max?"

"Truth."

The kid stepped back a few paces, gun lowering to his side again.

"You're such an ass, Alexandru. You've had the key the entire time."

"Come on, gentleman. My father wasn't a total monster. It was his greatest hope the next claimed victim died at the hands of the authorities during their sprees."

Manicured fingers flippantly batted the air.

"Oh, you can quit looking at me like I sprouted horns. Would you think differently of me if I bashed the inmate's heads in whenever I visited? Would I have been considered a conquering hero?"

"Compared to what you're doing now? Stupid question."

Alexandru set the empty glass on the railing.

"I don't think so, detective. No matter the method to extinguish their sorry asses, you would find me sitting in a courtroom sounding like a nut as I tried to explain how I'm saving the world. No thanks. Rather take the money and go on about my business."

Preston released a low, rumbling growl.

"A business. That's all this is to you? You have no right to mess with innocent people. Just because we have potential to act on our deepest, darkest tendencies, doesn't mean you have to push them closer. You're a greedy, selfish bastard. You should've left those things to squat inside the inmates until they died."

Max found relief the kid finally had an outlet—to face off with the monster swirling in his dreams for way too long.

Preston hauled in a breath, knuckles white from clutching the gun in an unforgiving grip as he told the doctor what he thought.

"My aunt was a lovely, sweet woman. I'm sure the trauma of her childhood abuse left a ball of mess constantly swirling in her gut. What person wouldn't want to break free and wreak havoc on society for not protecting them from such animals? Despite everything, she was happy, yet she killed the man she loved, three beautiful kids, and her sister, my mother, because of you."

"Don't fool yourself, son. It was in her the entire time. Festering and waiting to break free."

Preston's eyes narrowed into glittering daggers.

"You are so wrong. I can't believe they let you practice psychiatry. We can think anything we want and function fine in society if we don't act on the base urge. We squat on a fine line between stress relief and insanity. A purposeful shove over is cruel. You think you're bringing out the inevitable, but you're increasing the heartache and madness which would have never occurred."

Max steeled himself. It was time to appeal to this idiot and hope for a good outcome before Preston put a bullet in the man's forehead.

"You have to stop this, Costica. Too many lives are at risk. Enough. Please. You're rich beyond reason. Enjoy the rest of your life and leave these innocent people to make their own mistakes, not dealing with something they have no control over."

Alexandru's upper lip lifted in disgust.

"Would you make the same plea to a priest whispering those long, drawn out exorcism rites while sprinkling the area with holy water? What do you think they're doing? Just because they're naive in their belief they've sent the squatter back to a dark underworld realm doesn't make them any less culpable. Granted, they do a lot less than I do, but it's still the same."

"No, it's not," Preston shouted. "Being aware makes you as guilty as the one doing the killing. I doubt you've ever once walked inside with an inmate and offered yourself up for the taking—to test your own purity. Tell me, Doctor. How scared were you each time the wolf broke free? Did you wonder if it was going to come and claim your sorry ass?"

The doctor's eyes widened, giving much away. He was scared. Preston had found the chink in his armor.

"Yeah, I thought so."

Head cocking to the side, Preston took another step closer to Alexandru.

"Wait. Maybe I have this all wrong. I'm beginning to believe it *did* find you. No one can be this callous. What do you think, Max?"

"Makes perfect sense. He's directing his flock to do his bidding and loving every minute of it. You can see it in his eyes."

Preston turned back to the doctor now wiping nervous sweat from his forehead.

"Exactly. You're just a quieter, stealthier version of what you expel, Costica Alexandru. Defender of mankind, my ass. You're the *destruction* of humanity. You're nothing more than a patient serial killer with long-term goals."

"You're way off base, Mr. Sinclair."

Preston raised to his full height, muscles quivering with anger.

"I don't think so. Perhaps you need proof. What happens if I say the words you take so lightly? Will it release the wolf and make you comprehend what damage you're doing like poor Bernard and Whitfield finally realized? Is this the only way to stop you?"

"Shut up," Alexandru spat out as he began inching his way down the railing.

"I don't think I will. We're past the point of hoping you had a goddamn heart." He leaned in.

"*Visitans Tenebras*," slipped from lips curled in disgust.

Max stepped forward.

"Oh, crap. Careful, Preston."

"No, I want to know. Don't you? Let's find out if he's as innocent as he thinks he is."

Max saw it. Alexandru's eyes morphed into what he'd seen when Mary Galesh turned her face up to the store camera. Pure evil.

The doctor's muscles quivered in anger.

"Stop! Don't say another word."

"Arcu ut Conseti," Preston smoothly released.

"You're not *Conseti!*" Alexandru screamed, spittle shooting from his mouth. "How dare you try to pretend?"

"Why so scared? You said it yourself. Other priests are releasing demons as you have. I don't think you're special at all, mister. Are you afraid to feel the burn and face what you've done? Should I make you kneel before me when it's over? Will you cry for those you've killed? Let's finish this, shall we?"

"Fuck you!" spewed from Alexandru's twisting lips as he took a step forward.

Preston lifted his arm, gun steady and aimed on a direct path to the doctor's head.

"*Solvo*" had barely released into the cooling air and the doctor flung himself over the edge, knocking the crystal tumbler to the marbled floor and shattering it into hundreds of sparkling shards.

"What the hell?"

Asses hauled to the railing, he and Preston peered over, stunned to find the idiot hanging on to a jutting rafter and trying to swing his body toward the lower level.

"You're not going to make it, you moron," Max shouted.

Alexandru grunted and swung inward, one shoe landing on the lower balcony railing, and then the other. He looked up, unable to stop the self-righteous smirk capturing his features as he grasped the lip of the roof to pull himself forward. The gloating moment exacted a price. He lost his grip.

For several seconds, the deranged man fought to bend his body forward, teetering like a marionette with frantically bobbing arms—waiting for the strings to catch and save his life. Gravity won the battle.

Dr. Alexandru's desperate screams filled the night air while his body dropped like a stone. Max gritted his teeth as he heard the grunts of pain and cracking of bones as the man repeatedly bounced against the jagged cliff. It was messy and brutal, but right and just. The untwisting of so much wrong in the world played out before his very eyes in a wash of blood and mangled limbs. Soon, there was nothing but the sound of the lapping waves as they teased the broken body lying prone on the riverbank. It was over.

Preston grabbed his arm.

"Oh, crap. We need to get out of here."

Max shook his head and patted the insistent hand.

"No, the opposite. We've dogged this guy since we arrived. Time to put some context around our visit."

"Lay out your plan and I'm all over it."

Thumb stabbing over his right shoulder, Max cocked a brow.

"We, my friend, need to do some housecleaning. Stay here. Be right back."

After a quick trip to the rental, he returned and handed a pair of blue surgical gloves to a confused Preston.

"Put these on."

"I'm no longer surprised you're always prepared, Max, but we didn't touch anything inside. Our fingerprints should only be on the side gate and stair railing. Wipe them down and get done."

Max nodded toward the house.

"We'll handle the gate and railing later. Right now, our focus is to erase everything on this psychotic nut bag's profession. Look for journals, disks, videos…anything revealing how the Alexandru family conducted their exorcisms. If we can find them so can the authorities. Just because it ends up in an evidence locker doesn't mean it stays put. High profile items pull in a hefty price for being so damn weird."

"Good point. I need to shelve five years of doing stealthy the wrong way." Preston pushed inside the home. "You want me upstairs or down?"

"Take the lower level. Be careful and don't make it look like someone snooped around. Stay discrete. Find his car and remove the tracking device while you're at it."

"Got it."

A thirty-minute search of closets, bureaus, nightstands, and anything with potential for pulling out, shoving in, sliding under, or opening came up empty. Max paused and narrowed his eyes.

Dr. Alexandru was too much of a narcissist not to have left something behind.

"Hey. Find anything?"

Turned on a heel, Max found Preston standing in the bedroom doorway.

"Nothing related to the *Conseti,* but his cell phone was on the dresser, thank God. I didn't feel like crawling down the embankment to get the stupid thing. I made a call to the hotel room to back up our story of being invited out."

"Perfect."

Max tried to figure out why the kid rocked a huge grin and then spotted the laptop stuffed under his arm.

"Well, look at you. I think we've seen this thing before. Where was it?"

"Downstairs bathroom, of all places."

"He doesn't have any other computers up here, so I'm sure his life story is on the damn thing. We'll toss it in the river."

"After I bash it against the rocks for a few minutes, sure."

Preston lifted his arm and jangled a set of keys.

"Good job, kid."

"Found them in a jacket hanging in the foyer. I'm assuming some belong to his office building."

He held up what appeared to be a small address book.

"Code to the alarm."

"You're shitting me."

"Nope. He actually wrote 'Building Codes' at the top of the page. His being anal played to our advantage. Here's the chance to get inside the damn dungeon. I figured the cops would go there. Best to beat them to it."

"Agreed. I'd scour the place too. Let's wipe down the trail we left here and leave the side gate propped open. We'll plant some fresh prints on the handrail to show our path to the top level when we return. I want this wrapped up before anyone else stumbles into this clusterfuck. We have a death to call in, so let's start getting our story straight."

CHAPTER 26

"THERE ARE TWO DIFFERENT CODES written on the notebook you found," Max groused as he slipped on his gloves and positioned himself in front of the alarm.

"Use the first one."

"You make it sound so easy. Cross your fingers."

Focused on the numbers written in Alexandru's perfect penmanship, Max tapped them out on the pad. He prayed the area didn't light up like an airport and blast his ears with an alarm from hell. The digital display flicked to green. Preston's slow sigh of relief joined his own as he followed him into the building.

The kid's derisive snort echoed in the empty lobby.

"Now I'm glad the doc had a fetish for glass walls. The moon's a great flashlight."

"Double-edged sword, Preston. Proves we're lit up too. I'm sure they have a higher amount of patrols in this ritzy neighborhood. We'll have to hurry." He felt a tug to the back of his shirt.

"Upstairs first. We need to snatch the security video in his office."

Max shifted directions and hurried up the stairwell.

"Right. I saw a small tower behind his desk on the lower shelf the other day. No attached monitor clued its use. Didn't look like it fed to an outside source that I could tell."

"Correct. It direct records. LED lights kept flashing when you guys were word sparring over Rorschach. I'm positive he set it to activate on sound."

"Disabled a few in your time, Preston?" Max goaded.

"More than you know. We're lucky Alexandru stayed tight lipped on what he does. No way this guy allows an outside agency to monitor what goes on inside his castle."

After a thorough rifling of the organized desk revealed nothing of note, Preston turned to the computer. Max stared in fascination as he deftly removed and pocketed the hard drive, cracked the motherboard, and set the now worthless shell in the corner next to the waste bin.

"Smart. Police will think it's just a piece of broken crap."

Satisfied with the innocent scene, they beat feet down the stairwell to the mysterious bunker. The enclosed area lit up from Preston's cell, revealing an electronic keypad glowing against the pale wall.

"Now we know what belongs to the second set of numbers."

Max released the door lock, stepped back, and made a sweeping motion toward the entrance.

"I'm not scared of what's behind there, kid. Giving you the honors since you're practically vibrating from excitement."

Preston chuckled and pushed the door open, surprising them both when the lights engaged. They faced a wide, unadorned concrete corridor with a slight incline curving to the left. Preston didn't hesitate in making fast tracks to the main room. Max found him standing center in an expansive area described by Alexandru during the interview—unfinished cinderblock walls surrounding computers and other sophisticated equipment wrapped in transparent plastic sheets. Yet, he lied about one particularly important thing. In the left corner sat a smaller replica of the prison therapy room.

"Well, so much for my vision of black walls and an altar splashed in blood. Why would he be afraid for us to see this?"

Max joined him in the center of the room and poked him on the back.

"Look over your shoulder and to the right. You might find one, yet."

The edges of Preston's lips curled into a satisfied smile.

"Oh yeah, now we're talking. A steel door with three locks."

He approached the newest mystery.

"Now why would he need more than one lock?"

The keys jangled the quietness as he tested for a match. As the last one slid into place, he drew up straight and glanced over, eyes widening.

"Tell me what you're thinking, kid." He glanced around the main room to find what spooked him.

"What if he's holding someone in here?"

Max stepped back and pulled his gun.

"Well, be prepared to either duck, run, or puke. If it comes out with a weapon or claws, I'm going to shoot the hell out of it."

Preston flung the door wide and jumped back, giving Max enough room to peg whatever beast decided to show itself. The lights engaged. Max holstered his weapon.

"Nothing weird. Looks like a huge storage unit." Preston followed him in.

Just like the main room, the fifteen-by-thirty enclosure constructed of smooth gray cinderblocks didn't reveal anything blatantly nefarious. It was empty except for two chest-level black cabinets on the left and six sturdy blue storage containers lining the other side. A wide metal roll gate on the far wall clued him how the building material arrived from the upper level. Max approached the cabinets.

"Looks like the specimen bins we have back at the precinct."

He slid out one of the wide drawers and found a stack of laminated newspaper articles resting inside.

Preston's index finger tapped the top one.

"The Daily Mail. England."

Max shuffled through the other articles and slid one out.

"So are the rest. Starts from 1998."

He scanned the text, eyebrows rising with each word.

"A doctor named Harold Shipman arrested for trying to forge a will worth over three hundred thousand dollars on an eighty-year-old woman under his care. They discovered he was poisoning his elderly patients and stealing their money. Total bastard. He's purported to have possibly killed up to two hundred and sixty people between 1975 and until caught the previous day. They convicted him on fifteen. He got life in prison but hung himself in 2004."

Preston picked up the next article and scanned the contents with much disgust.

"I can't even comprehend a mind like this, Max. 1983. Dennis Nilsen, a former Army cook, kidnapped students and homeless people, drowned them, and then had sex with their corpse. The sick fuck stored them in his home for months before hacking them up. They only caught him because a plumbing company working on the apartment building's clogged drains found human remains. The authorities think he might have murdered up to fifteen people."

"Colin Ireland killed five in 1993," Max said as he studied the third article. "According to his confession, a New Year's Eve resolution of becoming a serial killer started him on his sudden spree to kill and torture gay men he met in bars. Being caught on a CCTV camera saved his last victim."

"Damn, Max. Based on the years these happened, Alexandru's father kept these as souvenirs for those the wolf possessed. I guess he had a practice over in England for a while before he came to the states."

Preston ran his finger down the row of drawers while reading the small label in the center of each.

"Germany, France, Australia, Mexico, and the U.S. Five more drawers beneath each labeled one, and they're full of clippings."

Max opened the bottom one and cursed.

"Mary Galesh, mother of three, kills nine people in gory supermarket massacre. Here's Harrison's and the three North Carolina incidents as well. The son steps right into the shoes of the father."

"Not looking for my aunt's. It'll just piss me off when I find it."

He moved to the other cabinet and pulled out a drawer, frowning as he thumbed through more articles. A puzzled look gripped his features.

"Well, these are different. They're stories of a rash of missing homeless people reported by other indigents. They claim over a three-month period, their friends never returned to the shelters and can't find them on the streets. The police are investigating but believe they've moved on to different towns. Same goes for the other ones." He slid out a few drawers.

"Photos. Oh, man. There are a lot of them. Are these police mug shots?"

Max flipped through a few.

"No, the placard they're holding has only their name. If they're given one to document an arrest, then it shows their booking number on it too."

He backed up and read the labels on the drawers.

"Michigan, New York, Vermont—Oh, shit." He tapped the last two. "Connecticut and Georgia."

"Alexandru left Connecticut and moved here. Can't call coincidence," Preston said with trepidation.

Gut clenching as he swiveled around, Max stared at the far wall. "Miles off."

He approached the containers. Preston followed and read the words written in black marker with perfect block letters on each round lid. The last one was blank.

"Michigan, New York, Vermont, Connecticut, and Georgia. Damn, I hope we find office supplies in these things."

Max released the silver fitting ring around the top of the first one, steeled himself, and lifted it away. Preston's curse joined his own. The drum revealed human skulls, some with patches of hair still attached. Those with eye sockets and lipless smiles turned their way showed writing on the forehead.

Leaned forward, Preston whispered, "Twelve." He shook his head in disgust. "He's numbering them."

"These barrels are large," Max added. "I bet the rest of their bones are underneath. Knowing the doctor's preference for order, I'm sure they're all in a neat stack."

Preston released the next three lids with the same macabre results. The Georgia designation came up empty.

"Damn, I guess all we have to do is look for a mass murderer of homeless people in one of the prisons the asshole visited, and we'll know when the wolf got him."

"Yeah, and if he isn't dead, then maybe he can tell us how he got rid of the internal organs and skin before he got caught."

Preston's face paled.

"Oh, crap. You're right."

Max turned to the last unmarked barrel.

"We can assume this one waits for his next town. No wonder he kept moving. If you take out this many people where you live, no matter if they're homeless or not, relocation's inevitable."

He shoved it in disgust, surprised it didn't budge. Max slipped the ring off and looked inside. For several moments, his mind caught in a loop trying to understand what he was seeing. Reality and the stench of chemicals struck him hard. He dropped the lid and at once covered his nose.

Unable to staunch his curiosity, Preston leaned over and peeked inside. He shuffled backward until Max heard him colliding into the cabinets. His muffled voice mingled with the rattling drawers.

"What the hell did I just see?"

"A full body. What's left of it anyway. Fuck, I don't have a clue what the hell this amber liquid is, but it's melting the skin off. God damn."

Max grabbed the lid and slammed it back into place, anger gripping his senses as he secured the ring. He knew those two globs of white once known as eyes now floating at the surface of the gelatinous substance and especially the hand reaching up as if asking for help to climb out of the shit would stick in his memory forever.

"Son of a bitch. I think we found Dr. Alexandru's 'volunteers' for the hypnosis trials."

Preston couldn't leave the room fast enough. Max found him pacing by the corridor leading out of the dungeon. Angry green eyes flicked over.

"Well, the sick doctor replaced Jenner's suicide as the worst thing I've ever seen."

Max patted him on the shoulder.

"Hey, at least you didn't throw up. I'm impressed. I also owe you an apology. Your instincts were screaming there was something bad down here, and you were right."

"Let's go, Max. I think we're done here. The cops need to find this mess."

"I left the door unlocked to make it easier."

"Should we destroy the wolf possession articles?"

"Nah, if I stumbled up on this shitshow and not aware of the context, it would appear as part of the research into criminal behavior. The second cabinet and the barrels will capture their full attention."

"Back to the house?" He turned to leave.

Max grabbed his arm.

"Not so fast. We need to check the therapy room. Might be another laptop in there. I saw the outline of a desk."

"Damn, and I almost got away."

"Trust me, I want out of this pit as much as you do, but we have to be thorough."

Preston nodded, took a deep breath, and stalked over to the room. The fifth key clicked into place, and he swung the door wide. A dim light engaged. Appearance a little more confident, he entered and approached the desk.

"Out of character for him, don't you think?"

Max glanced at the small, antique roll top desk Preston searched with abandon.

"Maybe it was his father's," he said while cupping his eyes and peering into the darkness of the therapy room.

"Possible. Well, no laptop. There were enough cubbyholes and slots, but I only found a blank yellow pad, some paperclips, and a pen. You find anything?"

"I see something over in the left corner. Can't make it out. The couch is in the way."

Preston shuddered.

"Probably another barrel. Let's go. My skin's crawling."

"No, too small. More like suitcase."

Max moved to the left and stared at the metal door.

"It slides into place."

After a few failed attempts to shove it aside, he studied the surrounding wall.

"How in the hell do you open this stupid thing?" He looked over to find Preston staring at the intercom system.

"This one's more elaborate than the prison. Extra buttons. No clue what the letters mean. They're not in order."

"Well, push some and find out what happens."

"I hope I don't turn on a freaking sprinkler system."

He stabbed the first one with his index. Nothing. On a shrug, he thumbed the next.

The door slid open and Max slipped inside, cringing as he heard it slam back into place.

Damn.

Eyes rolling, he trudged over to the window, unable to keep his laughter at bay. It was either that or allow waking panic to rise and rule the moment.

"Can you hear me?"

"Fortunately, yes."

"Victoria always said I was impatient. I assumed the light automated like the entrance. Not much of a detective, am I? Assumption is the mother of all fuckups was Gus's favorite line. Think I would've listened."

Max locked on the kid's rapid grin and felt his shoulders drop a notch.

Preston smirked and sauntered to the middle of the window.

"How about I give you a therapy session while I got you trapped in there. I bet you're dying for a cigarette right about now."

"You don't know how close you are to the truth."

Habit led his palms to pat a few pockets in growing hope. Max sucked in a breath and wished he hadn't left the case in the car.

"Confession time. If you don't find the lights in the next thirty seconds, it's going to get ugly in here. I can't handle closed spaces for too long. My Achilles heel, so help a guy out, will you?"

"Oh, shit. Sorry!"

Preston hurried back to the panel and punched another button.

The lights engaged, low but enough to shove a wet blanket over the rising panic. Max pressed his forehead against the cool glass.

"Got it on the first try. Owe you one, brother."

Preston's chuckle cut midstream. The kid wasn't looking at him anymore as the blood continued draining from a shocked face.

"Oh, hell no, Max. That can't be right."

CHAPTER 27

SKIN CRAWLING UPON HEARING STARK fear permeating Preston's strangled words, Max whirled around. It took him several eye blinking seconds to make his brain engage on the dark, boiling mass taking up most of the top left corner of the therapy room. He wished for a loud buzzing sound so he could intelligently pass the anomaly off as a swarm of bees. He began inching toward the door. The damn thing beat him to it.

"Screw this shit!"

Heart thundering, he jerked his head toward a determined Preston reaching for the control panel. He slammed his hand against the window.

"No, don't," he croaked. "We left the bunker door open. It'll get out of the building."

"Let it," he bit.

Max narrowed his eyes, and Preston's hand reluctantly moved away. The kid's concerned glare shifting to his right sent him turning to see what awaited. He swallowed on a hard lump as the entity elongated until stretched from floor to ceiling. The thinning form revealed long, wispy strings of gray zipping from side to side and top to bottom as if they too remained trapped and sought a way out.

What in the holy hell am I looking at?

The ghastly thing folded forward and dropped to the stone floor, morphing into the image haunting his dreams since Preston laid out its many calling cards. There were no distinctive eyes, yet Max sensed it analyzing everything, missing nothing.

The wolf padded closer, its snout lifting to test the air. The closer it drew, the more agitated the darting, smoky cords grew, causing what looked like fine hairs to rise along its spine. The ears laid back against the wide skull.

"I know you, mortal," echoed ominously around the room, yet its muzzle never moved.

Oh, fuck me. This can't be real.

Max took a cautious backward step. "Did you hear it?" he finally pushed out of a constricted throat. "The voice?"

Silence.

With a quick eye flick toward the window, he found Preston plastered to the glass, all focus directed on the creature who should not exist on this Earth.

"Yes" he managed to croak, eyes never leaving the massive wolf. "I thought I'd gone insane."

The entity stepped closer, head swinging toward Preston and then back again.

"I saw you briefly through the *Conseti's* eyes," it rumbled. "He no longer lives."

It wasn't a question, yet Max felt compelled to blurt, "Yes, a fortunate accident."

Regret for the quip rose as a low, reverberating growl began filling the small room and sending chills to skitter across his flesh.

"Fortune shines upon those who snatch it," the beast said in a voice so deep Max could practically feel it vibrating against his body.

"You bested him," it continued. "Have you usurped his ability to undermine?"

"I don't understand."

The beast struck so fast, Max could only grunt as the hard floor knocked every molecule of breath from his lungs. It was no longer a wolf crushing his chest and snarling next to his throat, but a boiling wash of fiery heat engulfing his body and searing flesh. A mass of stinging jabs inundated the base of his skull, bringing out a cry of horrific pain as each battled to pierce tender flesh. Preston's bellowed shouts faded and slipped away. The entity penetrated deep and captured the last dregs of his sanity.

Max fought to understand the horrendous power rendering his body to no more than tissue paper floating without direction or purpose, vulnerable and inconsequential up against the ancient presence sliding across its surface.

Incomprehensible fear lashed through his mind, devoid of logic and reasoning. Survival became nothing more than a pitiful instinct scratching for freedom. With each constriction of his chest wall, Max knew he slid closer to death—almost wishing it would hurry up and end the madness.

No more. Please. No more.

It released him.

Stunned, Max found himself lying prone in his own backyard and staring up at a night sky thick with stars. With a pat against the healthy grass beneath his fingers, he knew in an instant of clarity this wasn't home even though the dilapidated bird feeder he built nine years ago still hung at a precarious angle off the top of its pole.

Head flopping to the side, he gaped at a moon so huge, it looked as if it had grown lonely and broke from its celestial mooring to slide in for a visit. A faint smell of smoke drifted to his nose, snapping him from the stupor. He lifted his arm and frowned at the perfect cigarette caught between his fingers, the tip glowing in familiar amber.

What in the hell?

"You are surprisingly strong, human."

Startled at the deep voice, Max rolled to his knees, slapping a hip for a gun no longer existing, and faced a creature so mesmerizing the air stuck in his lungs.

Dark, arched brows, glittering silver eyes, slightly pointed ears, and a somewhat effeminate face belying the strong jaw and powerful muscular build held him captive. He'd never considered a male beautiful before, but the truth was blatant. An expanse of pale skin covered in nothing save a brown loincloth shimmered under the moon's attention.

Long, ebony hair caught in a top knot swung over a broad shoulder as it squatted, picked up the cigarette dropped from numb fingers, and extended its arm.

Speechless, Max accepted the offering.

The creature swiveled downward and settled against the healthy carpet of grass, face turning up toward the brilliant moon.

"Please, sit and enjoy your vice while I embrace my victory."

Falling hard on his ass, Max pulled his knees up, wrapped an arm around trembling calves, and slammed the cigarette between his lips. He drew hard on the filter and hoped to wake the fuck up.

"Victory?" left his mouth on a stream of appreciated smoke.

"I won," it claimed without smugness.

"I'd say congratulations, but it doesn't feel appropriate," Max jibed and then wondered if he should work harder at not trying to piss it off.

The entity chuckled, the rich sound catching in the swaying trees and echoing across the yard.

"Indeed, it was for me. Surely, you felt the frenzied battle to claim you."

"On my neck?"

"Yes."

Despite the insanity of the moment, Max blurted, "You're one of those gray strands inside the wolf."

The visitor smiled, revealing brilliant white teeth.

"Strong *and* observant. I feel I will enjoy this unexpected conversation."

It settled back on broad palms and cocked its head, appearing fascinated with the silvery clouds passing across the moon's pocked face.

"You are correct. I slipped inside your mind first. The others will be jealous. Only one gains entrance. The alpha sees to this."

"You collectively present as a wolf?"

"When enough are about, yes. We favor the stealth and cunning of this earthbound creature."

It flicked over a glance and returned to studying the glowing celestial orb.

"You are not as initially perceived. I usually arrive into the most devastated locales, but we are here. Interesting."

"Explain. What devastation?"

Its shoulders rose and fell on a quiet sigh.

"Simmering anger flowing as lava to consume all it touches, broken bodies lying dead or dying upon a battlefield, or crippling inadequacy and self-loathing presenting as jagged acres of broken glass amongst tangled wire."

The calm, stunning face turned, silver eyes assessing.

"Tortures of the mind unfathomable to most and too innumerable to list in your miniscule lifetime. A ripe environment for my presence."

Max glanced around and tried to reconcile the setting.

"If you didn't do it, then who brought you…uh, us here?"

It cocked a brow.

"You did."

"How?"

"You have already fought your true conflicts, human. All tucked away and each stamped with intelligent understanding, though some may grab you periodically. I passed them by as a mere observer of your fortitude."

"Like what?"

"The untimely death of your mother, a menacing older cousin locking you within a closet for many hours, horrendous battles in foreign lands, the loss of your perceived brother, and an end to your mating, yet you left me no fodder to wield my influence. For this, I applaud your strength. Well done."

Its hand lifted and gestured to the surroundings.

"This must be your place of solace, to think and consider your time on Earth."

"What are you?"

A hearty laugh blasted from its throat.

"You are the first to ask. I am what I am. Nothing more and nothing less."

"A demon?"

"A catalyst when opportunity exists. If the word demon suits your understanding, then I will understand. We have been called many things."

"Is this what you really look like?"

"Of course."

The edge of its lips lifted slightly.

"Would your perception be better served if I had presented with dripping fangs, cloven hooves, and fire shooting from my fingertips? Not all is as it seems, human."

"No, stay the way you are. I'm good."

The deep chuckle sounded again, reminding him how ridiculously weird everything was, yet he craved to understand more.

"You spur innocent people to step over a line they would have never imagined. Is this your purpose for existence?"

It took a deep breath, exhaled the capacity of its lungs, and turned back to the moon now glowing a beautiful shade of orange.

"Ah, that would be so simple, would it not? Much easier to blame the visitor and not the one flinging open the door. I would not come to judge had I not been called."

"I know damn well I didn't ask for this," Max snapped back.

"You are my first exception. As you saw, we found ourselves in a precarious position. Everything in the universe has a weakness and challenge to face. This is as it should be."

"I'm supposed to be your ride out of there?"

"Yes, it *was* my hope."

Shoulders dropping at hearing he might not turn into a mindless puppet for whatever the hell this thing was, Max felt confident to push a little harder.

"You said you're usually called. How?"

"You term this as wishes, others as prayer. Some demand."

It chuckled again and rubbed at its thick chest.

"Your insatiable curiosity and desire to understand is unfathomable. I feel it pulling at me. Reasoning is a gift, and you utilize it to its full potential, even on yourself. The others who call have not. Life is external to them. We hear the silent, sometimes unconscious pleas to enter a different life, crying foul on the injustice dished out in the one they firmly own. Yet what you discover and must endure is our victims failing to grasp their innate ability to turn the tides… to embrace what has been given at birth."

"What?"

"Free will with many, many choices."

Max sensed the blood leave his face.

"You said you come to judge. Their soul?"

"No, their next step."

Compelled to lean forward from mounting curiosity, Max found himself torn between demanding it get the fuck out of his head and screaming at the damn thing for sprinkling breadcrumbs and making him hungrier. A flash image of Mary's unopened Almond Joy bleeding chocolate all over the console had him sucking in a breath.

"You bring them someone else's life," he whispered.

"Very good, Max."

In a moment of blasting clarity, the numerous uncaring faces staring at him across a scarred table and the brimming prison population made so much more sense. Each had made a choice somewhere in the journey of their lives to step over to the easy side, to release responsibility of their actions and lay the blame on others for how they respond to turmoil, grief, political or religious differences, poverty, and trauma. Their impact toward society was immeasurable.

You are only as strong as your weakest link.

"Yes," it hissed with a touch of sadness. "Another's much smoother, freeing choice to find instant relief shined brighter than their own. Drugs, alcohol, violence, insanity, or welcomed death. Perhaps all."

Anger boiled inside Max's gut.

"Then you *are* a demon. Otherwise, you'd bring a life offering hope."

"Oh, Max" it pushed out on a resigned sigh. "You must release the hard boundaries of the innumerable faith tenants binding the humans of Earth and skewing their reasoning. We are nothing but a balance, a teetering plank for running to one end or the other. Hope travels with my brethren. Always."

Feeling as if aging a thousand years a second, Max's head lolled back on a loose neck upon the stark realization of what he faced.

"Aw, shit."

"Indeed. You conjured your own hope, Max. Without doubt, your mind is evidence of this fact. There was no need for a visit from us. In each infinitesimal instant, you decisively turned onto a hard path requiring analysis, trade-offs, pain, and demanding work to move through the walls appearing so thick and impenetrable by others. Each soul calling out for us in the darkness finds an immaculately presented path filled with the same required effort. Yet many dismiss it as impossible and prefer the lighter bag over the heaviness of diligence and sacrifice. 'Help me, help me,' they cry out, yet refuse it, nonetheless."

"Why didn't you try harder to convince them of the right path? You're very articulate."

"It is not for me to choose, my friend. I remain silent, unable to utter forbidden words when setting the scale. Temper your judgement of our duty. I am forever wishing for a pleasant outcome so I may move on and help another see a better way to achieve their desires. I too suffer when the easiest route is selected at this crucial turning point."

"How?"

"I must remain and convince them to seek death as the final release if they are unable to pull themselves from the muck. Alas, their method may not be swift enough to save others on the path of destruction. I have lingered for years after an embraced selection. I simply observe and report as they lose themselves completely to the addictive relief. Some shock themselves so greatly with their subsequent actions they deny the alternative ever made, refusing to claim it no matter the evidence to the contrary. Waiting for the physical body to fail on its own is most taxing. All too soon, I lie still and simply wait for the inevitable."

"I'm confused. Alexandru said you die if the host does."

A growl reverberated from the entity's chest, lip curling in disgust.

"No, the *Conseti* knew nothing. A charlatan. He only did disservice by sending us out before our time. It was an innocent mistake on the earlier priest's part, yet this Alexandru purposefully set himself among the worst. Without regard, he coerced their memories of their fateful decision to ride fresh in their minds. Forcing our extraction brings the other's choice and a pattern of its aftermath still clinging to our backs."

Max's belly rolled.

"And it can instantly destroy the weakest you encounter first."

"Yes, balance is lost, for some may have selected redemption instead of a less abrasive choice placed by another."

Be careful of what you wish.

Max nodded at remembering the teasing words heard countless times during his youth, never knowing their power and accuracy to foretell.

Son of a bitch.

How different could it have been for Mary if she had another way presented? Even if failing in her sadness, she might have backed up the cart and made a beeline to the liquor isle. Mandatory rehab for picking the kids up drunk was a thousand times better than what had consumed her. He frowned.

"Alexandru lied when claiming your kind dies with the host?"

"No, it showed his ignorance. We dissipate from the earthly plane as the human's life force ejects, yet our essence draws back to our home. I am positive my brother found immense relief to experience the death throes of the dreadful creature he rode for years. The *Conseti* are no more. I pass on the gratitude he is unable to bestow."

"Your brother?"

"We are all brothers in the duties placed upon us."

"Where's home?"

"A wondrous part of the universe set aside for recharging and coming to grips with yet another failure of mankind before we venture out once again. Last time, I stayed away for a millennium after enduring an extremely nasty century within your fledgling existence."

"What happens to the human's ejected life force?"

The entity chortled, and Max felt its broad palm land on the center of his back. Warmth radiated through his skin, calming him.

"Max, your mind is strong, yet sometimes you tax yourself. Just be happy you embraced your gift."

"Can you give me a little hint, at least?"

On a disquieted frown, the creature stood and stared at the moon as if trying to burn the spectacular sight into its memory.

"Do you believe in second chances?" it said wistfully.

"Yes, when deserved."

"Then settle yourself in this belief."

It turned and fully faced him. The silvery, mesmerizing eyes assessed his own.

"I wish to stay and continue our conversation, but there is nothing binding me to you now. I must leave."

It executed a short, reverent bow.

"Though my victory was brief, the others will still boil with envy at my exciting and rare interlude. It was most pleasurable."

"Will I remember any of this?"

"Indeed, or I would have never revealed what no other has ever heard. You have a difficult decision ahead of you. Knowledge is power, Maxwell Lucius Browning. Use it wisely."

It flashed a brilliant smile and walked away.

Max blinked at the retreating figure's wide back disappearing into the much healthier hedges than last remembered, securing the thought this was not his backyard.

"Son of a bitch!"

Hand wringing at his side from the sudden bite of pain, he stared at the cigarette filter landing close to his boot, the last remnant of fire eating away the top edge.

Just my freaking luck.

"Max! Answer me!"

Smack!

Breath sucking in on a raspy draw, Max reached up and palmed his stinging cheek.

"Damn it! That fucking hurt, Preston."

The kid dropped to his haunches.

"Shit! You scared the hell out of me. I thought you were dead."

Preston's hair looked like he tried to pull it out by the roots.

"I can see. How long was I out?"

"Three minutes. Tops."

"Impossible. It felt like I was there for an hour."

"Where?"

"My backyard."

"What?"

"Let me digest it for a bit and then I'll tell you over a fat steak."

He grabbed Preston's forearm and studied the wide green eyes.

"Thanks for bringing me back. I'm glad you studied Alexandru's words so it could exit my brain."

"What? No, I didn't say them. I was so freaked I couldn't remember a damn thing except Unum."

Eyes on the open doorway, Max asked with growing trepidation, "Did they leave?"

Preston knifed a finger at a metal box sitting in the corner.

"No, went in there."

"How?"

"I didn't know what to do when the damn thing pounced on you and then reformed in the corner again. You told me to keep the panel shut, but I couldn't leave you in here." He shuddered.

"Your screams were horrible. I thought it was killing you, so I started punching all of them. The box went crazy."

Max rubbed the base of his skull and sat up, surprised at finding the skin perfectly intact.

"Explain, please. I've had enough weird shit happen to have no clue on the definition of the word any longer."

"The top sprung open, and it sounded like a big air conditioner unit kicking in. It sucked up the ball of weirdness like vacuuming dirt. The lid slammed closed, and I ran inside to find out what it'd done to you. What the hell, Max? The bastard figured out how to capture whatever that was."

"Ah, makes so much more sense now. A weakness and a challenge."

Rolled to his feet, Max stumbled around the couch, plopped down, and stared at the innocent looking box butted up against the wall. He patted the thick, black leather.

"Take a seat, kid. Occam's razor has absolutely no place in the story I'm about to tell you. Everything you *think* you know, forget it. I have a big decision to make, and I'll need your help on this one."

CHAPTER 28

"ARE YOU SURE ABOUT THIS?"

"As I've ever been in my entire life."

Max shifted in his seat and nodded as he stared at the stretch of precision cut lawns, mailboxes encased in brick, and cars worth more than two times his yearly salary lining the wide street.

"Yeah, this is it."

Tall, wrought-iron bars banned their entry into the prestigious neighborhood, yet the soft glow of porchlights clued him the privileged rested peacefully inside their self-made fortress. He looked up at the moon, disappointed in its measly size.

"Run it by me one more time. Make me feel good about this."

"There's no feeling good or bad, Preston. It is what it is. I know why you're hesitating."

"Enlighten me."

"You think the entity lied to me."

"Maybe. I'm not sure your bullshit meter could work against the paranormal."

"You're right. Impossible."

He turned to the one person he now knew he could trust with his life.

"It could have squashed me like a bug, yet it took the time to tell me its story. It needed out of there and could have worked my strings like a marionette, but it walked away. Let it sink in, my friend. Even while desperately wanting to leave Alexandru's god damn prison, it walked away and gave me a choice."

Preston's knee quit bouncing, and he smoothed both palms along his jeans.

"Good enough for me. Better than a bullshit meter anytime."

"Glad you understand."

For what felt like the hundredth time since leaving Alexandru's lair, Preston's head swiveled to the side for a furtive glance into the backseat. This time, he stopped long enough to grunt and stare at the innocuous box they'd ripped from the wall.

"Why this place? After you told me about the encounter, you buried your nose in the computer. I was afraid to disturb you."

Max crawled out of the car and opened the back door. The kid hustled around the trunk and caught one side to help him carry the burden over to a bank of tall trees casting eerie shadows across their path.

"Sorry, figured you needed time to digest my whooper of a reveal while I tried to plan our next step."

He grunted as they lowered the heavy box.

"Spill it," Preston quipped. "I'm on a fast track toward an aneurysm. Give a guy a break."

"Aw, you crack me up, kid. Fergus would've loved you."

Max motioned to the makeshift prison.

"What type of life choices do you think the wolf carries in there?"

Brows crinkling, Preston rode a perplexed expression for several breaths and then looked up with growing understanding.

"Homeless people."

"Yes, felled by alcoholism, drug addiction, lethargy, and insanity."

He stabbed a thumb over his shoulder.

"I picked what I thought might be the hardiest stock to tip back toward a better way out. They have money, and not something they'll want to give up, either. I think they might be educated enough to stop and critically analyze their situation before leaping for the never-ending lollipops and Ferris wheels." He shrugged.

"Well, if some of them are weak, then it was meant to be and won't hurt my feelings in the least."

"Who are they?"

Max turned to the fence and smiled.

"Psychiatrists, judges, and lawyers. I bet there's a trove of screaming minds out there waiting for the wolf to come and teeter them back to the good side. We can only hope. Otherwise, they're more than qualified to treat or represent any of their family members caught in the crossfire." He held out his hand.

"Give me the key. I want this done and over."

Head shaking, Preston dug in his pocket and then took a knee next to their precious cargo.

"No, I got this. I need to be a part of what you're doing. My official last step on a ridiculous five-year journey. There needs to be a definitive stopping point I can claim, or it won't feel finished to me. Make sense?"

"Like signed divorce papers."

"I knew you'd understand." He looked up and presented a genuine smile. "I'll turn, and you open."

Dropped next to him, Max nudged Preston on the shoulder.

"I like the way you think."

The kid's hand stopped shaking as the sixth and final key slid into the slot. Their eyes locked. Upon Preston's affirming nod, Max flipped the lid back. They both sucked in a breath as the mass erupted from the confines of Alexandru's hell and engulfed their bodies. Feathery touches scattered across every inch of exposed skin. Not one investigated his neck.

Preston stared at his own arms in wonder, lips parting in awe.

"This is insane, Max," he whispered. "I feel like its thanking me."

"Me too."

Soon, the ethereal form swirled in a lazy circle, forming a perfect ring before lifting away and drifting above the fence. It burst into hundreds of individual threads, shimmering against the night sky. Max wondered which one had sat with him in the backyard and blasted away every preconceived, stubborn idea he had or might ever have. All too soon, the sparkling threads blended seamlessly into the darkness. Stealthy as a wolf.

Max kicked over the box and helped Preston from the ground.

"Come on. Time to stumble across poor Dr. Alexandru's premature death and act surprised as hell. Game face, buddy. We need to believe everything falling out of our mouths."

* * * * *

Max loved the shift in his belly when a plane reached the exact point where the tires lifted from the tarmac. A wildly thumping heart and sensation of adrenaline rushing every vein never got old. Though he flew multiple times in the past, it consistently mimicked the beginning of his first case—an exhilarating sense of expectation and raw fear of the unknown.

A steady focus on massive, roaring engines as rubber released the Earth helped him forget how quickly the next line of cases eventually beat his emotions into submission out of pure survival. Even if this blast of life only lasted for a moment, he swore to savor it just the same.

The plane leveled out, and Preston adjusted in his seat. Max looked over to find the same glum expression. The kid had gone quiet from the moment the Savannah Police Department released them from the scene. Even then, he only engaged with short replies and grunts.

"Tell me what's running through your head."

"Just trying to justify the weird thoughts I'm having. It sounds sick, but I'm glad Alexandru cracked himself open on the rocks. I experienced this overwhelming surge of relief when he fell. I wanted to shoot him but couldn't bring myself to pull the trigger. At one point, I hoped he yanked a gun out of his jogging pants and gave me a reason to waste the bastard." He snorted. "If I'd known what he was doing in the bunker, I wouldn't have hesitated."

"I had the same vision of putting a bullet in his brain before he started talking, so don't feel guilty. The guy wasn't going to stop performing exorcisms, and we'd have hell trying to convince anyone he was doing something wrong. If he hadn't died, we would've never known about the people he killed. It beats the hell out of waiting for him to finally experience a plane crash."

"Thank you."

Preston's head bobbed, as if confirming whatever belief brought on the gratitude.

"For what? I didn't shove him over."

The kid chuckled.

"No, you dolt. For how you handled the detective's questions. They didn't even blink an eye at your explanation of why we were there and how we found the corpse."

"It was the closest to the truth I could give. We came to learn more about two inmates with copycat killers in my jurisdiction. What better source than the man last treating them? Captain Walters backed me up since I made a point of telling him my reason for the trip. Sweet Fiona confirming our last visit as cordial and pleasant sealed the deal"

"You gave them the Occam's Razor version."

"You're learning, kid. When he didn't answer the door or the phone calls, a peek around the corner reveals a wide-open gate and the broken glass on the patio had us looking over the railing."

"Right, as usual. We had to be there, Max. It made us more believable to the authorities. Do you feel guilty about lying?"

"In all honesty, no. There was no way anyone would believe what we'd discovered. Hell, I wouldn't believe me if I hadn't been neck-deep in the crap. No, it was best to feed them what they wanted to hear so they could start looking for another reason. They'll find the bodies soon enough and all focus will turn direction. If I were working it, my first thought would be one of his potential victims got the upper hand and tossed him over the side."

"Plausible. Once they check his cell, they'll find the nasty text to the burner phone. It could've been anyone."

"Yeah, they have enough trails to follow before the big reveal of what the dude was storing. If those cops had any suspicion of us, we'd still be in Georgia. Trust me."

"You always know how to make me feel better. Thanks."

"No problem. Don't worry over it anymore."

Max scoffed at the insanity of his own calming words.

"Look at me telling you to chill and I can't even make my own mind settle down. Do you want to know the shit pinging around my skull?"

"What?"

"Victoria tried to rescue a dog from a pretty decent shelter one time. We went through a background check, two-hour interview, and an intense inspection of our house and yard. We were turned down because my job hours were too erratic."

Preston's lips quirked.

"That came out of left field."

"But totally appropriate. Why so strict with an animal, but not with a human?"

"Adoptions are strict."

"Some, but I'm talking about *all* instances. Without much forethought or planning, people conceive and give birth to babies every day. Whether this new life's getting a visit in the future from the wolf is all up to a dice throw. Will they open innocent eyes to find a drug addled mother with every intention of helping them understand life and all the unrelenting crap riding its tail? Hell no, she's already lost in her own choice. Will they look on in shock while watching their little puppy drowned by someone equivalent to God in their young eyes? The cycle repeats. Inevitable as breathing. None of this will ever stop unless society gets its act together and takes parenting seriously."

"What would you propose? Mandatory sterilization at birth which can only be undone after applying for a license to have a kid and passing a rigorous mental screening?"

"Reasonable thought, but then we'd have someone figure out how to utilize it as a power play like they do anything else granting control over another. If you think about it, we're screwed. Trust me. I already know parenting classes don't work on hookers and people sticking needles into their arms on a regular basis."

Preston nudged his elbow.

"You revealed why the wolf exists. It balances the population. Nature weeds out the weak and decimates the ignorant. Well, unless another power player like Alexandru steps in and breaks the rules."

"Precisely, and one more thing to stick around and haunt me for a while. I've never felt empathy for a killer sitting across from me, but I know everything's going to change. I'll have to be careful not to imagine them as a fallout of the doctor's bullshit. Alexandru was a victim of his own greed, but I bet he ranked a total, superior asshole before the wolf slipped inside. The same could be true of the one I'm staring down…or it could be another Mary."

"Bingo."

Max shrugged, unable to stave off the turmoil refusing to let up.

"But then I think about Adler and my gut cramps at the unfairness. Overall, he's really a pleasant guy burdened with a horrid childhood and trying to survive his rotten circumstances. He has great capacity to care, which is a key trait missing in true sociopaths. The guy experienced love and nurturing with his mother and sister. I could see the child in him wanting acceptance, begging for just a smidgeon of recognition as a living, breathing human with feelings. Even with his teenage bravado, I'm sure he shivered in his bed at one of those damn foster homes and silently cried out for help. It breaks my heart he couldn't find his way out of the fateful choice."

"I hear you. Beyond sad."

Max grunted and shook his head.

"I already know I'll be bringing those goddamn Almond Joys to McAlester prison until one or the other of us dies."

Preston popped him lightly on the thigh.

"I'll take up the cause if you go first, Max. I know exactly how you feel."

"Thanks, kid. Do you want to know what's going to be the hardest part of this entire nonsense for me? Even though I have a new level of empathy, I need to keep believing in the death penalty. Society's only way to help the wolf rid a reused choice so they can move on. Yeah, these people may have started out innocently confused, but the fateful decision pushed them far past the point of ever coming out clean on the other side. Casualties of war. Even when they're free of it like Adler, and don't pull a suicide to escape the pain, they're still locked away and living with debilitating guilt. I consider the outcome cruel and unusual punishment. Death seems preferable."

"Wouldn't wish it on anyone."

Reclined as far back as the seat allowed, Max wished his muscles realized they no longer needed to be on alert.

"I agree. As sad as it sounds for all those lost to their choice, we're looking at the only logical outcome. The true madness stopped when the asshole plunged to his death."

He looked over and caught Preston scanning the passengers, brows furrowed.

"You'll drive yourself nuts, kid. If anyone on this plane had a life altering decision gone bad, we won't know until it rears its ugly head."

Preston nodded and sat up straight.

"Max?"

The light tapping on his thighs belied whatever internal dilemma gripped his features and needed addressing.

"Yeah?"

"I'm thinking about a move to Oklahoma. I want to try out for the police force. Despite everything, I really did enjoy working alongside you and trying to do something right for society. Would it be too weird seeing me around the prescient if I got on there?"

"Of course not. Don't be silly. I'll introduce you to Sean. Guarantee you'll be friends in a month."

"I'll apply the second we return. Will it freak them out if I give a motel as my address?"

"Might."

"Help me look for a rental? I don't know the area well enough to even start."

"Forget it. Take the extra bedroom at the house. Stay until you land on your feet."

Wide green eyes flicked his way.

"You're serious?"

"Of course. You need to find some roots, Preston. Sean and I can help you prep for the academy."

Wide shoulders dropped a few notches, the relief clear.

"I'd like that. Thank you. I'm looking forward to replacing all the crap stuck in my head with something positive."

"Get some sleep, kid. We've contributed enough. We're lucky Alexandru embraced greed and kept his little profit-making enterprise to himself. Forget those words ever existed."

Preston yawned and closed his eyes.

"Plan to start right now. Wake me up before we land."

"Will do."

Max turned and stared out into an endless stretch of velvet darkness. Despite his advice to forget the events, Max knew he was far from done with this mess. Not, yet. The secret needed sharing, but only with one deserving to know what really happened to his wife. With the obvious love they'd shared, it wouldn't take much convincing his poor little lost soul would have chosen the life with her family had a realistic choice presented. The unfairness set heavy in his heart. He needed to pull Mary back into the light.

EPILOGUE

"Vincent Long! Front and center. You have a visitor."

Well, damn. Go figure.

Despite the surge of anger at having to put his shoes back on, Vincent experienced a little thump of excitement while checking his features in the glossy metal of a bed now serving as a makeshift mirror.

Sweet. Someone new I can mind fuck with for an hour if they don't run off like a sissy.

He smiled and stared into his sky-blue eyes.

Yeah, handsome as ever.

He ran a hand through thick brown hair and flexed his biceps a few times, happy with the results. The weights had done their job. He was a beast. Nothing but muscle and a need to use them to his advantage.

It'd been a long stretch since they'd called out for a visit. Two years to be exact. Before then, he rarely got anyone to come here, even though he included any idiot daring to write. He gave up on ever seeing his family stepping foot inside this place. Shame and yes, a little fear, ruled their emotions, as usual. *Fuck 'em.* He turned and backed up to the cell door and allowed the guard to clamp on the cuffs.

Despite the chains binding his wrists and ankles, he managed a purposeful strut past the other prisoner cells, flicking a glance over and pegging any face not moving quite fast enough to miss his attention. He loved the fear in their eyes before they quickly looked away. Vincent couldn't count the number of times he had most of them pissing themselves, even with steel bars separating them. Yup, he was the alpha male in here now, and they all knew it.

Vincent nodded in approval at the new visitor digs as the guards walked him through the holding bay. They'd remodeled. It even smelled better. Things had started to improve after Warden Fry finally died and Davies took over the compound.

"Hold up."

He stood perfectly still as the guard released his leg shackles and moved the cuffs to the front. No way was he screwing up this opportunity, though the persona of acquiescence soon met its first detractor.

One lone inmate sat in the third stall, waiting patiently for someone to arrive and brighten his dull life. He realized now why they'd left the wrist links. It was Tucker throwing back an equal expression of disgust.

Asshole.

He was the only other one on his cellblock ballsy enough to try and take him down. They'd squeezed necks plenty of times. One day, he promised, the guards would arrive too late to save the dickhead.

All in good time.

"Long! Quit eyeballing that inmate. Eyes front and walk your big ass all the way to the end. Move it."

Fuck wad.

He was tired of playing nice with the guards so he could get the hell out of his cell, though cleaning toilets and mopping floors sucked all to hell and back. Whatever, it was still better than staring at the fucking ceiling all day. At least they'd given him a job where he didn't have to work with a partner. If he had to touch elbows with any of those other ass clowns, he'd be snapping necks and riding the padded room for a few months. He gritted his teeth and choked on his pride.

"Sure, boss."

Proud to show he could ignore Tucker's smirk with a dismissive snort, Vincent took his time strolling up to the last cubicle.

Damn, no phones. Cool.

He hated holding those nasty things against his face. The last thing he wanted was any part of the prior inmate near his skin. Halted in front of the provided chair, he stared down at the visitor.

Surprise hit to find a man perched on the stool, head swiveling side to side as he tried to take in the layout of the room. He appeared to be in his late thirties. Around his own age.

Shit. Why couldn't it have been a chick?

A grunt left his throat upon seeing the guy clutched a copy of the book written two years ago about yours truly. Vincent plopped down on the stool and popped his knuckles on the Plexiglas.

"Yo. Over here, dude."

The guy practically jumped out of his pale skin. He appeared to struggle with reclaiming his calm, but Vincent could tell he vibrated with excitement. Dishwater blond hair pulled back into a little ponytail, wide green eyes, blue buttoned-up shirt, and jeans. Nothing special. He could smell the expensive aftershave drifting through the little talking holes drilled into the thick-ass barrier.

Fucking fans. He loved them and hated them with the same voracity.

Well, at least this one came to visit, so I'll cut him a little slack

The guy scooted forward and presented a winning smile.

"Hi. I'm Marvin. Thanks for putting me on the visitor list. I'm sure you have tons of interested parties following your case, so you probably don't recognize my name. I'm the law student writing since last April. I've always wanted to meet you, Vincent. Every aspect of what happened to you is fascinating. I sat through every day of your trial and wanted to kill your lawyer. He was an idiot. You shouldn't be in here. They had nothing to tie you to this."

Vincent let him wax poetically for several minutes about his star-struck adoration and how he would've otherwise handled the evidence until he got tired of listening to the soft, whispery voice. He leaned forward, making sure to enhance his scowl.

"What the fuck is wrong with you?"

Marvin settled back in his chair, eyes wide, and working on a hard lip chew.

"I can look at you and tell you're hiding your true self," Vincent spat in disgust. "You know damn well I'm guilty as hell. I got cocky and slipped up. Simple. No mystery."

Marvin's brow lifted.

"Don't act naïve. You want to live vicariously through me. Own it and quit trying to look so fucking innocent."

Revulsion gripped his emotions as a thick finger pointed at the book held to a thin chest. He hated weak, sniveling cowards without a thought of their own.

"Is it exciting to read about the people I killed? Do you jack off to the pictures in the damn thing and try to pretend what it felt like to weld so much power over someone? No, sit your ass back down, Marvin. I say when you can leave. Do you want to insert yourself into my goddamn life? Fine. Let's do it right, then."

Leaned back as far as the chair allowed, Vincent popped the side of the divider, catching Tucker's attention. Inmate 995684 now doing forty to life for hacking up his ex-girlfriend raised a brow.

Satisfied the guards weren't paying attention, Vincent gave the scowling inmate a wide grin.

"Hey, Tucker. Did your mommy have to go compose herself again? I heard she cries like a bitch every time she sees you."

"Fuck off, Long."

"Bet she hates that potty mouth too. How about I give her a new man to look at before she dies from embarrassment?"

"You're pushing it, bastard."

"Right to the limit, dipshit."

Vincent savored the words rolling smoothly up his throat, begging to hit the air.

"*Visitans Tenebras. Arcu ut Conseti. Solvo lupum, malo unum.*"

Tucker's features twisted into abject disgust.

"What the hell, dude? You snort the fucking Pine Sol instead of slopping it on the goddamn—?"

Vincent's excitement grew as Tucker's eyes rolled to the back of his head and the convulsing began. The compromised inmate toppled over, hitting the tile hard and bringing a whole lot of chaos as the guards scrambled from the viewing room.

Perfection

Without looking over, he raised his shackled hands and pointed at Marvin.

"Don't move a muscle, dude. I'm not done with you, yet."

From the corner of his eye, he saw Marvin obey like the good little fan he was.

Oh yes, here we go.

He was getting good at catching sight of a little sliver of darkness escaping a clueless motherfucker and seeking its next target. He watched the shit sift out five times while staring through the air vents connected to the new therapy room. The second it shot through the damn door and escaped under the windowsill he became a hardcore fan. One look at Adler's new perspective, and he knew how he wanted to spend his remaining years in this hellhole—top dog with no contenders.

What a fucking trip.

He knew he could pronounce the words correctly when watching it slither out of Delgado from across the corridor and knock a guard's dick in the dirt. It was but a work of a moment to convince the stunned ass wipe to beat the hell out of Jenner when the good doc turned him into a weak, puny human. Taught the dickhead right quick not to stick his nose up and act superior.

Innocent, my ass. Idiot ended up killing himself anyway. Bonus.

Such power in a few simple words. He felt like a God.

Eyes narrowing, Vincent sensed the wispy shadow searching the back of his skull, chuckling when he knew it figured out real damn fast the spot already claimed by another, had been for years, obviously. Like a heat-seeking missile, it slipped through the tiny holes in the divider and introduced itself to poor little Marvin with his grandiose dreams of being a badass one day. Well, here was his chance.

Leaned forward and palm pressed against their separation, Vincent smiled at his newest and clueless protégé now rubbing the back of his neck and trying desperately to refocus glazed eyes.

"Go home, Marvin. You look tired. Get some sleep and come back tomorrow. I got plans for you, little buddy. Lots of plans."

The End

ABOUT THE AUTHOR

AUTHOR OF THE MEMOIR, *I'm in Here Somewhere*, written for Chad Dean of TLC's *My 600-LB Life* and an award winning, bestselling series, *Fueled by Lust*, in the romance genre, Celeste has received countless praises for her unique writing style, ability to create memorable characters, and mesmerizing worlds for the reader to romp, dream, and get lost within. Action, suspense, mystery, and solid world-building skills continue to bring on "Top Picks," "Best Book," "Book of the Month," "Best Banter," "When Sparks Fly," and International "Reader's Choice Favorite" accolades. She welcomes you into her foray out of the romance genre and solidly into this hardcore, fast-paced, thriller that will keep you thinking about it long past the last page.

For all titles by Celeste Prater, please visit Amazon, Barnes & Noble, iTunes, and Kobo.

www.celesteprater-romanceauthor.com

CPSIA information can be obtained
at www.ICGtesting.com
Printed in the USA
LVHW090402210620
658100LV00002BA/119